BREATHLESS & BLOODSTAINED

The Chicago War, Book Four

BETHANY-KRIS

Published by Bethany-Kris

www.bethanykris.com

eISBN: 1-988197-09-8
eISBN 13: 978-1-988197-09-8
Print ISBN: 1-988197-08-1
Print ISBN 13: 978-1-988197-08-1

Cover Art © Jay Aheer
Editor: Dominique S.

For my hubby. My very own personal Damian, Adriano, Theo, and Tommas all rolled into one. Love you always, D.

CONTENTS

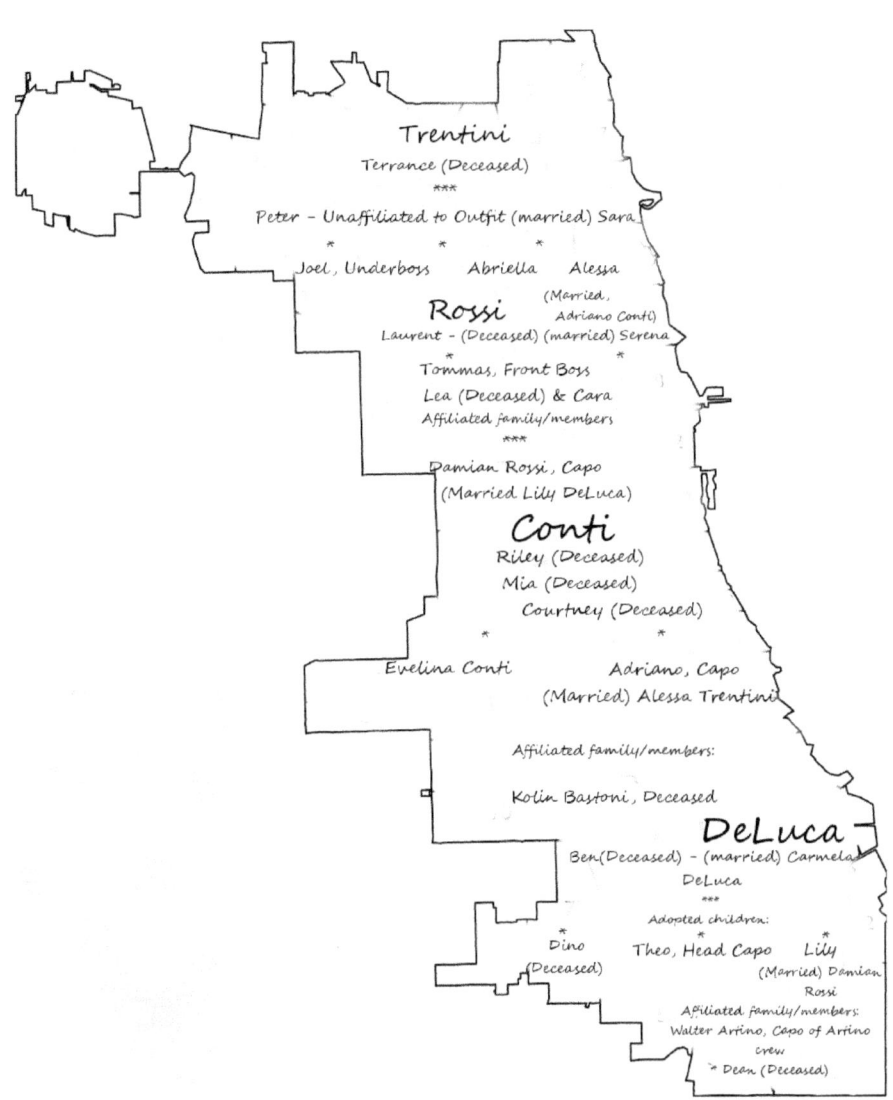

Trentini

Terrance (Deceased)

***

Peter - Unaffiliated to Outfit (married) Sara

*

Joel, Underboss   Abriella   Alessa

(Married, Adriano Conti)

Rossi

Laurent - (Deceased) (married) Serena

*

Tommas, Front Boss

Lea (Deceased) & Cara

Affiliated family/members

***

Damian Rossi, Capo

(Married Lily DeLuca)

Conti

Riley (Deceased)

Mia (Deceased)

Courtney (Deceased)

*

Evelina Conti   Adriano, Capo

(Married) Alessa Trentini

Affiliated family/members:

Kolin Bastoni, Deceased

DeLuca

Ben(Deceased) - (married) Carmela

DeLuca

***

Adopted children:

*

Dino   Theo, Head Capo   Lily

(Deceased)   (Married) Damian

Rossi

Affiliated family/members:

Walter Artino, Capo of Artino

crew

* Dean (Deceased)

PROLOGUE

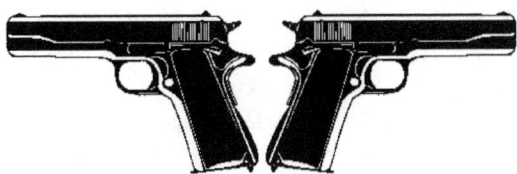

Abriella Trentini had been called a lot of things in her life. A *principessa*, a beauty, stubborn, and difficult. She had been praised for her tenacity, adored for her place as the oldest granddaughter of the Outfit's boss, and respected simply because of her last name.

What she had never been called was a whore.

Until now.

"Just like our mother," Joel snarled. "A whore, Ella."

Abriella flinched as if her brother had reached out and slapped her with his hand instead of his words. Squeezing Abriella's arm tighter, Joel dragged her down the dark hallway. His fingers dug so deeply into her skin that he was going to leave bruises. With every step they took, she could barely hear the thrum of the club behind them.

"Let me go," Abriella hissed.

She tried to jerk out of Joel's grasp, but he yanked her hard enough to make her stumble. The short club dress she wore did nothing to protect her knees when she hit the floor. Joel forced her back on her feet, sneering.

"Stop fighting, or this will get a hell of a lot worse," Joel warned.

Abriella sucked in a hard breath, wanting to stay calm. For the most part, she followed the rules set out by her family. Being mafia bred, meant women didn't get much of a choice when the men in their lives made calls on certain things.

The women who fought back lost.

The men of the Outfit won.

Always.

Abriella had too much stubbornness to go out like that. She'd always been close to her grandfather. There was no way in hell that Terrance Trentini would stand for his granddaughter being treated like she was worthless, no matter what she did. Terrance might have been the boss, but he loved her. He let her get away with anything, even if that meant he had to hide things for her. Terrance wouldn't stand for Joel acting like this.

"I want to call Granddaddy."

Joel barked a bitter laugh. "He's out of town. Shut up. Don't make me tell you again."

"I said—"

Joel kicked open a door and shoved Abriella inside before she could finish her sentence. Abriella fixed the skirt of her dress and spun around to face her brother, thinking she had just made the worst mistake yet. Her brother was angrier than she had realized. When he took a step toward her in the dark room, Abriella stepped backward.

Her back hit the edge of a desk, stopping her from moving further away. The room looked like some kind of office for the club. Joel flicked on a light, illuminating the space. A leather couch rested along the far wall. Black and white pictures of Chicago lined the walls in a haphazard fashion. The desk she bumped into was filled with paperwork, a laptop, and other personal belongings.

She had picked the wrong club tonight. With the help of high heels, a tight dress, and a fake ID, Abriella was able to get into just about any club she wanted. Eighteen wasn't legal, but her ID said she was twenty-one, and no bouncer would refuse her.

She just wanted a good time tonight.

Respirare was the newest, hottest club in town. She heard about it through her friends at college. Abriella checked it out, ended up dancing with a guy who bought her a few drinks, and then she found herself being shoved down a dark hallway by her brother. Abriella didn't even know how Joel found out she was there.

"Christ, look at you," her brother spat.

Abriella blinked away the tears stinging in her eyes. "I didn't do anything wrong, Joel!"

"Is that what you think, really? Where I stand, you didn't do a goddamn thing right. Is that what you want to be, a fucking whore like our mother?"

"No," Abriella said, forcing herself not to cry.

"Hey, come on."

A familiar form darkened the office doorway behind Joel. Abriella looked away from Tommas Rossi as he came to stand beside his friend. Tommas had always been respectful to Abriella when they crossed paths. The Outfit Capo was never rude, but he never went out of his way to talk to her, either. They were at two different spectrums in the family.

"Joel, chill out," Tommas said quietly.

Joel flipped a hand at his friend. "Stay out of it."

Abriella refused to let her brother see any tears. Joel liked that shit too much. Other people's pain was nothing more than amusement for him.

Joel waved Abriella's clutch for her to see before he opened it. Digging in the purse, he pulled out the fake ID. "Where did this come from?"

"A friend," Abriella said.

"Which friend?"

"Someone from school."

Joel shoved it into his pocket. "It's mine now."

She would have a new one in a week.

Fuck him.

"And as for you—"

"I want to call Granddaddy," Abriella interrupted sharply.

Joel scoffed. "You're an idiot. I told you, he's out of town. Our parents are gone for the weekend. I am the only one left watching you."

"Then I'll take a cab back to my dorm." Abriella shrugged, feeling worse the longer she had to stay in the room. "You can let Granddaddy know what happened. I'll deal with the consequences when he's back."

Abriella moved forward to leave and tried to push past Joel as she went. It was a stupid move. Joel had a short temper. Before Abriella had blinked, Joel grabbed her arm, spun her around to face him, and raised his hand. Abriella couldn't have gotten out of the way even if she tried to move, but she was too stunned to make the attempt.

No man had ever hit her.

None tried.

Abriella was a Trentini—no one touched a Trentini.

Joel's palm met Abriella's cheek with a loud enough crack to take the air from her lungs. The sting of the hit radiated over her face. Gasping, Abriella stared at her brother with her mouth open and a hand on her cheek where heat bloomed.

"You ..." Abriella started to say.

She tried to speak, begged the words to form, but nothing came out. Joel's hold on her arm loosened briefly. The two stared at one another for what felt like minutes, but was probably a few seconds.

Joel released her fast and let her go. "I-I—"

While Joel struggled with his own words, Abriella jerked back into reality.

"*You*," Abriella hissed. "You ... hit *me*!"

Joel stuttered stupidly. Abriella rammed her hands into her brother's chest hard enough to knock him backward. Shock flitted over Joel's features as he righted himself. Abriella shoved him again the second she could, forcing Joel away from her.

She didn't want him anywhere near her.

Abriella wasn't a dog to be beaten.

She was no man's toy.

"Don't you ever fucking hit me again!" Abriella screamed at him.

Tommas Rossi stared between the siblings, but stayed out of it.

Abriella took another step toward her frozen brother. "I might have done wrong being out tonight at a club, but out of the two of us, who do you think is going to take more shit for this? Me, with my slutty dress, or

5

you and the bruise you just left on my face? Huh, which one?"

Joel swallowed hard, his shoulders stiffening. "You shouldn't have—"

"I did nothing," Abriella snapped. "Don't blame your abuse on me. You are a piece of shit, Joel. Just wait until I tell Granddaddy what you did to me tonight."

Like someone had lit a fire under his feet, Joel lurched forward to come at Abriella again. Tommas Rossi moved faster, sliding in between the siblings and hitting Joel hard on the shoulder with a closed fist. The smack echoed in the quiet office. Joel froze on the spot. For the moment, Abriella felt safer.

She silently thanked Tommas.

"*Enough.*"

Tommas' one word was deadly quiet. A promise of violence that made Abriella shiver in her heels.

"Excuse me?" Joel asked.

"I said that it is enough," Tommas repeated, still quiet but firm. "Leave her be. You have done more than enough, Joel. She gets it. But I won't let you touch her again. Try it, and I'll physically throw your ass out of this room before I have the bouncers remove you from this club. Test me, Joel, you know I can fucking do it."

"That's how you want to play this?" Joel asked.

Tommas nodded once. "It is."

"She's—"

"Young, man. She's eighteen, trying to have a little fun, and made a goddamn mistake. You made your point. No more, Joel. It's *enough.*"

Swallowing hard, Joel flicked a hand in Abriella's direction as if to shoo her away like she was a piece of trash. "If you want to handle the little whore, then handle her. Make sure she gets back to her dorm. I have better shit to do."

"I bet," Tommas muttered.

Joel turned on his heel and stormed from the office. The pictures on the wall rattled when the door slammed shut with a bang.

Tommas' shoulders heaved. Abriella could practically feel the anger flowing from the man as he stared at the spot where Joel had vacated.

"Thank you," Abriella whispered.

Her throat was tight. As fast as her fight had come, it was gone.

Tommas didn't act like he had heard her.

Clearing the thickness away, Abriella said, "Tommas, thank—"

"Hush," Tommas interjected sharply.

Abriella stiffened, surprised all over again. "I beg your pardon?"

Slowly, Tommas turned on his heel to face her. "I said hush. It means be quiet."

"I know what it means."

"Then listen."

What?

Where had the man from two minutes ago gone to?

"Hey, don't be an asshole."

Tommas' brow furrowed, softening the sharp lines of his features as he grinned.

What was amusing?

It wasn't the first time Abriella had gotten a good, close-up look at the man, but it was the first time she took notice of how roguishly handsome Tommas truly was. His easy stance, tall frame, and broad shoulders that filled his suit perfectly, only added to the smirk he sported. From his steel-blue gaze, to his strong jaw, and his dark hair that was swept upward like he'd been running his fingers through the short strands, the man oozed confidence and …

Abriella blinked, caught in her daze of staring.

Sexy.

Tommas was sexy as sin.

She'd always had a bit of an interest in the quiet Capo of the Rossi family, but Abriella kept her distance for many reasons. One, because he was a goddamn Capo. Two, because he was her brother's friend. And three, because he was eight years older than her.

Abriella willed away the sudden heat flooding her cheeks and the rest of her body as Tommas looked her up and down.

"Stop that," Abriella said.

"Stop what?" Tommas asked.

"Staring at me like that."

"You're staring at me."

She was.

Abriella glanced away.

"So?" she asked.

"I don't mind," Tommas admitted. "I told you to be quiet, because I don't want you to thank me for doing that. Never thank a person for doing what is right, Ella."

Abriella's gaze snapped up to meet Tommas'. He'd never called her anything but her full name before.

"Okay," she said.

"And I'm sorry."

"For what?"

"Two things."

"Do tell," Abriella said.

"I should have stopped him sooner. Joel is an ass, I know. I didn't think he'd go off like that on you, especially not with someone here."

Abriella shrugged. "I guess you don't know my brother all that well,

7

huh?"

"Apparently not."

"What was the second thing?"

Tommas wet his lips with his tongue, drawing Abriella's gaze in again. A question passed through her thoughts so quickly, she almost missed it.

What did he kiss like?

Tommas' next words did not help to take away that errant idea. "I called him to let him know you were in my club. I shouldn't have done that. You were having a good time, it seemed like innocent fun, but I thought your brother should know you were out. That was my mistake. It won't happen again. You're free to come and go from my club as long as you can get in, Ella."

Damn.

"Thanks."

"One more thing."

"Yeah?"

"You're not, Ella."

She frowned. "Not what?"

"A whore," Tommas murmured.

Heat pinked her cheeks again. She didn't want to rehash all of that. It was bad enough that Tommas had heard what Joel said about Abriella's mother.

Sara Trentini wasn't an angel. Abriella knew her mother's darkest secret, but only because she'd accidentally stumbled upon some paperwork regarding Sara and Joel's father. Biologically, Joel belonged to Terrance, although their father Peter had claimed him as his son. Skeletons like those wouldn't stay hidden in the closet forever.

Abriella didn't judge her mother.

She couldn't.

Sara was her mother.

"I just … it doesn't matter," Abriella said lamely.

Tommas rubbed at his right temple. "No, it isn't. You're eighteen, and you can consent to whatever you want to do when it comes to a man. What you were doing tonight wasn't any different than what Joel does with whoever he picks up on any given night."

Abriella cringed. "I don't want to hear that."

"Well, it's true. Double standards are reserved for hypocrites and assholes only."

Unable to stop herself, Abriella laughed.

Tommas flashed her with a sexy smile. "That is a much better sight and sound."

"Huh?"

"Your smile. Your laugh. Not that the fight you showed wasn't good, because it was. A strong fight makes for a good woman, but I like your smile and laugh more."

Abriella's throat went dry. "Oh."

"Don't let anyone take that from you, either."

"I won't."

"Good. You're not a whore, Ella. Don't ever let a man call you that, or label you with that title unless you want him to."

Her mind blanked.

Tommas' sharp stare caught Abriella's as he asked, "Do you get what I'm saying?"

"No," she confessed.

"You're not a whore, sweetheart, but you can be anything you want to be for the man you want to be with. It's that simple. What you do in private with a man is nobody's business but yours and his. There's nothing wrong with it."

Abriella's bottom lip caught under her teeth as she took in his words. "You don't think so?"

"No."

Oh.

"Outfit daughters shouldn't act like who—"

"What did I say about that word, huh?" Tommas asked, taking a step forward.

Abriella tipped her chin down, but grinned all the same. "Sorry."

She didn't realize how close Tommas had come to stand in front of her until his fingers were sliding under her chin and tilting her head up. She decided right then and there that she liked the feeling of this man's hands on her skin.

That was so bad. Wrong, even.

But she liked it.

"Do what makes you happy, Ella. Let the assholes like your brother keep their judgment."

"Easier said than done. You know where I come from, Tommas."

"Tommy. I prefer Tommy."

"Tommy," she echoed.

"Let them keep it," he repeated. "Just get smarter about your ways, girl. That's all."

She didn't know how to respond to that.

"Are you encouraging me to break the rules?"

Tommas chuckled. The sound of his amusement rocked through Abriella. "If you want to call it that, then sure. The thing is, I have a feeling this wasn't your first time doing something you shouldn't and it probably won't be your last. Just get smarter about it; that's all. You want to have some fun. Have it. You want to go out. Go. Don't be stupid about it, though."

"Are you always this ... strange?" Abriella asked.

"No, sometimes I'm even worse. Moody. A prick. Quiet. Depends on the day."

Abriella wondered if she could find out more about Tommas.

"Huh."

"I do have a question for you, but you don't have to answer."

"Maybe I will, but you won't know unless you ask."

"A smartass. I like that, too."

Abriella smiled. "You're not the first to call me that."

"I'm not surprised." Tommas tipped his head to the side a bit and asked, "The man you were dancing with ... would you have taken him to your dorm or wherever tonight?"

"No," Abriella said instantly.

"Why not?"

"Because he was good for a little fun, but not much else. Two dimensional men are boring."

Tommas cocked a brow. "What would it take, Ella?"

Was he asking?

Because almost everything she learned about Tommas tonight was a great start. She wasn't an angel. She hadn't been one of those for years. She wasn't going to act like one now.

"The right kind of guy."

Tommas laughed. "And who is that?"

"The one who can give me what I want."

His gaze caught hers, holding strong. "Care to let me in on the secret?"

"I just want to be free, Tommy."

CHAPTER ONE

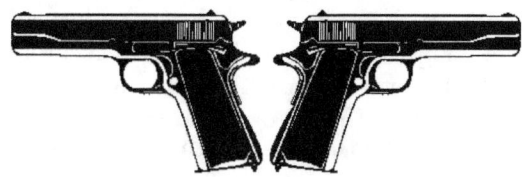

What good was family if they didn't storm in your home without knocking while barely saying a word to you as they went directly to where the food was?

"Cousin," Tommas greeted.

Damian strolled past Tommas' spot at the small kitchen table. His cousin hit up the fridge, his broad shoulders blocking Tommas' view of Damian as he dug to find food.

"You need to go shopping, Tommy."

"I'm aware, D."

"There's fuck all in here."

Well, there was, but Damian didn't like healthy food. He preferred junk food, and then he worked it all off with his crazy morning regime. Tommas had lived more than enough years with his cousin to know what the man liked.

"Eat an apple for once," Tommas said. "It's better for you. An apple a day and all that crap."

Damian popped up from the fridge, closing the door and biting into a red apple at the same time. "Not my first choice."

Tommas cringed. "Don't talk with your mouth full."

"You sound like my wife."

"She has better manners than you do."

Damian chuckled, swallowing his bite of apple. "She is my better half for a reason, I guess."

"Truth."

Tommas shut the laptop he'd been working on and pushed it away. Damian joined his cousin at the kitchen table, twisting the chair around so he could rest his arms over the back as he regarded Tommas.

"I went to your house first," Damian said.

"I haven't been there a lot lately."

His apartment was easier and safer. Joel Trentini wasn't aware of Tommas' second, much smaller place in the heart of the Trentini territory. Tommas had only picked up the apartment a couple of years back, because he wanted a safe place for Abriella to come to if she needed.

Looking around the two bedroom, one bath apartment was a bad idea for Tommas. There wasn't a single part of the apartment that was unmarked by Abriella in some way. Her little touches were all over it from the colorful artwork on the walls, to the black appliances in the kitchen. Tommas knew the things she liked and had picked accordingly to decorate. Abriella had added a lot over the years like the silver throw pillows on the sectional and the white chaise by the bay window.

"There you go again," Damian said. "Off into another world."

Tommas slammed back down to reality in a blink. "Hmm, what?"

"You're dazed, Tommy. You're out of it."

"I—"

"Don't deny it."

Tommas sighed. "All right, so I'm out of it. I've got a lot on my mind. What did you want coming here, anyway?"

Damian passed a look at the blankets on the couch. They were messy, like someone had been sleeping in them and hadn't bothered to fold them up. "Still sleeping on the couch, huh?"

It was easier than the bedroom.

She was all over that, too.

"What do you want, D?"

"To talk," Damian said.

"About what?"

"Whatever you're planning. I'd like to know this time around instead of getting surprised by whatever in the hell you're going to do like the last time."

Tommas ignored the heat of his cousin's tone. Trusting that Riley would do what he needed to do and kill Joel, Tommas had inadvertently put Theo DeLuca in the crossfire. The man nearly lost his life more than once, but shit happens sometimes, and people became casualties. Once Tommas had known about Theo's involvement with Evelina Conti, he'd changed plans and tried to correct what was already in motion because of Riley. Tommas was hoping Theo would see it the same way and move on.

Unfortunately, the war was far from being over.

"I apologized for Theo."

"Not to him," Damian replied.

"All right, that's true enough."

"When are you going to do that?"

Tommas shrugged. "Soon. What more do you want, man?"

"A guarantee it won't happen again."

"I don't know if I can do that."

Damian's shoulders stiffened. "Don't go stupid over someone you don't even have, Tommy."

"It has nothing to do with not having someone, Damian. It's getting what is mine. That's all."

"Is it?"

"Yes," Tommas murmured.

"I think you should make your way over to Theo's hospital room before he gets out," Damian said. "Make face, and give the man the respect he's owed for the shit he's had to go through the last few months."

Tommas nodded. "I will. I told you soon, okay?"

"He's getting out today, Tommas."

Oh. Well, then …

"And I think he might want to step out of this," Damian added quieter.

That caught Tommas' attention. "The war?"

"Yeah. He's never had much to do with it except to be used by people for their own gain. Theo is at a different place right now. This mess is the last thing on his mind. So yeah, he wants out."

Theo DeLuca was smart as hell for doing it, too. Tommas didn't blame the man.

"Does that mean he isn't taking any sides?" Tommas asked.

"I don't know, Tommy. You'll have to ask when you make your way over there."

Tommas scowled. "Mmm."

"Someone else to consider is Adriano Conti," Damian said. "What about him? Where does he stand in the mess right now between you and Joel? It would be good to know where he is in all of this."

Adriano Conti was a young Capo that Tommas had learned to respect over the last few months. For a long time, Tommas simply took Adriano's age and compliance to Riley as a weakness. Tommas was ten shades of wrong on both fronts. Adriano had more than proved he was capable of handling his own business without his father at his side. With Riley dead, Adriano hadn't even skipped a beat with his crew or life.

The kid was moving forward.

That was the important thing.

Tommas shrugged. "His wife's sister is stuck firmly on Joel's side of things, man. Think about it."

Damian scowled as he took another bite of his apple. Tommas waited his cousin out while Damian chewed and swallowed. The men sat in silence until Damian put his apple aside.

"Adriano won't do anything that risks Alessa, her family, or her happiness."

"Exactly," Tommas said quietly.

"But that doesn't mean he'll jump into Joel's side of things, either."

"Probably not. There's a lot of love lost there."

Damian leaned forward, letting his arms hang down over the back of the chair. "You're on your own against Joel Trentini."

Tommas chuckled dryly. "Not entirely. I've got you, D."

"True," Damian agreed, flashing a wicked smile. "But I still don't have the first clue what you're doing or where you're going, cousin. Joel, like he usually does, has made a lot of threats and sent out a bunch of warnings, but he's yet to put any of those words into actions. That makes me nervous. We don't know what he's doing or when he's planning on doing it. You need to make a choice where you're going, Tommy, before Joel decides something for you."

"Up."

"Up?"

Tommas passed the decorative glass bowl on the table a look. A handful of silver bangles had been tossed haphazardly in the bowl months ago by Abriella when she woke up early one morning to cook breakfast. She hadn't wanted to get her jewelry messy while she cooked. Tommas had driven her back to her apartment so she could make it to church with her sister.

No one suspected a thing.

No one ever had.

To get mornings like those back, the very best mornings he could ever remember, Tommas only had one option. He needed to take the empty boss's seat. He would have to clear Abriella's house of Outfit men, so that she was free to make her own choices.

Guilt still chewed at Tommas.

"A lot of people have died," Tommas told his cousin.

"I know."

"They shouldn't keep dying, D. They didn't cause this feud. The people have done nothing but be born or married to certain families."

"I never knew you to be the kind of man who worried about other people," Damian noted.

"I'm not."

"But Abriella is, right?"

"She is," Tommas said under his breath. "And I know she wouldn't want this to keep going. I can give it up, D. I can say fuck the seat, leave it alone, and let Joel take it."

Damian didn't give a thing away as he said, "And her, too, yeah?"

Yes.

"I could do it," Tommas said, meeting his cousin's gaze. "I could let her go if I thought she would be happy, or that she would find someone who could make her happy. I wouldn't mind. I could do it, D."

"Are you sure about that?"

"I know I could."

Because Abriella's happiness was all Tommas had ever cared about at the end of it all.

"But," Tommas added, "I know Joel. And he won't let her be happy. All the blood in that family is so sour that it stinks. They're poisoned against one another. Joel doesn't care about his sisters or his parents, he never has. He won't do a damn thing for her. If I let it all go thinking that he might give her the chance to be happy, I'll be sorely disappointed in the end."

"You're choosing to go up, then?" Damian asked.

"Up," Tommas echoed.

Damian blew out a quiet breath. "Then that's where we'll get you, man."

Tommas wondered if being up as high as he needed to go would be a lonely place. It certainly would be if he was alone once he made it there. What if he took the seat as the Outfit's next boss, and Abriella still pushed him away?

As if Damian could read his mind, he said, "It's a risk, Tommas."

"Nothing worth having comes easy, right?"

"Right," his cousin said. "Besides, the Outfit needs a change. A good change, Tommy. You could be that. Don't make this about only your selfishness, make it bigger than all that nonsense. We haven't been a *famiglia* for a long time. Do what needs to be done, man. Get us back to that place. You're capable."

Damian was right.

"Doing what needs to be done could be messy as hell."

Hadn't enough blood spilled?

"So let's play dirty." Damian laughed. "We can do that."

Tommas caught sight of the bangles again.

"I saw Abriella yesterday," Tommas admitted. "She was having dinner with her mother."

"Oh?"

"She didn't see me."

Damian chewed on his inner cheek. "What about it?"

"Love and business never mixes well, but I don't know how to make it about anything else right now. That's dangerous, D."

"Dangerous men are the best ones."

The problem with that was Tommas wasn't the only dangerous one. Joel was lethal, too. Erratic at times, demanding like a spoiled child, and unpredictable in his moves at best. That didn't make for a good situation when Tommas needed to carefully plan ahead to take the seat and the Outfit from Joel without spilling more blood than what was necessary.

"You could play it like Riley did," Damian suggested. "Best Joel in the areas he's most weak and cut him off at the knees when he thinks you're down and out. You've got to give Riley the credit where it's due, even if he did get killed in the end. He played one hell of a good game."

"I'm not Riley," Tommas replied.

Damian chuckled. "No, you're right. You're far too bloody for that."

Tommas didn't bother denying it. He had a taste for spilled blood when it was needed, and sometimes, even when it wasn't. Spilling blood always made a damn good point.

"Yeah, Bloody Tommas, right?" Damian asked.

"Right," Tommas agreed.

He hadn't earned that nickname for doing nothing.

"Just make sure to give me a heads up this time before you do something crazy again, all right?" Damian asked.

"Yeah, I got it."

"Good. And you know, be careful, Tommy. I want my boy to have some kind of family to grow up around. Something better than what we had, which was practically fucking nothing. Certainly nothing worth having. Next to Theo, you're going to be the only other family I really have for my son. It takes a village and all that."

Tommas froze in his seat, taking in his cousin's words. "A boy?"

"Shit. I said that, didn't I?"

"You did."

Damian smirked. "I wasn't supposed to tell. Lily wanted to do some kind of reveal thing."

"I won't say anything," Tommas promised.

"Thanks."

The shitty bubble Tommas had been floating in for the last few weeks suddenly burst without warning. All it took was his cousin reminding him that there was more to life than the Outfit and selfish desires.

Love wasn't always selfish.

Neither was family.

Tommas was thrilled his cousin and Lily's first child would be a boy. Damian was too high-strung for a girl, as far as Tommas was concerned. Damian would likely spend his life in a panic as his daughter got older, so a boy was a relief. But at the same time, it wasn't. Boys followed their fathers. Just like Tommas and Damian had growing up.

"This needs to be better," Damian said quietly. "The Outfit can't be like it is right now for my boy in the future, Tommy. Is that how you want your kids growing up? Is that what you want to hand off to them? This legacy?"

"No," Tommas said.

"I didn't think so."

"It's not that simple, D."

Damian frowned. "It rarely is. Are you doubting yourself?"

Tommas scoffed. "Hardly."

Being a boss hadn't been in his long-term goals, but Tommas didn't mind the added task.

"Her again?" Damian asked.

Tommas simply nodded, but said nothing. It was always about Abriella even when it wasn't.

"I could always try to scare Joel into compliance," Tommas said, more to himself than his cousin.

"That's an interesting idea."

"I'm sure we'll figure it all out."

Damian sighed. "I know what you're doing, man."

"What?"

"You do realize that with the boss gone, there's only a few people who could really fill the other seats for the front boss and underboss, right?" Damian asked.

"Obviously."

"And if Joel doesn't hand the boss's seat over, you'll end him."

"I might end him even if he does," Tommas said honestly. "I still want what is mine, D. He's got what belongs to me in a gilded cage. It's the one thing holding me back from slaughtering him when it's all I really want to do. I don't want to hurt Abriella, or worse, get her hurt in the process of making my moves."

"That's not my point, Tommy."

"Then what is?" Tommas asked.

"Don't make me your right-hand in this. I never wanted something like that."

Tommas didn't even blink at the statement. "But you're good at it. You've always been my right-hand, even when we were kids. This shouldn't be a surprise to you. Don't act like it is."

"That's not important."

"It is to me, Damian. And right now, that is all that matters."

Damian didn't even try to hide his displeasure. "You're putting me in a spotlight. You know I don't like that kind of bullshit."

"Comfort zones are only useful for weak men who are afraid of the unknown. Time to step out of yours, D."

"Point taken," Damian muttered. "So, what are you doing today?"

Tommas pushed out of the chair and stood. "Well, I have to check on my mother and make sure she hasn't gulped back enough alcohol to kill herself over the last few days."

"And?" Damian pressed.

Goddammit.

"And I'll head over to Theo's hospital room."

"I knew you would. Good men apologize when they do wrong, Tommy."

Tommas didn't reply.
Why should he?
He hadn't been good for a long time.

Tommas cringed the moment he pushed open the door to his mother's home. The pungent stench of rotting food, piss, vomit, cigarette smoke, and old liquor burned his nose when he inhaled. Tommas held back the automatic gag reflex that always seemed to act up whenever that smell invaded his senses. It wasn't the first time he got a whiff of that concoction, but it still felt like a punch to his gut.

Since his father's unfortunate death—or murder, depending on how someone wanted to look at it—his mother had only slid downhill with every passing day. Truthfully, Tommas was just waiting for the woman to drown herself in alcohol.

As harsh as it sounded, it would be easier for everyone, Serena included. Alcoholism was a disease that affected everyone and anyone it could touch. It wasn't just the alcoholic that felt the disease's dirty touch, but the people around the addict, too.

Tommas had felt more than enough over his thirty years.

Sure, he was more than capable of handling the issue of his mother if he wanted to go that route. He'd killed his father, after all. When Laurent nearly got Abriella killed in the crossfire of his attack on Riley Conti months back, Tommas lost all control.

His father should have expected it. Laurent should have seen Tommas coming with that one long before he actually pulled the trigger. How many times could a father hurt his son in one way or another before the abused finally struck back?

Simple as that.

"Ma?" Tommas hollered, letting the front door close.

Silence answered his call.

Strolling down the dark entryway, Tommas came to the kitchen. Light filtered in through the half-shaded windows, giving the space just enough light. It was a fucking mess. Dirty dishes on the countertops, filling the sinks, and empty bottles of wine everywhere in between. Half-cooked and uneaten food in pans and mildewed in containers on the cupboard. The fridge door was wide open, likely explaining a good portion of the smell.

Sighing, Tommas pushed down the irritation swelling in his gut.

The only good thing his drunk of a father had done when alive was care for his useless wife. Laurent made sure Serena was fed, filled with drink, and clean. The house wasn't immaculate back then, but it was bearable.

Serena was a lost cause.

Gone.

Tommas shoes crunched on the broken shards of what looked to be pieces of a wine glass as he stepped closer to the island to grab the unhooked phone. Hanging it up, he checked the last dialed number. The Canadian area code told Tommas that his mother had probably been trying to contact his only surviving sister in Toronto.

Pain edged around his senses.

Tommas forced it back.

Cara likely didn't answer the call. After the shooting that took away her twin, and Tommas' other sister, Lea, Cara wanted very little to do with her family in Chicago. Once in a blue moon, she would pick up a call from Tommas just to let him know she was still alive and doing okay, but nothing else. Tommas wouldn't hurt his sister by demanding more from her. He couldn't possibly bring her back here for the sake of their mother knowing it would only hurt Cara more than he could possibly imagine. She deserved to be free of this place.

Ghosts had a way of following behind, though.

Plucking up the phone again, Tommas hit redial. The call rang and rang before someone on the other end finally picked up.

"*Bonjour, ciao?*"

The gruff male voice was not what Tommas had expected. The French and Italian mix was even more shocking.

Tommas recovered quickly enough. "Is Cara there?"

The man on the other end mumbled something, and a shuffling sound followed. "No, she's in the shower. Who is this?"

"Her brother. Tommas. I could ask the same thing about you."

"Gian," said the man, his French accent shortening his Italian name even more.

Tommas stilled, taking in the name. It was familiar enough that he didn't have to think on it for long. "Gian Guzzi?"

"One and the same. What about it?"

Arrogant. Cocky. Sharp. Quick.

And the grandson of the Guzzi Cosa Nostra Don.

Fuck.

Tommas rubbed at his forehead, willing the throbbing headache to go away. He wasn't going to tell his sister what she could or couldn't do. It wasn't okay with him. He'd watched women be trampled on and treated like game pieces for his entire life.

But he still cared for Cara.

"I'm going to hang up the phone," Tommas said. "And we're going to pretend like we didn't talk, Gian. Does that sound good to you?"

"*Perfetto*, Tommas."

"Convince my sister to call our mother."

"I'll try."

Tommas took those words to mean his sister and Gian were close enough that he knew the truth about Cara's volatile relationship with her mother. Fantastic.

Not my business, Tommas reminded himself. He hung up the phone before his brain could convince him to do otherwise.

Tommas made his way through the lower section of the house and then to the upper level. At the upstairs bathroom doorway, he found a pool of mostly dried vomit on the threshold. He passed it by without giving it too much thought. Vomit wasn't uncommon for his mother when she drank. In fact, Serena seemed to like seeing how much she could imbibe before her stomach would revolt.

Alcohol poisoning be damned.

Tommas found his mother sprawled across an unmade bed in the far bedroom. She hadn't slept in her bedroom ever since she found Laurent dead. At least, that's what she told Tommas when she was in the midst of one of her stupors.

Who knew Serena had actually cared for her husband?

"Ma," Tommas said, coming to stand beside his mother's still frame.

She was breathing, but the sound was shallow. The pale, sickly color of her skin carried an ashy hue. Dried spit and vomit had streaked over the side of Serena's slack cheek and matted her dark hair.

Bending down, Tommas was eye-level with his passed out mother. He grabbed a few tissues out of the opened box on the nightstand and dipped it into the glass of half-filled water to wet them. Dabbing at his mother's cheek, he cleaned as much of the mess off her face as he could.

Despite how much he hated his mother and how she had treated him growing up, she was still his mother. She had birthed him, raised him, and at times, loved him. Tommas had essentially left Serena to survive on her own when he killed his father.

She was his responsibility.

"Ma," Tommas whispered. "Wake up, Ma."

Serena groaned, her hand coming up to push Tommas back. "Go away."

"Ma—"

"Shut up," Serena slurred. "Get out!"

Her waving hand smacked the glass of water on the stand, sending it flying on the floor. Tommas barely got out of the way of the water before the glass shattered on hardwood. He stood, exhausted already. He had to make nice with Theo DeLuca and get business done in the city, but he wanted to check on his mother first. Well, he'd done that.

She was alive.

For now.

"Ma, there's glass all over the floor. I'll send someone over to clean the house a bit. All right?"

Serena mumbled unintelligibly.

This was the most he could do for her. He'd already taken everything else.

Tommas wished he regretted it.

There were very few things in life that made a man worthy. Those things became lessened when a man was in the mafia. Instead of his value being counted in his actions and words, it was tallied by his deeds and possessions. It was determined by the number of men on his streets and the most red he could cover on a map to say he owned.

Tommas Rossi had always found it amusing how made men were called Men of Honor. There was nothing honorable about this life. The Outfit had forgotten honor a long time ago. Long before the war.

They breathed. They bled.

Life and death.

That's all this life had ever been.

The one thing in *his* life that had kept Tommas honorable throughout the years was just a few steps ahead of him, but still out of reach.

Tommas tugged his jacket tighter around his neck, determined to keep the cold February air out. Even with it being the last days of the coldest month of the season, he knew the weather wouldn't let up for another two. Probably. The bite of the wind was the only thing he seemed to feel lately. Maybe that was why he preferred to be outside rather than inside.

"No way," a familiar voice said down the way.

Leaning around the lamp post, Tommas watched the two women walk arm in arm down the street. His eye caught the taller of the two and the dark waves of her hair that flew wildly in the wind. For a moment, he felt something else.

His heart splintered.

It was an agonizing crack.

He hated it.

But he loved her.

"Not at all?" Abriella asked.

"No, I want to make sure it's all pale yellows and greens," Alessa replied. "No pink. I hate pink. No dark blues, either. I don't want to know the gender or make people think we do know what it is."

Abriella's laughter floated down to Tommas' spot, traveling in the wind. It was a sweet sound, and one so familiar to him that it soothed the deep ache inside his chest. But not for long. It never lasted very long.

He hadn't expected to see Abriella strolling out of the hospital with her sister in tow when he arrived to visit Theo. His plans to see the Capo had been forgotten while he followed the sisters down the street.

"I'm excited for you," Abriella said.

Alessa tugged her sister closer. "Me, too."

Tommas wondered if Abriella was smiling. The fact that he was the cause of her unhappiness lately, or the majority of it, sucked away what little soul he had left. People shouldn't hurt those they loved.

God knew he had grown up in a home where that's all he ever saw. His mother hating his father, and his father despising his mother. Violence. Drinking. Abuse.

Tommas wanted to be better than that, but then he'd went ahead and got himself mixed up with a girl eight years younger than his thirty years. Someone that the Outfit determined he couldn't have because of her status and last name. And because he wasn't good enough for her with his status or last name.

Fuck.

He knew better.

All those years ago?

Tommas wasn't stupid, but it had been fun. Just simple, honest fun with a girl who tasted like trouble all over and gave him a whole new thrill that had nothing to do with the streets, being a Capo, or the mafia. Somewhere along the lines, fun with Abriella turned into a private apartment with her clothes in his closet, scarves hanging off the bedpost, and her lotions in the bathroom.

It changed to comfort.

She seeped into his blood.

She infected him.

Tommas tried to cut her out a few times, just to see if he could bleed Abriella from his blood and let her do her own thing. He'd clearly failed, because comfort turned to love. Tommas had given Abriella something important. He'd lost a piece of him. She hadn't quite handed him the same thing back yet.

Sighing, Tommas pushed away from the lamp post that was keeping him hidden and strolled into the flood of people walking down the busy sidewalk. With his head tilted down just enough to keep his face shadowed from the view of others, he picked up his pace until he could hear the familiar voices in front of him again.

"So, yellows and greens for the baby shower," Abriella said.

"Yep."

"Adriano is good with that?"

"He's good with whatever makes me happy, Ella."

Tommas knew the feeling, but the girl he wanted to make happy wouldn't let him do it anymore. Not that she ever had before. Abriella had always kept him at arm's length in one way or another. She never let him too close, and when she did, he found himself shoved backwards.

"There's a nice little shop right around the corner for party stuff," Abriella said. "Do you want to check it out?"

"Sure." Alessa didn't sound like she was excited for shopping.

"What is wrong?" Abriella asked.

"I wonder if I should ask you that," Alessa said.

Tommas stopped his walk, glancing up at the girls as people passed him by. Abriella and Alessa had stopped walking, too. He caught the sight of Abriella's profile as she turned to stare at her sister with a frown tugging the corners of her mouth down.

This woman was crazy beautiful with her high cheekbones, blue eyes, her soft lines, and her pretty mouth. Her stubbornness, dark humor, and defiant personality had simply been the icing on the cake for a woman he'd never been able to stay too far away from.

Even now, with a feud raging around them and Abriella demanding he leave her alone, Tommas still couldn't do it. He needed to keep a watch. He wanted to make sure she was safe.

Damn it.

He needed to see her.

Yeah, *beautiful*. She had never been anything less to Tommas. Even when she frowned; even when she cried. *Christ*, he still wished she wouldn't do it at all.

"I'm fine," he heard Abriella say softly.

She wasn't.

Her tone coated her lies.

Tommas heard it. He knew those lies.

"Have you talked to him lately?" Alessa asked.

"Him, who?"

"You know who."

Abriella started walking again, untangling her arm from her sister's and going on ahead. Alessa quickly followed behind.

"Hey, wait up," Alessa shouted.

Tommas trailed behind, silent and unknown.

"I don't want to talk about that shit," Abriella muttered.

"Ella—"

"Just drop it!"

Alessa grabbed her sister's coat and tugged hard enough to stop Abriella. "Talk to me, Ella."

"I can't," Abriella ground out.

Tommas' chest began to hurt again. It was his only weakness. In a life filled with violence, mistrust, and foulness, he had but one good thing to call his own. One thing that was the light to his dark, the good to his bad.

Every little thing about Abriella that was wonderful for Tommas was also terrible for him. When they were good, they were so fucking good. Only when they were together, though, because when they were apart, they were worse than bad. Unhealthy, like an addiction that they couldn't fulfill. Being apart made them do stupid, awful shit to be together. They hurt each other a lot trying to just *be them*.

A *weakness*.

A spot to incapacitate, to destroy.

Abriella Trentini.

Twenty-two, blue-eyed, smart as hell, sweet like sugar, but poison to his soul.

Poison, because she kept killing him. She didn't even know it. She killed him when she refused him, and when she pushed him away. The one love in his life couldn't even tell him that she loved him, too.

Abriella always refused him those three words. *I love you.* On his knees with his fists tangled in her dress, and the words on the tip of his tongue, she still refused him. In a bed with her under him, her fingernails cutting into his skin while he used her the way she liked, she refused him those words. Begging for the truth, even if it was a lie, she would never give him what he needed from her.

It killed him.

Abriella controlled him. She was his flaw, bliss, and hate all rolled into one. He still wanted her.

"Talk to me," Alessa demanded.

Tommas slipped into an alleyway when his lover turned enough that he thought she might have caught sight of him.

"I can't," Abriella repeated.

"Why not?"

"Because then I miss him."

Tommas let his head rest back to the brick wall of the alley. It took one sentence from Abriella for all the control that Tommas had been maintaining in the Outfit to blow to bits. One single fucking sentence to ruin it for him. He'd kept a distance and tried to stay quiet while Abriella's brother, Joel, began to rally compliance and allies in an effort to take the boss's seat since Riley Conti's death.

That was over.

So done.

Abriella missed him.

He wanted her.

The answer was simple: he was going to have her.

Didn't she know?

Abriella Trentini had always been his.

Tommas pushed off the wall and slipped out of the alleyway into the flood of people. He didn't doubt that Abriella hadn't seen him as he began his trek back toward the hospital.

He would get her.

There was business to do first.

CHAPTER TWO

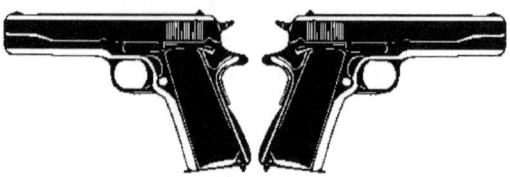

The faint hum coming from Abriella's left wouldn't stop no matter how much she wished it away. Rolling over just enough to wake from her sleep, she blindly waved her hand across the bedside table to find the vibrating cell phone. When she had it in her grasp, she put it to her ear and pulled the covers over her head.

"Hello?" she asked groggily.

"I'm going to fuck this all up, Ella."

Abriella cleared her throat. "What?"

"I'm twenty-one. How in the hell am I supposed to be a mom at twenty-one? The last time I held a newborn baby, I was eleven. I can't do this."

Alessa.

Abriella willed the sleep out of her voice and vision as she pulled the blankets off her head again. The darkness of her bedroom and the moon shining high in her window told her it was still early morning. Far too early for her sister to be calling.

"It's a little late for you to be panicking, isn't it?" Abriella asked. "I mean, your due date is in less than three months, Alessa. This isn't the kind of thing you can just tell to go away. The baby is coming."

Alessa groaned. "I know all that."

Abriella checked her attitude, knowing her sister needed something from her. Why else would Alessa call like this? Their brother, Joel, was an arrogant ass on his good days. Contact between the sisters was sometimes limited depending on Joel's mood that week. Sometimes, he acted like Alessa was golden to him, and other times, he treated her like a whore who had gotten knocked up by a rival family's son.

"I'm sorry," Abriella said, rubbing at her eyes. "You woke me up and surprised me. Tell me what is wrong."

"I don't know how to be a mom," Alessa blurted out.

Fair enough …

"Because you're twenty-one?"

"Yes, Ella. I said that already."

"No offense, but that's not a good reason, Lissa."

Alessa sighed. "You don't get it."

"No, I do. I'm just saying that your age isn't a good excuse. You've always been older than your actual years. You're mature. You've been ready for this baby and prepared to step up from the moment you found out you were pregnant. What is it really?"

"Nothing, you're right. I was being silly. What are you doing tomorrow?"

Abriella didn't believe that for a second. Her sister had attempted to change the topic far too fast for her liking.

"Seriously, what is up with you?" Abriella asked.

For a long while, Alessa went quiet on her end of the call. Abriella briefly wondered if her sister had hung up, but Alessa's soft breaths confirmed that she hadn't.

"I'm scared," Alessa finally said.

"You're going to be a great mother, and Adriano will be—"

"A great dad, I know."

Abriella laughed. "Just last minute cold feet, huh?"

"Maybe," Alessa said. "Adriano had something to handle tonight, so I couldn't talk to him. He always makes me feel better."

"What about Evelina?"

"Um ..."

"What?" Abriella demanded.

"You don't know?"

"Obviously not. What did I miss?"

"Evelina didn't come home with us after Theo got out of the hospital yesterday," Alessa explained. "She's living down in DeLuca territory."

"With Theo," Abriella said quietly.

"Yeah."

She wasn't surprised at the news. In fact, when Abriella visited Evelina while Theo was still in his coma, she had a sneaking suspicion that her old friend wouldn't be going too far from the DeLuca *principe's* side.

Love was funny in that way.

"Why didn't you mention that to me yesterday when we visited Theo?"

"I didn't think it made a difference," Alessa said.

"Who else knows?" Abriella asked.

"Adriano said it isn't anyone else's business but his, Theo's, and Evelina's. So, I guess no one really. They aren't hiding it, but no one is talking about it, either. Riley is dead, and Adriano gets to make the calls for Eve. He's letting her be free."

"Shit."

"I know," Alessa murmured softly.

"What does that even feel like, to be free?"

"I only got my freedom because you did it for me, Ella. But I still paid a price for it. It's never really as free as you think it is."

Alessa was right. A great portion of the Outfit had turned their back on the young Conti couple because of their choices and mistakes. The sneaking around and sleeping together could have been ignored, but the accidental pregnancy was a huge rule breaker. Abriella couldn't bear the thought of her sister being dragged through the mud for something as innocent as a baby, but she wouldn't allow Alessa to be abused by Joel's manipulation and behavior for another day.

So, she had done what she needed to do.

Alessa was free.

Abriella didn't have the first clue how to go about achieving her own freedom now that everyone else around her had gotten free of their cages. Lily Rossi had been forced into an arranged marriage, but ended up falling in love with her determined husband. She had found her way home after spending years running away. Alessa had surely taken heat for her choices with Adriano, but in the end, she still had him. And now, even Evelina Conti was breaking the rules and the Outfit's expectations by choosing a man she wanted, not one chosen for her.

Freedom.

It was a private dream of Abriella's that she wasn't sure would ever come to fruition. Not after everything that had happened. There was a time once, when her grandfather was still alive, that she thought maybe ... just *maybe.*

Not anymore.

"Abriella?" Alessa asked.

Shaking the depressing thoughts away, Abriella said, "Yeah, I'm here."

"I've been thinking a lot lately, too."

"Oh, about what?"

"A few things ..."

Blowing out a heavy breath, Abriella said, "Just tell me."

"Terrance, for one."

"Oh," Abriella mumbled.

"Yeah. Have you talked to Mom—"

"No, and I won't. I don't want to know what happened years ago. I live in the now, Lissa. Everything that happened back then has already happened. It's done and over with."

"But don't you want to know if it's true? Don't you want to know if we're really Peter's children, or Terrance's?"

"No," Abriella admitted. "I don't."

It was the truth. Abriella hadn't given her paternity much consideration ever since she found out the secrets of her mother's past involvement with her deceased grandfather. It just wasn't important, although things in her life had made a lot more sense after the truth came out.

Like how close Terrance had always been to her, why he let her get away with so much, and how he always treated her like she was the little queen of the family.

Yeah, she understood it all now.

"Okay," Alessa finally said.

"Is that not the answer you want?"

"It doesn't matter to me, honestly. You, on the other hand, I was curious."

"Who my father is doesn't make a difference to who I am, Alessa. I'm still a Trentini, either way. I don't see myself differently." Abriella pushed upward in the bed until she was sitting cross-legged. "You said there were a few things you were thinking about. What was the rest?"

"Our conversation yesterday when we were leaving the hospital."

"Tommas," Abriella said.

"Yeah, him. I just want to make sure you're okay, Ella. You've been messing around with Tommas for years, and I know you don't talk about him and all that business, but I worry. Especially now with the Outfit in an uproar after Riley's death, and Joel like he is. It makes me nervous. Tommas is in the middle of that—you're never far behind."

Abriella drew in as much air as her lungs could take until her chest burned. She refused to let the immediate rush of betrayal and anger wash over her again. She wouldn't allow the sadness and memories to take precedence over the lies and pain Tommas had caused her.

He ruined her.

She'd given him everything—anything she could that wouldn't destroy her. He'd taken her trust, the most important thing she had to hand over to him, and he tossed it away with one simple action.

All Tommas had needed to do was tell Abriella what he planned to do. Before the fake engagement to her best friend, he should have taken her aside. Anything other than what he did would have been fine with her.

Instead, he embarrassed her, hurt her, and his remorse meant little. At the same time, she couldn't quite say goodbye to him.

Control, she reminded herself.

It was something she found herself saying far too much where Tommas Rossi was concerned. Four years of her life had been tied into that man. Abriella had always held Tommas at a distance to where he couldn't get too close, not enough to cause her pain.

Their relationship had been a cat and mouse chase for years. Sometimes, she wasn't sure if she was the prey or the predator where he was concerned. Tommas always let her be whatever it was that she needed to be. Her little games with him over the years had spun wildly out of control, and by the time she realized what happened, it was too late.

They were supposed to be easy.

Done when it was over.

A forgotten thought.

Nothing was simple.

Tommas wanted one thing from Abriella. Just one. *Love.* She wouldn't give it—not freely. She wouldn't say it. He hadn't earned it yet. Abriella didn't know if he ever would.

And then he hurt her. Without care or concern, regardless of his motives to get closer to her, Tommas had shredded every bit of faith Abriella had in him. His promises, all of his declarations of love, his assurance of fidelity … it meant nothing.

Not anymore.

She couldn't let it.

Control, Abriella repeated silently.

She intended to keep it, no matter what. Even if it cost her the heart in her chest and the soul she didn't even believe she had. Tommas would never get her control again. He'd always had it before. Between them, he held the weight. He pulled the strings.

She was nothing more than a stupid girl caught up in a game with a much older man. She wrongly thought she had the power between them, and he proved her wrong in the worst way.

"Abriella, you didn't answer me," Alessa said, drawing Abriella from her thoughts. "Are you okay?"

"I'm not okay," Abriella said.

It was the first and only time she would say those words. Trentinis weren't weak. They didn't cry if they could help it, and they were too stubborn for their own good.

Abriella wasn't that kind of woman, anyway.

"But I will be," Abriella added.

"When?" Alessa asked.

That, Abriella couldn't answer.

She didn't know how.

"I thought I saw him following us yesterday," Abriella said.

"Oh? I didn't notice him."

"I almost wished he had been. I do miss him. I just don't know if I can trust him not to hurt me again."

"You look like shit."

Abriella hadn't even walked two feet into the kitchen, and already her day was starting out in a terrible way. After being woken up by her sister's phone call in the middle of the night, Abriella hadn't been able to fall back to sleep. Add in having to sit through breakfast with her brother, and Abriella just wanted to go back upstairs and hide.

"Is that the first thing you want to say to your sister when you see her in the morning?" Abriella asked.

"Seriously, you look awful," Joel said, tossing the newspaper on the table. "What did you do, stay up all night?"

"No, but thanks, Joel," Abriella said, smiling as sardonically as she could manage. "I never wonder why you can't find a woman to put up with you anymore. You show me exactly why every time you open your mouth."

Joel's smirk melted into a scowl instantly. "I don't have a wife because I haven't found the right woman who makes me want to marry her."

"Sure, sure."

Ignoring the glare her brother was leveling on her, Abriella strolled across the kitchen to the island. A plate of hot waffles smothered in syrup was waiting for her, cooked by their chef and maid. Thanking the chef quietly, Abriella walked to her seat at the opposite end of the table from Joel and sat down.

Figuring if her brother was in an asshole-ish enough mood to poke at her like he had, then maybe she should poke back.

"What about Chloe?" Abriella asked, cutting a triangle slice out of her waffle.

Joel's head snapped up, his gaze cutting in her direction. "I beg your pardon?"

"Chloe Belli. Why aren't you making something official with her? Or are you not messing around with her anymore? Was the fact she was playing whore to Riley Conti too embarrassing for you?"

"That's none of your business."

Abriella scoffed. "You wouldn't say the same thing if I was messing around with a guy."

"Because it isn't the same thing, Ella."

Right …

Double standards and all.

Their life was full of them.

"Actually, I know why you won't marry Chloe," Abriella said.

Joel's lips formed a tight, angry line. "Is that so?"

"Sure, because you've treated her like nothing more than a piece of ass for you to use when you want to stick your dick in something. Now, that's exactly how everyone else sees her. She isn't wife material because you've made her that way. Too bad, I think the girl might have actually liked you, Joel."

"Excuse—"

"And God knows there aren't very many people left who do like you," Abriella finished with a smile. "Not with the way you've treated and used all of us."

Joel's mouth dropped open as his gaze flashed with unhidden rage. Abriella wasn't frightened in the least, and certainly not in the face of her brother's anger. Over the years, she had learned that Joel was like any bully. Once you stood up to him and backed him into a corner, he would quit.

Cowards always did.

"That's quite enough," Joel said, his tone dark with a warning.

Abriella shrugged. "Whatever you say. Frankly, I just think it's sad. You could have your pick of women, Joel. Anyone you wanted, you could have. If you loved her, even better. What is so wrong with you that you're more focused on making everyone else miserable instead of making yourself happy?"

Joel's palm hit the table before he stood fast from his seat. "I said that's enough, Ella."

Despite his anger, Abriella could see a hint of sadness in her brother's eyes as well. Joel was an asshole, a royal one, but he was still human. He hid his feelings well, sure, but he still felt them like any person did.

She almost wished that knowing what she did about Joel was enough to make her feel sorry for him, but it didn't. He'd done this to his family, to himself, and to anyone else he touched.

The man was rotten to his core.

Poison.

"Have you ever considered that what would make me happy might just be something that makes everyone else miserable?" Joel asked quietly.

Abriella continued cutting her waffles into triangles. "Then all that makes you is a useless excuse for breath, brother. You've never gave a damn about any of us, so it's not a big surprise. The last thing you would ever do is care, never mind put someone else first."

Joel flashed a cruel smile. "Why should I, Ella?"

"Because we're your family. That's what family does."

"This family lies."

She would give him that, but not much else.

"That doesn't mean you have to go out of your way to purposely hurt us, Joel," Abriella said calmly.

"Why shouldn't I?" he asked. "My whole life has been nothing but stains of shame from our parents and being dismissed by the man who helped to bring me into this world. They raised me this way—they created me. And you expect me to give a damn about any of you? When you make a monster, Ella, you don't complain about having to live with him."

Abriella swallowed hard, taking in the hatred coating her brother's every word as he spat them at her. "I didn't do any of that."

"You didn't have to." Joel's coldness was back in a flash, replacing the anger he had previously shown. "You, like Alessa, don't have the first clue of what it feels like to be the unwanted one, to be the mistake, and the shame everyone tried to cover up."

Abriella held back from shouting the truth of her own unknown paternity at her brother, but only because she didn't want to give him anymore ammo to hurt people with. He'd already done enough of that.

She finally understood him, though.

"You're jealous," Abriella said. "That's it, isn't it?"

Joel's jaw clenched. "No."

"Liar. You're just like the rest of us, Joel, a goddamn liar. And sad—a fucking *pity*. You hate our mother for nothing more than the fact she birthed you instead of aborting you. You hate me and Alessa simply for being alive. And you hate everyone else because your behavior and attitude is so vile that they don't want to be anywhere near you. Deny it, Joel."

Between the three siblings, Abriella was the tough one. She knew it, and so did her brother and sister. She wasn't afraid to speak up, step out, or cause a problem if need be. She also wouldn't let Joel push her around if she could help it. Their whole life was nothing but Joel's attitude and anger. Years and years of his verbal abuse ripped out chunks of their family and left them bleeding on the floor.

Abriella refused to let Joel keep doing that to her. He had already practically taken her sister from her given that she could only talk and spend time with Alessa when Joel agreed. Her relationship with her parents was strained because of how awful Joel treated them while refusing them any say in Abriella's life. She had no friends that she could turn to, no life of her own to control or live, and even her choice to love was not her own to make.

"If you want to talk about making monsters, Joel," Abriella said, keeping her cold smile in place, "... then look no further from the one you've created in your own house."

Her brother stared at her, and did nothing else.

Then, very quietly, Joel said, "Get out of my face."

He could dish it, but he couldn't take it.

Abriella wasn't surprised.

"I'm eating."

"No, you're *leaving*. I want you gone."

Abriella sneered. "Be careful what you wish for, brother."

Grabbing her messenger bag with her laptop and textbooks from the upstairs library, Abriella sent off a text to her enforcer. It was her way of letting the guy know that she would be leaving the house soon. She knew better than to simply skip out with no notice, because the fool would report back to Joel in a heartbeat.

Abriella wasn't interested in that nonsense.

Once a day was enough.

Half-way down the second floor corridor, voices from the upper level traveled down to Abriella's spot. Her mother and father, actually. Confused at why her parents weren't in their own wing of the Trentini mansion, she rounded the stairs instead of going down like she had planned.

Midway up the stairs, Abriella was able to see over the top few stairs. Down the hall, her parents stood toe to toe, with Sara backed into the wall and Peter barricading her there with his arms on either side of her body. Tears streaked down her mother's cheeks, but Peter was quick to wipe them away.

"I'm sorry," Sara whispered.

"Don't," Peter said, softer than Abriella had ever heard her father speak. "I know it's hard for you, sweetheart. I've never assumed differently."

Abriella knew, somehow, that she was intruding on something that she shouldn't be seeing. Her parents had never been anything but respectful and kind to one another. She had never witnessed the two publically fight as she grew up. Her childhood had been a relatively happy one.

But this … *this* felt laced with something else entirely.

"You can talk to me, Sara," Peter said. "Just tell me anything."

"I keep coming back here. I shouldn't and I do."

"Punishing yourself."

"Maybe."

Abriella's gaze flitted past her parents to the large oak doors they stood just beyond. It had once been her grandfather's office, and where he had ultimately been killed. Sara had found Terrance that morning with a gunshot to his face, and his matter coating the walls.

For the first time since Terrance's death, Abriella found herself questioning her mother's reason for going to the office that morning. Sara had not needed to go to the office to see Terrance unless that was something she regularly did. Abriella hadn't known her mother to do that, but apparently there was a lot about her family that she wasn't aware of.

The affair between Sara and Terrance had lasted for years. If both of the Trentini sisters' paternity was in question, then it was possible the affair has lasted a lot longer than anyone actually knew.

No wonder Alessa was curious.

Sara sucked in a ragged breath. "It's no wonder Joel despises me. Look at what I've done, and who I am."

"Someone who loves?" Peter asked quietly.

"Don't, Peter."

"Well, what else do you want me to say? Do you want me to lie, to call you a whore like Joel has done and like your father did? I've never done any of that and I won't. I can't let you do it, either. Self-deprecation looks good on no one, sweetheart."

"You know what I've done. You have every right to call me those things if you wanted."

"But I won't." Peter sighed heavily. "I never understood, Sara, but I wasn't in your mind. I know you love me, and that you loved him. You didn't want to choose, but I was happy as we were. I made my own mistakes with other women because it was easy and I didn't have a reason not to. I pretended like I didn't know what you were doing. What was already there just grew and no one even noticed. That was my fault."

"I'm sorry," Sara said, barely above a breath.

"Me, too."

"It hurts you, though."

"But I love you," Peter said like that was the only important thing.

"I know." Sara smiled sadly. "And I do love you. Sometimes, that's what makes it worse. I was so over my head, Peter."

"You're still above water."

"Barely."

"Stop coming back here," Peter told her firmly. "You can't keep doing this, because it does nothing, Sara."

"You're wrong. It does do something."

"What then?"

"It reminds me that there was a time when it wasn't different, when it was marked by him, and not his ... his body and his blood. But then it hurts again."

"No more tears," Peter murmured. "Please."

"Why don't you hate me?" Sara asked.

"Because I love you. And that was enough for me to overlook what you did to me, Sara. All your lies, the affair, and our daughters."

"I don't know who the girls belong—"

"I know, but they've always been mine," Peter interjected quickly.

"Don't you want to know for sure if they are or aren't yours?"

"No."

Sara slumped back against the wall. Abriella watched the man she knew as her father wipe more wetness from her mother's cheeks with a tenderness that spoke of familiarity and love. Not for one second did Abriella doubt what she heard Peter tell his wife.

Turning away from her parents' private moment, Abriella headed back down the stairs as quietly as she had walked up them. She shouldn't have listened for as long as she did.

Their situation was difficult. It was one Abriella didn't understand, and clearly one she wouldn't ever be able to sympathize with. Some would call her mother a whore, and her father a weak man.

Abriella wouldn't. She wouldn't judge her parents for their errors and poor judgment. She wouldn't hurt them for their secrets, or use them for her own gain. They had suffered enough from their choices and actions toward one another.

Her mother was human.

Her father was human.

Humans make mistakes.

They forgave.

They loved.

Abriella knew she wasn't the same as her parents. Her forgiveness was not easily handed out, and her understanding only went as far as her pain did. Tommas' name echoed right along with her punishing thoughts that constantly revolved around a man who never left the back of her mind.

Because Tommas was always there.

He'd gotten under her skin long ago.

Abriella almost wished she could hate Tommas enough to stay away.

But she couldn't.

The itch was back under her skin with a few simple thoughts about Tommas and nothing more. It was a constant ache Abriella couldn't get rid of, no matter how hard she tried. Twice since the Christmas party when she had told Tommas to stay away from her, Abriella found herself seeking him out to soothe the urge beating in her heart.

Just to be close and just to see him. Being close led to a touch, and once he touched her, Abriella was lost.

If her father was strong enough to forgive and trust after all that his wife had done to him, why wasn't Abriella strong enough to give her lover the same thing?

She was going to fail at staying away from Tommas.

Again.

CHAPTER THREE

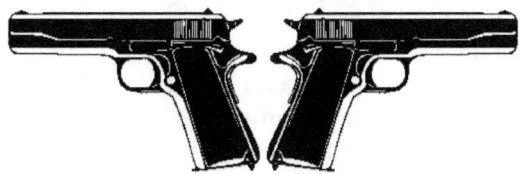

Tommas cleaned his desk area of paperwork, sliding documents back into their respective files until he could get back to them another evening. *Respirare* was the only one of his clubs that he managed hands-on. His dozen others were looked after by hired managers who were paid a decent wage to turn their cheek to any illegal happenings when it went on.

Respirare, however, was Tommas' safe zone. He could personally control who came in and out because he worked there every night the club was open. He controlled the workers and their loose lips when he needed his secrets kept quiet.

Secrets like Abriella.

Lately, there hadn't been a reason for his workers to get their extra bonuses on their checks what with Abriella not coming around like she sometimes did.

Tommas chanced a look at the decorative clock hanging on his office wall. At well after two in the morning, the club was closed. The business's schedule was tight. Last call came just before one, and the patrons had to be out of the venue twenty minutes later at the latest. Cleanup and prep was quickly followed by the staff before they were out of the joint by two.

His floor and bar manager was always the last person to leave. The man let Tommas know when he was locking up for the night. Tonight had been no exception.

Leaning back in his chair and closing his eyes, Tommas pressed the pads of his fingers into his temples to relieve some of the tension headache that had been plaguing him for the last week and a half. There wasn't a pain killer or drink on hand that would make the damned thing go away.

"Tired?"

Tommas straightened in the chair, his boots snapping on the floor with a crack as his eyes flew wide. He found where the voice had come from almost instantly. Damian stood in the doorway with a lit cigarette dangling between two fingers and a curious glint in his gaze.

"Someday, you're going to get your ass shot for doing nonsense like that," Tommas warned his cousin. "You almost gave me a goddamn heart attack, D."

Damian smirked. "That's kind of hard to do when the whole reason I sneak up on people is usually to kill them, Tommy."

True enough.

His cousin was the hit man, after all.

Tommas let it go.

"What are you doing here?" Tommas asked.

"I couldn't sleep." Damian lifted his cigarette, took a drag, and exhaled a cloud of smoke into the office. "You're predictable, by the way. You need to change that."

"Pardon?"

Damian waved a hand high. "This place, your club. Your schedule is predictable. You make it easy to find where you're at on any given night. On weekdays, you're usually at one of your restaurants. On the weekend, you're always here."

Tommas cleared his throat. "It makes for an easy target."

"Yeah. Maybe change it up for a while. At least until things calm down and we know what's going on."

"I spend my weekends working here for a reason, D."

Damian's expression was unreadable. "I'm aware. Keep that shit up and she'll get you killed for it, too."

Tommas couldn't find it in himself to be surprised that Damian knew exactly why he spent weekend after weekend running his club. It was two of the only days when Abriella's dogs were a little less watchful of her. Joel usually spent time away on the weekends, and Abriella used that to her advantage to lose the enforcers trailing her.

She always came here to Tommas.

Or she used to.

"Yeah, I get it," Tommas finally said. "When did you show up?"

"A few minutes ago. I figured I should make sure you're still alive, since you've been as quiet as a mouse for the last little while."

Tommas relaxed into the leather office chair. "I've been taking some time to think everything over."

"Think what over?"

"When I visited Theo a week and a half ago, it made me realize something."

"What is that?" Damian asked.

"I don't have a great deal of allies left in Chicago," Tommas said quietly. "The DeLuca crew is out until they have a new boss to answer to, and the Conti side of things is Switzerland when it comes to everyone else."

"Unless provoked, you mean."

"I won't provoke a man with a pregnant wife into aligning himself with me just so that I might have a better number to go against Joel with, D. Yes, I could easily force Adriano Conti's hand into turning on Joel, but unless it's absolutely needed, I can't see the point. Widowing Alessa

Trentini before her child is even born isn't the right thing to do here."

"Fair enough," his cousin replied.

"But on the upside," Tommas continued, running his hand through his short, dark hair, "… Joel is in the same predicament that I'm in. No allies to name. A crew of his own to protect and streets to manage. We're on equal footing where that is concerned."

"What is the problem, Tommy?"

Tommas chewed over his thoughts. He'd always been the kind of man who thought before he spoke, because that was the way of a smarter man. Emotional people liked to shoot off at the mouth first and then deal with the consequences later. He didn't have time for that nonsense.

"What about outside of Chicago?" Tommas mused.

Damian glanced away at the question.

Tommas didn't miss it.

"What?" Tommas asked.

"I think that could be an easy route to take if you went to the right families with the best offers."

"A family like the Marcellos?"

"Just like them," Damian confirmed. "I know who they don't want as a boss down here; I also know that if shit doesn't start quieting down soon, they've promised to make their way here and finish it up themselves."

"Huh," Tommas said under his breath.

"But be careful of who else you talk to where other families are concerned, Tommy."

"Joel is a snake."

"He is, and he's done those rounds outside of Chicago when Riley was coming at him. Be mindful of families that haven't already taken issue with Joel in some way outside of Chicago. You don't know who might be aligned with him until it's too late and you're in their den."

"Thanks for the info."

Tommas cleared off his desk and put the laptop he used into the bag hanging off the office chair. Standing, he slung the bag over his shoulder.

"Time for some sleep. I've got an early day tomorrow," Tommas explained.

Damian nodded. "How's your mother doing?"

"Drunker than ever. I hired a girl to look after the house. Half of the time, Serena doesn't even realize someone is there with her. But it makes me feel better to know someone is keeping an eye on her when I can't."

"Sorry."

Tommas shrugged. "I couldn't do it, man."

"Hmm?"

"Kill her," Tommas said lower. "Laurent was easy, like breathing. Maybe it was because he'd never really felt like my father for a long time, so pulling the trigger was simple. He fucked me over when he went off half-cocked and almost got Abriella killed in the process. But my mother? I know she's not a saint, D, and I know she put us kids through hell as we grew up, but she's a victim in her own way, too."

Damian blew out a heavy exhale. "You want me to do it? It'd be quick, painless, and no mess if you want. It could look like a suicide, for that matter."

As cruel as it made Tommas, he actually considered the offer.

"No," he settled on saying.

Damian didn't question Tommas on his answer. Tommas was grateful.

"By the way," Damian said.

"Yeah?"

"I didn't have to mess with the locks to get in earlier."

Tommas tossed his cousin a look. "Pardon?"

"You have a guest out on the floor, man. She must have let herself in with the keys you gave her or something. I'll see you later."

Tommas was already leaving the office before Damian had even finished talking.

"Ella."

Tommas dropped his messenger bag on the bar and took a couple of steps toward the woman sitting on the edge of the stage. *Respirare* sported a raised platform that rested four feet above the club's floor in the center of the venue. Depending on the night, the platform could be used for a variety of things to entertain the guests with.

"Later," Tommas heard Damian call from his far right.

Out of the corner of his eye, Tommas watched his cousin disappear out of one of the side exits. Once he was alone with Abriella, Tommas gave her all of his attention. The sight of her sitting there, waiting for him like she had done so many nights before, was all too familiar to him.

It soaked into his system like a drug.

Comfort.

Need.

Hunger.

It wasn't anything new, but it never felt old.

Abriella's fingers wrapped tightly around the edge of the platform until her knuckles were turning white from the pressure. Tommas kept the distance between them to a couple of feet. It'd been a good month or more since she had come anywhere near him.

Why was she here?

"Hi," Abriella said.

"Hi."

Abriella grabbed the tumbler glass resting beside her and lifted it for a drink. "I hope you don't mind, but I poured myself something while I was waiting for you to finish up in the back."

Tommas didn't give a damn. "As long as it's not a rum drink, Ella."

"Yeah, I know."

The girl couldn't drink rum if her life depended on it.

"Is your brother out of town or something?" he asked.

Abriella sipped from her drink before setting it back down. "No."

"But you came here anyway?"

"I turned the cameras off and the alarm for the back door. I walked for a bit and then I called a cab. I wasn't going to come. I wanted a break or something. Time to breathe."

Tommas' fingers ached to reach out and grab his longtime lover, but he forced the urge back. "Is that so?"

Abriella laughed bleakly. "Before I even realized it, I was already walking in this direction. The cab brought me the rest of the way."

"You shouldn't be here."

"I'm aware, Tommy."

"You told me to stay away and to leave you alone. You're making it terribly goddamn hard on me to do those things when you keep seeking me out like this, Ella. You'll leave here, like you have the last couple of times, making me feel like I did something wrong; you'll fuck me, but you'll leave me feeling dirty, making me think you hate me all over again. If that's your goal tonight, get your pretty ass off that stage and get out. I don't need you to fuck me up like that again. I have enough problems right now, girl."

Abriella blinked, a wetness coating her bottom lashes. "I'm so angry with you."

Her voice was nothing more than a whisper. Pained, filled to the brim with longing, and so tired, but it was still just a breath of air whispering to him.

"I'm not going to keep apologizing," Tommas said.

"Why not? Don't I matter enough for you to want to keep apologizing until I forgive you for being such an asshole?"

"You know you matter. You don't need me to tell you how much you mean to me, Ella. I've told you for years in a hundred different ways. I won't keep apologizing to you because it won't make a difference. Your stubbornness won't allow you to let your anger go enough that you can see beyond it all. Your bitterness is bred too deep. It's your only fucking flaw, but I never cared until you turned it on me."

"I—"

"Don't bother," Tommas interrupted sharply. "We both know it's true. So I hurt you, Ella. I hurt you because I'd hoped that what I was trying to do with Riley and Evelina would outweigh your anger about it all in the end when you were free of your brother to do what you wished. I did it for you and you know it. I can't help that it didn't go according to plan."

"I just wanted you to tell me," Abriella said, anger heating her eyes when she turned back on him. "And what you did instead was prove to me everything that I already knew."

Tommas barked out a laugh and took a step forward. "Exactly, Ella. You've been waiting for four years just to see me fuck something up. You've been waiting for me to prove how little I care about you. You want me to be just like everybody else because that would be so much fucking easier for you than admitting that you might actually give a shit about us, or that you might love me. Right?"

Abriella's lips drew thin. "You don't know a thing."

"I know everything that's important about you. I know why it hurt when I didn't tell you about the fake engagement to Evelina, because you've never been able to be even close to the same thing with me publically. We've had to hide it. Privately, you've always been mine, but you always felt that if people knew the truth, they would compare you to your mother. And when someone else had to stand at my side, even if it was just for show, it made you feel like exactly what you were trying to hide: my whore.

"I know you're lonely as hell; I know that you miss me like nothing else, and that's why you came here tonight." Tommas moved forward until he was close enough to Abriella that could see the flecks of navy in her sky blue irises. Tears welled in her eyes, threatening to fall. He wouldn't relent, he refused to. "I know that, as much as you want to pretend differently, you *care*. Tell me I'm wrong about any of it, Ella. Go on ahead and do it."

Abriella glanced away. Tommas wouldn't allow her to hide her truths simply because she was stubborn as hell. He was close enough to touch her, and he did, reaching out to grab her chin and tilt her face back so he could see her.

Her tears streaked down to trembling lips.

Tommas held her chin tighter when she tried to move away. "Don't, Ella."

"I hate this."

Well, at least she hadn't said that she hated him.

"Hate what?" Tommas asked.

"*This*," Abriella whispered, her hand coming up to lie flat to his chest.

"I don't want to depend on you, but I can't even stay away from you long enough to stand on my own. I'm so fucked up around you."

Tommas moved closer to Abriella until she was parting her thighs to let him stand between her legs. Her hand slid up from his chest to his neck, stopping briefly over his pulse point before moving to his jaw.

"Don't say that," Tommas murmured. "You can't hate us, Ella."

"It's not the same thing."

"Isn't it? All the things you just said make exactly what we are, babe."

Abriella's thumb swept a tender line over his cheek. "I miss you."

Tommas' tension drifted away with those words. "The apartment feels empty."

He released her chin to grab onto her wrist. His fingers curled around hers, stopping the stroking motion to his cheek. Holding her hand tight to keep her still, Tommas used his free hand to ghost the tips of his fingers over her frowning lips.

"I wish you wouldn't do that," Tommas said.

"I don't know what you're talking about."

"Frown, Ella. When you're with me, you should never be sad or angry."

Abriella sighed shakily. "Why do you do that, Tommy? Why do you have to say things like that when I'm sad and angry with you? It's not fair."

She batted his hand away from her face.

"And that, too," Abriella added, forcing his hand down between them and not allowing him to touch her.

"What?"

"When you touch me, I go fucking stupid. I want more. I want you to keep touching me. I forget about all the reasons why I don't want you to touch me, and everything you did that made me so angry with you. I didn't come here tonight for this, Tommy. It's not fair at all because you know what you do."

Tommas chuckled. "You've never played fair with me, babe. What makes you think I won't play dirty with you to get what I want?"

He tugged his hand free from her grasp and quickly intertwined their fingers tightly together. For any other couple, an action like holding hands was innocent. A fairly easy way of showing affection and support.

For Tommas and Abriella, something as simple as holding hands was sacred and rare. An action that they could only do in private. Affection they couldn't give freely. As much as their sex could be rough, dirty, and dangerous, something like holding hands could be the exact same thing but in a different way.

Abriella swallowed thickly, her tongue peeking out to wet her bottom lip. "I do miss you. That's why I came tonight, but if you keep this up, it might turn into something else, Tommy."

Despite her words, Tommas felt the tug on his arm when Abriella pulled on his hand. He moved closer until her thighs were closing around his waist and locking him in. The wool dress hugging Abriella's curves slid up her hips, letting him feel the heat of her sex beneath the cotton panties she wore.

There were no keys to her prison.

Tommas didn't mind.

In love, freedom was a myth.

Abriella's hand still hadn't left his cheek. With her warm, smooth palm pressed tight to his skin, and her other tangled up with his, Tommas was grounded.

"You're crazy coming here tonight," Tommas said.

Abriella bit the inside of her cheek and replied, "I know."

"I am sorry, Ella. I lied. I'll keep saying it until you don't need or want me to anymore. You know I will."

"Of course, you will."

Tommas smiled. "There's no hiding anything from you, is there?"

"Well, you can't."

"I wish you would let me know when you're coming. I could meet you somewhere safer. I don't know on any given night if someone is watching this place, Ella."

"I was careful. I snuck in through the back alley and used the keys for the emergency door like you showed me."

Tommas' fingers tightened with Abriella's. "That's not the point. Nothing is safe right now, Ella. I have no idea what your brother is planning, or rather, what he might already have planned. I don't want you in the middle of anything that might get you hurt."

"Tommas—"

"Hush, and listen."

Abriella's mouth snapped shut. "Fine."

"I fucked up the first time around with the engagement and the boss, Ella. I thought for sure that Riley would take out Joel, and that would leave you free to do what you wanted."

"With you," she said softly.

Tommas had never been a liar. "Yes."

"All you had to do was tell me and not let me find out in a room full of people, Tommy."

"You wouldn't have listened no matter when I told you."

Abriella opened her mouth to argue, but Tommas wasn't in the mood to fight with his lover. They had done enough of that over the last couple of months. The worst kind of fighting was the kind that was silent and non-verbal, separated by people and space. He preferred Abriella's anger, even violence, over her silence and distance.

Instead of allowing her to argue the point with him, Tommas leaned forward and caught her opened mouth with his own. Her silky lips pressed back to his, returning the kiss, and almost instantly, their softness was gone. Abriella's fingernails dug into Tommas' cheek the second his tongue found hers when he deepened the kiss. He fisted her dress and pulled her closer, wanting her to feel the hardness growing under his slacks.

Simply being close and touching Abriella was enough to make Tommas harder than steel and fucking stupid in the head.

Tommas caught Abriella's bottom lip and bit down hard enough to leave the imprints of his teeth behind. She gasped the sweetest sound, a high whine following right behind. The spikes of her leather high-heeled boots dug into the small of his back, stinging in the best way when she left her own mark on his cheek with her nails.

"You wouldn't have listened," Tommas breathed against her trembling lips. "No matter what I said or how I told you, Ella, you wouldn't have heard a thing I said. All you would have heard was that someone else would stand with me, and not you. Someone else would be thought of as mine, and not you. Someone else who wasn't you, Ella. It wouldn't have made a difference how fake it was, and that I never intended to follow it through, because it wasn't *you*."

Abriella's lashes fanned her cheeks, and more tears escaped the corners of her eyes. "You're right, but it still hurt me, Tommy."

"Hurting you kills me, babe. You know it does. It was easier for me to do it the way I did. I knew you would be forced to control your reaction and ..."

"Keep going," she demanded.

"And I didn't want to see your face when you heard about the engagement."

Abriella didn't even seem surprised. "That was selfish of you."

"The word you used was cowardly, actually."

"You're not a coward, Tommy, but you are terribly selfish."

"When it comes to you, yes. I'll always be that way. You've made me like this, Ella."

"And what about the monster you turned me into, huh?"

Tommas leaned down, nose to nose with his lover. "I adore the monster in you."

The sadness in Abriella's gaze was replaced by a feisty fire. This was the woman Tommas loved; she was the woman that he wouldn't trade for anything. There was no one on earth like Abriella Trentini. She was fucking gorgeous, as sharp as a razor's edge, and smarter than most men in the Outfit.

She was perfect.

Crazy wonderful.

Abriella bent forward and kissed Tommas hard, driving her booted heels into his lower back and pushing him into her body. His tongue tangled with hers, their familiar dance falling in tune like it always did between them.

There was nothing like this.

No one else but Ella.

"Goddamn," Tommas groaned into her mouth. "I thought you said that you hadn't come here tonight for this."

Abriella's laugh was high and airless. "Should I go somewhere else for it?"

Tommas let loose a sound that came off a hell of a lot like a growl. He grabbed her waist with enough force to leave his fingerprints behind, but he knew she liked it. Abriella preferred him rough and dirty, not soft and sweet.

"Excuse me?" Tommas asked. "Do you want to repeat that a little louder, babe?"

"Is that a no?"

"That. Is. A. Fucking. No."

Abriella flashed a wicked grin. "You're so jealous."

He was.

He was damned awful.

"You love it."

Abriella's smile fell. Tommas' frustration skyrocketed at the sight. All it took was one word for his girl's walls to climb back up high.

In typical Abriella fashion, she went for a deflection. Tommas decided to let her.

"You weren't the only one who lied tonight," Abriella said.

"Oh?"

"No. I didn't actually sneak out. Joel's been in his office for a couple of days. He barely comes out of it. I don't know what is up with him, and he's not that important anyway."

"Hey," Tommas said quickly, quieting Abriella instantly. "Don't underestimate your brother. Too many other people have done exactly that and they've ended up in a grave because of it, Ella. Joel is an asshole, but he is not a stupid man."

Abriella tipped her chin down. "Sorry. You're right. I just meant that he's not important to us right now, Tommy."

Tommas disagreed entirely. Joel was the one and only reason why Tommas couldn't have Abriella in every possible way that he wanted to have her. Joel was the one thing keeping Tommas from everything that mattered in his life. Joel was the road block to the highest seat in the family and the wall keeping Abriella's heart locked up tight.

Joel was the problem.

Abriella didn't understand just how much her brother was really in the way. Regardless of Tommas' thoughts about Joel, he wouldn't argue with Abriella about her feelings on her brother.

"Keep talking," Tommas said.

Abriella smiled. "I was actually at Alessa's to help her with the final plans for the baby shower. It was late. Joel called over and said I might as well stay there. Alessa helped me to sneak out."

"And you came here."

"Yeah. So, I lied. A little."

"I don't mind."

Abriella rocked into his groin, reminding Tommas of how damned hard and aching he was. "No, I don't suppose you do mind."

"Stop that. This stage is awkward to fuck on. We learned that once, remember?"

Her shiver was a gift to him.

"Take me home," she whispered.

Tommas cupped her face in his hands. "Yeah?"

"Yeah, Tommy. I want to go home with you. I want to sleep in our bed. I miss you."

Shit.

Tommas didn't know how to deny Abriella when she said things like that. He knew it was stupid as hell and more dangerous than he could explain, but he just didn't care. His bed was fucking cold, and his sheets didn't smell like her.

That was worse than anything else.

"Go put your cup on the bar. Meet me out in the parking lot. I'll warm up the car."

Abriella's face lit up with happiness and a sexiness curved her lips. She trailed a hand down his middle and grazed her fingertips across his erection straining the zipper of his pants. A shot of heat and lust coursed through Tommas' cock.

"Quickly, right?" she asked sweetly.

"*God*, yes. Quickly, Ella."

Tommas helped a laughing Abriella down from the stage. He pulled the car keys attached to the auto start for his Mercedes from his pocket.

"Grab my bag," he yelled over his shoulder.

"Got it."

Tommas was already half-way to the side of the club where a second exit door led straight into the parking lot when he heard Abriella call for him to slow down. Pushing the door open, he tossed his lover a wink over his shoulder. Abriella couldn't run in heels, and he told her that he wanted to get out of there.

She would catch up.

The girl always did.

Pointing the car starter as he opened the exit door, Tommas hit the ignition button to start his vehicle at the other end of the parking lot. His foot barely hit the slush covered pavement when he was blinded by light and heat. Tommas' ears rang from the level of the blast. His breath was gone the moment his back hit the building and his head snapped against the bricks with a sickening crack.

In the background of the sudden pain ricocheting through his body and the confusion muddling up his mind, he could still hear Abriella's screams.

Fuck.

Predictable, Damian had said.

Joel was going to answer for this one.

CHAPTER FOUR

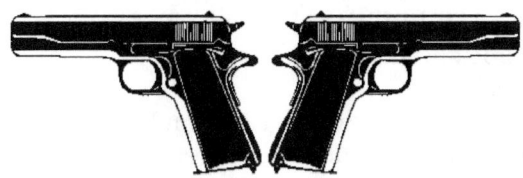

The boom was volcanic. It was so loud that it made Abriella's ears ring even inside the club. Her hands flew up to cover her ears, and she crouched low on the floor out of instinct. She was only a few feet away from the door, but the instant reaction of the bomb was unmistakable. Heat, blinding light, and flinging metal.

Abriella's scream caught in her throat when the exit door was blown wide open from the pressure of the blast.

"Tommas!"

Dropping the messenger bag on the floor, Abriella shot toward the exit and where she had just seen Tommas only seconds ago. She stumbled in her heels, a pain blooming in her ankle when it twisted hard to the left. A sickness rolled in her stomach when she caught herself on the floor. In her chest, her heart raced as tears streaked down her cheeks.

He had been right there!

Abriella finally gained traction on the hardwood floor and scrambled to the threshold of the exit door. On wobbly legs, she staggered out of the building only to find a still burning Mercedes at the other end of the vacant parking lot. The surrounding brick walls were shadowed with marks from the blast, and pieces of the car rested in various spots around the parking lot.

God.

It was almost like a daze had settled over Abriella as she stupidly stared around at the smoldering mess and the black plume rising toward the sky. The world around her moved slower than what was normal as she took a hesitant step forward, and then another.

Abriella couldn't breathe.

"*Tommy!*"

"Ella."

Tommas' quiet call came from Abriella's left. Still feeling sluggish and confused, she turned to find her lover on his knees with one hand pressed to the pavement and the other wrapped around his chest. Even with his head bent low, Abriella could tell there was something wrong.

Somehow, she managed to make it to Tommas' side without falling again. Her knees hit the wet, slushy pavement and she reached for him. Something stopped her hands from grabbing him at the last second.

A dark trickle of red oozed down in a thin line behind Tommas' ear.

"Oh, my God," Abriella cried. "You're bleeding."

Tommas shook his head. "I'm okay."

"You're not."

"I am, Ella. Give me ... just give a second, okay."

His words came out mumbled and slow. All of Abriella's training from school came rushing back in a blink, but she didn't know where to start.

"Chill out," she heard Tommas whisper.

"Look at me," Abriella demanded.

Coldness seeped through her dress and chilled her skin, but Abriella barely felt it at all.

Tommas' slate blue gaze lifted again. The dilation of his pupils were worrisome. Abriella held up one finger and moved it back and forth.

"Can you watch it?" she asked.

"Stop it, Ella."

"Tommy, come on. Don't be difficult."

"I see your fucking finger."

"Then why won't you follow it like I ask?"

Tommas didn't answer. Abriella didn't need him to. He couldn't follow it. He was trying, she could see how his eyes flicked in the direction they wanted to go but quickly zoned back in on her.

"How many fingers am I holding up?" Abriella asked.

Tommas swallowed hard. "Four."

Wrong.

Two.

This whole situation screamed bad to Abriella. She believed that Tommas had suffered some kind of concussion. He had been a great deal closer to the car bomb than she was when it went off. The pressure of it probably sent him flying right off his feet.

"Did you hit your head?" Abriella asked.

"Yeah."

"On what?"

"The wall, or maybe the door. I don't know."

"Sit down for me, please, Tommy."

"Kind of hurts to move right now," he confessed under his breath.

Damn.

"When you breathe?" she asked.

"Yeah."

"Too bad. You've got to sit up or lay back."

Despite his protests, Abriella managed to get Tommas rolled over onto his back. His hands shook and his eyes became unfocused the more he moved. Abriella used his jacket and placed it under Tommas' head to give him support and keep him higher. With Tommas on his back, Abriella could see that he sported a nasty, bleeding cut on his right cheek directly under his eye.

As she was removing her hands from under his head, something warm and sticky coated her fingers. She had a feeling she knew what that substance was—blood. Pressing the tips of her fingers gently along the base of Tommas' skull, she found a lump that was hard and hot to the touch. Behind his ear, she found the spot that was bleeding.

"Does this hurt at all?" Abriella asked.

"No."

That couldn't be good.

"How's the breathing on your back?"

"My phone," Tommas mumbled.

"In a second."

"No, you need to call—"

"Tommy, shut up," Abriella barked. "Just answer my question."

"What question?" he asked, confused.

Well, that actually answered a lot of things for Abriella. She asked about his breathing not even five seconds before. Tommas should have remembered what she just asked him. Her fear climbed higher, but her resolve never wavered.

"You need to go to a hospital, Tommas," she told him quietly.

"I'm fi—"

"You're not fine, so don't even start. At best, you've got a concussion. At worst … It doesn't matter, but we need to get you to a hospital."

A calm head, a firm demeanor, and confidence was the best thing to show in a bad situation. Tommas had taught her that a long time ago. Abriella couldn't forget it even if she tried.

"Christ, what is that sound?" Tommas growled.

The only sound that Abriella could hear was the siren of the club going off, and the hisses and pops from the burning car across the lot. Other than that, a lot of Abriella's senses still felt numb to her, dulled like she was under water.

He tried to push up from the ground, but a confusion settled over his features before he dropped back down just as fast. He pressed his shaking hands into his eyes and mumbled something unintelligible.

"See, you can't even sit up," Abriella said. "Where is your phone? I'll call for an ambulance."

"The cops are going to come," Tommas forced out through gritted teeth.

"What?"

"Cops, Ella."

It took her far too long to understand what he was saying.

"So?"

"You need to go."

Abriella's fingers fluttered over Tommas' hands to push them away from his face. She held on tight to him, making him look at her. "I can't go, Tommy."

She had to make sure he was all right. She needed to see him go into a hospital. She wouldn't leave.

"Abriella … babe, you gotta go. It's okay, sweet girl." Tommas' hand found Abriella's cheek and his thumb swept under her eye. "Don't cry, Ella."

"Don't make me go."

"Here …"

"What?"

Tommas dug into his pant pocket with his trembling hand and pulled out his cell phone. The screen was cracked, but it turned on when Abriella hit the home screen.

"Call my cousin, Ella."

"Damian?"

"Call him. Go back to your sister's place."

"Tommy—"

"Do it, Ella."

"But your head, Tommas."

"Cops. You need to go."

Abriella cried harder, sobs catching in her chest. She didn't even have to ask who had done this, because she knew without question that this attack had Joel's name written all over it. How was she supposed to wake up tomorrow and face her brother only to act like she didn't know and like she hadn't been here?

"I hate him," Abriella whispered.

"Go, Ella."

"No."

"*Go.*"

For the next thirty or so seconds, Abriella watched as Tommas' clarity and wakefulness began to drift away. Tommas stared beyond Abriella, like he wasn't seeing her at all. The paleness taking over his usual olive-toned complexion was worrisome. Laying on the wet, cold pavement couldn't be helping anything, either. He needed a hospital, and soon.

A siren blared in the distance, waking Abriella from her stupor. She recognized the sound instantly as a police cruiser.

Someone was coming.

Someone would help.

She still held tight to Tommas.

Go.

His voice was louder in her head.

"I'm sorry." Abriella bent down to quickly kiss Tommas' mouth. She wiped a bit of the blood from his cheek with her thumb. "You're not allowed to die, Tommy. You're not. You're mine, okay? *Mine.* So, I'll go, but you can't."

She rambled, knowing it was pointless.

Abriella still hoped Tommas had heard it.

Abriella fell into an alleyway, frozen and shaking. The numbness that had been plaguing her was finally gone, but now she was left feeling useless and incapable of doing anything else. The cell phone in her hand practically burned against her skin. With trembling fingers, she turned the phone on and typed in the passcode.

Tommas hadn't changed the six digits in four years.

Somehow, through teary eyes and chattering teeth, she found the number tagged onto Damian Rossi's contact information, and hit the call button. Abriella pressed the phone to her ear, and three rings later, Damian picked up.

"Cousin," Damian greeted. "Have you left the club yet?"

Abriella choked out a sound that even she couldn't decipher.

Instantly, Damian reacted. "Who is this?"

"Abriella."

"Where's Tommas?"

"Something happened—Joel, I think. We were getting ready to leave, and Tommy went out first to start the car. It was really, really fast and loud. I didn't see what happened until I got outside, but he must have hit the wall or something. He was so confused and talking slow. He hurt himself and—"

"Slow down," Damian hissed.

Abriella sucked in a deep breath, desperately wishing she could calm herself. "He made me go, but I didn't want to."

"His car, you said?"

"Yeah."

"Start there, Abriella."

"Someone blew it up. Tommas hit the car starter and it just … blew up, Damian."

Damian cursed severely. "Where are you right now?"

"A couple blocks away from the club."

"You're not with him?" Damian roared.

"He made me go! I didn't want to!"

"Of course, he did." Damian laughed a bitter, angry sound that cut Abriella straight to her core. "He's so fucking in love with you that he's stupid. Do you realize that, girl? He could be on the ground dying, and he would still think about you before himself."

Abriella's sobs caught in the back of her throat. "I know."

"Why do you have his phone?"

"He told me to call you."

"And you're just a couple of blocks away from the club?"

"Yes. I heard the sirens just before I left. He'll be okay, right?"

"I fucking hope so," Damian grumbled. "Do you have a street name or something to help me out here?"

Abriella could hear the sound of tires screeching in the background of the call. Obviously, Damian had still been driving.

"I'm in the alley beside the pizzeria two blocks away."

"The one Tommas likes?" Damian asked.

"Yes."

"All right. Stay out of the weather. It's cold as hell."

Abriella's shaking only increased at the reminder of the chill in her body.

"I didn't want to leave him," she said again.

Her chest hurt something fierce, and her fingers ached with the need to hold Tommas again. She had never been any good at praying even though she went to church every Sunday. Praying wasn't meant for people like her, because Abriella's religion had very little to do with a God up above, but rather, a man two blocks away.

"I'm sorry, Damian."

Damian sighed. "I'll be there in fifteen, Ella. Stay out of sight like he told you to."

Damian reached over, aimed the vents toward Abriella's vibrating form, and turned the heater on high. Thankfully, the car was already warm. It didn't take the vents long at all to begin blowing hot air on Abriella.

"Shit, look at you," Damian muttered to himself.

Abriella wouldn't look the man in the eye. It was bad enough that he had come into the club earlier when she was waiting for Tommas. There were very few people that knew about her relationship with Tommas, and she preferred it that way. The one thing Abriella never wanted to be seen as was a whore. She was terrified of being looked at like her mother had been.

"Just don't say anything, okay," Abriella said.

"About what?" Damian shook his head and pulled off his coat. He handed the item over to Abriella and said, "Put that on. You're going to catch pneumonia. Tommas would kick my ass all the way back down to the other side of Chicago if he thought I let you get sick."

Abriella took the coat and practically hid under the weight of it. The thick tweed did help to warm her up. "Thank you."

"How in the hell am I supposed to get you home without your brother knowing?"

"I was staying with Alessa and Adriano for the night."

"That makes things easier," Damian said.

"Okay."

"Tell me everything that happened."

"About the bomb?"

"Yes." Damian's gaze narrowed as he pulled the car out onto the road. "And things that may have been happening lately at home with your brother. Has he been difficult, or different in any way? Things like that."

"Yes, more so than usual. And yes, but sometimes he does that."

"How so?"

"He's spent a lot of time in his office. He makes a lot of private phone calls. He's moodier than normal, and quick to lash out at me or my parents if they get in his way. Even the cook has asked for some time off because Joel is unbearable."

"Have you overheard anything that might suggest Joel had been planning something like this on Tommas?"

"Other than Joel's normal nonsense, no."

"What does that mean?"

"It means that ever since Riley died, and even before, Joel hasn't trusted Tommas. He hasn't trusted him since the night that Adriano was caught in Tommas' club, and the Artino guy was killed in the fight that broke out."

"So?"

"When Joel doesn't trust or like someone, he gets increasingly paranoid about them and what they're doing. Eventually, he goes after them. Like our grandfather, for example."

Damian's jaw clenched. "I can assure you that your brother did not kill your grandfather, Abriella. I hate Joel, make no mistake about that, but he was not the person who went after Terrance."

"Then who did?"

"Me."

Abriella's gaze cut to the man and she froze in her seat. "What did you just say?"

Damian cleared his throat and repeated louder, "Me."

"You—"

"I had to protect myself and my wife. I made a bad decision and your grandfather suffered from it. I regret it, but there is nothing I can do about it except to protect the people that my wife and I care about now. That is it, Abriella. I'm sorry, but you asked. I'm so tired of keeping secrets for other people and for myself. So yes, I did it. And trust me when I say that your anger is nothing compared to my guilt."

Abriella felt the tears well and slip from the corners of her eyes. She didn't know what to say, but her heart clenched in her chest, taking away her air and making her feel like she was burying her grandfather all over again.

"I know you two were close," Damian said. "I know Terrance cared for you a great deal."

"I loved him. He was a good man in his heart."

"I know. Tommas doesn't let me forget it."

Oh.

Abriella's bottom lip quivered. "Tommy knew?"

"I had to talk to someone. I needed to make sense of what happened and what I did. Tommas is one of the only people I trust. So yeah, I went to him."

"He didn't tell me."

"Tommas wouldn't hurt you if he had a choice about it, Ella."

She wanted to be angry that her lover had hidden something as important as the killer behind her grandfather's murder, but she couldn't be mad at Tommas. Nothing Damian had said was a lie.

Abriella wiped the mess of tears from her face. "So you went into his home and …"

"Yes."

Anger swept her under the current, but she kept control.

Somehow.

"Why?"

"I trusted the wrong person," Damian admitted quietly. "I did it because I didn't have a choice in the end. It had already gone too far."

"He must have seen you coming or known it was you."

Damian nodded. "He did."

"What did he say?"

"He forgave me."

Abriella wasn't surprised to hear those words. Terrance Trentini was not a perfect man, but he was a forgiving one.

"I can't say the same," Abriella said through her haze of anger and pain.

"I don't expect you to. I am sorry."

She did believe that.

Damian's phone rang in his lap. He picked it up and checked the screen before answering the call. "Damian Rossi speaking."

Abriella watched a rush of relief wash over Damian's features.

"Thank you," Damian said after a moment. "I will be right there."

Once the call was ended and the phone had been forgotten in his lap, Damian shot Abriella a small smile.

"Who was that?"

"Presbyterian ER. I am Tommas' emergency contact on his medical file and there was a secondary card in his wallet with my name on it. They just brought him in."

Abriella's air rushed from her lungs in a whoosh. "Yeah?"

"He's stable. You can't risk going, though. Not tonight. If your brother did this, and we both know he did, Joel will be watching, Ella. You need to stay safe. That's what Tommas would want."

"I will."

"Good. I'll get you back to your sister's place before I head over to the hospital."

"Tell Tommy something for me, please?"

Damian shot her a look. "What is that?"

Three words stuck like glue to her tongue: *I love you.*

It should have been simple.

Obvious, even.

Easy.

It was true. She did love Tommas.

Why couldn't she say it?

"Tell him that I'm sorry," Abriella mumbled.

Fumbling with keys, Abriella managed to stick the right one in the lock and open the door to her sister's apartment. She wasn't concerned about someone seeing her arrive back to the building.

Adriano was always particular about enforcers watching his place when he was home, and he didn't like it. Alessa wasn't one to be followed now that she was a married woman. Her husband only asked for her to have guards if there was significant danger. It was one of the reasons why Abriella hadn't been worried about going out to see Tommas.

She wasn't quiet when she got inside the apartment. Her heels smacked the wall loudly when she kicked them off. She dropped the keys and her clutch on the floor with a thump before her back hit the closet wall.

Abriella's face met her palms, and she cried.

Hard.

Loud.

Unrelenting.

Her tears flowed freely, and her pain came out in catching sobs and gasps of breath. She despised weak women who cried at every little thing. She never wanted to be one of those women, but life wasn't giving her much of a choice lately.

Before she knew what happened, Abriella's backside met the floor and her tears just kept on coming. One by one, the lights in the apartment started to turn on. She didn't bother to try and hide her presence or fix the mess that her face was.

"Ella?"

Alessa's soft voice traveled down the hallway. Abriella waved a hand blindly, hoping her sister would take it as a hint and leave her alone.

She didn't.

Alessa padded down the hallway quickly and dropped down to her sister's level. Abriella found her hands pulled away from her face, and then she was buried in a tight, familiar embrace. Alessa's rounded stomach kept her from pulling Abriella in too close, but it was still good.

Safe.

Home.

Good.

"What in the hell is going on?" came a grumbling voice.

"Shut up, Adriano," Alessa said.

Abriella sniffed away her tears. "I'm okay."

Alessa forced Abriella to look up at her. "You sure?"

No.

"Did something happen?" Adriano asked.

Abriella hadn't actually told her sister or her new brother-in-law where she was going earlier. She suspected that they knew, but they hadn't asked. She didn't want to out the fact that she had been with Tommas, or what happened.

The less people knew, the better.

Tomorrow, word would pass.

They could make their own conclusions.

"Nothing," Abriella said, pushing her sister back and standing. "It's nothing."

Alessa's brow furrowed. "Ella, you can talk to me."

No, she couldn't.

She wouldn't be able to talk to anyone and feel safe about it until this whole mess was over. It only took one wrong word to ruin everything. She was beginning to learn that lesson the hard way. Inadvertently, her own family could cause more harm than good.

It was better not to know.

It was better to pretend like you didn't know.

"Something happened," Adriano said, frowning. "What was it?"

Abriella shook her head. "I don't know what you're talking about."

Alessa glanced back at her husband. "Don't push, please."

"I just want to go to bed."

Lies.

She wanted to go to the hospital.

She wanted Tommas.

She wanted to kill Joel.

Alessa reached up and wiped at a spot on Abriella's cheek. "You don't have to tell us anything if you don't want to."

"Thank you," Abriella said.

"But let's get that blood cleaned off your face," her sister finished quieter.

Shit.

"Yeah, I should do that."

Abriella managed to walk down the hallway on her shaky legs without tripping. She didn't look Adriano in the eye as she passed him by.

Behind her, she heard her sister ask, "What just happened?"

"I don't know," Adriano murmured.

"I've never seen her like that before."

"Shock is hard to deal with, Lissa."

"Tommas, you think?" Alessa asked.

"Probably."

"I want to know what happened, Adriano. Find out for me."

Abriella let the bathroom door slam loudly behind her.

Abriella tried all she could not to glare at her brother. Joel sat at the other end of the restaurant table, spooning scrambled eggs into his mouth. After a particularly quiet morning spent with her sister, their brother had shown up at the apartment and asked them to breakfast.

As much as Abriella wanted to refuse, she couldn't.

Joel was more chipper than usual, flirting with the waitress and being as nice as he could be to his sisters. Abriella suspected she knew the reason for Joel's good mood, but she didn't know what to do about it.

"A month to the baby shower?" Joel asked.

Alessa nodded. "Yes."

"Good. I'll send out the invitations for the party. It'll be good to have something to celebrate in the family."

Abriella's head snapped up. "Now the baby is something to celebrate?"

Joel's gaze narrowed. "I beg your pardon?"

"Up until recently, Alessa's pregnancy and the baby has been nothing but a nuisance for you, Joel. If you didn't outright ignore every situation that came up about the pregnancy, you couldn't say enough bad things about Alessa and Adriano. What's changed?"

"Abriella, don't," Alessa said quietly.

Joel waved his sister's warning off. "It is fine, Alessa. She asked. What is the harm in answering?"

"Well, why then?" Abriella demanded.

"A boss should always celebrate joyous occasions in his family, Ella. Sure, this pregnancy and the marriage was an issue for us at first, but that was only because of the way it came about. Being the dominating family means we no longer have to worry about that little problem anymore. The first *principe* or *principessa* of the next generation is about to be born. Of course, we should let the Outfit celebrate the child."

A show.

That's all it was to Joel.

It was something else for him to show off and brag about. Now that Alessa's pregnancy and the soon-to-be born child could garner him some respect and admiration, he was willing to hold the baby and marriage up as something wonderful and joyous.

Abriella was so disgusted that she could spit.

"I see," Abriella said, not bothering to hide the hatred in her tone. "I wasn't aware there had been a change in the Outfit that suddenly made us the dominating family again."

Or for you to be the boss, Abriella added silently.

"Ah, you know better than to be asking things about the Outfit. Careful, Ella."

Abriella scoffed. "Right. My apologies."

"You're awfully touchy this morning," Joel noted.

"You're awfully happy."

"I can't be happy?"

"Not when you're usually so unbearable that even sharing a meal with you is emotionally exhausting."

Alessa pinched Abriella's leg under the table. No doubt, Alessa had learned of the events from the night before at Tommas' club. It had been all over the news that morning. Abriella watched from a distance, panic seizing her heart and anger boiling in her blood.

She still hadn't heard from Tommas.

It took all she had not to go to the hospital as soon as she could. Someone would see. People were always watching. Abriella couldn't risk it.

"Why the change, brother?" Abriella asked.

"Things are looking up for the Trentini family and the Outfit," Joel said as he leaned back in his chair. "Now, I need the rest of my family to fall in line and help out a little bit. If there is one thing I am good at, Abriella, it is forcing the hands of those around me to get what I want. I've certainly learned enough from the men in this family to know how to play dirty. I don't know why you're acting like you are this morning, but I suggest you cut it out before it becomes a habit."

Was that what her brother had done? Had he tried to force Tommas' hand into giving Joel a seat that wasn't even taken yet? Was the bomb simply a promise of what was to come if Tommas challenged Joel?

"And what if I don't cut it out?" Abriella asked.

Joel flashed a cold smile. "Then I will correct it for you."

Alessa passed Abriella a quick look that begged for her to be quiet. Abriella, as much as she hated to do it, picked up her fork and forced a bite of ham and eggs down her throat.

Even eating was a chore.

Silently, the three siblings went back to eating without another word. The only sounds in the restaurant were the scraping of utensils on plates, the shuffle of feet, and quiet murmurs from other tables. The screech of a cell phone damn near made Abriella jump out of her chair.

She still couldn't shake the jumpy feeling.

It hadn't left since the bomb blew.

Joel glanced down at the ringing phone on the table. "I'll be right back."

The moment their brother was gone from the table, Alessa turned on Abriella. "What in the hell is up with you this morning?"

Abriella scowled down at her plate. "You watched the news."

"I did."

"Then you know what he did, Lissa."

"Yes, but—"

"But nothing. Privately, he's celebrating because he thinks he's won. Joel believes he's gotten exactly what he wants."

Alessa frowned. "Don't push him. Wasn't it always you who told me to tread carefully where Joel is concerned? He turns on people faster than anyone we know, Ella."

Abriella was aware.

The bigger problem was that she couldn't let her brother win.

What would that mean for her?

For Tommas?

Alessa glanced down at her lap. "Oh."

"What?"

Her sister waved a phone before it disappeared under the table again.

"Adriano just got out of the hospital. He went to see Tommas on the low when he thought it would be safe to do so."

Abriella's shoulders tightened. "You told me he was working!"

"So I lied. Back off."

"Well, what did he find out?"

Alessa looked down at her phone again. "Tommas wasn't there."

"What?"

"That's what it says. There was no Tommas Rossi checked in at the Presbyterian, Ella."

Where was he?

"A different name, maybe?" Abriella asked.

"I don't know. Your guess is as good as mine."

Abriella thought about the cracked phone in her purse. She had turned Tommas' phone off to save the dwindling battery. She had the right contacts to find out where Tommas really was when she got the chance to use them. Before she could consider the phone more, Joel returned to the table. The angry scowl he sported now was far more familiar to Abriella than the smile he had been wearing earlier.

"Bad news?" Abriella dared to ask.

Joel's cheek twitched. "Mind your business, Ella."

She took that as a good sign. Bad news for Joel was great news for her.

CHAPTER FIVE

"Rossi, it's nice to see you again."

Tommas clenched his teeth to keep from barking at the detective. The familiar man strolled into the room with his smirking partner on his heel. Ignoring the pain in his chest and the dizziness when he stood too fast, Tommas moved from his spot at the end of the hospital bed.

"I didn't invite you into my hospital room. Leave."

"Nope," the cheery man replied. "Detectives Crown and Delog from—"

"I know who you are," Tommas interjected sharply. "I said get out."

"We had to make some calls to figure out which room you were in, Tommas," Crown said. "Using an alias. Nice trick. I never knew you to be a frightened man, but you must be if you're hiding out in a hospital."

Tommas crossed his arms, refusing to give the man a reaction. "Concussion, a cracked rib, internal bruising … frightened, same thing."

"That's what we're saying," the other detective, Delog, said with a grin.

Knowing it would only exacerbate his cracked rib, and make his pounding headache twenty times worse, Tommas held himself back from forcibly removing the detectives from the hospital room. It wouldn't be the first time he had done something of that nature to these men.

These fools had been following him around ever since he was twenty-two and earned his button into the Outfit. He figured it was because they saw him as an easy target, what with his drunk parents.

They wanted a rat.

They needed an in to the Outfit.

Tommas wouldn't be it.

"Haven't you gotten the hint yet?" Tommas asked.

Crown fiddled with a phone on the moveable table at the foot of the bed. "Got what hint, Tommas?"

"You two fools have had me on your radar for eight years, and our meetings keep ending the same way. You want something, I make you leave. It's not going to change. Get out."

Crown placed the phone back on the hook. "Let's talk instead."

"There's nothing to talk about."

"Don't be like that, Tommas," Delog said. "You nearly died early this morning. They've been waking you up every half hour, refusing you food, and you've been demanding to be released for the last three hours. You're tired—we know. Let's just do this quickly, easily, and you'll be on your way."

"With what, a wire taped to the crack of my ass?" Tommas asked cuttingly.

"Oh, stop. The bomb, who set it?"

"I don't know."

"I think you do," Crown said.

"I don't know for *you*," Tommas replied with a sneer.

"My guess," Delog drawled, "was that Joel Trentini set it. See, we're watching, Tommas. You know we are. The new boss is dead, and his biggest challenge for the seat was Joel. Now, Joel probably has it in his head that he needs to go after it, but maybe you're in the way somehow. Are you in the way, Rossi?"

Tommas shrugged. "About as much as you're in my way. Which isn't a whole lot."

Crown shot his partner a look and nodded.

Delog turned his attention on Tommas again. "We can give you what you need, Tommas. Safety, a new life, and freedom from this. Anything."

"And as I've told you several times, I like my life just the way it is. But thanks."

"We can get—"

"Me straight into a makeshift grave," Tommas interjected coldly. "Your efforts would be better spent trying to find a way to get me behind bars instead of attempting to use me to turn rat against the Outfit."

Crown shook his head, sighing. "Be careful what you wish for, Tommas."

Was that supposed to scare him?

It didn't.

"You know, when the police didn't question me early this morning or afternoon, I figured you two fools would be around. If I didn't already have a few enemies coming at me from behind, I might actually think that you two set the bomb in my car."

Delog laughed. "Now that's just rude, Tommas."

"No more than you are. Please leave."

Crown waved a finger in Tommas' direction. "We will get what we want, Rossi. Eventually. It doesn't have to come from you. Anyone with the right access can give us all the information we need to eradicate the Outfit from Chicago."

Tommas nodded. "Yeah, yeah. The war on crime. I'm aware. What's in your bonuses if you put a few mobsters in for life, huh?"

"Depends on the mobster," Delog answered. "But the fact is, we really don't need you Tommas. We simply like you. You can either be the one we put away, or the one that helps us put them away."

Obviously the police had a hard-on for the Outfit again. It wasn't the first time they had tried to infiltrate the Chicago mob in an attempt to take down the organization. Joseph DeLuca had fallen into that trap when Tommas was just a teen, and the man lost his life for it.

Despite his young age at the time, it was an event that Tommas couldn't forget. He would never turn rat no matter how bad shit seemed.

Never.

"Find something on me," Tommas said quietly, "and I'll do my time, boys."

Crown smiled. "We'll see you again, Tommas."

"Make sure it's when I'm in handcuffs, or don't bother. And when you go past the front desk, make sure they correct the nonsense about my room. I don't need or want to hide. My name can be on this room. They refused to change it for me. You two aren't nearly as smart as you think."

Once the detectives had vacated his room, Tommas fell back into the closest chair with a groan. It had taken all he had just to keep standing and not show the fact that he was dizzy as hell, in some serious pain, and not up for a verbal sparring match with the officials.

The quiet creak of the bathroom door made Tommas' head pop up. He found his cousin leaning in the bathroom entryway with a scowl and a glare focused on the spot where the detectives had gone.

"Snakes," Damian muttered.

"You're lucky they don't pester you."

"They tried once. I seriously considered killing one of them just to make a point so they wouldn't do it again."

"Did they try anyway?"

"No," Damian replied. "Our meeting ended in a way that made it clear I was not open to play."

"Good thing."

"I am surprised that it was them who put the restrictions on your room. Especially the name change thing and all. That could look really bad on you if someone found out it was the officials who cooked up that nonsense, Tommy."

"I'm more concerned about what they said before that, D."

Damian's gaze narrowed. "Like the fact that they felt it was necessary to point out how they didn't need you."

"Yeah. It makes me think they might already have someone else or they're working on it."

"But who?"

Tommas winced as he stood from the chair. "Hard to say."

"Tommy, you can stay another couple of days in here. I'll keep an eye on your room."

"No, I'm safer if I'm out, D. Besides, you've got a pregnant wife to get home to. I'm going to force the discharge and get the hell out of here."

"When you do …"

"What?" Tommas asked.

Damian glanced away. "Just be careful about certain people, okay."

"People like who, D?"

"You know who."

Abriella.

"She is not who they were talking about," Tommas said, his tone heating instantly.

"I never said that. But I do want you to be mindful. You get stupid and crazy when that girl is involved, Tommy. You don't think shit through and you make rash decisions."

"You're one to talk. Look at what you did in this whole mess."

Damian straightened fast. "I—"

"Don't deny it. You helped to start a war between the families under the idea of something, not the truth of it. You could have ended it before Terrance and saved everyone a hell of a lot of trouble and bloodshed, but in an effort to keep your wife safe, you finished the job."

"I don't know how to leave a job unfinished. I wasn't taught to work that way."

"My point is that you're no better than me, D. Judgment looks well on no one. Before you start pointing dirty fingers in my direction, make sure the ones pointing back at you have been cleaned."

"There's a difference," his cousin said quietly.

"Do tell."

"I have my wife."

Tommas stiffened. "So?"

"You don't have Abriella at all."

He had her in all the ways that mattered.

For now.

"I'm working on that," Tommas settled on saying.

Damian sighed. "Well, get smarter about it. Joel did exactly what I thought he would do, Tommas. He gave it some time, he waited it out until he thought you were distracted and focused on something other than him. And frankly, he couldn't have hit you at a better time. If you don't start hitting him back, his next move might be the last one he has to make where you're concerned."

Damian was right on every single point. Tommas wouldn't deny it.

"Just … get smarter about this," Damian repeated. "You've never been a fool. You know how to play this game. They don't call you bloody for nothing, Tommy."

"I'm working on that, too. Go get my fucking discharge papers."

Tommas had shit to do. He wasn't staying in the hospital for a cracked rib, a couple of bruises on his internal organs, and a headache.

"Before I go force them into giving you the discharge papers, we should talk about what happened when I picked up Abriella," Damian said.

"What about it?"

"She was out of it, Tommas. She didn't know if she was coming or going."

Tommas' chest ached at that admission. More than anything, he wanted to find Abriella and let her see that he was okay. Unfortunately, that couldn't happen. It wasn't safe. His second biggest concern was making sure no one knew just how much that really bothered him.

"Let me worry about Abriella," Tommas said.

"She's got your phone."

"I know."

"Make sure that girl knows you're okay."

"Back to the two-seater, boss?" Nate asked.

Tommas slid into the passenger side of his Jaguar F-Type. "I prefer this car, anyway."

"It's not—"

"Safe," Tommas interrupted the enforcer. "Yeah, I got it. Until I can have the Mercedes replaced in a couple of weeks, this will have to do."

"Don't get your fucking panties in a twist because you know this car makes you a goddamn vulnerability."

"Lay off, Nate. I've got a massive headache and you're not helping it."

"Got it, boss."

As much as Tommas liked his main enforcer, who also acted as his driver in the daytime, he was not in the mood for another discussion about what he should or shouldn't be doing.

Quietly, Nate asked, "What did the doctors say?"

"Bad concussion."

"That all?"

"And a cracked rib, some internal bruising on my liver and right kidney, but that's it."

"No drinking, I guess."

Tommas chuckled. It hurt like hell, but it felt good, too. Leaning back in the comfortable leather seat and enjoying the heat warming his back, Tommas closed his eyes and wrapped his arm around his chest to give the injured rib a bit of support.

Anything was better than nothing.

"No drinking," he agreed. "My liver won't take it right now."

"You're one lucky son of a bitch, Tommas."

"Thanks." Tommas looked Nate over. "Did you grab me a clean suit from my house?"

"Yeah, boss. It's in the trunk."

Nate frowned, his hands tightening on the wheel like he was thinking about something. Tommas would recognize that nervous action in his enforcer on any day of the week. He and Nate had been friends for years, way back when Nate was just a street kid trying to keep his head above water and Tommas was still learning the streets.

Tommas trusted Nate more than most people in his life.

"Spit it out," Tommas demanded.

"I'm sorry, boss."

Tommas' eyes popped open. "I wasn't expecting that. What are you sorry for?"

"Last night—I asked for it off. If I had been around, nobody would have messed with your car."

"Nate, you have a life. I should have known better than to leave my car unattended like that for hours out in the club parking lot. It had been way too quiet. It was a stupid move on my part that had little to do with you taking the night off to spend the evening with your kid."

Nate nodded. "I know, but—"

"But nothing. You only get your daughter a couple of days a month. And a club isn't the kind of place for you to be bringing her. I should have had someone else keeping an eye on my car. Shit, had I parked it in the front lot, I would have caught whoever it was on camera."

"Did you get anyone to check the cameras?" Nate asked.

"Damian went into the system this morning online. The cops took the hardcopies. There was nothing to see. Whoever it was probably went in through the back alley, came up to the car from the other side, tricked the alarm with a wireless program, and set the bomb."

Easy fucking pickings. Tommas had set himself up perfectly for that goddamn bomb. The more he thought about it, the more agitated it made him.

Thankfully, the cameras outside of his club were not positioned in the back where Abriella had come in, and the ones inside were strategically placed as well. Abriella knew the black zones.

"Is it really a *whoever* kind of situation?" Nate asked.

Tommas kept his expression a blank mask. "No. We know who did it."

"Joel."

"Joel," Tommas confirmed. "He even had people at the hospital trying to get info, he put word on the street wanting to know if the Rossi Capo was down and out, and he went about his morning like nothing was amiss."

Which apparently included taking Abriella and Alessa to breakfast. Yes, Tommas had people watching. He also knew where Joel had gone after breakfast.

Nate took a corner a little too sharply for Tommas' injured rib. Cussing low, Tommas smacked his enforcer as hard as he could.

"Slower, asshole."

"Sorry, boss."

Tommas grunted as he resituated his frame in the seat. "Speaking of Joel."

"What about him?"

"I have something to do today that involves him. I need you to take me. I'm not supposed to drive, and I want to get this done before I go home and pop my painkillers."

"Whatever you want, boss," Nate said.

"Church," Tommas replied. "I want to go to the church."

"What does that have to do with Joel?"

"Every Saturday afternoon he goes to church. Confession, that sort of thing. It's a habit I've never known Joel to break. If he wants to start playing games, I'm good with that."

Not that it mattered, Tommas thought.

Not even God would save Joel, now. Tommas just had to bide his time, make his moves carefully, and strike when Joel was at his weakest.

"Is that how you see almost getting killed by a bomb, as a game?" Nate asked, not sounding the least bit amused.

"No, but that's how Joel sees it. To win the game, you've got to play it."

And play it well.

Tommas carefully buttoned the cuffs of his clean suit jacket. Too much movement caused him a great deal of pain, and he didn't want to show just how much agony he was actually in. The more pain he felt, the dizzier he became. The last thing he wanted to do was end up back in the hospital because he had a goddamn spell. At least, he didn't want to end up back at the hospital before he got one thing done.

Tommas had quickly changed in the Jaguar while Nate had a cigarette a couple of blocks away from the church. The first thing that Tommas had noticed when they pulled into the familiar parking lot were the two cars parked close to the front steps.

Joel's and his enforcer's car.

Tommas hadn't even gotten out of his car before the Trentini enforcer had pulled out a cell phone. By the time the guy was talking into his phone, Tommas had already climbed the steps and entered the church. Knowing what he did about Joel's routine when it came to church and confession, Tommas planned on using it to his benefit. Joel rarely used the confessional room like the other parishioners did. Instead, the man liked to have his chat one-on-one with the priest while sitting in a pew.

Tommas never understood Joel's need to confess his sins. The man had no intention of changing his behavior or ways. But who was Tommas to judge? He had no intention of changing, either.

Taking another breath to will away the dull ache in his chest from his cracked rib, Tommas pushed the main doors open to walk into the church hall. Bright light filtered in through the stained glass windows, bathing the floor and pews in a rainbow of colors.

Instantly, the sight made Tommas light-headed. He'd been instructed to avoid bright lights, a lot of movement or noise, and to have someone close by to monitor his physical state for the next forty-eight to seventy-two hours.

This was not helping his migraine.

Ignoring the nauseating sensation settling in his stomach, Tommas strolled down the middle of the aisle between the pews. He found the man he was looking for at the very front, sitting alone. Making sure to be heard as he rounded the last few rows, Tommas cleared his throat. Joel didn't turn around at the sound of Tommas' approach.

"Afternoon, old friend," Joel said quietly.

Tommas sat in the pew directly beside Joel's. The moment he was sitting, he felt better and not so unsteady like before. "Where is the priest? I wasn't aware confession could be done alone."

"I'm supposed to be doing my penance."

"Ah."

"It's a little stupid for you to come here, don't you think?" Joel asked. "I could have you killed before you even left the parking lot."

Tommas hummed a dismissive tune. "No. You see, Nate is outside.

He's watching your man. I'm not concerned."

"You never are."

"Well, I try not to be."

Joel glanced to the side, likely taking in Tommas' appearance. "At least you're not dead. I didn't hurt you too badly, huh?"

"Water under the bridge, Joel."

"Funny."

Tommas smiled. "You know how it is."

"I know you think you want to be the boss because you believe you're the only man left in the Outfit good enough to fill the seat, but you're wrong. You could just give me the seat and save us a lot of problems, Tommas."

"The same could be said for you."

"It's not yours."

Tommas chuckled dully. "It's just as much mine as it is yours, Joel. You have no more or less of a claim to the boss's seat than I do. The one difference between you and I is the fact that you believe it is a birthright and I understand that is it earned. You wanted it handed to you, like everything else in your life has been, while I want it because I have earned it."

"Doing what?"

"Everything that you couldn't," Tommas said simply.

Joel straightened in the pew, glaring straight ahead.

Ouch.

An angry Trentini was a dirty one.

"Hit a nerve, did I?" Tommas asked.

"You know nothing," Joel snapped.

"I know your temper and your lack of control will kill you someday. I know if someone else doesn't do it soon, it will eventually happen, Joel. You're not worthy of this spot. You simply want it because of your blood and not because it's who you are."

"My blood makes it who I am, Tommas."

"A father does not make his son, Joel."

Joel released a harsh breath. "What do you even want to be a boss for? You're a Capo. It's all you've ever been. It's all you're ever going to be, just like your father."

Tommas let those words roll off his shoulders. Joel was only showing his stripes, like every tiger eventually did. Or rather, like a child being denied what they wanted. Joel's temper tantrums were always quick to show.

It wasn't a shock.

"Then I suppose it's a good thing that I spent far more time being raised by every other man in the Outfit besides my father," Tommas replied calmly, pretending like his head didn't feel as if it was going to explode. "I'll offer you the same thing you gave to me, Joel, and nothing more. Let me take the seat with no issues, and save us a lot of problems in the process. You know the Outfit won't give it to you unless you force them into it. For me, however, they'll hand it over willingly."

Tommas was lying through his teeth. No matter what, Joel would have to go. His life would end by Tommas' hand. It was simply a matter of when. But for the sake of everyone else, Tommas wanted to make that happen as cleanly and easily as possible.

"It's an easy choice to make, Joel," Tommas added.

"You're wrong."

"You know I'm not."

Joel's jaw clenched and his fists balled tightly at his sides. "You—"

"I won't discuss or argue this with you, Joel. I've given you my offer and that is that. You'll either hand me what I want, or I will take it by whatever means necessary."

Tommas stood from the pew, ignoring how his vision swam when he was upright once again.

Joel stared up at him, hatred brimming in his eyes. "Good luck."

"Don't bother. I don't need it."

"I nearly got you this time, Tommas. You didn't even see me coming."

Tommas smirked. "I learn fast."

Joel nodded. "Until the next time."

Clearly, this was the way that Joel wanted it to go. Bloodstained until the very bitter end. Tommas didn't mind. He liked a little blood.

Turning to leave, Tommas said, "Hand it over, Joel, and make it easy on everyone. You know how this is going to end."

"Actually, I don't."

"Then allow me to enlighten you. Once I step outside of this church, you are a dead man walking. The bomb was a nice little wakeup call. I needed it. But if there is a next time, if you really want to play this game with me, I will slaughter you, Joel. And I will fucking enjoy every single last second of it."

Joel didn't look back as Tommas walked back down the aisle.

It didn't matter.

His words were still heard.

Loud and clear.

Tommas barely got the passenger door to the Jaguar closed without falling over. He bent over at the knees and pressed the heels of his palms to his eyes, willing away the vomit that had suddenly rose in his throat.

"Boss?" Nate asked cautiously.

"Drive," Tommas croaked.

"What?"

"Drive!"

The car lurched forward, and Tommas threw out a hand to catch himself from falling over in the seat. It had taken all the willpower he had to keep from vomiting inside the church when his migraine only seemed to get worse. Then, as he was walking out, the dizziness and nausea had returned with a vengeance.

"Jesus," Tommas mumbled, pushing against his temples to take some of the edge off.

"You okay?"

No.

Tommas tried to check where their current position was, but the sight of the buildings flying by them was enough to send bile spilling into his mouth.

"Pull over," Tommas said hoarsely.

Nate jerked the car hard to the right. Tommas pushed the door open just in time to spill the contents of his stomach, what little there was, on the ground. Shaking and confused, Tommas breathed deeply in an attempt to clear his head and calm down.

"Yeah, Ghost? Hey."

Tommas fell back into the passenger seat and eyed the enforcer talking on a cell phone.

"What are you doing?" Tommas asked.

Nate ignored him. "We've got a fucking problem. Tommas is messed up. They shouldn't have let him out."

"Get off the phone, Nate."

The enforcer didn't even look at him.

Tommas' agitation level climbed a notch.

"Yeah, he was holding onto his head, he's green as hell, and he just puked on the side of the road. If he had that bad of a concussion, then he needs to go back—"

"Get off the phone!"

"Shut up," Nate barked.

The sharp, high level of Nate's shout made Tommas' head split with pain again. Wincing, Tommas clenched his eyes shut and grabbed at his head again.

"Oh, yeah, he's going back. Meet me at the hospital?" Nate asked. "Good. Later, Ghost."

"You're about to lose your spot as my enforcer," Tommas hissed when the car began to move again. "You don't get to call my cousin like I'm a child in need of handling, Nate. If I had thought that I needed to stay in the fucking hospital, then I would have stayed there. I am fine."

"You're not fine. You're going to make your concussion worse. Shit, there might be something else already going on. I'm taking you back."

"You're taking me home!"

"You did what you wanted to do, boss," Nate said, sounding entirely unaffected by Tommas' anger. "You showed Joel that you were fine, you made your point. What else do you want, Tommas? There isn't anything else you can do or need to do right now."

Yes, there was.

It was incredibly important.

She was important.

"Ella," Tommas said quietly.

He still had to talk to her—see her, maybe. Anything. Tommas couldn't remember a lot from the moment the bomb had gone off, but he could vividly bring back the image of Abriella above him, touching his face and crying.

He'd told her to go.

She hadn't wanted to.

"I need to … go see her," Tommas said.

"What? Listen, I'm sorry for yelling at you and all. Dammit, boss, sit up and look at me!"

Abriella.

Her name was the last thing to pass through Tommas' mind before the world went black.

CHAPTER SIX

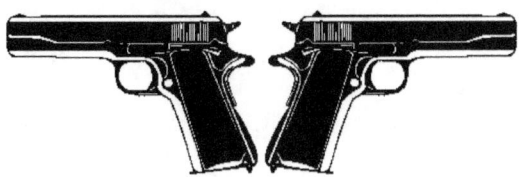

Checking the rearview mirror, Abriella hit the gas harder and flew past a half a dozen cars on the freeway. It was not an easy thing to lose a car trailing behind your vehicle when you drove something as massive as a Hummer. Abriella had gotten rather good at it over the years.

It was almost like a game.

Swerving in between another set of cars and ignoring the horn that blared behind her, she watched the black vehicle that belonged to one of her brother's fools get in the row, too. They were back a couple of cars, though.

Abriella didn't know if they would ever learn.

Seeing the exit sign for next ramp coming up, Abriella swerved out from between the vehicles and hit the gas again. Her Hummer zoomed past an eighteen-wheeler and a sports car. The vehicle belonging to the enforcer who always trailed her wasn't too far behind. She wanted him going faster—too fast to take a turn at the last minute when he couldn't possibly know it was coming.

Pulling in between another set of vehicles when there was a big enough opening, Abriella caught sight of the enforcer following her lead. He was right behind her now and going a good twenty over the speed limit. The black car was so close to her bumper that she could practically see the scowl the man wore.

Poor guy.

Abriella almost felt sorry for him.

Except ... nope.

He picked the job of watching her, after all.

When the exit ramp came, Abriella took the turn with no warning. She didn't put on her blinker to signal she was leaving the freeway, or even slow down for the turn. The enforcer behind her clearly hadn't been expecting the move because he flew on past with no available time to turn with her.

Laughing, Abriella watched the brake lights on the black car light up. She simply hit her gas and sped down the exit ramp leading back into the city. There was no way the guy could turn on the freeway without causing some kind of accident. He had another few miles to go before another exit ramp would come up.

This wasn't the first time that Abriella had pulled this kind of stunt. She knew without worry that the enforcer would probably drive around looking for her, and wouldn't call Joel unless it was absolutely necessary. That might cost the guy his life.

Mistakes in their world were corrected with bullets, not apologies.

Easy.

Like child's play.

Once she was off the exit ramp and a safe place to pull over came up, Abriella took it. Putting the Hummer in park, she leaned down and pulled the latch for the hood.

If there was one good thing that came out of the friendship between her brother and Tommas for all those years, it was the knowledge Tommas had gained and passed onto Abriella. Like the fact there was a GPS tracker hooked to her Hummer that her brother had put in after she got the vehicle for her eighteenth birthday. The enforcer had an app he could log into with his phone to check Abriella's whereabouts, but once she disconnected the right wire, her vehicle position would be lost except for the last known destination.

Climbing up on the bumper of the Hummer, Abriella balanced on her scuffed chucks and tried to keep the dirt off her skinny jeans. She stuck her hand down along the side of the battery, knowing the computer for the Hummer was in the same spot, and was careful not to touch anything that might be too hot. Once she found the wire, she pulled it higher to make sure it was the right one, and then yanked it from its home.

She stuffed the wire back down into place before jumping off the bumper. Wiping her hand off on her tweed coat, Abriella grabbed the hood and slammed it shut. That was another thing off her list for the day.

There was only one thing left, now.

Tommas.

"Where are you?" her sister asked.

"Uh, out," Abriella said.

"You were supposed to meet me for dinner."

"I know. I'm sorry. Tomorrow?"

"Aren't you at school? I thought you weren't taking March break because you had a bunch of stuff to catch up on. I could just come over there and we could grab something."

Abriella searched her brain for an excuse as she parked her Hummer. She didn't think it was fair to drag her sister into her affairs. Alessa didn't need to be hiding secrets for anyone, and certainly not Abriella. The girl had enough to worry about with her pregnancy and new husband.

"Ella?" Alessa pressed.

Abriella decided to tell part of the truth. "I'm not at school."

"But it's Monday."

"Thanks. I'm aware of what day it is."

"Hey, don't be a bitch. I was just saying."

"Alessa, I'm not at school. I can't meet up with you today. Tomorrow?"

Her sister sighed. "Did you skip out on your enforcer again?"

"Maybe."

"Are you in Wicker Park?"

Abriella smiled.

Wicker Park was where the apartment that Tommas kept for her was located. It was a smart way of her sister to ask, but no, she was wrong again.

"I'm not in Wicker."

"Oh," Alessa said sadly.

"Don't worry about me, Lissa. I just need a break. Joel has been crazy these last couple of days. I want some time away from his stupid ass."

Alessa was terribly lucky that she didn't have to live at the Trentini mansion anymore. Joel made even the simplest of tasks like watching television unbearable. He had men coming and going from the mansion doing his bidding and reporting on people's whereabouts and actions. He raged at the dumbest things, and he made demands constantly.

Joel was planning something. Abriella didn't know what exactly, but it was something.

"He's been worse since the Tommas thing?"

"If you want to call it that," Abriella replied. "I think he's pissed because his plan didn't work, but that doesn't matter. I need to skip out on life for a day. If, by chance, Joel calls because the fool following me calls him—"

"I'll say you're with me."

Abriella grinned, loving her sister a little bit more. "Thanks."

"Be careful."

"I always am."

Alessa laughed. "Right. And say hello to Tommas for me."

Before Abriella could even deny that she was going to see Tommas, Alessa hung up the call. She shouldn't have been surprised that her sister knew the truth. Abriella had never hid things from Alessa.

Growing up in the lifestyle they did, sometimes all the sisters had were one another. They survived in a world that looked glamourous and mysterious from the outside, but was smothering and caustic on the inside. For a profession that claimed to tote honorable men within its rankings and families, what it really held were liars and cheats.

Tired of her own thoughts, Abriella tossed her phone on the passenger seat of the Hummer. Grabbing her bag, Abriella got out of the Hummer and made sure it was locked up tight. Chances were slim that the enforcer would actually find the vehicle, but if he happened upon it by a stroke of luck, then it was parked in a paid lot that could be used by anyone. It was also a few miles away from the small suburb where Tommas' home was located.

After calling Damian Rossi repeatedly, Abriella finally got an answer back from the man. She had hoped that Tommas would be at the apartment he kept for her, but he was at home instead.

It was riskier than normal.

Well, *their* normal.

Nothing about her and Tommas was safe.

Tommas' home wasn't unknown like their apartment was. Anyone could see her Hummer in the driveway and recognize it. Tommas regularly had visitors to his house. Men from his crew, family, or friends.

Abriella didn't care. She had to see him. A quick phone call from his cousin to reassure her that he was out of the hospital and fine was not enough for her.

Tommas should have known that.

It pissed her off and worried her at the same time. Abriella never did very well when she was angry and anxious. It was a terrible combination for a woman who liked to know everything and be in control.

Stepping onto the sidewalk, Abriella threw her hand high and whistled as a line of yellow cabs drove past. The very last one stopped for her and she jumped into the back seat.

"Where to, Miss?" the guy asked.

Abriella rattled off Tommas' home address. "And take me around the back."

"Not the front?"

She couldn't remember a time when she entered Tommas' home through the front door. The back door was safer with the ten foot high privacy fence surrounding the rear of the property. Abriella had keys to enter the back as well as the house and through the front.

Sometimes, the reality of needing to sneak around like they did made her feel like a dirty little secret.

Or a man's whore.

She refused to think on it for long. It only hurt her.

Why?

Because even being Tommas' whore was out of reach for Abriella. A man's mistress could be taken out, shown off, and cared for. She could still have some semblance of a relationship with her man. Abriella didn't even get the pleasure of having those things.

Tommas had told her a long time ago that she could be whatever she wanted with him or for him. He would never judge her, or for that matter, take their private business out for everyone else to see and pick apart. He had mostly kept that promise—he gave her what she asked for, when he could, he let her lose control when everything in her life had to be kept just so. He let her be his lover in a way that most men wouldn't understand. She liked it that way. She loved that Tommas gave her the kind of freedom to be his private slut, that he never treated her like she was precious china, or a princess that couldn't get dirty.

He let her be.

Abriella needed it.

She just wished she could also be his equal in public.

"No, take me to the back of the house," Abriella said.

"The back it is, Miss."

Pushing the silver key into the deadbolt was so familiar to Abriella that it soothed her in a way. She had a dozen other memories with Tommas that started exactly this way by simply sliding in a key and turning the lock.

Their entire relationship, whatever it was, had always been private, behind closed doors, and away from prying eyes. The outside never touched them when they were together. It was easier to pretend like what they had was real that way.

The back door didn't make a sound when it swung open. Abriella stepped into the quiet home and listened for any noise. She couldn't even hear the sound of a television. Tommas always kept his TV on even when he wasn't home.

Was he not here?

Had Damian lied to her?

Abriella's messenger bag made a soft thump when it hit the cherry hardwood. She toed off her chucks and kicked them into the corner. Padding down the hallway, she peeked into the small office as she passed only to find it dark and empty. The living room was in the same condition.

The end of the hall veered off into two separate rooms. One was the kitchen, and the other was the entryway that led to the front of the house or the stairwell for the second level. When she turned to take the kitchen corner, Abriella heard a floorboard creak.

That was it.

Then a gun was in her face. All she saw was a flash of brushed silver, the black butt enclosed by a fist, and the cold blue eyes of her lover.

Gasping, Abriella stumbled back with a shout. "Tommas!"

Immediately, Tommas' gun dropped to his side. "Jesus fucking Christ, Ella. Are you trying to get yourself killed?"

Somehow, Abriella had backed into the wall without even knowing it. Her heart was in her throat, pounding like it was about to leap right out. Blood rushed in her ears as she tried to calm down and speak.

"You asshole," Abriella managed to say.

"Me? You came in here—"

"I came to see you!"

"Without telling me you were coming?"

"I thought your cousin did."

Tommas' brow furrowed as he rubbed at his forehead. His brief distraction gave Abriella the chance to look him over for injuries. There wasn't much to see except the cut under his eye and the bandage wrapped three times around his chest.

That made her realize he wasn't wearing a shirt.

Abriella's mouth went dry as her gaze traveled over the cut expanse of his chest and straight down to where a pair of cotton sleep pants rested low on his hips. Tommas was tall, lean and built like a man who ran a ten-k every day with his roped arms and defined chest. The bruising from the attack were the only marks on his skin.

Tommas shifted on his feet, ran his fingers through his hair, and glanced at Abriella. The simple movements took the worry out of his eyes, made him seem happier for the moment, and even sexier in a blink. Abriella's stomach clenched, reminding her how long it had been since she had this man between her thighs.

God, she wished he was wearing something. Abriella didn't think very clearly when Tommas was barely clothed, grinning like he was, and looking at her like he missed her.

"Didn't Damian tell you I was looking for you?" Abriella asked, finally finding her voice.

"No, but that doesn't surprise me. He's been on my ass ever since the second hospital round. He practically barricaded me in this house for forty-eight hours waking me up every time I even thought about drifting off to sleep, the dick."

"At least you have someone who cares."

Although, Abriella wished she could have been there for Tommas.

"Yes, if you want to see it that way."

"Damian cares. He just shows it differently than most people."

"You didn't come here to talk about my cousin, did you?"

"No," she replied, grinning.

"Good," Tommas said, chuckling. He waved his gun. "Sorry about that."

"Are you really?"

"Ella, I didn't know who the hell was coming into my house. I've been out of it for a couple of days. I finally sent Damian home this morning after I was able to keep my breakfast down and could stand on my own."

"You're not supposed to wrap ribs, Tommas."

"The nurses said that, too."

"But it feels better, right?"

Tommas nodded. "Yeah."

"Let me take it off."

"Listen, little nurse in training—"

"Stop it," Abriella cut in, cocking a brow. "You're not supposed to wrap your chest. Is it a break or just a crack?"

Tommas sighed before he tossed his gun to the small, decorative table in the hallway. He lifted his arms up, allowing Abriella to begin unraveling the bandage. "Just a crack."

"And what about the rest?"

"A couple of bruised organs. A bad concussion that could have been a lot worse."

Abriella tried to hide her frown as she placed the unwound bandage on the floor, and failed miserably. "And what does that mean?"

"It means that I forced my release from the hospital before I should have. The doctor made it clear I shouldn't leave, but I signed the disclaimers and every other fucking paper they wanted me to and went."

"Oh, Tommy."

"I didn't even make it two hours out of the hospital before Nate rushed me back in after I passed out in the car."

Abriella cupped his cheek and ran her thumb over his strong jawline. The scruff of his unshaven cheeks tickled her skin. "Stupid man."

"I couldn't stay in the hospital, Ella."

"Yet, you went right back."

"Only because I didn't have a choice."

"Why on earth did you force a release if you knew you weren't ready?"

Tommas' jaw tightened under her touch. "I made a point to go see your brother."

Jesus.

"And?" Abriella dared to ask.

"And it's not over."

"Of course not."

Tommas grabbed her wrist, stopping the stroking of her hand. "Yes, of course not. Do you understand what it would mean if I did bend to Joel's demands and wants? Don't you know what that would do?"

"Yes."

"Do you? Do you *really*?"

Abriella bristled at Tommas' dark tone. "I said yes, Tommy. I'm not a fucking idiot. I know what my brother would do to the Outfit if he had control."

"No," Tommas said harshly, grabbing her wrist even tighter. "Not the Outfit. I don't give a fuck about that in the end, because without you, the Outfit would mean nothing to me anyway. I meant to us, Ella. As it is, you're just a woman with a last name in need of being changed. You are his chess piece to move as he wishes to advance himself in the game. That is it. Nothing more."

"Oh."

"You know all this."

"I do," she agreed.

"And yet, *we're* the second thing on your mind when it comes to what is wrong with your brother taking control. Second place is the first to lose, Abriella."

She stepped back from him, needing the space. "Don't say that."

Tommas waved at her. "That's how it feels. Like we're the runner up. Like we're just not good enough to be the thing you're concerned about."

"Don't say that!"

"I—"

Abriella moved back in front of Tommas and jabbed a finger into his chest, right over the spot where his heart beat. She didn't think about if it would hurt him, but he didn't give off any indications that it did.

"Don't. You. Say. That."

Tommas' fingers encircled hers and held tight. "I didn't mean it like that, Ella. I'm frustrated and concerned about you, us, and a lot of other people. I don't mean to lash out."

"Not good enough," Abriella said heatedly. "That is not a good enough excuse, Tommas. You know better—you know that I care about you more than anything. Do I say it just the way you want me to? No, but that's not because I don't want to. It's because I'm not allowed to."

"Not allowed?"

"Yes, exactly. Not allowed. I have never been free to date, or to pick who I want to give my time and love to. Instead, I've been told to sit down, shut up, and be pretty until the right last name comes along for my family. That name hasn't arrived yet, but he might. And I thought …"

Tommas stepped closer, letting his hands trail up Abriella's sides until he was holding her so tightly that it ached and relieved at the same time.

Home.

She found home in his touch.

Always.

"Don't do that," Abriella said weakly.

Tommas smirked, his blue eyes gleaming with mischief. "Hmm, what?"

"Touch me, Tommy. I'm trying to talk."

"So talk. Let me help. You thought ..."

Abriella wet her lips and said, "I thought that keeping you at a distance would force you to keep me at a distance, too. It never did. You kept bringing me closer. You draw me in over and over again. I adore you, but that frightens me. It has always scared me. You have all the control here, and I have none."

"I love you," Tommas murmured. "I have loved you for years, Ella."

"I know you do."

"What you know, Ella, is what I want."

For her to say it back.

Yeah, she knew.

Abriella tipped her chin down. "I need to keep this one thing for me, Tommy."

"It drives me crazy. You've given me everything else. Whatever I wanted to take, you handed over. Your body, your secrets, your words ... *everything*. I already know you do, Abriella, just fucking say it for me."

She couldn't.

It hurt because the words practically clawed their way out of her chest. They wanted out. Her heart screamed for Tommas when they were apart, and it only got louder the closer she was to him. He'd won her over by daring her to be the rebel she wanted to be, and then sealed the deal by allowing her to be whoever she needed to be with him.

They were insane.

Sometimes volatile.

Dirty liars—secret keepers.

Sneaks. Lovers. Best friends.

But it was beautiful.

She wouldn't ruin that. She refused to take what they had, make it better, but then turn around and destroy it when she was forced away from Tommas because of someone else's demands. How awful would that make her?

"I can't," Abriella finally said.

Tommas' shoulders dropped. The sight hurt her more than she could explain. She hated being the one thing that weakened Tommas, but she loved being the one thing that could control him at the same time.

It was a bad mix.

They were bad.

"Why not?" he asked.

"Because how can I give something to you only to take it away, Tommy?"

Tommas blinked, recognition and surprise lighting up his handsome features. "Oh."

"I'm sorry."

"Don't be. I'll just have to fix it for you."

Abriella laughed sadly. "It's not that easy."

"It really is."

"I'm sick of people being hurt, Tommas. I don't want to keep being separated from my friends, and watching them bury family member after family member. This needs to end. No one even knows what they're fighting for in this war."

He leaned down close enough that his nose skimmed hers. "I do."

"I'm sure. A title, right? The highest seat. Control and power. Useless things, Tommas."

"Wrong."

"Am I?"

"Entirely, babe. I'm still fighting for you."

Abriella's air caught hard in her chest. She had known his answer before he even whispered it, but it still struck her right in the heart, taking away her ability to breathe. His fingers dug into her sides again, making her body sing with want and need. Just the sensation of his fingertips pressing into her skin promised the sex, security, and love that only Tommas could give her. With a single stroke of his digits, Abriella was spun, happy, and home.

Tommas' hands ghosted up her sides, skipped under the jacket she wore, and pushed it down over her shoulders. Then, his fingertips danced along the spot where her shirt showcased her collarbones.

She still couldn't catch air.

He made her breathless under his touch.

"And if that means taking it all down with me to get you," Tommas continued, ticking a finger under her chin to make Abriella look up, "... then that's exactly what it means, Ella."

"Don't do that for me, Tommy."

"Don't ask me not to."

Abriella frowned. "I don't want—"

"I know what you don't want. You don't want people hurting, you want to go back to living in your pretty gilded cage where safety is a lie, and where everyone believes that we're all compliant, happy little sheep. That place doesn't exist, Abriella. It never has. Glass houses only stay standing until rocks start getting thrown. I want you. That's the one thing in my goals that has never changed. Just you, babe."

"Just me?"

Why did she like that so much?

"Always you, Ella."

"I've never been a sheep," Abriella whispered as Tommas' thumb trailed over her bottom lip with a tender swipe. "You know that."

He laughed huskily. "No, I guess not. My little rebel Trentini queen, right?"

"Don't call me that."

"You like it."

"I—"

"Love it," he murmured.

Abriella sucked in a sharp breath when Tommas pushed her back into the wall with a hard thud. "I've chosen to ignore it, actually."

"You're so good at lying, baby."

"I learned from the best, Tommy."

"Don't ask me not to fight for this," he said, pressing his body to hers.

Every single inch of Abriella reacted to the pressure of Tommas' frame pinning her to the wall. From her fast breaths, to the pulsing between her thighs, she wanted him. It came on fast, like it usually did. It was almost always overwhelming for her.

Like a fucking hunger she couldn't control.

"You're so bad for me," Abriella told him.

He could kill her. Ruin her. Hate her. Hurt her.

All it would take was a few words whispered to the wrong person, and Tommas could destroy Abriella like it was nothing.

But she knew he wouldn't.

He loved her.

"You're the best thing for me," Tommas said lowly. "And you know that's why you can't ask me to stop fighting for this—for us. I know what you want. Give me time."

Wasn't time running out?

Abriella decided to ignore her inner voice.

Her heart spoke louder.

"I came here today, didn't I?"

Tommas grinned a dangerous sight. It was enough to make her panties wet.

"You did," he said. "You didn't know it, but I needed you to do that, Ella. Come here, I mean."

"Me, too."

The words barely escaped before Tommas' mouth was crushing down on hers. Sucking in a gulp of air, Abriella's lips opened the second Tommas' tongue struck against the seam of her mouth, demanding entrance. There was no asking for her kiss, he simply took it with hard strikes of his tongue and the nip of his teeth to her lips.

He marked her with his kiss; he owned her.

Tommas' hands grabbed onto her jaw and his fingertips bit into her cheeks. Abriella tilted her head back a second before Tommas' digits began to roam over her neck.

Christ.

She couldn't breathe again.

It was crazily familiar.

His dark eyes watched her like she was prey, his kiss turned harder, and the scruff on his jaw was sure to leave marks behind. It was so good, and her body trembled under his weight.

"Missed you," Tommas breathed, peppering softer kisses along the seam of her lips.

"I missed you."

"I needed you, Ella. I need this—*you*. Forever, babe."

God.

It was terrifying and lovely.

She needed this, too.

CHAPTER SEVEN

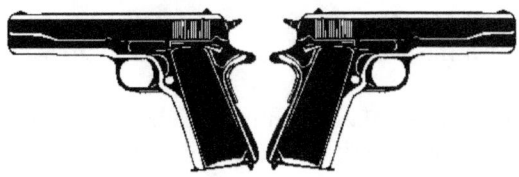

"Be careful."

Tommas barely even heard Abriella's whisper as he lifted her effortlessly against the hallway wall. She was mumbling about something or other when he kissed her quiet. He loved all her sounds, particularly the ones she made when he was fucking her, but he wasn't even at that point, yet.

"Tommas ..."

He forced her head back so he could stare down into her ice-blue gaze. He grabbed her throat tight in one hand, and her chin in his other. She would feel the imprint of his fingers pressing into her skin for days, like invisible fingerprints had been left all over her body.

Tommas had gotten smarter over the years where sex with Abriella was concerned. Once, he'd left a mark on the spot behind her ear, red and clear from his teeth and lips, and someone had seen it. Joel, probably. Abriella never really said. She simply asked him not to do it again, because she couldn't explain something so obvious away to others.

He hadn't minded correcting that for her.

Marks that could be felt but not seen were far more effective between them. He would fuck her hard enough that she could feel him long after he was gone. He would leave bite marks on her inner thighs, ones that would fade but a sting would remain, and his kisses would cover every inch of her.

It allowed Tommas to wonder ... When she wasn't with him, did she still touch the spots that he had? Did she wear the invisible aches and marks with her usual pride because he left them on her to keep until the next time?

"Christ, Tommy," Abriella mumbled as he nipped a path along her collarbones. Her back arched off the wall while her legs tightened around his waist. Tommas drove his hands down her sides and fisted her shirt. All the blood in his body was rushing straight down to his cock, making him sore and as hard as fucking steel. "You shouldn't—"

"Shut up and let me love you."

"But your rib."

"No hits. No pressure. No sleeping on my stomach. No wrapping them. I was told nothing about fucking someone, Abriella."

"Someone?"

Tommas couldn't have missed the heat in her tone for a second. Popping his head up to meet her gaze, he smirked. "You, not someone."

"Better be *only* me, Tommy. I would rip out a bitch's throat if I found out otherwise."

Tommas didn't question her on it. Abriella was horribly jealous where other women were concerned. Not that Tommas had any other women, but he worked in places where he employed a lot of younger females. Abriella never hid her contempt for those women whenever they were around.

"You're pretty when you're jealous, Ella."

"You're an asshole when you're jealous."

Tommas flashed a smile. "I know. And you love it."

Abriella didn't say a thing. Instead, she ground her jean clad hips into his growing erection, making a wave of pleasure course through Tommas' cock and straight down into his balls.

"Jesus," he breathed, wanting more of that.

"You might aggravate your rib, Tommy."

"It's not broken. It's a very small fracture. It has little to nothing to do with how badly I want to feel your sweet pussy squeezing the very life out of me while I fuck you raw. It's not going to make a difference to how hard I fuck you, how loud you're going to scream for me when I put you on your knees, or how many times you come today. It isn't. Okay, Ella?"

Abriella blinked, her pretty pink lips falling open. "Okay."

Her breathless response only made Tommas harder. He reached up and swept his thumb over her bottom lip. Her tongue struck out to taste his skin, and then she moaned when Tommas flexed his hips into her center.

"Not another fucking word about my rib," he warned.

Dark lashes fanned her cheeks when Abriella closed her eyes and let out a soft sigh. "Nothing. I promise."

Tommas never knew Abriella to follow the rules, but he believed her this time. Stepping back, despite how much he hated to let her go, Tommas helped Abriella drop back down on the floor safely. A twinge of pain reminded him that his rib was still tender, but that was about it. The pain killer he'd downed with his breakfast would keep that nonsense at bay for another couple of hours.

"How long do you have?" Tommas asked.

Abriella smiled. "Most of the day."

"Are you sure?"

"Technically, I'm supposed to be doing catch up work for school which isn't even in-class work. I could be anywhere doing that, Tommy. It's not my fault that my enforcer drives like an eighty-year-old woman."

Tommas laughed hard. "Get upstairs. You better be fucking naked before your back hits my bed, Ella, or I'll turn your sweet ass red."

Abriella bit her bottom lip and grinned sinfully. "Promise?"

Good God.

This woman would kill him someday.

Tommas was sure of it.

"*Go.*"

Abriella's gaze widened at his husky order before she turned to disappear around the corner leading to the entryway and stairwell. Tommas took his time to grab the gun on the table and the bandage that Abriella had dropped. He put the bandage on the table and slipped the gun into the waist band of his sleep pants.

Satisfied that he had given his lover enough time to follow his demands, Tommas turned the corner to take the stairs. He froze at the bottom of the stairwell at the sight of Abriella waiting for him at the top.

She was naked but for a black lace thong. She'd let her hair out of its messy bun, and the waves drifted far below her shoulders to cover her breasts. With the tip of her thumb stuck between her teeth, and a wicked smile curving her lips, she looked like sin.

Sex.

Heaven.

And *sin.*

"That is not my bed," Tommas said, taking the first few steps.

Abriella shrugged. "You're not upstairs yet, Tommy."

"And you're not completely naked, Ella."

"I'm working on it."

Tommas licked his bottom lip and sucked in a hiss of air. "Work faster."

Once he was at the middle of the stairwell, Tommas stopped walking. Abriella had dropped her hand from her mouth to hook her thumbs under the waistband of her thong. With slow, unhurried movements, she pulled the lace down around her thighs. A simple shimmy of her hips, and the thin scrap of fabric fell on the floor.

"I'm keeping those now," Tommy told her.

"What, like a memento?"

"Something like that. I have five steps left before you need to be on my bed, Ella."

"Maybe you should walk a little faster."

The peach and cream tone of her skin was highlighted by the morning winter light filtering in through the upstairs windows in the hallway. It bathed her in color and warmth, showcasing every beautiful curve and dip of her body.

Perfection in flesh and blood.

That's what Abriella was for him.

Young. Vibrant.

Vital to his life.

Taking the last few steps two at a time, Tommas pulled his gun from his pants, set it down carefully on the step, and then fisted the waistband of his sleep pants. He shoved them down roughly. The moment his foot hit the second level, Abriella turned on her heel and shot for the bedroom with a breathless laugh tumbling from her lips. Kicking off the only article of clothing he had on, Tommas grabbed the heavy length of his erection in his palm and stroked his cock.

By the time he stepped into the bedroom, Abriella was on his bed like he had told her to be. She wasn't on her back, but he let that go considering she was on all fours with her sweet little ass high in the air. Tossing him a heated glance over her shoulder, Abriella winked.

"God, that took you long enough."

"You're such a fucking smart mouth," Tommas growled. "Always teasing me like you do. I think you do it just to see how far you can push before I snap. You like that, Ella. You always have."

"I know. It's wonderful."

"What's wonderful is when I fill it full, Ella. And I think I might just do that, babe. Make you get down on the floor, fill your mouth, and make you serve me like you do. Strip you of everything just the way you like, fuck your throat until your eyes water, and watch you lick me fucking clean."

She groaned low, the sound originating from deep within her chest. "Is that how you want to do this, then?"

"No."

Her gaze met his.

"No?"

At the foot of the bed, Tommas stopped walking. He was close enough to Abriella that he could reach out and touch her if he wanted.

"No," he repeated.

"But—"

Tommas didn't give her a chance to argue with him. Reaching out, he snagged her ankles in his palm and yanked her to the edge of the bed before she could react. Abriella's gasp echoed in the room as her hands flew out to find purchase on the bed. She came up empty as her hair billowed out in all directions.

Pinning her flat on her stomach, Tommas climbed on the edge of the bed so that his legs kept Abriella in place and unable to move while his hands could wander. His palm skimmed up her back while his other reached back to slide between her thighs.

He found her wet, hot, and sensitive to the touch. She jerked with a loud cry the moment his fingertips came in contact with her wet slit. Stroking her from the entrance of her pussy up to her hard little clit, he felt her body shudder beneath him. She squirmed under his weight, and soft whimpers muffled into the bedsheets.

This was how he liked her. Under his control. However he wanted to take her. Obedient in a way, but defiant all the same. Dirty, begging for it, and a little crazy.

She liked it, too.

To be used.

To be his.

Even if it hurt. Even if she would be called a slut for it. Even if it left them filthy deep in their souls.

She wanted it.

"I need—"

"What, Ella?" he interrupted darkly. "To move, to be fucked, or to come? All of the above?"

"Oh, Christ."

"No, *Tommas*."

His words were punctuated by two of his digits thrusting hard into her pussy. Knuckle deep, her walls flexed around his intrusion while her honeyed juices slicked up his fingers and palm. His other hand grasped the back of her neck when she tried to push up from the bed. Her shoulders strained while her cries turned louder, sweeter. The pace of his fingers fucking her was brutal and fast, no mercy. He wanted her to come pinned down like she was, unable to control herself, and then he needed her to beg for more.

It got him off like nothing else.

Tommas got his wish.

Abriella's orgasm came on fast and hard as she shook under him. Her tartly sweet-smelling arousal soaked him wonderfully. Nothing was better than feeling her break apart around him.

"Tommas ... *please* ..."

As quickly as he'd climbed on the bed to hold her down, Tommas stepped back off it. Abriella sucked in a gulp full of air as her fingers curled tightly into the bedsheets.

"Love it when you do that to me," she breathed.

Tommas laughed quietly. "I know, baby."

"Drives me crazy."

Before she had even fully caught her breath and recovered, Tommas was pulling Abriella back to the edge of the bed again. He let her feet drop on the floor. Next to whatever grip she could get on the bed, it was the only stability she would have when he fucked her.

She liked it better when he had all the power.

Abriella pushed up a little on her hands to watch him behind her. Tommas stroked his cock in a tight grip using the same hand he'd fucked her with. The juices from her sex smeared along his length with every tug. Despite her earlier performance on the stairs and her smart mouth, Abriella was quiet and waiting now.

He enjoyed breaking this woman's will. She gave it to him willingly. He liked to steal her kisses, her orgasms, and her screams. She always handed them over with a smile.

Tommas needed to fuck her raw, until she was nothing but a mess in his sheets. Abriella never asked for anything different.

They were so good like this. The very best. They were fantastic when they fought, better when they were quiet, and happy all the times in between.

But like this?

Like this they were *perfect*.

Tommas hooked an arm around Abriella's waist and pulled her higher again until her ass was level with his steel-hard cock. The tip of his erection drove into the fleshy lips of her sex as he bent down and nipped at the middle of her back. Abriella's hiss quickly melted into a low moan of pleasure when his fingers dug into her sides.

It's better when it hurts, she had once told him. *It's better when I ache.*

Tommas always gave her what she wanted, after all.

His tongue struck out to taste her skin. Above the spot where he'd tasted, a scar caught his eye. Small and circular, the discoloration was the only blemish on his lover's body. Tommas kissed the spot where the bullet had entered her back months ago. Abriella stilled until his lips pressed on her scar. A shiver worked its way over her body.

"It's okay, Tommy," he heard her say.

"It is now."

"Leave it alone, hmm. Another time."

She backed into his cock, seeking and wanting more. Tommas refused to give it to her until he was fucking ready for it.

This wouldn't last forever.

She still had to go.

"I miss you," he whispered against her spine.

Tommas was sure he had said it too quietly for Abriella to hear, but apparently not.

A tremor wracked her body.

"I know, Tommy. I know you do."

A tightness circled his chest, making his air disappear for a moment. Tommas got his breath back the second he flexed his hips and found his home between the heaven of Abriella's thighs. Her wet, tight heat took his length in one long, hard thrust. Her body was made for his. There was no give, she simply took what he gave.

And it was wonderful.

Driving his hands into her long hair, he tangled the strands around his fists and pulled her up. Abriella's back molded to his chest as her body slumped in his hold. He wouldn't let her go—she wouldn't fall in his hands.

Ever.

"Oh, my God," Abriella mumbled brokenly.

Tommas' exhale came out shakier than he intended. "You take me so well, babe. You're so fucking full, stretched open with me, Ella. Christ, do you feel that? You're soaking wet and squeezing me so tight I can't even *breathe.*"

Another flex of his hips and Abriella whimpered his name. Tommas pulled her even closer and slammed into her harder, reaching deeper. Her hands reached back to grasp onto his thighs. The sensation of her fingernails scratching into his skin was enough to drive him downright insane.

"Keep doing that, Ella," Tommas said as his pace picked up.

Her rolling cries mixed in with the sounds of their bodies meeting. The faintest sheen of sweat had gathered at the base of her neck and down her spine. Under his hold, her body vibrated like she was a coil ready to break.

"Come on, Tommy, give it to me like I want it," Abriella whispered almost tauntingly.

"My girl," Tommas murmured into Abriella's ear. "So fucking dirty, Ella. Is that what you want me to tell you, huh? How much I love when you let me fuck you like you're nothing more than a slut? When I use you like this?"

Abriella sank into his touch, sighing. "*Yes.*"

Because in his bed, she could be whatever she wanted. She could be his lover with sweet words and soft love. She could be his enemy with harsh words and a rough fucking. Or she could be his slut … with no fear that he would ever take that private desire of hers outside the safety of a bedroom.

Simple as that.

He adored her more for giving it to him, and for letting him have her like that. No one else would understand the way they sometimes loved, but he didn't care.

Abriella had always been his.

"I'm going to …"

"Come," Tommas finished for her.

Abriella nodded. "Yeah."

"Get it for me, baby. I want it. Give it to me, Ella."

He caught site of his lover's teeth cutting into her lip as her body began to shake. Tommas let go of the hold on her hair with one of his hands so that he could grab her jaw. He tugged her lip from her teeth, and then Abriella sucked his digits into her mouth.

In her ear, Tommas' murmured the words he knew Abriella wanted to hear the most. The things that would make her come fast, hot, and harder than ever.

Take that fucking cock, Ella.

My pretty little slut.

Show me how bad you want it.

His fingers stuffed in her mouth and his hand around her throat muffled the sounds of her scream as she came around his cock. The feeling of her lips sucking his fingers and her pussy milking him was enough to send Tommas over the edge.

He came trembling, weak, and with his teeth buried into the junction of her shoulder.

Abriella came for a third time.

She loved being used

Loved pain.

Tommas didn't mind providing it.

Tommas ghosted the pad of his thumb across Abriella's cheekbone. Her lashes fluttered as her smile grew. Despite the fact that her eyes were closed, he knew that she had been awake for at least a half an hour.

It had become a habit for Tommas to care for Abriella after sex. He cleaned the traces of their fucking from her body, massaged the spots on her that were sore from his roughness and handling, and did whatever else she wanted or needed.

This time, however, she seemed content to pretend to sleep.

Whatever she needs, he thought with a grin.

"How long are you going to stay like that?" Tommas asked.

"Maybe a little longer."

"You look like a kitten wrapped up in my sheets."

Abriella's eyes opened. Humor danced over her features as she asked, "How so?"

"You stretch here and there like a kitten would. You grab onto the sheets like they're a lifeline or something. It's cute."

"Tommy."

"What?"

"Be quiet," she mumbled. "I need quiet."

"Whatever you want, baby."

Abriella's smile grew when his thumb trailed over her soft lips. She kissed the tip of his digit and closed her eyes again.

"You know I'm yours, don't you, Tommy?" she asked softly.

The statement took Tommas by surprise. It wasn't like Abriella to say things of that nature. It was too close to the walls she kept firmly stuck around her heart, a place she wouldn't let him touch all that often.

"Yes," he replied.

"But I don't feel like it sometimes."

Ouch.

Tommas hid how that cut at his soul, but barely.

"What have I done that makes you feel that way, Ella?"

"Nothing," she confessed. "But I don't get to be yours outside of this. I want to hold your hand, I want to stand close to you, and I want people to know. I can't have that, and it kills me."

Maybe he got it then …

At that moment, Tommas figured he might have finally understood why Abriella kept three little words from him. Sure, she might have to take them away someday, but she was doing her damnedest to never have to take them from herself, either.

"Abriella," Tommas said, catching her chin between his forefinger and thumb.

Through thick lashes, she watched him silently.

"I love you more than you could ever know," he told her. "I love you far more than the breath in my own body. I have always loved you, sweet girl. You are the light in a mostly dark life. This …" Tommas waved between them. "Abriella, this is what you've chosen to give me and I've taken it because I can't do without it. Don't you understand that? I've only taken what you've given. If you want something else, then give me more. Tell me you want something beyond this."

"I do," she said so low he strained to hear. "I just don't know how to give it."

"That's it?"

"It's everything to me, Tommy."

"I'll give you whatever you want, Ella."

"I know you will. That's what scares me the most."

Unsure of how to respond, Tommas rolled onto his back. The only thing separating the two was a thin sheet. Tommas felt the tips of Abriella's fingers glide over his chest before her palm settled on top of his heart.

"You deserve everything you want, Tommy," he heard her say.

"Do you even know what it is that I want?"

"I think so. I know who you are and the things you could be. You're so sure of me and us that a lot of other things are forgotten about. There are other things—more important things—than us."

"Not to me."

"The Outfit?" she asked. "Being the boss? Isn't that a part of what you want?"

"I already told you."

"It's nothing to you without me. I remember. But you can't rip everyone else apart in the process of trying to get what you want, Tommy."

Couldn't he?

The moment Tommas woke up in his bed, he knew he was alone. The coldness of the sheets and the ache in his chest told him that he had passed out for a while and his pain meds from the morning had worn off.

Rolling over to check the digital clock, he saw his cell phone resting where it hadn't been before he went to sleep. Abriella had taken the phone the night the bomb blew. She must have brought it for him to have. He also found a small note on top of his gun. She obviously carried the weapon into the bedroom before she left, too.

I had to go.
You looked too good to wake up.
Next time.
Soon.
E.

Falling to his back, Tommas rubbed at his forehead and stared at the note a while longer. Frustrated that he hadn't gotten to say goodbye, he dropped the note on the sheets and pushed up from the bed. His sleep pants had been folded up and placed at the foot of the bed. Tommas tugged the pants on, stood, and searched the room for any other sign that Abriella had been there.

Nothing.

She was far too good at coming and going from his life.

Before he could dwell on that nagging thought any longer, his home phone rang a shrill tune. Tommas grabbed the cordless phone from the cradle and picked the call up on the second ring.

"Rossi speaking."

"Cousin, we've got a problem."

Tommas perked at Damian's voice on the other end of the call. "What in the hell is that supposed to mean?"

"Stuff about the club. I just got word, and we need to chat before your friends from the hospital make a trip to your house to talk about it."

Friends from the hospital?

The detectives, Tommas realized.

Goddammit. What now?

"What is it, D?" Tommas asked.

"We need to meet up and soon. It shouldn't be talked about over the phone. Are you good enough to leave your house or what?"

Nothing that Damian said made much sense to Tommas. It only aggravated him more.

"Yes, I'm fine. Better than I was this morning."

At least that wasn't a lie.

"Good. Meet me at your downtown restaurant. Twenty minutes?"

"Is whatever it is that bad?" Tommas asked.

"It could be. I don't want to talk about it over the phone. The cops are around too much."

"Yeah, I got it. Also, I've got my cell phone back from Ella. No more calls on the house phone. Twenty minutes, Ghost."

"Sounds good," Damian replied.

The call hung up without either man saying goodbye. Tommas made quick work of cleaning his face in the attached bath, tossing on an acceptable suit and pair of Italian leather shoes, and gathered his things to leave.

Downstairs, he stilled at the sight of something missing from the hallway table. Abriella must have taken the bandages he'd left resting on the furniture.

Smart girl. He would have wrapped his rib the moment it started aching again. She took away the option altogether. Abriella was dirty like that, but Tommas didn't mind. She kept him in check.

Chuckling to himself and forgetting that she had left without saying goodbye properly, Tommas opened the front door to his home and stepped outside. It was the first time he'd left his house since he got out of the hospital the second time.

Tommas wasn't the least bit surprised to find Nate already waiting for him with the car.

CHAPTER EIGHT

The moment Abriella stepped out of the cab, she knew that she had made a very terrible mistake. A familiar black car was parked beside her Hummer. Her throat constricted with panic as she grabbed onto the cab's back door and considered jumping back inside the vehicle.

"Miss, I gotta go," the cabbie shouted.

Abriella barely heard the man. She was too focused on the driver's window of the black car as it rolled down a few inches. It was just enough to give her a glimpse of a very pissed off enforcer sitting behind the wheel.

How had he found her?

She'd been careful and smart like always.

Right?

"Miss," the cabbie barked.

Abriella released her hold on the cab door and stepped away. The cab's tires screeched when it pulled out onto the busy street.

Tossing another look at her waiting enforcer, Abriella kept her expression calm. She didn't want the man to know that she was worried. If she acted like she had something to hide, then he would search for it. Not that skipping out on him wasn't hiding something, because it was.

Excuses could be made for that.

Something that wouldn't lead back to Tommas.

Abriella readied something appropriate to say as she strolled across the parking lot and tossed her messenger bag over her shoulder. The enforcer opened his car door and stepped out with a severe scowl that was dark enough to send a weaker woman running.

Trentinis didn't know how to be weak.

Certainly not Abriella.

"Darryl," Abriella greeted.

Standing just a few feet away from the man, Abriella was forced to look up at him. He towered over her by a good few inches. The guy was built like a linebacker, and he usually seemed as stunned as a football player that had taken too many shots to the head. He wasn't necessarily a handsome guy, but he was a mean looking motherfucker.

Abriella still wasn't scared of him.

Men didn't have that effect on her.

"Where in the fuck have you been?" the enforcer asked.

"Shopping," Abriella lied.

"Where are the bags then?"

Abriella shrugged. "Didn't find anything worth buying."

"You're lying."

"Prove it."

Darryl's lips thinned in his frustration. "That little show on the highway earlier was ridiculous, Abriella. You nearly got me fucking killed when the eighteen-wheeler behind me almost introduced the trunk of my car to the back of my head."

"Maybe you shouldn't drive so fast. Reaction times and all."

"That's enough of your smart mouth."

Abriella held back her smirk. She had the guy right where she wanted him. Darryl was good for scaring people, but he seriously lacked the wit to have an argument with Abriella. That, or the man just didn't have the patience.

"You know the rules," Darryl continued angrily. "You make sure that your vehicle is visible, that I can follow behind at a safe distance, and that you don't pull shit like you did today."

"I have no idea what you're talking about. I wanted to go shopping."

"You told your brother that you were studying and playing catch up for school."

"Did I?"

Darryl's gaze narrowed. "Stop playing word games, you little—"

"Careful," Abriella interjected swiftly. "Your next words might very well be your last. If I broke the rules, prove it and I will handle it, but your disrespect will never be tolerated."

"Oh, you think?"

"I know."

Darryl grinned a cruel sight. "What I know, Abriella, is that your brother has very little patience for this sort of bullshit. I know he expects you to be above all reproach and act the same. You stepped out of line today. As far as my language, if you're going to act like a bitch, then you'll wear the title like one."

Abriella's jaw clenched so hard her molars ached. Silently, she reminded herself to play nice with the man to keep him from running his mouth to her brother. It didn't help much.

"What are you going to do, run to Joel and tell him how you can't manage to keep up with little old me?" Abriella asked sweetly.

"No."

"I didn't think so."

Darryl shrugged, and his smile deepened. "I don't have to, Abriella, because your brother called me. You fucked up today. You left your phone inside the Hummer."

Abriella stiffened in the cold air. "So?"

"Didn't you realize?"

"Realize what, Darryl? Stop messing around."

"When you had your phone updated to the newest version last month, Joel paid for an added locator feature in the apps on the account. Because he has control over the account, the app can be downloaded wirelessly without him even needing to touch the phone. It could have downloaded while you were sleeping. You probably didn't even notice it since it just looks like a regular preloaded app in the list that you would scroll right on past."

Abriella's heart stopped. "He didn't."

GPS on her Hummer was one thing.

She had never let her brother touch her phone. She would go to the store, pick out a new one, and the account would be charged.

Jesus Christ.

How could she be so stupid?

Quickly, Abriella went over her travels for the past month. Darryl had said the GPS app had only been on her phone for that amount of time. She had a habit of leaving her phone in the Hummer when she left the vehicle. It was one thing in her favor. The night she had gone to Tommas' club, she had left her phone in her bag in the Hummer parked at her sister's apartment.

She was positive there was nothing else.

Right?

Fear choked Abriella silent.

Oh, God.

"Yeah, that's right," Darryl said. "It's not so hard to find you now when you pull stupid stunts, Ella."

"You're an asshole," Abriella spat.

"Maybe so, but I'm not the one in trouble. I hope whatever you did today was worth it, sweetheart, because you won't have another one like it for a long while."

Abriella kept her mouth shut, but it was goddamn hard. She wanted to scream and lash out at the enforcer. More than anything, she wanted to rip her brother's throat out for tricking her like he had.

Steeling her spine and refusing to give the enforcer the reaction of anger and fear that he clearly wanted, Abriella stood straighter. "Let's go. Home, I take it?"

"Straight home."

"Fine."

"In my car," Darryl added.

Abriella opened her mouth to argue, but Darryl's lifting hand stopped her.

"Not a word," he said. "You lost the right to have an opinion and to drive yourself around when you disappeared today."

"I am not a damned child," Abriella hissed.

"Your brother thinks that your actions today disagree."

"Fuck you both."

"What did you do?" Abriella's mother asked.

Abriella glared at the enforcer standing beside her. "Nothing. I took a little detour and went shopping."

"Keep saying that," Darryl muttered. "No one believes it."

Standing outside of her brother's office, waiting to be allowed inside like Joel was a wanted man, Abriella's frustration grew to epic proportions. The drive back across Chicago to her family's mansion had been tense at best. Darryl continued to question her about where she had been all day. Abriella wouldn't give the man a damn thing.

Let them search.

They would find nothing.

Turning back to her mother, Abriella asked, "Why are you here?"

Sara frowned. "Your brother was on a rampage. We happened to be one of the people he called when he finally got word that you were found."

"We?"

"Me, too," a voice said from behind Abriella.

Her father came to stand at Sara's side.

"Dad," Abriella said quietly, avoiding her father's stare.

Peter had always been a good father. He rarely, if ever, raised his voice. He had never hit his children, treated them badly, or acted like they were anything less than loved.

Abriella knew that as she and her siblings grew up, her father had mostly been a bystander in their life. While he adored them and cared for them, he had been forced to stand on the sidelines while other men in their family took control. Men like her now deceased grandfather, Terrance, and now, Joel.

Peter never had much of a say with his children. He allowed family decisions to be made without his input, even when it came to his own offspring. It was one of the things that Abriella disliked about her father, although she did love him.

She just couldn't help but wonder why he didn't care *enough*.

"You worried your mother," Peter said.

Abriella let out a soft sigh. "I was fine. I'm twenty-two, not sixteen. I have a license and a car for a reason. I didn't do anything wrong."

"You told lies," Darryl put in. "You acted like a fool."

"Would you shut up?" Abriella snarled at the man.

Darryl shook his head and said, "I have had just about enough of your attitude, Abriella."

"Is that so?"

"Yes, so cut it out before I—"

The office doors opened, interrupting the enforcer before he could finish. Joel stood inside his office, sporting his usual scowl and with a cell phone in one hand. His rage filled gaze landed on Abriella, and for a brief second, she wished she could disappear.

Just as fast as that feeling had come, it left.

Her brother didn't frighten her. He could take her things away, call her names, abuse her with his words and choices, but he still couldn't own her. Fear was a possession to Abriella—one she wouldn't ever hand over to her brother.

"You," Joel said, still glaring at his sister.

"Yes?" Abriella asked.

"Get in my office."

Abriella strolled on past her brother. Joel reached out and snagged her messenger bag off her shoulder. Immediately, he began to dig through the bag. When he couldn't find whatever it was that he was looking for, Joel dumped the bag upside down and the contents spilled on the floor.

Her notebook, laptop, keys, makeup, tampons, and everything else that was inside her bag clattered across the hardwood. The rolled up bandage that she had taken from Tommas was also added into the pile, but Joel didn't seem to notice it. Cursing under his breath, Joel tossed Abriella's purse on top of the rest of her things, too.

Anger rushed through Abriella's bloodstream at the very sight of her belongings being discarded on the floor like garbage. Where did Joel get off acting like that?

"Hey," Abriella shouted. "What in the hell is that all about?"

Joel turned on Abriella with a fire lighting in his eyes. "Where were you today?"

"Out."

"Where?"

"Shopping."

Joel's jaw ticked. "Where are the things you bought?"

Abriella tossed Darryl a cool look over her brother's shoulder as she repeated what she had told the enforcer earlier. "I didn't find anything worth buying."

"You must think I am one stupid fucking idiot, Ella."

No.

In fact, Abriella thought the very opposite of her brother. Tommas had always warned Abriella never to treat Joel like he was dumb. Joel was anything but stupid. He was slick, dirty, and quick on the ball. That made for a dangerous man, not to mention the sometimes erratic behavior her brother showcased when making decisions or reacting to something.

No, Abriella didn't think of her brother as stupid. She was too smart for that.

"Well?" Joel demanded. "Do I look like an idiot to you?"

"No," Abriella said. "Not at all."

She just happened to be sneaky, too.

"You purposely tricked your enforcer, lost him, and then disappeared for an entire day. Why did you do that, Ella?"

Without missing a beat, Abriella replied, "Because I wanted a chance to be normal for a day, Joel, without all of this nonsense. Twenty-four-seven, someone is watching me. Someone is following me. I never get to actually be alone. So what? I took a day off, walked around Chicago a bit, window shopped, and relaxed alone. Who cares?"

"I do, and I'll tell you why." Joel took a step forward. He was too close for Abriella's liking, but she wouldn't back down. "Because you're a goddamn liar, Ella. You're sneaky, girl. You've pulled stunts like this before, and everybody knows it. If you want to run around acting out or whatever it is you were doing, then you'll answer the consequences for that kind of behavior."

"What behavior?"

Joel sneered. "Are you playing dumb today?"

Jesus.

Her brother was working every nerve she had. Abriella tried her hardest to keep her cool, but she was three seconds away from blowing.

"Who cares if I was out alone, Joel?"

"I just told you. I care. It looks bad on me. I won't have my sister running around and causing me issues. I won't have people looking at you and wondering what you're doing when people aren't watching. That is how rumors start, Abriella. That is how stories spread. And once you get a title on your back, there is no getting rid of it. You'll stain me—stain your family with your actions and I won't have it. You might not mind what people have to say behind your back, but I do. It stops now."

Abriella blinked, stunned. "Excuse me?"

"You're not deaf. You heard me. I won't have others spreading lies about us simply because Abriella is bored with her life and wants a change. You might not care if people call you a whore and stain your name with rumors, but I won't allow it."

"Joel," Peter said harshly. "Watch yourself."

"Shut up," Joel said, dismissing his step-father with a flick of his wrist.

"Joel!"

Abriella's mother's cry was ignored.

Peter stepped up beside Abriella, glaring at his step-son. "You are out of line. What did Abriella do, other than worry us with her little disappearing act, to earn her that kind of language, Joel?"

"You have no voice here," Joel said dully. "In fact, I don't want you here at all, Peter. Take your wife and go back to the other side of the mansion."

Peter opened his mouth to say something, but Darryl stepped between Abriella's father and Joel. Immediately, Peter quieted with a scowl.

"Make sure they lock the connecting doors," Joel said to the enforcer.

"Will do, boss."

Abriella nearly gagged at that title being given to her brother. Joel was no boss. He wasn't made to be a boss. No man heading a family acted like her brother did. Power-hungry, vindictive, and foul. A proper boss concerned himself with every man's worries, not just his own.

Joel couldn't be a boss. He was far too selfish, malicious, and ignorant to fill the role. He would run the Outfit into the ground. Abriella could see it happening already.

Pointing over the enforcer's shoulder, Peter said, "This isn't over, Joel. I'm done with your nonsense, son."

"Son," Joel said, scoffing. "That's rich."

"He's never treated you like anything different," Sara spat from behind Abriella.

Joel's face remained cold and impassive. "He didn't have to. Your disgusting actions were more than enough shame for me to wear my whole life, Sara. Once a whore, always a whore, right?"

"Watch it!" Peter barked.

Abriella took a second look at her father, shocked out of her wits. Never had she heard him speak to anyone like he had just then. He was typically a quiet-mannered, good-natured man. The anger in his features darkened Peter and made him look far more dangerous than she thought him to be.

Where had this man come from?

Joel also seemed too stunned to speak.

"I won't have you treating your mother that way," Peter said sharply. "She has loved and provided for you, Joel. She has held you when you were sick, sang your nightmares away when you were a child, and adored you for every moment in between. You may not like how you came into this world, but you are here because she refused to abort you when your grandfather demanded it. She loved you even then. She loves you when you are at your most vile. She will go home tonight and still love you. Do not call her a whore one more time in my presence."

Joel's sneer remained firmly in place. "I—"

"Shut your mouth," Peter snarled. "I've heard more than enough. The only reason I am still standing here dealing with another round of your bullshit is because of your mother and sister, Joel. Otherwise, I could be chewing on glass and be happier than I am when I stand in a room with you."

"Dad, it's okay," Abriella said softly, finally finding her voice.

Peter passed Abriella a strange look. "Ella."

"It's okay, Dad. I'm fine."

"It's not fine," Peter muttered.

"You're right, but ..."

But she didn't want her parents to be the next victims of Joel's wrath simply because they stood up to him to protect her. She knew, without any doubt, that her brother would turn on their parents if he thought that Peter and Sara were getting in his way.

It was psychopathic.

Cruel, even.

It was Joel Trentini all over.

"Go to your wing," Abriella settled on saying.

"Yes, go," Joel said, drawling out his words with a threatening undertone.

Abriella glanced up at her father. "Please."

With a tight jaw and a heated glare shot at Joel, her father turned on his heel, took his wife's hand, and stalked from the room.

Joel sighed. "Thank God that mess is gone."

"They're our parents, not a mess."

"They're always a fucking mess for me."

Darryl cleared his throat and held out his hand. Abriella's cell phone rested in his palm. Joel took it from the enforcer with a knowing smile.

"Thanks, Darryl."

"No problem, boss."

Joel bent down and picked up Abriella's keys from the pile of her things on the floor. "And I'll take these as well, Ella."

Abriella crossed her arms. "Take them."

Her words were all bravado and little else. She was now without a personal cell phone and her vehicle. Her gilded cage, locking her away from freedom, had just become a little bit smaller. She couldn't breathe, but God knew she hid it as best she could.

Joel didn't deserve her anxiety. He would like it too much.

"Darryl will drive you to and from wherever you need to go," Joel informed.

He looked Abriella's cell phone over. She was glad that she had gotten into the habit of deleting her text and log files for calls and messages. She also had very little contact information for anyone in the phone.

"School included?" Abriella asked.

Joel nodded. "Of course. He'll be close. You won't outrun him the next time, I'm sure."

"I didn't outrun him this time."

"Keep lying. It looks good on you."

Abriella clenched her teeth to keep from spitting every vile thing inside her head. "Is that all? I'm tired."

"No, that isn't all." Joel glanced up from the phone and met Abriella's stare. "I suggest you curb whatever rebellious bullshit you've got going on right now, Ella. I don't have the time or patience for it. Frankly, if you keep it up, I'll find someone else who will teach you how to behave just to get you out of my hair."

Her heart leapt into her throat.

He couldn't be saying what she thought he was. Surely he wouldn't.

Not yet.

"Guessing by the look on your face," Joel drawled, "you understand me perfectly fine. Cut out your nonsense, Ella, or you'll find yourself walking down an aisle in a white dress to meet whatever man I deem suitable to marry you. I've had a few offers from some families outside of Chicago, and even from some close by that would like a way into our business. You're skating on very thin ice, sister."

Goddamn him.

Abriella felt like she was going to throw up. She literally had to force herself to say, "Okay, Joel."

"Okay, what?"

"I'll behave."

"Good," her brother stated. "You can start by getting the fuck out of my face."

Abriella didn't have to be told a second time. She left the office and her things behind. The door slammed almost as soon as she was out of it. Behind the wood, she heard her brother curse. Then, something crashed into the wall. Typical Joel behavior. When he was angry, he acted out like a child.

"Rough day?" Darryl asked, his voice muffled slightly.

"Worse," Joel grumbled. "I don't have time for that spoiled little bitch's nonsense."

"I think you scared her straight."

Joel scoffed. "Right. You don't know my sister all too well. Keep close to her. You never know what Abriella might do next. I don't trust her. She was lying her ass off. I'm going to send someone out to see if they can find out where she was."

Fuck.

Abriella ignored the dread climbing up her spine.

"I can do it when she's in class," Darryl said.

"Sure. Make sure she sees you outside of the class when she goes inside. Mess with her head a bit. Abriella never was any good at playing mind games."

Wrong, Joel.

Abriella was terribly good at beating her brother's games. The fool.

"Is there anything else?" Darryl asked.

"Yeah, there is."

"What?"

"Someone was at the club that night with Tommas when you set the bomb."

Darryl grumbled under his breath before saying, "Man, I set that up right. It blew. I can't help it that he used the fucking car starter."

"No, not that, you idiot," Joel snapped. "Someone else was there. Inside. I had guys doing the rounds, trying to get info about the investigation at the club. I guess there was a set of footprints in the slush outside the exit door that were small like a female's. Plus, there was more around Tommas. And inside the place, Tommas' bag had been dropped halfway down the hallway leading to the exit like someone had just let it go. Tommas was outside. Why wouldn't he have his bag on him?"

"Someone was carrying it for him."

"I'd say so."

"Who?" Darryl asked.

"A woman, apparently. I want to know who she is."

Darryl grunted in agreement. "Did they say anything about who it might be or who Tommas is messing with?"

"Not a thing," Joel answered.

"What about the cameras?" Darryl asked.

Abriella's heart stopped and her mind raced.

"The club was dark and the cameras inside don't do well with the dark, only the ones outside. Plus, the place only had cameras set up in the important locations like above the cash at the bar and at the entrance. I know Tommas does business in there, so he probably doesn't want it being caught on camera."

"So we know nothing."

"No. But we're going to work on finding something out. Tommas is hiding his involvement with a woman, for whatever reason, I don't know."

Abriella's heart started beating again at that statement. She hadn't even thought about the fact that she might have left something behind that night at the club, some kind of evidence of her presence.

"But if he cares about her, I want to use her. Get him where it hurts, after all. He's always been private and quiet about females, and that sort of thing," Joel finished.

"I can ask around," Darryl said.

"Do that. Now, get out of my office. I need a drink and a smoke. Maybe I'll give Chloe a call, too."

Abriella cringed.

"Still fucking with her, boss?" the enforcer asked.

Joel laughed. "She fucks like a pro. You're still here, Darryl. Don't you have something to do, now? Like get me some info on Tommas Rossi and whatever female he's dipping his dick into?"

"I guess."

"Then do it."

That was enough for Abriella. She tiptoed down the hall and slipped into a spare bedroom that was only used for guests. Closing the door just enough to leave an inch crack for her to peek through, she listened as the office door opened and shut. Squeaks of footsteps echoed down the hallway and then traveled over the staircase before quieting completely.

With her back pressed to the door, Abriella took in the information she had learned. She needed to tell Tommas and soon. Especially about the club and Joel's plans.

Hours ago, Abriella had been sure she wanted the war to end. She didn't want to see more bloodshed and people hurting because of others' selfishness and power-hungry ways. Now, she was ready to do whatever she had to so that her brother wouldn't get what he wanted.

Joel wasn't ready for Abriella.

But she was still coming for him.

Abriella caught the cordless phone charging on the bedside table. She quickly crossed the room and picked up the phone to turn it on. She never called Tommas from a phone inside the mansion just in case someone overheard her conversation or picked up another line and listened in.

This time, she didn't have a choice.

Joel's office had a different number from the rest of the wing. He'd said he was going to make his own phone call, and Abriella was positive her brother was distracted with that. Hopefully, he would be for a few minutes.

Dialing a familiar number, Abriella watched the door she'd left cracked open and waited when she put the phone to her ear. Tommas would likely recognize the number as a Trentini one, considering their home phone for the wing wasn't a private number. She wondered if he would even answer.

Her cell phone? Absolutely.

A Trentini number? Maybe not.

Abriella also wondered if Tommas was pissed off about her earlier disappearing act. Her time had run out, and she woke up with little to spare as it was. Had she woke him up to say goodbye, the man would have dragged her back to bed and she wouldn't have been able to refuse him.

How else would she get ahold of Tommas?

Pick up, Tommy.

He didn't disappoint.

"Tommas speaking."

Abriella let out the breath she'd been holding. "Tommas, we've got a problem."

"Ella?"

"Yeah. Sorry I left earlier without saying goodbye. I couldn't stay."

"It doesn't matter. I love you, crazy girl. Now, what's the problem?"

"What else?"

Tommas sighed. "Joel."

"Joel," Abriella confirmed.

CHAPTER NINE

Tommas hung up Abriella's call, a heaviness settling in his chest.

"What was that about?" Damian asked.

Turning on his heel, Tommas faced his cousin. He'd met Damian for dinner at one of his downtown restaurants before they went to Damian's club that was closed for business during the daylight hours. They had needed to talk over whatever problem had come up. Privately.

"Abriella called," Tommas explained.

"So?"

"She just gave me the same news you did an hour ago."

Damian frowned. "About the police?"

"Yeah. Seems like someone is poking their noses into my business, and they shouldn't be."

"How did Abriella find out?"

"Joel," Tommas said.

Damian cocked a brow. "Huh."

"That's not good, D. It's one thing for you to be able to get information because you've got a couple of contacts, but for Joel to find out that the police suspect there was another person with me the night my car got blown up—a woman, for that matter—is a bad thing. It means he's got someone inside, too."

"I'm aware of what it means, Tommas."

Shit.

Tommas could feel the panic rising in his gut, threatening to close off his throat. If the police had information that there was a second person with Tommas that night, then they were just a few steps from finding out who that person was.

Worse yet, if Joel had access to someone on the inside of the police department, and the police found out that Abriella was the mystery woman, then Joel would know, too.

It screamed bad in ten different ways.

"I had enough attention from the cops before the bomb," Tommas said, rubbing at the headache beginning to form at the base of his skull. "Now, it's even worse. A little digging, maybe going back on the security cameras if they get a warrant beyond the day of the bomb, and they could find out it's her, D. They would *know*."

"Yeah, I get it."

"What in the fuck am I going to do?" Tommas asked.

"Chill out." Damian pushed an unopened bottle of beer toward Tommas. "Have a drink, we'll chat it out."

Tommas eyed the beer with as much disgust as he could manage. "You know, I bet that's exactly how my mother and father started out by thinking like that, too. Just a drink to take the edge off, nothing too serious. Before they knew it, they were knee deep in addiction with four kids they couldn't take care of."

"Whoa. This is … new."

"Not new, D. I don't want the beer. I want to figure out how to keep Joel from getting any more info from the police."

"Well, you can start by keeping a distance from Abriella."

Tommas scowled. "That's your grand fucking plan?"

"It's a start, Tommy. It's like this, man, she's dangerous for you right now. There's too much attention, like you said. And frankly, you're not very goddamn safe for her. Let some of this settle down. Maybe the cops will question you again, maybe they won't. What I do know is that if you keep taking risks with Abriella for the sake of dipping your dick and feeding your heart, then you're both going to end up killed."

Easier said than done.

It was more than sex.

More than love.

Tommas needed Abriella like he needed air to breathe.

"Joel took away her stuff," Tommas said quietly.

"Abriella's?"

"Yes. Her phone, the Hummer, and whatnot. She uh …" Tommas trailed off, cringing. His cousin wasn't going to like the fact that Tommas spent the day shacked up in bed with Abriella, especially not after this. Damian was all about protecting family, after all. "She came over today after she lost her enforcer. I guess the guy found her car using the GPS app Joel had the phone company install on her cell during a routine update."

Damian's face grew stony. "Where was her Hummer parked?"

"I don't know. Nowhere near my house. She never parks it close. She always takes a cab and comes in through the back."

"You're a fool," Damian grumbled.

"I didn't know she was coming over."

"You knew. After the hospital incident, you knew she wouldn't stay away for long. You get off on that shit, Tommas. You love it that she's crazy in the head over you, just the same as you are for her. Sometimes, I wonder if your relationship with that girl is even a little bit healthy, or if you're both just fucked up beyond repair."

"Wouldn't that mean we're the perfect pair either way?"

"Keep looking at it like that," Damian said as he tipped his beer up for a drink.

"My point is, how am I supposed to look after her or do anything for her if she has no way of contacting me or even driving herself around?"

"No, the better point is that you need to stay away until shit dies down a bit. I guess you can thank Joel for making it easier on you. Take the break from Abriella Trentini. You could use it to get your head back where it needs to be."

Tommas was seriously beginning to dislike his cousin.

But ... Damian could be right.

"A week, two tops," Tommas said, "but then I'm going after her."

"Don't get yourself killed over that girl, Tommy."

"You're one to talk."

Damian's mouth snapped shut audibly.

Tommas took that as a battle won.

The next two weeks, however, were sure to be hell.

"We've got a problem, man."

Tommas sighed harshly, more frustrated than he had been in a long time. Those were the last words he wanted to hear from his cousin. After two weeks of being quiet, staying under the radar of police, and dodging the asshole detectives requests for interviews, Tommas didn't need more problems.

It was bad enough that he hadn't spoken to Abriella in thirteen damn days.

Nothing was doing it for him when he woke up from dreams, and smelled her on his sheets. Not his hand, a cold shower, or the most mundane thoughts he could think of. He was like an addict without a fix.

Just her voice, her sarcasm and humor, would be enough.

Tommas wasn't even getting those things.

It drove him crazy that he had to wonder and worry about his girl. Was Joel being his usual asshole self? It was enough to make Tommas insane with anxiety and anger, but Damian was never far behind. Damian liked to point out that the cops were still trying to find out who the mystery woman was, and someone was feeding Joel information.

The asshole.

"Can't I enjoy my breakfast in peace?" Tommas asked.

The eggs, toast, and bacon on his plate were hot, fresh, and begging to be eaten.

"Eat while I talk," Damian said, pulling out a chair and sitting down.

"You didn't tell me there was a problem when you said that you wanted to meet up this morning."

"You wouldn't have met me if I did."

Tommas didn't even bother denying it. "I've got enough stress without adding to it."

"You're about to get more."

Great.

Tommas shoved a mouthful of eggs in and waved the fork at his cousin.

Damian took the hint and said, "Adriano gave me a call this morning and gave me a head's up about something. I think what he was really looking to do was get some kind of guarantee on his side, you know what I mean?"

Swallowing back the food, Tommas said, "Not really."

"The kid wants someone backing him. He doesn't want to run into problems with Joel."

"Over what?"

Damian cleared his throat and rubbed his hands together. The actions spoke clearly of Damian's nervousness, which was abnormal for the former hitman turned Capo.

"Well ..."

"What did I miss?" Tommas demanded.

"Nothing. Even I didn't know. Theo gave Adriano a call to let him know it would be happening today, and nothing more. There wasn't even an option involved, although I don't think Adriano cares. He's happy for his sister."

"Are you purposely being vague? Because if you are, I'm going to shove my foot up your—"

"Theo and Eve got married at town hall as soon as it opened this morning," Damian interrupted.

Tommas dropped his fork on the table with a loud clatter. Several patrons of the restaurant turned to look in the direction of his table, but he didn't give a shit. He owned the place, did a heck of a lot of work in it for the Outfit, and if people didn't like him making a bit of noise, they could take their business elsewhere.

"Seriously?"

Silently, Tommas praised Theo for breaking the rules and taking what he wanted. But he was also concerned for what that could mean for Adriano. The young Capo was the man heading the Conti family, and Joel

113

fancied himself the boss of the operation. No marriage should happen without Joel giving some kind of approval.

Especially one between families as influential as the Contis and DeLucas.

"Theo hasn't kept his relationship with Evelina a secret," Damian said.

"No, I guess not."

"Joel hasn't kept secret his dislike for the fact that Adriano is letting his sister run wild with a man of her choosing, either."

Tommas leaned back in the chair, tapping his finger to his mouth as he considered his cousin's statements. "Adriano wants someone backing him here, you said?"

"Yeah. You, likely. He knows Joel is going to throw a fit that he told Theo to go for it. Did you hear anything about Joel putting pressure on Adriano to marry Evelina off to him?"

"To Joel?" Tommas asked.

Damian shrugged. "I guess so. Adriano refused. He's been making nice with Joel, or as much as he could before this, but he wouldn't do that."

"Making nice for Alessa's sake. Family. Nothing more."

"This could be bad," Damian said.

"But it could be really good for us," Tommas pointed out quietly. "Or for me, I suppose. DeLuca sways to my opinion even if Theo won't actively put a hand into the war. Adriano is outright saying he needs an ally right now. Who does that leave Joel with?"

"No one."

"He's got a decent sized crew, but this could be exactly what I need to force him into a situation where he goes crazy and messes up in a bad way."

Damian cringed. "Be careful doing that, Tommas. Joel is unstable."

"I know, I just wonder if he's unstable enough to turn on himself."

Pushing up from the table, Tommas dropped a few bills down for the waitress and his unfinished meal.

"You're done eating?" Damian asked.

"Yes. I have a Capo to see."

"Don't get Adriano killed in the process of fucking around with Joel."

Tommas smiled. "That's not my plan."

But first, Tommas had other plans.

It'd been two weeks.

Tommas had done the time that his cousin wanted to stay low and out of the view of the police. That was over. He had his girl to see. Chances were, Joel knew about Theo and Evelina getting married and was on one of his rampages. That meant Joel was distracted, and likely wouldn't have a handful of enforcers watching Abriella.

But even if he did, Tommas would have to take the chance.

Two weeks was too fucking long.

Abriella would be at school. Tommas had spent a week planning to safely see her.

It wouldn't be too hard.

Hopefully.

Tommas shrugged off his suit jacket, laid it over one of the chairs, and sat down on the edge of one of the many tables.

Checking his watch, Tommas noted the time was cutting close to when the class was expected to start in this very room. He wondered if Abriella was going to show up, or if she'd somehow missed school that day.

His girl needed a new way to contact him.

Tommas hoped to fix that little issue today. He'd picked up a prepaid burner phone on the way over to the college. As long as Abriella kept it out of Joel's sights, then she should be okay.

Five long minutes of waiting later, and a knock on the classroom door brought Tommas from his thoughts. Pushing off the edge of the desk, he walked over, stood to the side of the door, and opened it to let who he knew had to be Abriella in without her being able to see him at first.

"I'm not late," Abriella said as she strolled right past a slightly hidden Tommas. "I'm five minutes early, so I don't know why you closed the door on me. I know the rules, thank you very—"

Tommas slammed the door shut, making Abriella jump and spin in her heels.

"Oh," she breathed.

A beautiful smile bloomed on his girl's features.

Tommas answered it with a grin. "How long was it going to take you to realize that the classroom was empty?"

"Not very long."

"Mmhmm. And what was all that attitude you walked in here with?"

Abriella dropped her bag on the floor and stuck a hand on her hip. "What about it?"

"Are you always like that when you waltz into a classroom?"

"None of your business, Tommy."

"Get over here, babe."

Abriella didn't need to be told again. She flew into Tommas' opened

115

arms, and let him lift her right off the floor. Her jean clad legs wrapped around his waist like she didn't want to let him go. Keeping a firm hold on her backside, Tommas used his other hand to grab Abriella's chin and draw her mouth to his. The soft touch of her lips was all he needed to forget the nonsense of two weeks missing, thinking about her, and worrying his ass off.

Just a kiss.

That simple kiss quickly turned into something hotter when Abriella's teeth nipped on his bottom lip and sent a shock of lust straight down to his cock. Tommas groaned, and Abriella took the opening he gave to deepen their kiss until neither of them could breathe and blood rushed in his ears. Beneath his trousers, his cock twitched to life, hardening more by the second. The gentle friction of her body rubbing against his length only added to the need beginning to thrum hard and fast through his body.

"God, I missed you," Abriella mumbled against his lips.

Tommas chuckled. "I figured. It ate me up thinking about being away from you for two weeks and not even calling you somehow. Damn, Ella, I was going crazy."

Carefully, Tommas let Abriella drop back on the floor. She didn't go very far. Her arms snaked around his chest and hugged him so fiercely, his heart ached. She didn't seem to want to move away, so Tommas held her, kissed the top of her head, and stayed still until she was ready to release him.

That time didn't come.

"How did you get in here, and where is the rest of my class and the professor?" she asked.

Tommas shrugged. "Maybe I paid some kid in the office to hack the computer, get a list of the students in the class and their cell phone plus email contacts, and sent out a message that the class would be held in the fourth hall."

"Seriously?"

"Maybe."

"And the professor?"

"Minor water leak. That's what his message said."

Abriella's laughter was light and airy. "How did you manage to find someone who could do that?"

"I know some people," he said vaguely. "And I had two weeks to get the details figured out."

"You've been planning to come see me?"

Tommas put two fingers under Abriella's chin and tilted her head up. Her blue gaze shined with her emotions. As much as it was something he adored about her, it was also one of her flaws. All a person had to do was look into Abriella's eyes and they would see her truths.

"I've thought about coming to see you every day since you left my place, Ella."

Abriella bit her bottom lip. "Yeah?"

"Why wouldn't I, babe?"

"I don't know, I just … It's not important. You know Joel's enforcer is probably outside the class, right? He usually stays down the hall by the soda machines."

"Which one?" Tommas asked.

"Darryl."

"Don't worry about him."

Abriella frowned. "So you're only here for a little while and then you have to leave?"

Tommas sighed, nodding. "Yeah. Just for the period. Something came up that I have to handle. I'm working on stuff, though. Know that."

"Working on what, Tommy?"

The only thing that mattered to him.

"Us, Ella."

Abriella glanced away quickly. Tommas wouldn't let her do that— hide from him. She was too good for that nonsense.

"Hey, look at me," Tommas demanded.

Abriella did, but her frown had deepened. "I've only ever looked at you."

Tommas flinched, a memory rushing his mind before he could stop it. He could still see Abriella on the floor, bleeding from a bullet hole in her back from her brother's stupidity. She'd almost lost her life—Tommas would have followed his girl in a heartbeat if she had died.

Simple as that.

But those words … She'd told him those words when she was on the floor, bleeding and dying.

"Who else is going to save you, right?" Tommas asked.

Abriella shrugged. "Bang on, Tommy."

"Crazy girl."

Glancing around the quiet, empty classroom, Abriella asked, "What are we supposed to do?"

"Whatever you want. The hour is yours. I just wanted to see you, be close to you, or anything that I could have for a few minutes. Like I said, it was driving me crazy being away. I don't like it."

"Me, neither." Abriella wet her lips, adding, "But I don't always want to keep hiding, either."

Tommas heard her unspoken words loud and clear. "We won't. Not forever."

"Don't make promises."

He'd never broken one before.

Not to her.

"Stop," Tommas told her. "That's not important right now."

"You're right."

"I have something for you."

Abriella's eyes lit up instantly. "Oh?"

Laughing, Tommas pulled the prepaid burner phone from his pocket. It was simple in design with a touch screen and a black casing. "Here. There's a fifty dollar card on it right now. Next time I see you, I'll bring another one for you to activate. Fifty was the highest the store had right then, or I would have bought you something unlimited. If you have to toss it for whatever reason, then don't worry about it as nothing can be traced."

Her breath caught as she took the phone from him. "Thank you."

"I need to be able to have contact with you, Ella. It fucking kills me when I don't know how your day went, or if you're okay. You know I'll always take care of you."

"Your girl, right?"

"Right," Tommas echoed with a smile. "My girl."

Abriella's gaze lifted to meet his. "Only yours, Tommy."

A possessive heat curled in his stomach, reminding him of just how badly he loved and needed this woman. Something as simple as an innocent phrase could make his yearning for her grow into a goddamn monster in a second.

It was kind of ridiculous.

Tommas didn't mind.

"I know what I want to do for the next hour," Abriella said, grinning slyly as she shoved the phone into her jacket pocket.

"What's that?"

Anything she wanted, he would give.

"You, me, this classroom, and anyway we can defile it for the next fifty or so minutes."

Tommas' throat closed around the appreciative groan wanting out from his chest. "Yeah? Because that's kind of bad."

"You hacked into a computer system, tricked a class full of students and a professor just to get me alone in here. Which one is worse? I'm just taking advantage."

"You're wicked, baby."

Abriella winked and stepped closer to him again. Her hands trailed up his chest to his neck, and then back down his body. The graze of her fingernails through his silk shirt was enough to get his cock harder than steel and ready for something wet, hot, and tight. Keeping her stare locked on his, Abriella's hand dipped lower, the tips of her fingers ghosting over the line of his erection straining against his trousers.

Damn.

Tommas wasn't even ashamed.

Abriella should know what she did for him.

"Fuck, Tommy," Abriella whispered, leaning up on her tiptoes to kiss his mouth.

Her hand palmed him through his pants, making him swallow the lump forming in his throat. It wasn't often that Abriella took the reins between them. Tommas usually made the first move, demanded from her, and then took great joy in watching her control shatter under his wants and needs. She got off on it, but sometimes, she needed something different.

"You're so hard."

"It's all for you, Ella. You're wicked," he repeated.

Abriella's smile was downright sinful. "Someone made me this way, remember? Some strange man told me once to do what I wanted, what would make me happy, and fuck the judgment of others. He made me like this—I kind of like it."

Tommas let out a shuddering exhale, and fought off a shiver as Abriella's hand slipped under the waistline of his pants and boxer-briefs and found his cock. She tugged on his member with quick, firm strokes that made his throat tighten and his cock pulse.

"Good God," Tommas moaned.

Her hand stilled instantly.

"You know," she began in a whisper, "when we first started this four years ago, you kind of were like that for me, Tommy. I didn't realize it at first, but I definitely revered you like one."

Tommas grabbed Abriella's waist and dragged her closer. "Like what?"

"A God."

"I'm not one of those."

"You were mine in a way. I put you on a pedestal like one, and only saw you as this perfect, untouchable being. It was crazy, but it was exactly what I needed at the time."

"Putting people on pedestals only means they'll break when they fall off, Ella."

Abriella laughed. "Tell that to an eighteen-year-old me. Christ, Tommy, I adored the person I thought you were back then."

Tommas leaned down enough to rest his forehead to hers. "And you don't now? What did I do that changed who you thought I was?"

"You got better," she said, smiling in that way of hers. "My fascination got worse, but you got so much better. Worship is not a good enough word for what I felt."

"Like a religion."

Abriella's tongue peeked out to sweep her bottom lip. "Yeah. Just like that."

"Do you still feel like that about me?"

"Everyday."

Tommas' smile spread slow and easy over his lips. "Yeah?"

"Does that make me stupid?"

No.

Not at all.

It just meant she loved him, and needed him. It was simply Abriella's way of doing it, and telling him.

"If that makes you stupid, then I'm a goddamn fool, Ella. I've worshipped the ground you walked on for years, sweet girl."

Abriella watched him through those thick lashes of hers, beautiful and quiet. "We're so fucked up."

"Maybe so, but we're fucked up together which is more than a lot of people can say."

"You don't care, do you?" she asked.

"No." Tommas' hands tangled into Abriella's wavy dark hair and tugged firmly. Her sexy little sigh shot right down through his gut and into his cock, reminding him of how good it felt to have her mouth around his dick. "Do you want to know what I would like?"

Abriella blinked at him like she was coming out of a daze. "What, Tommy?"

He tugged on her hair again. "Get on your knees and show me how you pray."

With a sly grin, Abriella nodded and began to drop down to her knees. She shrugged off her leather bomber jacket, and let it fall on the floor behind her.

Tommas reached down and unsnapped the buttons on his pants before undoing the zipper. He was thankful the classroom door only had one small window at the top, and it was too high for anyone to get a good look inside. The door also locked automatically when it was shut and could only be opened from within the room.

That didn't make the situation any less hot.

They could still be caught.

Time was running out.

Abriella's hands pushed Tommas' pants and boxer-briefs down enough to free his erection. Her palm and fingers enclosed his shaft with an almost painful grip, waking him up all over again. Keeping a firm grip on her hair, Tommas tugged his lover closer to the head of his aching cock until he could feel her breath wash over his member with every exhale.

"Open up and let me fuck it properly, Ella."

She parted her lips enough for Tommas to slide his cock inside her mouth. Wet, soft heat engulfed his length, sending him spiraling straight into a familiar dark bliss. Her tongue flattened to the underside of his shaft as she took his cock in deep enough that he could feel her muscles constricting around his length.

Abriella stared up at him, waiting. One of her hands held onto his wrist, while her other slipped between his legs to palm his sac with a teasing, promising touch.

The sight of her on her knees always did it for Tommas. It made him fucking primal inside, made him want to fuck her mouth until her eyes watered and she was swallowing every drop of his come that she could take.

"Shit," Tommas forced out, his teeth clenching. "I'd forgotten how fucking good this is, Ella. Do you want me to fuck your mouth, or do you want to suck me off?"

Abriella answered his question by flicking her tongue against the base of his dick and then opening her mouth a little more. That was clear enough for Tommas. Keeping her rooted in place, he slowly began to thrust in and out of her mouth at a pace he liked to start with. It let his girl get used to having her mouth stuffed full of his cock and having no control in the process.

Abriella's hum continued as Tommas picked up the pace. He used his free hand to grab her under her jaw, and keep her steady.

"Eyes wide, Ella," Tommas demanded. "I love fucking your mouth, so you better watch me while I do it, or I'll stop. I bet you missed this, didn't you?"

Her gaze snapped up to meet his, a tiny smile trying to form on her pink lips. Pulling on her hair a little harder, Abriella whined in response, her mouth closing tighter around his cock and her teeth adding to the friction for a brief second.

"You want more of that?" he asked.

Without being able to talk, the only thing Abriella could do was nod for him. But her eyes spoke entirely of lust and need. The blues of her irises burned brightly with her want. Being on her knees, having her mouth fucked in a public place, and having no power or say as to what Tommas would do next was one of Abriella's favorite things.

Tommas knew it—she liked these games.

Some might call it debasing.

Abriella practically begged for it.

For Tommas, it was a gift of sorts to see Abriella, someone he loved and adored, at his mercy, trusting him, letting him use her for his wants, because that's what she wanted, too. Her compliance, her need, made him fucking wild.

The gentle graze of her fingernails against his sac had a coil beginning to twist and burn in his gut. The more of that he allowed, the quicker he was liable to shoot his load down her throat. More than anything, Tommas wanted to be inside his girl and fucking them both into oblivion.

With a groan, Tommas pulled his cock from Abriella's mouth with a pop and pulled her up from the floor to stand.

"God, you know I love your mouth, girl. But I love the feeling of your pussy squeezing around me and your body shaking as I fuck you good and hard even more. That's what I want right now. If you don't, then you can get back on your knees and finish what you started. Otherwise, take your fucking clothes off and give me what we both want."

Silently, Abriella glanced over her shoulder at the closed door before she began to take off her clothes. In no time at all, Abriella stood naked in front of him, and her clothes rested in a forgotten pile behind her.

"Christ," Tommas appraised with a low whistle.

He stepped close enough to get his hands on the most beautiful woman he'd ever seen. Abriella's body was a piece of art to Tommas. Her curves fit his hands perfectly, from the dip in her waist to the swells of her hips and breasts. The pixie-like features of her face always radiated with her sensuality and sexuality. She was made for him. Every single inch of her was his perfect match.

Abriella shivered the moment his hands came in contact with her sides. Tommas dragged his palms over her waist, across her stomach, and up to her chest where he could roll his thumbs over her pebbling nipples. Goosebumps bloomed over her flesh as her head tilted back and she hummed contentedly.

"You were right. I missed this, too," she murmured.

"I'm sorry that we don't have more time."

Abriella shook her head. "This is good. It's what I needed. It's perfect, Tommy."

Tommas caught her mouth with his own, taking his time to love her properly. Her tongue tangled with his, promising and sweet, making the heat in his gut grow into a raging fire out of control. Her fingers twisted into his shirt, drawing him even closer.

"I'll figure something out so that it can be just you and me for a whole day," Tommas told her, his lips brushing against hers with every word. "Nothing but us and whatever you want, Ella. Something, I don't know, but it's a promise."

She sighed shakily. "As much as I love it when you say things like that, because I know you will, I hate it, too."

"Why?"

"Because it makes it harder for me with all of this—us, mostly."

Everything about them was hard and difficult. Tommas understood what she meant without making her explain further.

"But I don't ever want you to stop making promises," Abriella added after a quiet moment. "Because you always keep them, and you're the one thing in my life that I can count on for that."

Any control that Tommas had was lost. He loved this woman entirely. All the things about Abriella Trentini that made up who she was inside and out were wonderful, crazy, and sometimes strange.

Picking her up from the floor without warning, Tommas pressed his lips to hers again, taking another kiss without asking. Abriella's legs wrapped around his waist and her heels dug into the small of his back. As he walked a few steps to the closest table lined with chairs, her body jostled against his, allowing her wet sex to grind against his bare erection.

Abriella's back met the table hard. Air rushed from her lungs with her low moan as Tommas kicked the chairs out of the way. Before he could demand that she open up for him, Abriella spread her legs wide, exposing her pink, wet pussy to his gaze.

Tommas grasped her thighs, his fingertips digging into her creamy skin hard enough to leave his marks behind. He yanked her to the edge of the table, close enough that his cock rested along the fleshy lips of her pussy. With just the right flex of his hips, he'd be balls deep in his girl and fucking them both fast toward heaven.

Naked, with her lips a bitten and kissed red, with her hair billowed out across the table and messy from his hands, and a shiver rolling over her skin, Abriella was a sight to see. Sexy as hell. Shameless in her lust. Reckless in her need. It goddamn near hurt him to look at her, but he couldn't help it.

Tommas had only ever looked at Abriella.

No one else ever caught his eye like she had.

"Christ, look at you, baby."

Canting her hips upward at the edge of the table, she said, "Come on, Tommy, fuck me the way I like."

"How am I supposed to make you beg when you ask like that, huh?"

"I'll beg another time. You know I will."

He did.

"Wider," Tommas said, his tone husky.

He pushed Abriella's legs open until he was sure she would feel it in her bones and muscles for days after. Her responding grin as she rolled her hips, making her pussy grind into his cock, told him that she was liking it a little too much.

"Fuck me, Tommy. Make me see the stars. You know how much I love that when you do it."

That was it.

That was all Tommas needed.

Grabbing his cock at the base, he slid it back through the sliver of her slit to her entrance. Then, he held onto her waist and pulled her onto his dick with one deep, hard yank. Abriella's shout of surprise, heated with her pleasure, was muffled into her palm. She whined for more as Tommas began a punishing pace that rocked the table back and forth every time he slammed into her.

Abriella lifted her hips to meet him thrust for thrust. She held onto his wrists, her fingernails biting into his skin, as he plowed into her. The crescendo of her soft cries filled the empty classroom, and Tommas.

He adored all her sounds.

They made fucking her all the more better.

"Ah, fuck," Tommas muttered, watching the sight of his cock disappearing into her pink pussy. Her arousal coated his length, and the sounds of her pussy taking him in as he stretched her full of him was incomparable. "You take my cock so goddamn well, Ella."

Lifting her one leg over his shoulder, Tommas leaned down so he could kiss her while he fucked her. He kissed and bit a path down over her neck and across her collarbones. Her breathless pants matched the constricting flutters of her inner walls hugging his cock tighter than he could take.

"Oh, my God," Abriella cried. "I'm going to come."

"Damn, you're so tight and wet for me. Get it, baby. I want to feel your pussy coming all over my cock while I fuck you through it. Ride that cock, Ella. Show me how badly you want it."

She didn't disappoint. When her cries turned louder, and her trembling made the table shake even more, Tommas caught all her noise with his mouth. He fucked her harder through her orgasm, but his wasn't too far behind.

Tommas came with a hard, long moan that he buried into Abriella's neck. His knees gave out at the intensity of his own orgasm, and he fell over Abriella's body. Her tremors subsided slowly, but her hands never left his body and her sweet kisses dotted his cheek and jaw when she pulled him up to look at her. Her tender touches and whispers soothed him until he felt strong enough to hold his own weight again.

"I love you," Tommas told her.

Abriella's lashes fanned her cheeks as she replied in a whisper, "I've always loved you."

It was everything Tommas wanted from her. He had everything else, her body, her needs, desires, thoughts, and wishes, but not those words.

"But I don't want to regret it someday, Tommy."

"You won't," he said.

"Promise?"

"I've never broken one yet, Ella."

CHAPTER TEN

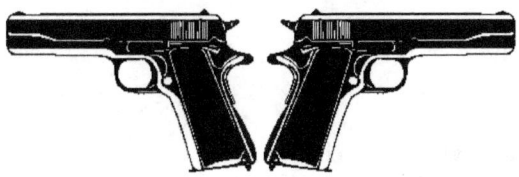

"Why now?" Tommas asked.

Abriella shot him a glance over her shoulder, confused at his question. As she finished tugging on her jeans, she asked, "What do you mean?"

Tommas rested on the edge of the table he'd fucked her on, cool and seemingly aloof. It was one of the things Abriella loved best about her man. Panic could be eating him up inside, or he could be raging mad, but Tommas would never show it on the outside.

Maybe it was his raising that left him impassive and outwardly numb. Abriella wasn't sure, but she did know that his calm demeanor, smooth talk, and dark personality drew her in like nothing she had ever experienced before.

People easily fell in line with a man like Tommas. He could be charming, or in a blink, he could be violent.

He was a trap.

She fell head first.

"Why now, Ella? What's so different now that you feel like it's okay to tell me that you love me when you've never wanted to say it before?"

"Maybe it wasn't a matter of not wanting to, Tommy," Abriella said. "Maybe it was a matter of me fooling myself into believing that love wasn't important enough to keep whatever we are together. Because love doesn't get a say, right? Why let it?"

"That's not really an answer, baby."

Abriella tipped her chin up, defiant in all aspects of her life. "I don't have a choice in loving you; I'm only now realizing it. That still doesn't mean it's enough no matter how much I would like for it to be. But you know what?"

"What?"

"I would rather go down—however this ends—knowing I loved you, than pretending like I didn't."

A hint of bitterness curved Tommas' lips into a smirk. "You're so convinced we're doomed to fail, Ella."

"Do you see this ending differently?"

Tommas didn't answer.

Abriella didn't really need him to.

From the moment they started their secret, crazy relationship almost four years earlier, she suspected that it would never become much. How could it when she was the oldest daughter of a major crime family with values that were thoroughly tied up in keeping their place in the mob and little else?

Abriella had always been Tommas'.

But she never really was at the same time.

"I do love you," Abriella said quietly, turning to face her lover.

Tommas slid off the desk with the grace of a predator. He was the kind of man who had the patience of a saint. Strolling across the room, he caught her hand in his, and pulled her into his chest. Abriella didn't mind being there at all.

"Love is enough," Tommas told her. "It always has a say."

"This life says differently."

Tommas shrugged. "This life is wrong."

God, how she would like for that to be true.

More often than not, the mafia life won.

"I'm working on ending this," Tommas said, his arms squeezing tighter around her frame. "And I know you want me to do it without hurting more people, but I might not have the choice. It needs to end, Ella, but I have to do it the right way."

Abriella sighed. "And what way is that?"

"Not the way Riley did it, I can tell you that. He left his biggest competition and his worst enemies free to do as they wished, and that came back to bite him hard."

"Joel?"

"And Theo," Tommas said.

Abriella shivered, remembering the night Riley had been killed. It was one of the few nights that Abriella sought out Tommas during their short separation—if that's what someone wanted to call it. Holding nothing back, Tommas had explained to her exactly who killed Riley Conti, and why. It was more than just the Outfit. It was years of abuse and hidden secrets. Theo just couldn't do it anymore, and he was desperately trying to protect Evelina in the only way he could.

Abriella didn't blame Theo.

Not one bit.

"You know," Tommas said, bringing Abriella from her thoughts, "... I'm just trying to do what I have to do here, sweet girl. Nothing more."

"What was it that you said? Everything you do is for me?"

"Exactly that, Ella."

It took Abriella a second to realize it, but she was in no better of a position than Evelina Conti had once been. She was trapped in a life that wasn't of her making, with a future that was uncertain and not of her choosing. She was not a person to the men in her family, but a move to make when the time was right.

"Can you end it with just one more death?" Abriella asked, refusing to say her brother's name.

It would hurt her family.

Her mother, certainly, and maybe her father.

Joel had cut enough scars into their family over the years, and he'd caused a handful of pain to each person he touched. Did that warrant his death? Abriella couldn't answer that. Was she selfish enough to let her brother die on the off chance that she might be set free to have what she wanted?

Abriella met Tommas' blue gaze.

Her heart clenched.

Her breath caught.

He was hers.

She wanted him.

Abriella absolutely was that selfish.

"Can you?" she asked again.

Tommas nodded. "I can."

"Don't tell me when, okay?"

"I won't," he said softly.

Abriella passed the ticking clock on the wall a glance. It was five minutes before her final class of the day was supposed to end and she would have to leave. Tommas caught her stare and sighed heavily.

"I'll figure out something else to get us away for the day," he said.

Abriella laughed. "You better. One more kiss?"

Tommas conceded to her request. He cupped her jaw, tipped her head back, and pressed his lips to hers with a ferocity that spoke entirely of possession and love. By the time he pulled away, Abriella was breathless and high.

"If you leave a little early, before the actual end of class, you could get past Darryl by telling him you needed to use the bathroom," Tommas suggested.

"Good idea."

"You have to let me go, Ella."

But she didn't want to.

Reluctantly, Abriella stepped away from Tommas. She hid her frown as she picked up her messenger bag and slung it over her shoulder. "Again. Soon."

"Soon," Tommas echoed, winking.

Unsteady on her feet after the intensity of their hookup, and ignoring the tenderness between her thighs, Abriella left the classroom without a look backwards. Each step she took down the hall closer to where she knew Darryl was waiting just around the corner reminded Abriella how insane she actually was.

Her relationship with Tommas was a lot like playing with fire.

Always hot.

Dangerous to touch.

Fantastic to watch.

A beautiful tragedy just waiting to happen.

"You're early," Darryl noted, glancing up from the phone in his hand when Abriella cleared her throat.

"I have to use the bathroom. The class might as well be over."

"Learn anything new?"

How fun it was to fuck on an unstable table?

Abriella shrugged. "No. It was basically a 'what to expect over the next few months' kind of thing."

"Huh." Darryl stood from the bench. "Do you think wasting your time working toward med school is really worth it when you're probably not going to use any of it?"

"Do you think being a sheep is worth it if you might end up being led off a cliff?"

Darryl's brow furrowed. "A what?"

"A sheep."

Follow the herd, idiot.

"I don't get it," the enforcer said.

Abriella wasn't shocked. Nobody said that Darryl was the most intelligent man in the Outfit. "Never mind. Let's just go."

"Goddammit!"

Joel's roar had Abriella jumping in the kitchen chair. Miss Cathy, the Trentinis' cook, clicked her tongue chidingly from where she was working at the island.

"That man has the temper of the devil, I swear," the cook muttered.

Abriella laughed bitterly. "You have no idea."

"I feel badly for whatever woman finds herself married to him. I can't imagine Joel as a very loving or caring man."

Neither could Abriella.

Joel cursed loudly again, and something crashed on the floor right after. Abriella wondered what had happened this time to cause her brother's temper tantrum. When it came to Joel, it could be practically anything.

"That asshole," Joel spat as he came into view of the kitchen.

Holding back her frown, Abriella asked, "What's wrong?"

"We have fools for family, that's what. Idiots, the bunch of them. I don't know if he thought I wouldn't find out, but I did. Word travels fast."

"And you're not making sense."

"Our *brother-in-law*," Joel said, drawling out the words with twisted sarcasm.

"Adriano?"

"Yes. He's the only fucking brother-in-law we have, isn't he?"

"That doesn't tell me what's wrong, Joel."

"It doesn't matter. The fact is, he fucked up."

Okay then …

Abriella made a mental note to call her sister with the cell phone that Tommas had given her earlier that day and find out what in the hell was going on.

Joel's cell phone beeped in his hand. Looking down at the device, a wicked grin spread over his cheeks. "Fantastic."

"What now?"

"You know what, I think I will tell you. We're going to crash a party, Ella. Get dressed."

Abriella didn't like the sound of that at all. "Why?"

"Because I said so, that's why."

"You sound like a child, Joel."

It wasn't anything new. Man-child Joel always came out to play when he didn't get something he wanted.

Joel didn't act like he'd heard Abriella's comment. "Fucking ridiculous. Thinking I wouldn't find out about this shit, or that I would agree to it if I did know. Unbelievable."

"Seriously, what happened?" Abriella asked again.

"Adriano," Joel barked. "That little shit went against everything I told him. That's what, Ella. He's as much of a fool as his father was. I've had enough of it. I've been nice for Alessa's sake—"

"Nice? What do you call nice?"

"Shut up and get dressed. We're going out, I said."

Abriella snapped her mouth shut, and forced back the urge to claw her brother's eyes out. Her fingers still twitched with the need, however. "To where?"

"The old DeLuca property, apparently."

That was where Lily and Damian lived now.

Abriella struggled to put two and two together to try and figure out what might have occurred to put Joel in such a rage. The only thing that really linked Adriano Conti and Damian Rossi was the not-so-secret relationship between Theo DeLuca and Evelina Conti.

What did they do?

"Why are you still sitting there?" Joel snarled. "Are you fucking deaf or stupid? I told you to move, Abriella."

"Jesus Christ, chill out."

"Get ready!"

"You're not permitted entrance," said the guard at the gate.

Joel glared at the man from inside the BMW. "Listen, Kirk, I get you're doing what Damian told you to do, but if you don't get that asshole on the phone and tell him I'm out here waiting, you won't see your wife tonight. Do you understand that?"

"Joel," Abriella hissed.

The DeLuca enforcer was just doing his job.

Joel flicked his hand at Abriella as if to silence her. Then, he turned back to the enforcer. "Call him right now and tell him."

Huffing, the enforcer pulled out his cell phone and dialed a number. He muttered a few words into the phone, and kept his eye on Joel all the while.

"Yeah, Skip," Kirk said. "What do you want me to do?"

"I could drive right through the fucking gate if I didn't like the paint job on my car as much as I do," Joel said under his breath.

Abriella rolled her eyes. The iron gate was reinforced with concrete and brick pillars. It could probably withstand a few hits. She hoped her brother wasn't serious, because her body couldn't withstand him ramming his vehicle into an iron gate and bricks.

Under her annoyance, Abriella's anxiety simmered on low. It was never good for someone to invite themselves to a party where they weren't wanted. It only caused more issues in the Outfit than was needed.

Joel didn't seem to care.

"Okay, I'll let him through," Kirk said before he ended the call.

"Thank you," Joel said, sneering. "Now open the goddamn gate."

Without a word, Kirk hit a button on his cell phone and the gate began to open automatically. Joel hit the gas pedal hard the moment he could fit the BMW through the opening, spinning rocks and making the tires screech.

"Calm down," Abriella told her brother.

It felt like she had said that exact thing fifteen times since they left the house.

"You don't get it," Joel growled. "I specifically demanded Adriano keep his sister in line, or better yet, set her up in a decent marriage to strengthen the families, and he went behind my back—"

"Eve is a grown woman, Joel. I don't know what she did, but you don't get to control her life."

"See, you don't get it."

Abriella chose not to argue it any further with her brother. It didn't matter as she already had a pretty good idea of what was going on. Evelina took her freedom and ran with it—with Theo DeLuca.

Good for her.

Up ahead, Abriella could see at least ten or more parked vehicles. She recognized a few immediately. Lily's yellow Maserati. Damian's blue Porsche. Tommas' Jaguar. Evelina's new electric blue BMW. Another handful of cars and SUVs were scattered in the driveway, too.

"Nice crowd," Joel noted.

"Are they having a dinner or something?"

"Or something."

Abriella scowled at her brother. "Can I wait out here?"

"No."

That was that.

Abriella got out of the car once her brother had parked and shut off the engine. She followed behind Joel, feeling entirely uncomfortable at having been forced to crash whatever was happening—a celebration, likely—at the DeLuca family home.

If it was what Abriella believed it to be, a wedding celebration, then the last thing she wanted to do was sully Evelina's day with Joel's jealousy and nastiness. Evelina deserved happiness. Abriella wasn't the kind of friend who would ruin that simply because others didn't agree with the marriage.

As they strolled up the front steps, the door opened. Theo DeLuca stood in the entrance with cold eyes and a tight frown.

Joel smiled. "Aren't you going to invite us in?"

"No," Theo said quietly.

Abriella fidgeted, and kept a few feet between herself and her brother.

"You won't allow me to congratulate you and Evelina, Theo?" Joel asked bitingly.

"I don't want your fake platitudes and cheers, Joel. You didn't come here because you're happy for my wife and me, but because you're pissed off that neither me, nor Adriano, gave you any say in the matter of my marriage. It is none of your business. Take that and run with it for all I give a damn."

"That's awfully big coming from a Capo with no pull in this family."

Joel's words were meant to mock. Abriella bit the inside of her cheek, hoping Theo caught onto Joel's games.

"You're not important to me," Theo said simply.

"I—"

"Let him in," came a voice from somewhere behind Theo.

Abriella's shoulders relaxed at the sound of Tommas' dark, rich tenor.

Theo, on the other hand, looked ready to kill. "I don't want to upset my wife."

"He was bound to show up. Eve knew it was a possibility."

"Fine." Theo's gaze cut to Joel, a promise of violence flashing in his brown eyes. "Disrespect my wife on her wedding day, or upset my pregnant sister in her home, and I will gladly take the prison sentence when I put a fucking bullet between your eyes. There are a lot of people here tonight—some unconnected. Mouths will run, but I don't care. Evelina would be a little pissed at me, but I hear conjugal visits are worth a try. Do you understand that, Joel?"

Joel tipped his chin up, flashing his teeth in a sneer. "I get it."

"Make sure of it."

Abriella tipped her wine glass up for another drink as her sister slid in beside her in the far corner of the room. She had been trying to stay out of view as her brother made the rounds with his false smile plastered on, and his passive-aggressive congratulations following right behind.

She was not going to be a part of his mess.

Abriella didn't want to be connected to him tonight.

"You could have given us a heads-up," Alessa said.

Abriella's back straightened. "Well, I would have, except Joel took away all methods of my communication."

Alessa blinked, her mouth falling open. "Oh."

"Yeah, oh."

"I'm sorry. I shouldn't have assumed. It was just that Lily and I thought it would be nice for Eve to be able to celebrate with Theo a little. They didn't even tell anyone until after. We didn't want them to feel like they had to hide their marriage. They adore each other."

"I can tell," Abriella said softly, finding Evelina in the crowd dancing with her new husband. "She looks happy."

Evelina wore a short, flared white dress with matching pumps and a crown of small roses in her hair. With her eyes darkened by kohl, and her lips painted red, Evelina looked like a sexy young woman ready for her life. Her skin was flushed from laughing and moving so much, but her eyes were only on Theo. The couple rarely stopped touching one another.

Now that was love.

Abriella was so filled with envy, it stung.

She wanted to be able to do that with Tommas, too. She wanted people to see how happy and radiant Tommas made her when they were together. She wanted to smile for just him in a crowd of people. She wanted to celebrate what they had.

It killed her that she couldn't do any of those things.

"I do have a burner phone," Abriella said, needing to get away from the sadness in her mind. "Tommas gave it to me to use, but I can't let Joel see it. Joel didn't give me a chance to call you or anyone else before we left the house."

"You're wearing a dress," Alessa said, looking Abriella over.

"Yes, one I put on while Joel waited outside the bedroom and banged on the door to tell me to hurry the fuck up. I'm sorry, Lissa. Honestly."

"I believe you. So ... Tommas, you said?"

Abriella tried to find her lover in the crowd, but failed. Maybe he had moved into the kitchen. Adriano didn't seem to be in view, either.

"What about it?"

"He met up with you?"

"Pulled some strings," Abriella clarified, keeping her voice down.

"You're messing with him again?"

Abriella laughed weakly. "I couldn't stay away."

"Yeah, love sucks like that."

"Tell me about it."

"What is Joel even hoping to gain by coming here tonight?" Alessa asked.

"I don't know," Abriella admitted.

That was the scariest part. Joel was unstable on his best days. He thought life was a game. Those who played it with him usually lost. Abriella didn't want her friends to be one of them.

Needing a breather, Abriella took the chance to escape from the immediate sights of the guests and her wandering brother by entering a hallway that led to the back of the house. In the darkness, she rested her back to the wall, closed her eyes, and tried to relax for a second.

It didn't really help.

"God, he's really got you on pins and needles," came a whisper in her ear.

Abriella shivered, smiling slightly. She'd felt Tommas' presence before she had even heard his voice. His familiar cologne, a woodsy and spicy mix, alerted her the moment he rested beside her.

"What are you doing?" Abriella asked. "You're going to get me into trouble."

"Joel is occupied with Adriano currently. I'm taking the chance to make sure you're all right, Ella."

"I'm not."

"I figured. You looked disgusted out there. You weren't even trying to hide it."

"He had no business coming here, Tommy, and doing this to them."

Tommas scoffed. "I know, but tell that to your brother. Joel believes he has every right, because he thinks of himself as the boss of the Outfit. We all know he isn't, and that the seat is still open, but to Joel, it's his."

"It doesn't matter. This wasn't about him. Eve and Theo are just trying to start their lives."

"And they will," Tommas said. "I'll make sure of it. Don't worry about that."

But what about Abriella and Tommas?

Would they get their start, too?

Tommas' hand found Abriella's in the darkness. He wove their fingers together a second before he tugged her into his side. Abriella put her head on his shoulder, soaked in his familiar comfort, and let her worries bleed away.

"You care about these people, right?" she asked.

"Of course, Ella."

"Why?"

"Because most of the men—Damian, Theo, Adriano, and even others—are good people doing what they can to provide for their families in the only way they were taught. They should be given a safe chance to do that, not have to worry about picking sides or being killed. That's not what the Outfit is supposed to be about. I believe in this life, and I have faith that it can be better."

Tommas would make a damn good boss.

She wondered if he knew that.

"Joel is probably going to come looking for me," Abriella said, stepping away from Tommas' side.

Just as fast, he pulled her back in, only that time, he spun her around and brought her into his chest. Without a word, Tommas grabbed Abriella's jaw, made her stand on her tiptoes, and pressed a fast, searing kiss to her lips. Abriella fisted his suit jacket, wanting him closer the moment his mouth touched hers. A quiet moan escaped from her chest, letting her lips part. Tommas deepened the kiss, allowing Abriella a taste of the whiskey that he'd been sipping on earlier in the night. He didn't pull away, and he held tight, refusing to let her move as he kissed her like he owned her with hard strikes of his tongue and scrapes of his teeth to her lips.

It was fucking wonderful.

For a moment, Abriella forgot about where they were. Despite the murmurs of people just twenty feet away, she only heard the ragged breaths from Tommas panting in her ear. She released his jacket to tangle her hands up into his hair. Tommas grabbed her thigh and lifted her leg to curl it around his own.

With nothing but her thin black dress and satin panties, and his slacks between them, she was able to feel the thick, hard ridge of his erection driving into her pelvis. Abriella couldn't help herself, she lifted her hips the best she could, rubbing against his cock. The little bit of friction sent sparks of shivers running down her spine.

Tommas answered her quiet gasp by grabbing her hips, lifting her a little more so that she was standing on her tiptoes, and then grinding his cock against her center.

"I bet your fucking soaked," Tommas mumbled against her lips. "Fuck, what I wouldn't give just to taste you right now, or slip my cock in and let you ride me against this wall. Wouldn't you like that, Ella? We're so close to those people, someone's bound to hear or see something. Does that feel good for you, baby, rubbing on me like that?"

Abriella whined softly, the sound muted by Tommas' mouth. It felt damn good. Her body was overheating with every stroke of her satin covered sex on his pants. The outline of his erection was more than enough to stimulate her throbbing clit, and the ache between her thighs from their earlier fucking reminded her of his cock pounding into her.

"Goddamn," Tommas muttered heavily. "You want a little help?"

Abriella nodded, still chasing that high rushing her veins.

She felt his hand untangle hers from his hair. Quickly, Tommas stuck her hand between their bodies.

"Get your fingers into that sweet pussy, Ella. I want to see the marks of your come on my pants when I take this jacket off later. Make sure your fingers are good and wet so I can clean them off before you go."

Abriella had all she could do to keep quiet. She did what he said, slipping her fingers into her panties and driving two hard into her clenching, slippery sex. Her inner walls hugged her digits tightly as Tommas drove his tongue into her mouth to hide all her sounds. With his hips still rotating against hers, forcing her wrist to rub over and over into her clit, Abriella was close to falling off the precipice.

"Holy hell," Tommas breathed in her ear. "You're fucking shaking, baby. Let it go for me. Hurry, before someone walks into this hallway and sees what a fucking little slut you are rubbing yourself on my cock with your fingers stuffed up your pussy. Is that what you want, Ella, for them to see that?"

God.

He knew just what to say to make her hotter than ever and teetering on the brink of her own personal insanity.

It was debasing.

He degraded her.

Being caught would be humiliating.

Dirty.

Fucking awful.

She loved it

Abriella just couldn't find it in herself to care that it was all true, too. She finger-fucked her way to an orgasm with Tommas grinding against her body and whispering the dirtiest things in her ear. She shivered and buried her face into his neck, biting down hard on his pulse point to keep from screaming out.

Why did he always make it so bad?

Why was it always so fucking good?

It was moments like this that reminded Abriella how well Tommas knew her. He'd given her a distraction, but he'd handed over much more, too. Stolen moments like these were marked all over their relationship. She loved how Tommas used her for this, and that he took great pleasure in making her run back for more.

"There you go," Tommas whispered, his lips brushing against her temple. "You're going to need to go back out."

Abriella ignored the stinging in her eyes. "Yeah, okay."

"First, though …"

Tommas snagged her hand, pulled it from her panties, and let her drop to the floor. With a sinful grin, he stuck her two fingers in his mouth and cleaned them with a hum.

Abriella's throat went dry.

"Sweet like candy," Tommas murmured when he released her digits. "And as filthy as fucking sin. You good, baby?"

She nodded.

What in the hell else was she supposed to do?

Stepping out of the shadows of the hallway, Abriella was met by two familiar faces. Alessa and Lily both crowded the entryway to the hall with their fronts turned to the people. To anyone else, it might have seemed normal, like the girls were just chatting, but Abriella could see the truth.

One of them must have noticed she'd taken off down the hall, and that Tommas followed. Her heart swelled at the fact her friend and sister helped to hide her secrets. Embarrassment quickly followed at the thought of what they might have seen.

Alessa laughed at Abriella's red cheeks. "Hey, we didn't spy."

"Not even a little bit," Lily confirmed.

Abriella smiled. "Thank you. Where did Joel disappear to?"

"I've been wondering that myself," Lily muttered.

Alessa frowned. "I think he went outside to talk to Adriano in private. When their voices started getting louder, Theo made them go outside."

Oh, shit.

"Did Joel even say hello to you?" Abriella asked her sister.

"No," Alessa replied. "But he did tell me that I was dead to him."

Abriella's heart hurt for her sister. "I'm sorry."

"It's all right. Joel is what he is."

"A fucking asshole," Lily said under her breath as she rubbed her rounded stomach with her hand. "The baby is giving my insides hell because of all the noise, so I'm going to go find Damian and let him know I need to rest."

"You'll be at Alessa's baby shower in a couple of weeks, right?" Abriella asked her friend.

"Yes. But will you?"

"She's my sister."

Alessa sighed. "Joel might not—"

"I'll be there," Abriella said quickly. "No matter what."

Fuck Joel.

"Rebel," Alessa teased.

"You know it."

"I would like to leave the hall," came a voice inside the darkness from behind Abriella.

She had forgotten about Tommas waiting to come back out.

Laughing, Abriella waved her sister and friend off, and disappeared into the crowd. She made a point of not looking back over her shoulder as she walked through the throng of people toward the front of the house. Chances were, if Joel had gone outside with Adriano, then her brother was ready to leave. She grabbed her jacket and tossed it on as she passed the lines of hooks in the entrance.

Unsurprisingly, she found Joel and Adriano in an intense stare down in the middle of the driveway. The younger man didn't look like he planned on backing down, and Joel's glare was fiery enough to melt ice.

"You screwed up this time," Joel said.

"I gave you no guarantees," Adriano replied. "My father's dealings were not mine. If you thought for even one second that I would marry my sister off to a man like you, then you are much stupider than I realized. Evelina is a grown woman who made her choice. It's over."

Joel barked out a laugh. "You're right, we're certainly fucking over here. Don't come looking to me for someone to back you when you need it, Adriano, because it won't happen. Run to another man's crew."

"I never came to you, anyway."

"Don't forget whose sister you knocked up and turned into a whore-made-wife, asshole."

Adriano's jaw ticked. "You know what, that's the last time you're ever going to say a bad word about Alessa. She doesn't deserve it, and I am sick and fucking tired of playing nice with you for the benefit of others. Stay the hell away from my wife, Joel. She doesn't need or want your kind of family love, trust that. If you try to cause me problems, you'll find a hell of a lot more for yourself waiting there in the mess."

With those very obvious threats said, Adriano turned on his heel and stalked toward the house. He offered Abriella a sad smile and a nod as he passed.

"What are you waiting for?" Joel snapped from the driveway.

Abriella hugged her jacket tighter to her frame. "Did you get what you came for?"

"Mind your damned business."

Story of my life, Abriella thought.

CHAPTER ELEVEN

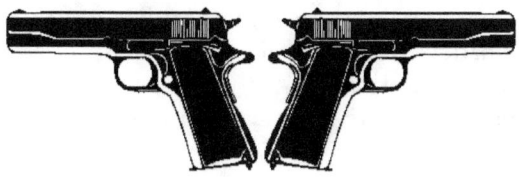

"Tommas! Tommas, where are you?"

Tommas nearly dropped the glass of water he held at the shrill shriek of his mother echoing through his house. There was nothing like the voice of Serena Rossi to put a man on edge first thing in the morning. Setting his cup down to the counter, Tommas rubbed at his forehead with his free hand to soothe the sudden headache he had.

"Tommas!"

Jesus.

"In the kitchen, Ma," Tommas said, sighing heavily.

Serena stomped into the kitchen looking like she'd just rolled out of bed not too long ago. Crumpled clothes, haphazardly done hair, and smeared makeup topped off her morning drunk ensemble. Tommas tried to pull forth some kind of sympathy for his mother, but he couldn't.

He had none left.

"How come—" Serena swayed, her words stopping abruptly as she grabbed onto the edge of the table. "I'm fine."

Tommas lifted a brow high. "I never said a word."

"You were thinking it."

Perfect.

This was exactly how he wanted to spend his morning.

"How did you get here?" Tommas asked.

He'd taken away her car and his father's old Cadillac. Serena had no way to drive around drunk with nothing to use to do it with. It was one of the smaller ways Tommas was trying to help the world. And his mother, too.

In a way …

"I took a fucking cab," Serena spat. "It's not like you make any effort to come to my home, thank you very much."

Tommas cleared his throat, trying to keep his cool. "Ma, I came over yesterday when the housecleaning lady said she found you in the hallway in a pool of vomit. Her job is to clean the house, not you. Who do you think cleaned you, got you in bed, and left the water and Tylenol for you this morning?"

Serena's gaze narrowed. "Oh, that little bitch. Yeah, about her. I want her to stop coming to the house. She moves things, and I don't like that I can't find something when I need it."

Unappreciative, as always. His mother didn't even mention a thing about the fact he had been there to take care of her.

Tommas wasn't surprised.

"You mean when you're sober enough to need something other than liquor?" he asked quietly.

"You little—"

"Bastard? Try something new, Ma. You've been calling me a bastard since I fell out from between your legs."

Serena's eyes widened, a false sadness coloring her still-drunk features. "I would *never*, Tommas."

Manipulation was a game Serena was terribly good at. Tommas had simply gotten better at recognizing it over the years. Instead of urging his mother on in whatever nonsense she had planned, he decided to go a different route.

"What do you want, Ma?" he asked.

Putting a fist to her hip, and using the table to balance her weight, Serena replied, "The Conti baby shower is in a few days. Why wasn't I invited?"

"You were."

"Nobody thought to tell me."

"I tossed your invitation in the trash," Tommas explained.

Serena's mouth tightened a second before she said, "Well, then ..."

"You're not sober, Ma. You have a bad habit of causing problems at these events. The upcoming party is about Alessa and Adriano celebrating their unborn baby, not your issues. It should be a happy, quiet day for them and nothing more. So yeah, I threw it in the trash."

Without a word, Serena fell into the closest kitchen chair with a loud sigh. She fiddled with some of Tommas' papers on the table, never meeting her son's gaze as he came to sit in the chair across from her.

"But Adriano is my nephew," Serena said quietly.

"Sober up and you can come with me. Simple as that. Otherwise, my choice is firm."

"Fine."

Tommas was surprised his mother had given up so easily.

Standing from the table, Serena waved at the large kitchen. "When are you going to fill this home with a wife and children, Tommas? It's empty."

"When I get around to it," he lied.

He had someone to fill the house with. It just wasn't the right time.

"Sure," Serena drawled, a slight slur sticking at the end of her tone.

"Go home, Ma. Get some more sleep."

Thankfully, Serena went without an argument. Tommas walked his mother to the front door, said his goodbye, and opened it to watch her leave. A running cab waited out front for her. It made Serena's sudden appearance all the more confusing. Clearly she hadn't meant to stay for long.

Once Serena was gone from the driveway, Nate poked his head around the corner of the house. Nate's most important job was to keep an eye on things when Tommas was at his house, and even when he wasn't, unless directed to do something different.

"Sorry, boss," Nate said. "I was going to stop her from going in, but she's your mom and all."

Tommas frowned. "It's fine, Nate."

"What did she want?"

That was a damn good question.

Tommas wasn't entirely sure of the answer.

"Maybe she wants attention," Tommas settled on saying. "Without Laurent, her house is full of nothing but her."

"And alcohol," Nate added.

"And that."

"You good, boss?"

"Great. You want something to eat?" Tommas asked his enforcer.

"Nah, I picked up a sub on the way over."

"All right."

Tommas closed the front door, shutting out the early April wind, and made his way back to the kitchen. The cell phone in his pocket rang as he sat back down at the table. Pulling it out, Abriella's new burner phone number flashed across the screen.

Smiling, Tommas picked up the call as he reached for the note that he'd kept. The note Abriella had written for him the day she came to his house and then left before he'd woken up. He liked to have it close, because it reminded him that Abriella was there in one way, even when she wasn't.

"Hey," Tommas said.

"Do you miss me?" Abriella asked.

"Always, baby."

Tommas' hand came up empty as he dug some more under the papers for the note. Confused, he flipped the pile over and began looking through each one in case he missed it. He hadn't.

The note was gone.

"You there?" Abriella asked.

Unsettled over the missing note, Tommas brushed it off. "Yeah, I'm here."

"You sound … different. Something happen?"

"No," he said, hoping that was the truth.

The only person who had touched the papers was Serena.

Why would she take his note?

"Tommas?"

"Yeah?"

"I miss you."

Tommas forgot about the note and his mother. Abriella was more important.

"I already told you that I miss you," he replied, chuckling.

"Have you figured out a way to steal me for the day yet?"

"Working on it."

Quite literally.

Maybe for longer than just a day.

Tommas chose not to tell Abriella that, however.

"Joel is trying to keep us from the baby shower on Saturday," she said sadly.

"Us?"

"Mom, Dad, and me."

"I'm sorry," he said honestly. "I know you want to go for Alessa."

"Oh, I'm going," Abriella replied, a fierceness that he loved coloring up her tone. "I'll be there, Tommy."

Tommas laughed. "Is that so?"

"We're going. Mom, Dad, and me. It's not for Joel to decide. He's not ruining this for Alessa. Simple as that."

He filed that information away, knowing Joel would probably be alone. It was the best time to strike a man.

"I'll be there, too," Tommas said.

"Sneaking me extra pieces of cake, huh?"

"Goddamn right."

A few days later, Tommas strolled out of his home to meet Nate waiting with the Mercedes. Just as he pulled open the back passenger door to get in, two familiar figures came up behind him.

"Tommas, we should talk, old friend."

Tommas scowled at the voices of the detectives. Delog and Crown just wouldn't get the damn hint. In no way would Tommas talk to police. Not about the bombing, not about the Outfit, and not for fun, either.

They could go to hell.

"Kind of busy today, boys," Tommas said, slipping into the car.

Detective Crown grabbed the car door before Tommas could close it. "Wait a sec, Tommy."

Tommas eyed the man with as much disdain as he could manage. "*Tommas*. It's Tommas."

"We don't know one another well enough yet to be on a nickname basis?" Delog asked.

"I would prefer if we weren't on a first name basis, asshole."

"Ouch," Crown said. "Nasty today, are we?"

Tommas pulled on the door slightly, just enough to tell the man he wanted to close it. "As I said, I have a party to get to. My cousin's baby shower. Nothing that you need or want is more important, I can assure you."

"Now, now," Delog drawled, shaking his head. "You still haven't come down to the station again for a follow up interview about the footprints at your club or the other things we found. It's been a month since the bombing happened."

"And in another month, you'll be here demanding I go down to the station again. Talk to my lawyer, it's what I pay him for," Tommas growled.

These damned investigators were seriously getting on his nerves. Tommas had noticed them following him more often, and they'd even question some of his employees at his businesses that had nothing to do with the club.

It was getting out of hand.

Tommas was going to have to handle these assholes at one point or another.

"You're actively impeding our investigation, Tommas. Just make it easy on everyone and tell us who was with you that night at the club," Crown said.

"As far as I can remember, no one was with me."

"That's what your lawyer keeps saying, too," Delog stated, cocking a brow. "Funny, we don't believe either of you. See, the problem we have is that whoever it was cared enough about you to be directly beside you when you were bleeding on the ground. We found smudged handprints on the inside of the exit doorjamb, which means whoever she was had been inside the club. She was also carrying your bag."

"So maybe I hooked up with a girl that night and was going to take her home. It is a club, idiot. Beautiful, young women are a given. But, I can't say for sure. I can't remember. Ask the doctors."

"We know you paid the man off to say whatever you wanted."

Tommas smirked coldly. "Prove it."

Delog's cheek twitched.

Cops didn't like being outwitted.

"We'll get the info one way or another, Tommas," Crown said lowly.

"I don't see what difference it makes," Tommas replied. "Other than the fact you two fools have been on my case for years, and you're still trying to find something valuable enough to make me turn rat. Newsflash, boys, it isn't going to happen."

Crown held tight to the door. "I guess the boss's seat is looking pretty damn fine from where you're standing, isn't it?"

Tommas' shoulders stiffened. "I don't know what you're talking about."

Delog waved two fingers at Tommas. "Have a good day, Tommas. Enjoy the party. See your *people*. We'll be around, looking into things like always."

"What is that supposed to mean?"

Crown let go of the door, finally. "It means the more you ignore us, the more we gather against you to use. We'd much rather have you work with us, than someone else."

Someone else?

Tommas clenched his teeth and slammed the door shut. From the driver's seat, Nate watched his boss warily in the rearview mirror.

"You okay?" Nate asked.

"Drive."

"Tommas—"

"*Drive!*"

Nate pulled away from the detectives, letting the Mercedes tires squeal on damp pavement. Once they were far enough away that Tommas' anger had faded, he relaxed into the seat and took a deep breath.

"Fucking bastards," Tommas said to himself.

"They're just digging for nothing, boss."

"They're looking for something."

"They'll still get nothing."

Maybe.

Maybe not.

Tommas simply wanted to protect Abriella.

"It doesn't matter," Tommas said, waving his hand as if to shoo the problems away. "We have to focus today."

"Right," Nate agreed.

"Are you good to do the job? Can you do it?"

Nate scoffed. "Have I failed you before?"

"No."

"And I won't this time."

Tommas smiled, knowing that was true. "Make sure you arrive back at the baby shower in lots of time to pick me up after you've finished the job."

"Will do," Nate said. "I'll make sure it's done, get out clean, and come back in lots of time to get you, boss. By the time they hear what happened to Joel, you'll be back at your house planning the meeting for the Capos so you can take the seat. Simple."

The remainder of Tommas' stress melted away at his enforcer's assurances. Nate was a good man—loyal to Tommas like nobody could ever possibly understand.

"One step closer," Tommas murmured, staring at the buildings passing them by as they drove.

"Hmm, what's that?" Nate asked.

"This is just one step closer to where I need to be."

"Being boss?"

No, having Abriella.

Tommas didn't correct the enforcer.

"Well?" Damian demanded.

Tommas brushed his cousin off, continuing his stroll around the food table. He picked from several desserts to fill the plate in his hand, and kept an eye on the woman across the room all the while. Abriella sat beside her sister, smiling and happy.

She had made it to the baby shower, as she said she would. Tommas had called the day before, just to make sure she was going to be there.

"Tommas, quit ignoring me," Damian growled.

Setting his plate aside, Tommas said, "Nate will call me when it's done."

"And you've thought of everything."

"Yes."

Damian's lips drew thin. "How can you be sure—"

"I'm sure that everything will go fine because I trust that Nate has been watching Joel enough to know the man's habits. It's a done deal, cousin. Leave it alone."

"A done deal," Damian echoed. "Then why do I feel like something bad just crawled up my back?"

"I don't know. You always were strange like that."

Leaving his grumbling, scowling cousin behind, Tommas strolled across the restaurant floor to greet the hosts of the day. Adriano had opened up one of his restaurants for the baby shower. There were no games to be played and no silliness happening. It was just a dinner between families and friends to celebrate the upcoming birth of their child.

"Oh, come on," Abriella groaned when Tommas was close enough to hear her sweet voice.

"We don't know, Ella," Alessa said, laughing.

"Don't know what?" Tommas asked, butting into the conversation.

Adriano bent down to press a kiss to his wife's cheek before he stood, and offered Tommas his hand. Tommas took the handshake, and handed his plate to Adriano.

"Here, feed your wife," Tommas said. "I hear she's craving sweets."

Abriella shot Tommas with a pointed look. She had let that little fact slip about Alessa's pregnancy the last time they chatted.

"Thank you," Adriano said.

"Now, what am I missing about knowing something?"

Alessa flashed a smile. "The gender of the baby."

"She won't tell anyone," Abriella complained. "How are we supposed to buy the right colored stuff if she won't tell us?"

"You buy me things all the time for the baby!"

"But cute girly or boy things, Lissa." Abriella sighed. "You don't get it."

"If I knew the gender, I would tell you," Alessa said.

"You know."

"I do not."

"You do," Abriella muttered.

"She doesn't," Adriano said quietly. "But I do."

Abriella's smile turned almost predatory as her sights landed on Adriano. Tommas had to hold himself back from laughing. If his girl wanted something, she would get it come hell or high water.

"Do tell," Abriella said.

Adriano chuckled. "I—"

"Adriano!" Alessa said loudly, smacking her husband in the thigh. "Be quiet. That was a mistake and you sneaked a look in the file. Now shut your mouth."

Adriano made a zipper motion over his lips, shrugged, and then said, "I'm just gonna … go find Theo."

"He's being pestered by Lily at the bar," Tommas said.

"She worries about him all the time," Alessa put in.

"No, she loves him," Adriano argued. "There's a difference."

"He has a wife, now," Tommas said quietly.

"Eve says Theo owes Lily, for whatever reason." Abriella smiled, adding, "So, I don't think she cares what Lily bugs Theo about as long as he's alive, you know."

"You coming for a drink?" Adriano asked, his hand landing on

Tommas' shoulder.

Subtly, Tommas passed a look in Abriella's direction. She was chatting quietly with her sister, seemingly oblivious to his attention. It was likely that she did know he was watching her, but they had always been damn good at this game.

There were far too many people at the baby shower. The restaurant was filled with family, friends, and last minute people who had heard about the party. It wasn't the kind of event where Tommas was willing to risk being caught with Abriella. He'd done it before, sure, but today he was trying to watch his cards a little more carefully.

"Sure," Tommas finally said. "But I'm not drinking."

"Whatever you say, boss."

Tommas stiffened at Adriano's casual use of the term, but hid the reaction quickly enough. It had been said so easily that even Adriano didn't catch his slip. Or maybe he knew exactly what he'd said, and he meant it.

Either way, Tommas liked it.

He just wasn't the boss.

Yet.

A round of drinks later—minus Tommas—and laughter was shared between Capos and old friends of the Outfit. The men had gathered around the bar, snacking on whatever had been brought into the other side of the venue, while the women relaxed in the restaurant side with baby gifts and all that nonsense. An MMA fight played on the large flat screen television, earning bets from Damian, and Theo.

"Three grand on Jarv," Theo said. "The man is a fucking beast. I had the pleasure of seeing him fight in Vegas a couple of years ago. Damn he's good."

"Yeah, but Louis has skills that Jarv doesn't," Damian noted. "Consider that. He's what, Kung Fu, Mixed Martial Arts, and Kick Boxing, right?"

"Jarv is still a beast."

"Take Jarv, asshole."

"I am," Theo said. "Get that cash ready."

Damian tried to smack his brother-in-law in the back of the head, only to be dodged by Theo's defensive maneuver.

"Ha, you're getting too slow for me," Theo taunted. "Age is working against you, D."

"Let's go outside and see you say that," Damian said, cocking a brow.

Theo smirked. "Later. Right now, I'm working on making you go broke."

Amused by the men, but not wanting to get in on their bet, Tommas rested his back to the bar and watched the fight begin on the television. He was thankful for the invitation from Adriano to the baby shower. While it might seem like a small thing, it was anything but. Now that Joel was in one of his rages because of Theo and Evelina's recent marriage, and Adriano was supporting his sister, Joel felt like Adriano had picked a side.

Tommas' side, of course.

Offering Tommas the invitation to the baby shower only added to it all.

Out of the corner of his eye, Tommas caught sight of a smiling Abriella stand from her chair. She looked like she was getting ready to greet someone, but Tommas couldn't see who it was. Alessa tried to stand as well, but Abriella waved her sister down.

Curious as to who it was that had the sisters looking as happy as they did, Tommas moved between the entryway of the restaurant's two sections. He didn't think the men would notice his absence considering how involved they were in the television.

Abriella's smile made a lot more sense as Peter Trentini walked across the restaurant with gift bags in hand to greet his daughters. He set the gifts on the table as he hugged Abriella, and then bent down to kiss his younger daughter on the cheek.

Briefly, Tommas wondered where Sara was. When he talked to Abriella, she made it clear both her parents were coming. A trickle of concern ran down Tommas' spine. His plans did not factor in someone else being with Joel today other than the man's enforcer. Joel often left the Trentini mansion to do the most mundane things like run to the store, or make a trip for coffee. Nate had been watching. Tommas' plan had been an easy, clean route of taking Joel out when his family wouldn't be in any way involved and Nate could get out quickly.

"Where's Mom?" Alessa asked.

Her question brought Tommas from his thoughts with a bang.

Peter frowned, avoiding his daughter's gaze. "She stayed behind. She was trying to convince Joel to come, show face, and make an effort. He seemed like he might before I left. Sara said if he didn't come, that she would just take her car, otherwise, she would drive over with him."

Tommas' throat tightened to the point he couldn't breathe.

Shit.

Abriella didn't look pleased. "We could do without Joel, Dad."

"Maybe, but you know how your mother is. She loves him even if he acts like he despises her. He's her son. Let your mother try. It makes her sad, but if she doesn't do something with Joel, it makes her feel even worse."

"Yeah," Alessa said softly. "We know, Dad."

Tommas' chest suddenly felt like someone had placed a heavy weight down on it. He slipped away from the guests and the party, making a beeline straight for the back of the restaurant. Taking Joel out was one thing, but Sara Trentini was quite another. She was an innocent, and nothing more.

It would still be a clean hit.

Joel would still die, likely.

Tommas would still get both the boss's seat, and his lover.

But at what price?

Her trust?

Her mother?

Her happiness?

Tommas couldn't do that.

He just pushed the back exit door open as the cell phone in his pocket dinged. That was Nate's sign. His first text was to say he had the hit in progress because he had Joel in a good spot. The second would be to say the job was done.

Pulling the phone out, Tommas dialed his enforcer's number. He put the phone to his ear, rested his forehead to the outside brick wall, and listened to it ring.

Over and over.

It kept ringing.

Tommas knew it wasn't Nate's fault.

The man was just doing what he'd been told.

Finally, the call picked up. It was the answering machine. Tommas' heart dropped. This was not what he wanted to happen. This was not how it was supposed to go down. There was a very good chance his lover's mother was inside the same vehicle as Joel that was about to be lit up in a random drive-by shooting.

One that he'd ordered.

One that he planned to make sure this sort of thing wouldn't happen.

No mistakes.

Good, clean, and over before anyone knew what happened.

How would he tell Abriella?

How could he apologize for this?

"Nate's phone, get it out and I'll get back to you," the enforcer's answering machine said.

Abriella pushed open the exit door at the same time the message finished and a beep sounded. Tommas met his girl's concerned gaze. She must have seen him rush out of the restaurant, and when she got the chance without being noticed, followed him.

I'm sorry, he wanted to say.

I love you, Ella.

"Don't do it," Tommas said into the phone, hoping Nate would see the message and take it before doing the hit. It wasn't likely. "Nate, call it off, man. Please."

Abriella's brow furrowed as she held the door open. "Tommy?"

He hung up the phone, ignored Abriella's outstretched hand reaching for him, and dialed the phone again.

The enforcer still didn't pick up.

"Tommas, what's wrong?" Abriella asked gently.

I'm so sorry, baby.

He met her gaze, unsure and cold in his heart.

Colder than he'd ever been. Frozen like ice because he was about to lose the one thing he wanted more than anything else in the world all because of one mistake.

Abriella wouldn't understand.

This wouldn't be forgiven.

CHAPTER TWELVE

Something awful and terrible welled in Abriella's stomach as she watched Tommas' face fall from the usual confident mask he wore to the expression of a heartbroken, guilty man.

"Tommy?" she asked in a whisper. "What happened?"

His mouth opened to speak as he glanced down at his phone and then back at her. No words came out. He didn't even look like he was breathing. His hand clenched so tightly around his phone that his knuckles had turned an ashy white from the pressure. He shoved the phone into his jacket pocket.

The sickness rolling in Abriella's middle only got worse and picked up speed until bile was rising in her throat.

"I fucked up," he finally said.

His words came out so quiet that she barely heard them.

"I'm sure whatever it is can be fixed, right?" she asked.

Tommas shook his head. "No, baby. Not this time."

Abriella swallowed hard, her chest tightening in reaction to his agonized tone. Tommas rarely showed emotion for anyone outside of the people he cared for. That list was short. She knew that without a doubt, she was at the top. His family and very few friends came after her. Even still, Tommas was the kind of man who could hide whatever he needed to when the situation called for it.

Why couldn't he do that now?

"I need you to tell me what happened, Tommas," Abriella said softly.

"I'm so sorry," was all he managed to say.

Abriella's heart cracked.

It wasn't from her own unknown pain, caused by something she didn't understand, but because of the wetness gathering in her lover's eyes. Tommas never cried. Not once had Abriella ever been privy to him in that kind of state.

It ached.

It made her sick.

It was all wrong.

"Don't do that," Abriella said, stepping closer to him. She immediately reached for his face and wiped the wetness away. The moment she touched his tears, Tommas tried to jerk away from her like he'd only realized at that moment he was crying. Abriella refused to let him go. She held him tighter, letting her fingernails dig into his jaw and forcing him to stare her in the eyes. "Don't do that, please. It can be fixed, right? Whatever happened, you can fix it. You always make it better, Tommy."

He shook his head again, a ragged exhale escaping his lips. "I don't think so."

"Nothing is unfixable—"

"This wasn't supposed to happen," Tommas interrupted. "I had it all accounted for, Ella. Every. Fucking. Step. This was the end, baby. Of everything. Done. No more fighting. No more bloodshed. No more war. Just you and me like it was always supposed to be. I had his every move down!"

Abriella flinched at the sudden rage in his tone. "Joel?"

Tommas nodded. "I've worked for two weeks to make sure this went down perfectly. I didn't want mistakes. I needed it to be clean. It should have been good. Just him, he'd be the last one to go in this fucking war. That's all we needed, Ella. I am so sorry."

A painful, swift fissure began to tear over Abriella's heart and soul. It was nothing like anything she had felt before. Abriella was not a stupid woman. She had never been a fool to the games of the men surrounding her.

She knew how they played.

She could play them, too.

Never once had she thought Tommas would back off from Joel. Abriella knew that her lover would make a move eventually, one that would permanently end the fighting and the bloodshed.

"Was it going down today?" she asked. "Whatever you were going to do to Joel, was it going to happen today?"

"Yes," Tommas admitted.

Abriella physically recoiled at what that might mean. Her father's words about her mother staying behind and likely coming with Joel in his vehicle rang heavily in the back of her mind. Her stomach twisted in sickness and disbelief. A numbness settled in her limbs.

Tommas grabbed hard to Abriella's wrists, keeping her locked in place. "I didn't know about Sara until five minutes ago, baby. I swear to God, Ella, I didn't. I never would have—"

"Stop," she breathed.

Abriella needed space. She needed to take in more air than her lungs were giving. Her body was cemented in place, but her mind felt a million miles away.

Nothing was right.

Everything seemed foul and bad.

"I tried," Tommas mumbled, holding onto her tight enough for it to hurt. Abriella didn't mind. It kept her from falling on the ground. "I tried to stop it the moment I thought there was chance someone else might be with him. It's not for sure, Ella. He might be alone."

"But he might not be."

"He might not be."

"My mom …"

"I tried," Tommas repeated weakly.

Abriella couldn't control the reaction. It bubbled up too fast for her to try and stop it. She jerked away from Tommas and spun on her heel in just enough time to bend over and spill the contents of her stomach on the ground. In her heartache and pain, she gagged on vomit and the sudden flood of tears.

No.

No, no, *no*.

This was not how it was supposed to be.

Her fingernails cut into her palms, making her skin break and bleed. She shook with the force of her sobs as familiar, strong arms circled her middle and held strong.

Tommas pressed his face to the middle of her back and whispered his apologies over and over. Abriella believed him. Every word he spoke was coated heavily in his pain and his honest grief for her agony. She had seen the regret in his tears and the confusion in his earlier words.

She knew he hadn't meant for this to happen.

It didn't help.

She wanted it to.

God, she needed it to.

"I'm sorry," Tommas said, holding her tighter. "I'm so sorry, baby. I wanted it to be over. I need it to be over for you and for me. Please, Ella, please don't hate me for this. I love you more than anything. Don't you understand? I'd rather be dead than without you. I tried to fix it. *Please, Ella.*"

She still believed him.

She still loved him.

Abriella just couldn't bring forth enough emotion through the haze of her grief and numbness to tell him. Wiping the sickness from the mouth with the sleeve of her dress, Abriella stood. She turned to face her lover, wiped the mess of tears from his face, and took a breath.

"Stop," she said quietly.

Tommas sucked in a hard breath. "Okay."

"I can't … I can't do this right now. And neither can you. Stop it, Tommas."

His shoulders stiffened and his back straightened. "You're right."

"This is not about us today. That party in there is not about the Outfit. It is the one day my sister has to feel happy and good about her baby. I can't take that away from her."

He reached out to stroke her cheek, but Abriella moved out of his way. She couldn't let him touch her. If she did, then the sudden, strange calmness she had managed to gain would shatter again. She would break and crumble. Her heart would tear back open.

She needed to be okay for just a little while longer.

For her father.

For Alessa.

For herself.

"Ella—"

Abriella held out a hand. "Don't."

Tommas cringed like she had slapped him. "I'm sorry."

"I ... I need to go back to my sister," she said.

A buzz in Tommas' pocket broke their staring contest.

Tommas dropped his gaze, but didn't reach for the device.

Another splintering crack settled across Abriella's heart.

"Answer it, Tommas," Abriella said.

He didn't.

"I don't need to," he said softly.

"Why not?"

Tommas didn't answer. Abriella didn't need him to. She knew what the call likely meant. The job was done.

Without a word, Abriella spun on her heel, opened the restaurant door, and left Tommas behind.

Control.

She needed to keep it.

If only for a few more minutes ...

Abriella ignored the enforcer sitting outside of her brother's hospital room. She knocked on the door a second before pushing it open. Joel sat on the edge of his bed, dressed in casual clothes with a black leather bag resting on the floor between his feet.

Setting the water bottle in his hand on the bedside table, Joel turned to Abriella with a blank expression. "Managed to make your way over, did you?"

Abriella didn't bother giving him a response to that statement. Joel didn't deserve it, frankly. He'd been in the hospital for nearly a week since the shooting that took their mother's life, caused Darryl to wreck the car he was driving, and almost took Joel's life as well.

The problem was, Joel showed no emotion.

He didn't ask about their mother after being told she had been killed by a gunshot to the head. He didn't seem to care at all that her life had been forfeited for his. Joel never had cared a damn ounce for the woman who gave him his very breath.

Abriella hurt every day. Her grief was constant and near unbearable. Sometimes, she found herself staring at a wall, unable to breathe or think, and an awful lump had welled in her throat. She found her father alone and crying more times than she cared to count. She'd comforted her sister in Alessa's pain.

All the while, she planned her mother's funeral. She made the arrangements necessary with the undertaker, the church, and the graveyard. She designed the headstone of a marble angel resting in a deep sleep with her mother's name engraved on the front. She picked the plot, wrote the check, and chose which dress would be the final one her mother ever wore.

Abriella never cried. She choked on her agony, swallowed it back, and kept moving because she didn't have a fucking choice.

Who helped her?

No one.

So no, Abriella had no fucks to give for Joel or the broken rib he suffered, the concussion he had, or the bullet he took to the left side that narrowly missed his heart.

She cared *nothing* for him.

Abriella would give anything she had, everything that was hers, if she could turn back time and make her brother die instead of their mother.

Whatever God would take, she would hand over.

"Darryl is outside with the car," Abriella finally said. "If you're ready, then he is."

"Why are you here then?" Joel asked.

Abriella didn't want to answer him. Joel deserved no explanations as to what she had been doing this last week while he took his little time out from the rest of the world.

"Abriella," her brother said, "I asked you a fucking question."

"I had to stop at the flower shop. Some last minute thing came up with the arrangements for Mom's funeral. They wanted to make sure it was okay."

"So?"

That one word right there, so uncaring, cold, and distant, was why Abriella hated the very breath her brother was still capable of breathing.

No, she wasn't happy with Tommas. She was angry over his error that cost her someone she loved. She was mad that the mistake happened at all.

More than anything, she wished his plan hadn't failed. She wished that she was burying her brother tomorrow and not her mother. Abriella couldn't find it in herself to feel guilty for those desires.

"So, I'm not allowed to go anywhere without my babysitter," Abriella said, letting the sarcasm haunt her voice. "And since the funeral is tomorrow, I needed to give my okay today. Darryl had to come here to get you. He decided to kill two birds with one stone."

Joel pushed up from the bed. "Wonderful. Everything is taken care of then?"

"What do you mean?"

"Sara's arrangements. That's all done?"

"Yes."

Abriella practically had to force the answer out.

"Is my suit dry-cleaned?" Joel asked.

"Waiting in your office."

Joel picked his bag up from the floor, ripped the hospital bracelet off his wrist, and then tossed the discarded piece of plastic on the bed. "Great. I'm ready."

The closer he came to Abriella, the more she wanted to rip his fucking throat out. Her anger and sorrow was damned excruciating, but she was holding it in. She hid it well enough to manage day by day.

Abriella was ready to fucking blow.

Maybe she should blame Tommas.

Maybe it was all his fault.

But she hated Joel far more.

Abriella hated her brother for his untrue ways, his manipulations, and his games in the war. She despised the fact that Joel had stained his hands with almost every death over the last few months in one way or another. She detested his lack of empathy, his greed for nothing more than power, and his selfishness.

He made her sick.

This time, just by fucking *surviving*, Joel had pushed Abriella a little too far.

"What are you waiting for?" Joel asked.

Abriella put her mask back on, letting her brother believe that she was just another one of his compliant little sheep. "Nothing. Let's go."

For a mid-April day, the rain held off for Sara's funeral. Abriella found herself silently grateful that the sun was able to peek through gray clouds and color up the sky as her mother's casket was lowered into the ground. Her mother deserved a little beauty for her final resting place. Something more than wet dirt and pretty flowers.

Sara was everything that Abriella had never wanted to be. Her mother had made mistakes. She'd been called a whore for most of her life. Her past transgressions had been held over her head as the people they called family whispered behind her back. She was shunned, shamed, and mocked.

Unfortunately, those were the things that some people would remember about Sara Trentini before anything else.

Abriella, on the other hand, would remember a strong, enduring woman who cared and loved far more than should have been possible. A woman who offered forgiveness and friendship to those who didn't deserve it. A kind soul who gave life to three children, and despite how they had come to be, she never stopped loving them.

She would remember her mother. That woman ... that imperfect, tender, devoted woman ... was who Abriella wanted to remember.

And maybe being like Sara wasn't such a bad thing.

At Abriella's right, Alessa stood quiet and still. Tears streaked down her sister's cheeks while her hand held tight to Abriella's. Placed atop her eight month pregnancy swell, Alessa's other hand rested with her husband's, their fingers intertwined.

Thankfully, Joel had managed to reign his asshole in for the day and allow his younger sister and her husband the chance to be at the funeral and burial.

At Abriella's left, her father stood like a broken statue. Full of cracks, withered, weather-beaten, and ready to fall. Peter hadn't said more than a few words since news of the car shooting and accident had come to the guests at the baby shower the week before. He barely moved, ate, or slept.

Abriella constantly worried about her father. Peter seemed lost without Sara.

The sound of a metal spade shovel being driven into dirt woke Abriella from her stupor. She watched the two groundskeepers as they started throwing shovelfuls of dirt into the grave. Most of the funeral had passed Abriella by without her even noticing.

On the other side of the grave, Joel gave one last glance at the grave with his usual disinterest present, and turned on his heel to leave.

He was the first person to go.

Shortly after, the other guests began to take their leave as well. Some stopped to give the sisters and their father a supportive word or hug. Abriella recognized the faces of her friends, Lily and Evelina, their husbands, and other people, but she couldn't muster up the ability to thank them or even smile.

"You ready?"

Abriella heard Adriano's question directed to his wife, but barely.

Alessa squeezed Abriella's hand. "You okay?"

Faintly, Abriella nodded. "Yeah."

Liar, her mind taunted.

She was two seconds away from shattering, from letting all her anger and distress out, or from breaking down completely. So close.

"Call me, okay?" Alessa asked softly.

"Sure," Abriella whispered.

Once her sister was gone, Abriella was left alone with just her father and the sounds of shovels digging into dirt over and over. Quietly, over the spades slicing through the mound of earth, soft, choked sobs began to echo. Abriella glanced up to see wetness streaking down her father's cheeks. Peter didn't try to hide his pain, he simply let it be free. Abriella wished she could do the same.

"I miss her," Peter said brokenly.

Abriella's heart splintered. "I know, Dad."

"I didn't tell her enough. Not nearly enough."

She didn't have to ask what her father meant. His heartbreak and grief was so clear to see that it only added to her own pain.

Drawing in a deep breath, Abriella pushed down her own suffocating emotions and the welling tears. She leaned her head to her father's shoulder, and wrapped her arm around his to hold tight.

"It'll be all right, Dad," she told him.

Peter shook his head. "No, it won't. It really won't."

She knew her father was telling the truth.

As much as she knew that her own lover had been the cause of her mother's death, she couldn't imagine standing at his grave to bury him. Tommas was every good and bad part of Abriella's heart—something she desperately needed and wanted, but could rarely have. The one thing she had chosen to love entirely, the man who owned her soul and her very breath.

Tommas was her shadows in the daylight, and her color in the darkness. He knew her secrets and her stories, he loved her defiance and her spirit. He let her be true to who she was, loved her fearlessly, and tried to give her what he thought she deserved in the only way he knew how.

She couldn't do what her father had to do today.

Abriella just *couldn't*.

"I'm sorry, Dad," Abriella mumbled.

"Me, too, Ella. Me, too."

A short while later, Abriella helped her father into his waiting car. Once she was sure he was settled in the back seat, she gave the enforcer waiting behind the wheel a nod to say he could take a somber Peter home. Closing the door, she stepped back from the car and waited as the black vehicle pulled away.

Heavy in her heart, Abriella looked for the car that should have been waiting to take her home as well. Joel had opted to have Darryl drive him home when he was ready, and allowed Abriella to have a separate car and driver waiting for her.

It was something else her brother managed to get right.

For once.

She quickly found the waiting car at the end of the winding road. The enforcer who must have been her driver was sitting on the passenger side of the hood with what looked to be a cigarette dangling from his fingers as he chatted on the phone, completely unaware.

Something—or rather, someone—caught Abriella's eye on the other end of the road, far away from her waiting car. A familiar Jaguar was parked with a man leaning against the passenger door.

Tommas.

His head was bent down too low for her to see his eyes. She knew he was watching her.

Inside, every single inch of Abriella screamed out for Tommas. She clung tight to her control.

She needed to keep it for just a little while longer. Abriella wasn't sure that when she gave up the control she had managed to keep since finding out about her mother's death, if she would be able to come out of it unscathed.

Her heart wasn't ready.

Abriella held tighter to the clutch in her hand. Inside rested the cell phone Tommas had given her. His text message that morning had been the same message as it was all week:

I love you.
I'm sorry, Ella.
I'm here when you're ready.
Tommy.

Simple.

Honest.

And exactly what she needed.

The phone was running low on minutes, and it needed a new card. She hadn't had time to pick one up when she wasn't being followed or watched by Darryl. Hopefully, she would be able to get one soon, but until then, she planned on saving the last few minutes she had on the phone card for when she couldn't take it anymore.

When she finally broke.

When she really needed him.

Tommas would understand.

Raising her hand slightly, Abriella waved to her lover.

Tommas tilted his head up a little, just enough for her to see the camber of his frown and the tightness in his jaw. He lifted his hand in return, and that was enough.

It was enough for her to keep it together for a little while longer.

Abriella shifted the messenger bag over her shoulder, hoping to ease the weight of the contents a bit. Walking around the hallway corner, she met up with her waiting enforcer. Like always, Darryl sat on the bench looking bored and annoyed at the same time.

"Finally," Darryl grumbled.

"The class ran a little late," Abriella explained.

She didn't apologize for making the enforcer wait because she didn't give a damn. It was his job to watch after her. It wasn't her job to make sure everyone around her ran on Darryl's time.

Darryl held out his hand, and without question, Abriella handed her bag over to him. She stayed quiet as the enforcer pulled out the laptop she used for taking notes and then grabbed the bag back. Joel still hadn't given up on keeping a close eye on everything Abriella did. Her idiot brother wouldn't give back her phone, either.

She had the one from Tommas, thankfully, but there still hadn't been an opening for her to grab another card for it.

"We're late, so hurry it up," Darryl said.

Abriella tampered her flare of irritation. "Late for what?"

"Your brother has a meeting."

"What does that have to do with me?"

"Your presence was demanded."

Abriella's brow furrowed as she took in those words. Not requested or wanted. No, *demanded*.

"What kind of meeting?" she asked, choosing her words carefully.

"A dinner with the Rossi asshole," Darryl informed.

Abriella swallowed hard. "Like a sit-down?"

"Could be. I wouldn't know. You made us late and I got the phone call about it last minute."

Darryl didn't offer any more information before he turned on his heel and walked away. Abriella slung her bag over her shoulder and jogged to keep up with the man. What was he so goddamned edgy about?

It wasn't like Abriella was having the best fucking day.

A week after she buried her mother, and Abriella was more restless than ever. Between checking up on her father, trying to manage to stay out of Joel's way, and being without Tommas, she was barely keeping it together.

Going back to school to resume classes had been just one of her attempts to keep herself and emotions under control.

Abriella was failing.

She could feel it in her blood.

Dying inside.

Breaking apart slowly.

Without air.

Existing.

It wasn't long at all before Abriella was in Darryl's car, and they were speeding through the city toward Trentini territory.

"Which restaurant are they at?" Abriella asked.

"They're not at a restaurant. They're at home."

What?

Was Tommas fucking stupid? Why would her lover think that it was okay for him to hand Joel enough faith and trust that he could be inside the Trentini mansion for a dinner?

"Who is all there?" Abriella asked, hoping she was being subtle.

"A couple of people for Tommas. Joel has a couple of men. Nothing huge. It was quietly offered by Rossi, I guess. That's all Joel said to me. Quit fucking asking questions. Just be quiet. I have a damned headache, and your voice doesn't help it."

Abriella glared at the enforcer. "You're not a great companion, either, asshole."

"Yeah, well, you're fucking stuck with me."

Wonderful.

Abriella rested into the seat, watched buildings fly by, and tried her hardest to ignore the worry beginning to compound in her chest.

What had Tommas done?

CHAPTER THIRTEEN

"How's the cognac?" Joel asked.

Tommas tipped the balloon glass in his companion's direction as he said, "It's been a while since I've had one of Terrance's twenty-year bottles. It's a shame to waste good liquor, but you know I don't like to drink when doing business."

"Terrance liked to save them for special occasions."

"How many have you cracked open since his death?"

Joel smirked. "A few."

"It's a good drink."

"It is."

Tommas leaned forward in the chair, set his glass on the corner of Joel's desk, and rested back again. "But like I said, I don't drink and do business."

Joel held up a hand, smiling slightly. "No offence taken, old friend."

The nut, spice, and earthy flavors of the cognac still rested heavily on Tommas' palate. He'd gotten a taste of the drink, and that was more than enough. Cognac was a particular favorite of his, and Joel likely knew it. Before Tommas would realize it, he might have three glasses down and be working on a damn good drunk.

That was not the way he wanted to go tonight.

Just being inside the Trentini mansion was enough to put Tommas on edge. This was his last resort. He didn't want to be there, and he certainly didn't want to make the choice he was going to end up making, but his options had run out.

That, and he needed his girl.

One way or the other, Tommas would have Abriella.

A beep echoed from the intercom on the desk. Joel reached over, pressed the button, and said, "Yeah?"

"Ghost is here," replied a gravelly voice.

Joel shot Tommas with a questioning look.

"He's the only man I invited to come inside," Tommas said quietly. "He has no idea what I'm here to do or offer, Joel. As far as I know, he was having dinner with his wife when I asked him to come over."

"Let him through," Joel said into the intercom.

"Sure, boss."

Tommas barely managed to hide his external reaction to someone handing the title of boss over to Joel Trentini without so much as a hesitation. The man was so far from a boss that it was disgusting. A good boss—an honorable one—cared about his family as a whole and not just his own selfish desires.

Joel worried about no one but himself.

It didn't matter.

Tommas pushed his opinions aside.

He was out of options.

Last resort, he reminded himself silently.

"You know," Joel drawled, leaning back into his office chair, "… you still haven't told me why you're here, Tommas."

"I did … in a way."

"You want to settle this peacefully. That's what you said. It doesn't tell me much. It certainly doesn't tell me how you plan to do that."

Tommas drew in a long, deep breath. He needed the fucking strength. He needed the reminder that he was still alive in this whole thing, and for that matter, so was Abriella. More than anything, he wanted to keep both him and her that way for as long as he could.

Alive.

Forever.

Even better if they were doing it together.

Guilt was a terrible monster to carry. Tommas didn't wear his well at all. From the moment he knew that it was his plans—his call—that had put his lover's mother into the ground, Tommas' guilt began to climb. With every passing day that Abriella didn't answer his messages, with every ignored call, he came closer and closer to giving up.

He was out of plans.

Joel had won.

Tommas still had one more card to play.

God forgive him, but he hoped Abriella didn't hate him for it.

"I should begin by apologizing for your mother," Tommas said quietly.

Joel glanced up from the cognac he was swirling inside a glass. "Don't bother."

"It's only right that I do."

"If I cared for the woman, then the apology would mean something. Since I don't care, it means nothing. I don't need or want it, Tommas. Don't bother."

Tommas wasn't surprised.

Joel wasn't the person Tommas wanted to apologize to, anyway. Abriella needed to hear Tommas' apology, and if she was willing to forgive his mistakes, then maybe his choices today would be a little easier for her to swallow.

Damn.

Maybe she would even … understand.

Another beep echoed through the intercom.

Sighing, Joel hit the button again. "What now?"

"Your sister and her enforcer have just arrived, and Ghost is being let into the foyer."

"Wonderful." Joel turned off the intercom. "Seems like everyone that you wanted is here."

"Seems so," Tommas agreed.

"Let's get started."

"Find a spot to sit," Joel said, waving a hand toward the long dining table. "The cook will be serving supper in a few."

"A little heads-up about this would have been nice," Darryl said.

Tommas ignored the enforcer as he pulled out a chair to sit in. Under his lashes, he sneaked a peek at a confused, quiet Abriella. She twisted her hands together and glanced between her brother and Tommas subtly. No one else would have noticed her quick look, but he did.

He noticed everything about her.

"I agree," Damian said gruffly.

Tommas shot his cousin a look, silencing him. "Sit, D."

Scowling, Damian strolled past a statue-like Abriella to grab a chair. Once his cousin was seated, Tommas felt a little bit of his anxiety begin to drift away. While he fully suspected that this dinner-slash-meeting would go off without any issues, it helped to have a backup.

Damian was a good backup.

No matter what, the man would make sure Tommas got out of the Trentini mansion alive. Damian didn't even need to know what he was there to do, but he would make sure his cousin was safe. That's just how their lives worked.

As kids they looked out for each other.

As adults, that hadn't changed.

"Abriella," Joel snapped.

Abriella's head popped up fast. "Yeah?"

"Are you going to stand there all goddamn day looking like an idiot, or are you going to sit down like you were told to do?"

"Sorry."

Abriella quickly found a chair to sit it. It happened to be the one directly across from Tommas. Now, he could watch her throughout the dinner, gage her emotions and reactions to what was about to happen, and go from there.

Her being closer was better.

She'd been too far away for too long.

"Thank you," Joel said, his tone oozing with sarcasm.

Tommas' jaw clenched, his only show of irritation. He had all he could do not to snap at Joel, never mind beating back his annoyance. How the man could outright disrespect his sister like he did, without even a care for her feelings, was beyond Tommas' understanding.

Abriella deserved people in her life who loved and adored her. Those who would care for her, treat her with kindness and respect.

That wasn't Joel.

It couldn't be anyone but Tommas.

"I have men outside," Joel said, drawing Tommas from his thoughts.

"I'm aware."

"How many did you bring along?"

"A couple," Tommas admitted.

"Peaceful, right?"

"Absolutely, Joel."

Joel nodded. "Okay then."

Ten painfully awkward and silent minutes later, food was brought into the dining room. The cook served each person with a smile. She accepted Tommas' thank you with a gracious pat on his shoulder. Once the woman was gone, utensils scraped to plates as napkins were flicked over laps.

"I have an offer," Tommas said.

Joel was just beginning to cut into his steak. "Go on."

"I want to end this. All of it."

"I'm willing to do that for the right price," Joel said simply.

Tommas knew what the price was.

The boss's seat.

Glancing at his lover across the table, Tommas noted Abriella wasn't touching her food. She had her hands in her lap, and her stare stayed stuck firmly on the same place. He could tell by the thin set of her lips and the tightness in her jaw that she was unsettled and confused.

He didn't blame her.

Tommas wished he could soothe her worries.

All for you, Ella, his mind whispered. *All for you.*

Forcing himself to look away from Abriella was harder than Tommas expected. He pushed the potatoes around on his plate, trying to settle the way his thoughts and heart warred. His head wanted one thing while his heart wanted another.

He wasn't sure which was right.

"I'm waiting," Joel said.

Tommas cleared his throat, needing to get back into the right mindset for the dinner. "Sorry, I'm distracted lately. It's been a difficult couple of weeks."

"Oh?"

Damian passed his cousin a curious look, asking a million questions without even saying a word. Tommas didn't have a single answer for his cousin.

"Yes," Tommas said to Joel, smiling slightly. "But nothing I can't handle."

"I'm waiting to hear your offer," Joel replied.

Was it the right one?

Tommas didn't know.

"You can take it," Tommas said quietly. "The boss's seat, the Outfit, and the claim. Take it, Joel. I don't want to fight for it anymore. I'm done."

Abriella's head snapped up at Tommas' statement. Her blue eyes burned into his, a disbelief and anger darkening her irises.

No.

He could practically hear her screaming it inside her head.

No. No. *No.*

Tommas gave his girl a lopsided smirk, wanting to reassure her that everything was perfectly fine. To anyone else, it probably seemed like an afterthought to his statement about giving Joel the seat. Abriella would know better.

He hoped so, anyway.

"Tommas?" Damian said, two seats away from Abriella.

Tommas met his cousin's gaze. "This is the best choice, D."

Damian didn't look like he believed that at all. "Are you—"

"Before you ask, yes, I am sure."

"Okay," Damian murmured.

"I like that offer," Joel finally said, approval thickening his voice. "However, offers usually come with a clause, Tommas. What it is that you want in all of this?"

The only thing Tommas had ever wanted.

He was only now beginning to realize that to get what he wanted, to get Abriella, he was going to have to give up something else.

"A guarantee," Tommas said.

"Of what?" Joel asked.

"My position. Nothing more."

Joel sucked in air through his teeth, and leaned back in his chair. "Why are you giving up, Tommas?"

"Because I have nothing left to lose."

"I haven't taken very much from you, old friend. I would say you've taken far more from me, actually."

Joel had no idea what he had taken from Tommas, but she was sitting just across the table with wetness shimmering along her bottom lashes and her teeth cutting into her bottom lip. Everything that was anything to Tommas Rossi was three feet away with her heart bleeding and her soul crying.

Tommas had done that.

He simply wanted to fix it.

"I'm tired," Tommas admitted, shrugging. "I don't want to do it anymore, Joel. What else do you need to know?"

Joel clasped his hands over his midsection. "A guarantee, you said."

"Yes."

"Like what, Tommas?"

Tommas smiled. "Like a marriage. There's no better way to cement loyalties, offer forgiveness, wipe slates, and apologize in this life than a marriage, Joel."

"Between you and who else?" Joel asked quietly.

"You know who," Tommas said. "I wanted her to be here for a reason. Your sister. I want a marriage to your sister as a guarantee for what I'm giving you, and nothing more."

Abriella sucked in a hard breath. The sound echoed in the near silent dining room. It felt laced with pain, rage, and disbelief all rolled into one. Tommas had all he could do not to look at his lover again.

He was doing this for her.

Didn't she understand?

"It's certainly an interesting offer to—"

Joel's words were cut off by the screech of chair legs against tile. Abriella stood from her chair with her hands clenched into tight fists at her sides.

"No," she whispered. "Absolutely not."

Joel cocked a brow as he regarded his sister. "I beg your pardon, Abriella? This isn't your choice to make. Sit down."

Tommas swallowed the lump forming in his throat that threatened to keep him quiet. "Please sit, Abriella."

She didn't. Her gaze never moved from Tommas, either.

"I won't marry him like that," Abriella said "I won't marry him at all for those reasons."

The pain her words caused was the harshest kind of pain. It was the kind of agony that you didn't immediately feel ripping into your nervous system, but instead, the shock of the immediate injury left you numb all over and unable to think, move, or react. Then, when the numbness subsided and you could finally feel again, the pain was immeasurable.

Unbearable.

Tommas hid his well.

Somehow.

"Abriella!" Joel snarled. "Sit down!"

"Not like that," Abriella repeated, still looking at Tommas.

His pain ebbed away.

Not like that.

She wouldn't do it like this.

He heard her unspoken words.

Tommas finally took a real breath.

Abriella glanced to the side, her gaze cutting into her brother. "I won't do it."

With those words, she stepped aside, slammed the chair into the table, and left the room without a single glance back. Joel spluttered to come up with a response.

Tommas found Damian staring at him, waiting for something— anything.

Slowly, Tommas stood from his seat. "We'll go."

Damian followed his cousin's lead, standing and pushing his chair in without a word.

"She'll do as I tell her to," Joel said.

Tommas shook his head, knowing Abriella far better than her fool of a brother did. "I won't force her down the aisle to meet me."

Joel's gaze narrowed, but the man said nothing.

Tommas didn't mind. "Damian?"

"Yeah?"

"I think this dinner is over. Let's go."

Damian nodded. "Whatever you want, Tommy."

"Your offer is still on the table, isn't it?" Joel asked.

Tommas looked at Joel, cold and numb inside.

He didn't answer.

But frankly, Tommas didn't have to.

"Boss?"

Tommas' attention on the buildings passing the car by as it sped through the city was enough to lull him into a daze. It was one of the things he hated the most about being in the backseat of a car while someone chauffeured him around. Boredom found him far too easily. Add in the fact that Tommas had gotten his new Mercedes to replace the old one, and couldn't sit in the front like he preferred, and his annoyance jumped higher.

"Boss?"

"What, Nate?" Tommas asked.

"The streets are quiet," the enforcer noted.

"Is that a problem?"

"No. I was just making an observation. You're awfully quiet lately, too."

Tommas sighed, rubbing at his right temple with two fingers. "You know I'm not angry with you, right?"

Nate swallowed audibly. "Yeah, boss, I know."

"You did what I told you to, Nate. There's nothing else to say. Stop trying to fill the silence and pick my brain to find out if there's something I'm not saying to you. It's done, man. It happened. You did your job."

"And fucked it up at the same time."

"Yeah, well—"

Tommas' words were interrupted by the ring of his phone. He recognized the unfamiliar tune instantly. It was only unfamiliar because he'd changed the tune for the phone number, and that number hadn't called his very damned much.

Abriella.

He hadn't seen her since the dinner two evenings ago.

Tommas pulled his phone out and pressed the device to his ear. "Ella?"

"Tommy?"

His relief felt as good as sex and damn near like being high.

He'd waited for her call.

Wanted it.

His fingers itched just hearing her voice.

Fuck, why was he so goddamn crazy like this?

What was it about Abriella that made Tommas so insane?

"Yeah, baby," Tommas said, "it's me. Who else?"

Abriella's laugh was quiet, strained, and broken at the end. The sound tore into him, promising to hurt and feel damn good at the same time. "Where are you?"

"Just driving. Nothing important."

"I'm at school."

"Okay."

"How far are you from the college?" she asked.

Tommas' heart clenched at her whispered question. "About twenty minutes. Why?"

"Darryl had an appointment during my third and fourth period class. It's a two-hour class, no break. Maybe he thought it would be safe and I wouldn't know. I'm not sure, but I heard him telling Joel about it this morning. I left the class knowing he wasn't outside watching for me. Tommy?"

"What, Ella?"

"I really need you."

Tommas' fingers dug into his thigh through his dress pants hard enough to hurt. "Why? What's wrong?"

"I just ..."

"Ella, tell me."

"I'm not okay," she said, a sadness coating her every word. "I've tried to be okay, and I pretended for a long time. I just wanted to feel like I was in control, because everybody else needed to hurt and I had to be strong. I can't do it anymore. Please come get me. I'm at the west wing exit. I need to breathe for a while."

Tommas didn't even question her.

He understood.

Christ.

Of course, he did.

His lungs were finally taking in air again simply because she called.

Tommas barely had time to swing the back door open and Abriella was tumbling into the seat on top of him. Her messenger bag fell on the floor of the car as the door slammed shut. She seemed to forget all about her bag the moment she had Tommas in her sights.

Something was wrong with his girl.

Her gaze was pained.

Tears dampened her lashes.

A tiredness edged around her eyes.

Tommas' air was knocked from the lungs when Abriella's arms found his middle and hugged tight. Her embrace was strong enough to hurt, but he reveled in the ache. He held her tight, too, wrapping one arm around her back while his free hand tangled into her hair and rooted her against his form.

She trembled all over.

Her breaths stuttered.

Quiet, breathless sobs slipped from her lips while her shoulders heaved. Abriella buried her face into his chest, he felt her teeth clench, and the wetness of her tears soaked into his dress shirt.

"*Shhh*," Tommas said, murmuring the words into Abriella's sweet-smelling hair. "Whatever it is, it's okay. I got you, Ella."

She nodded, but her soft crying continued. It cut him to the fucking core, making him bleed on the inside where no one else could see. This woman shouldn't cry—not with him.

"Boss?" Nate asked from the front.

Tommas sucked in a deep gulp of air, remembering who else was in the car with them. "Drive, Nate."

"To where?"

"Anywhere. Just drive. I'll tell you when to stop."

"All right, boss."

Abriella's crying eventually turned into painful, gasping sobs as the car sped through quiet streets. Tommas barely recognized the buildings passing them by as he was far too focused on wiping the streaks of tears from his lover's face.

"Ella, talk to me," he demanded gently.

"My mom," she managed to say.

Tommas flinched, remembering her words from the earlier phone call. She had to be strong, she'd said. Everyone else wasn't. He'd seen her at the funeral, hiding her pain and seemingly more distant than ever in her blue eyes.

Did she think her grief didn't matter?

Were her tears held at bay for others to cry instead?

"Oh, baby, I'm sorry."

Abriella shook her head, hid her face from his view, and curled into his embrace until her legs were tucked to her chest and he was cradling her in the back seat. Tommas didn't mind. Not at all.

"I just want to breathe, Tommas," Abriella mumbled. "Please let me breathe."

"Whatever you need, babe."

"Tighter."

"What?"

"Hold me tighter. I keep feeling like I'm going to break apart. Don't let me do that."

"I got you," he told her, kissing her forehead.

"Who else does?" she asked.

No one.

"You could have called me long before this, Ella," Tommas said.

"I couldn't. If I did, I would have broken all apart. I couldn't, Tommy."

Sometimes, his lover was strange with her ways. Control was something she tried to maintain at all costs. Tommas understood because he was the same way. How could he judge her for what she needed? He couldn't.

"Okay, baby."

Abriella moved her face enough that she could look up at him. "Would you have done it?"

"Done what?"

"Joel, the offer … would you?"

Tommas' arm tightened around Abriella's back. "Had you not said no, then yes, I would have done it."

"Why?"

"For you, Ella. I thought I didn't have a choice. I was trying to make a new one."

"He can't have it, Tommy. Joel can't win."

Yeah, Tommas knew that, too.

"Nate," Tommas said, willing the thickness out of his voice.

"Yeah, boss?"

"Not too far. Somewhere private enough that we won't be bothered. Then take a walk."

"Got it."

"When do you need to be back?" Tommas asked.

"Not important."

"It is. I don't want you having more trouble to manage alone. When?"

"A little more than an hour."

It wasn't much time.

Tommas would take it.

Abriella's back rested against Tommas' chest. After his enforcer had found a quiet parking lot, parked the car into a back corner, and left the vehicle, Abriella had made herself a comfortable spot lying with Tommas. His back was to the door as his fingers played with the strands of her silky hair. He went back and forth between running his fingers through her waves and stroking the soft skin of her neck.

The simple touches seemed to calm his lover, so he kept it up.

Abriella fingered the sleeves of her sweater as she asked, "What were you supposed to be doing today?"

"Nothing more important than this, sweet girl."

"I'm sure."

Tommas chuckled. "I had some money to collect from Damian, a dinner to go to with Adriano, and then I needed to drive my mother to her AA meeting."

Abriella stilled. "Your mom is going to AA?"

"It's a recent development. I found her in my house the other night when I got home. She blurted out that she'd been thinking about it for a while and wanted to talk to me. I overlooked the fact she used her emergency key to get in."

"Oh. Do you think it will last?"

"No."

Abriella tilted her head up enough for Tommas to see her frown. "I'm sorry."

"Don't be. It is what it is."

"It's more than she's done before, Tommy."

That was true enough.

"Yes, but Serena does nothing without a reason. Usually that falls in line with her manipulation like it always does. None of that matters, Ella. Just you today, huh?"

"Okay." Abriella sighed as Tommas' fingers stroked her cheek. "I was so angry with you."

"I know you were."

"But I was angrier at Joel," she whispered. "And I knew that it was a mistake; I knew you tried to stop it all, Tommy."

Tommas pressed his lips to Abriella's temple. "Yeah."

"But I still couldn't breathe. I didn't want my father or brother to see me break down, and I didn't want Joel to know how much it hurt me. I couldn't do it anymore. I was so close to just skipping out for a day, even if it would get me into shit. I wanted you. After the dinner the other night, I thought ..."

"Tell me."

"I thought that you were ready to give up, and that you didn't care."

"Ella," Tommas said, her name coming out like a growl. "Don't ever think that. There is no soul on this earth that matters more to me than yours does. You are every part of me that is good. Every single part. I did that for—"

"Me," she interrupted softly. "I figured that out, but I still couldn't let you do it."

"I'll figure something out."

"Please don't make anyone else bury someone they love, Tommy."

Tommas kissed Abriella's temple again. "I won't, baby."

CHAPTER FOURTEEN

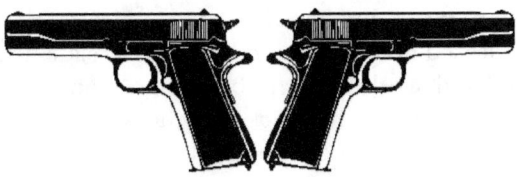

"**D**on't stop," Abriella whispered when Tommas' fingers stopped their travels through her hair. She'd been enjoying his attention. It wasn't nearly often enough that she had his love and time on only her. When she did, Abriella felt like the queen of his world. "Keep going, Tommy. Please."

Tommas chuckled, the movement rocking them both. "I thought you always said that whenever I touched you, you couldn't think and you went stupid."

"I do."

"Well?"

"That's what I want right now. Not to think. To be stupid over you. Please?"

Tommas' lips ghosted over the shell of Abriella's ear as his fingers began to wander again. "Anything you want, Ella."

The backseat of the Mercedes was large enough for them to stay snuggled together comfortably. It certainly wasn't the first time she had found herself stealing a moment away from the rest of the world in the back of a car with Tommas Rossi.

Abriella smiled, sighing just a little when Tommas' fingers skipped under the collar of her long sleeve shirt. The pads of his fingertips grazed her collarbones, making her shiver as her skin burned hotter.

Innocent.

Sweet.

But with them, it was neither.

"Ella?"

"Hmm?"

"Be stupid over me, or *with* me?"

His voice was a dark, deep melody in her ear. Through the haze of her comfort, Abriella could get lost in Tommas' voice alone. She could pretend like it was just them for the moment and that no one else existed.

"Ella," Tommas pressed when she stayed quiet. His hand slipped lower under her shirt, finding her breasts. His fingers pinched her nipples under the silk bra she wore, making her gasp sharply. Her legs tightened in an attempt to soothe the sudden ache between her thighs. "Be stupid over me, or with me, baby? Which one?"

"With you," she mumbled, tilting her head up to press a kiss on the underside of his jaw. "Always with you, Tommy."

"That's what I wanted to hear."

Tommas released his grip around her waist to slide his hand down her stomach. As his hand worked at the button and zipper of her jeans, his mouth kissed a hot path over her neck and cheek. Abriella felt the palm of his hand push into her pants, down under her panties, and then his fingers were there.

Touching.

Stroking.

Exploring.

Gentle flicks of his fingers to her clit made her jerk in his arms. Swipes of his fingertips through her folds drew her wetness over the lips of her sex. A nip of his teeth to the sensitive spot behind her ear made her shake.

"You're teasing me," Abriella accused.

"There's nothing better than hearing you whine and whimper for more, Ella."

Another sweep of his fingers, and two pressed a little deeper into her slit until the tips of his digits were entering her sex. It wasn't nearly enough to give her what she wanted. It was only enough to make her beg for more.

"*God*, Tommy."

"Love your sounds."

"I'll give you more if you fuck me with those fingers instead of teasing me like that."

Tommas laughed a husky sound a second before his tongue stuck out against her skin to taste, and his fingers sunk knuckle deep into her clenching pussy. Abriella whined low in the back of her throat, loving the sensation of being filled by Tommas' fingers. He didn't have a lot of room to move with her tight jeans keeping his hand confined, but he had just enough to give her what she needed.

Fast, short thrusts of his fingers while he opened them wide on the withdrawal, and his palm rubbed against her throbbing clit had Abriella widening her legs and melting into his arms. Tommas' voice was a whisper in her ear, urging her on while he finger-fucked her quick and deep.

"Get it, Ella. Fuck my goddamn fingers until you come. Take them how you want. Show me how bad you want to come right now. Give it to me, baby."

Nothing was better than that.

She loved hearing him talk; needed his throaty tone and his dirty words.

Abriella craved it.

"Oh, my God," she breathed. "I'm right there, Tommy."

"Hurry up then, and I'll let you climb on top of me, fill you full, and let you ride me until you're soaked in my come and sore all over."

Abriella shuddered. "Yeah?"

"Promise, baby. Give it to me. I want your fucking come on my hand, all over my fingers. I want to smell like you all over by the time we're done. I like being a little dirty with you, Ella, walking around with your come stains hidden under my jacket. Nobody knows but me, and it gets me so fucking hard for you."

"Jesus, *yes*."

That was bad.

So bad.

"Come on," Tommas growled, his fingers curling hard into her wet walls on the next thrust. He hit her G-spot perfectly, making Abriella fly. She felt her sex clamp down as her juices soaked his fingers in a rush of heat and bliss. His name slipped past her lips in a broken cry. "Shit, yeah, baby. I got you."

Mush.

Abriella's limbs felt like mush as she tried to catch her breath. Why was it that the simplest of orgasms, the ones that her lover provided with no roughness to his touch and only for her own needs, were the ones that left her feeling shattered?

"Come here," Tommas urged.

Abriella turned under his hands, blinking rapidly to clear her foggy vision. A wetness had coated her lashes when she'd squeezed her eyes shut and trembled her way through the intense orgasm. It was so blindingly good that she didn't want to let the feeling go.

"More," Abriella demanded.

Tommas caught her chin between his forefinger and thumb to pull her down to his kiss. His hand fisted into the ends of her hair, holding tight as his lips bruised hers with a kiss that relieved as much as it hurt. The bite of his teeth to her bottom lip took away what lingering stress was still floating through her wayward thoughts.

"To breathe. That's what you wanted, Ella."

"Yeah."

"I can do that for you. Just for a little while."

"I'll take anything you give me."

She found his steel-blue gaze, her fingers sweeping over his jaw.

"Anything?" he asked.

"Everything."

Because he was everything to her.

Tommas let go of her hair and face just long enough to fist her pants and yank them down around her hips. His movements were frantic and rushed. The denim of her jeans tightened to her skin, making her ache with his roughness.

God.

She didn't even care.

Shifting on his lap allowed her to feel the hard ridge of his erection straining against his slacks. She rolled her hips, letting the weight of her body grind into his cock. Tommas' responding groan started somewhere in the back of his throat, making it all the more heady and wonderful. Then, he was yanking her sweater off, too, leaving her in nothing but her bra and panties.

His gaze darkened as he looked her over, his teeth gritting beneath his clenching jaw.

Sexy.

Fuck.

Didn't he know how sexy he was?

"Faster," Abriella hissed.

"Lift up."

She raised above him, allowing him to pull her jeans lower. Abriella pulled one leg free before she was able to get the other one out, too. Her silk panties were soaked from his fingers and her orgasm earlier. She didn't even bother to pull them off.

Instead, she tugged them to the side and drove two of her own fingers into her pussy, wanting to give herself something to soothe the ache inside her sex. Tommas worked his pants down around his hips, and pushed his boxer-briefs lower until his cock was free and he was fisting his length with firm, long strokes.

"Fuck, let me see that," Tommas said softly.

Abriella lifted higher, giving him a better view of her fingers driving over and over into her pussy. The sucking sound of her wet sex taking her fingers in faster, harder was enough to make her moan.

"It's not enough," Abriella mumbled.

"You want my cock, not your fingers."

"Yes."

"Take what you need, baby."

Abriella withdrew her fingers, but kept her panties pulled to the side as she climbed back over Tommas' lap. She was grateful for the dark tinted windows as she braced one hand on the glass and lowered down on his length faster than she normally would have.

She liked to take her time when she rode him.

She liked to feel his cock stretch her open, fill her full, and hit every fucking spot that would make her scream.

What she needed more was to fuck.

Just fuck him.

"Christ," Tommas said in a breath of air. "You feel like you're squeezing me to death here, Ella. Your pussy is goddamn tight right now. Take a second and—"

"No," Abriella said, her hand coming up to push against his mouth. "Shut up, Tommy. Just let me fucking feel."

Tommas kissed the tips of her fingers a second before his teeth bit down hard on the digits. Abriella whined from the pain as a heat traveled down her spine. She rolled her hips up and down, back and forth, working his cock deeper until she was seated tight to his groin and her pussy ached.

"I'm so full," she told him.

Tommas sucked her fingers into his mouth, his tongue sliding between her digits to sweep and clean her arousal from earlier. His moan vibrated against her hand, making her shudder all over. On top of him, her pace picked up, faster, harder.

She wanted it to hurt.

She wanted to come again and again.

She needed to feel him when she was gone.

Tommas' hands found her ass and squeezed hard. His fingernails bit into her skin while his other hand slid lower. Abriella sucked in a hard breath a second before one of his fingers slid into her tight ass. He didn't give her the chance to prep for the added intrusion. The sting was more than enough to make her blood heat up to a boiling point.

Then, another of his fingers stroked her wet sex. She could feel the pad of his digit massaging her sex and his cock as he lifted from the seat to meet her rhythm. The sensation of his finger stroking her pussy while she rode him and his other buried deep in her ass had Abriella shouting out as she came yet again.

She pulled her fingers from his mouth.

Tommas sucked in a ragged inhale as Abriella grabbed his jaw. She fingers dug into his skin, her manicured nails leaving crescent marks behind.

"Again, harder," she told him. "I want to fucking *feel*, Tommy. Give me what I want."

She found herself lifted off his cock, turned around, and then her face was buried into a leather seat. Abriella's hands were caught in Tommas' hands and pinned to her lower back. The strain of her shoulders hurt, but she moaned, wanting more.

He pushed in, taking her deep in one thrust. Abriella trembled. Her knees slipped on the seat.

"Jesus Christ," Abriella groaned.

Her skin burned as silk was ripped from her body. He didn't even pull out. He just ripped the fucking panties right off.

It was damn good.

She blinked a second before she felt the soft material being pushed against her lips. The wetness and scent of her own come assaulted her nose before she opened her mouth to her lover's silent demand.

Tommas used two fingers to stuff the panties into her mouth.

"Pinch my hand if it gets to be too much," she heard him say.

It wouldn't be too much.

Abriella wouldn't need to pinch him.

"Please," she mumbled around the panties.

Tommas' other hand found the back of her neck, pushing her further into the seat. Then, it was just a blink, and he was pulling her into him. Over and over.

Deep enough to hurt.

Fast enough to take her air away.

She couldn't think. The tips of her fingers were numb. She could taste her own come in her mouth. She came harder than ever.

It was humiliating.

He used her wonderfully.

This is my fucking pussy.

You're such a slut letting me fuck you like this.

You better come, Ella.

Right fucking now.

God, did she ever.

Crying, shaking all over, and with his come leaking out of her. She came hard.

Abriella dug through her messenger bag. Panic seized her throat when she couldn't find one of the things she was looking for. Checking through the few items, she realized something else was missing as well.

"No," she said, leaning into the closest wall.

Both a textbook she needed for class, and the burner phone that Tommas had given her was missing from her bag. In their frenzied hookup and her rush to make it back to class before Darryl got back and noticed she left school, her stuff must have fallen out of her bag.

She'd left Tommas with a hard kiss, his promise for more soon, grabbed her bag, and sneaked back in so she wouldn't be late for her class.

"Dammit," Abriella grumbled.

Just outside of her last class for the day, she needed that science book. She could probably use her partner's for the day, but she had tests coming up and had to go over the book chapters the class had already gone through.

Out of the corner of her eye, Abriella took note of Darryl as he slid a dollar bill into the vending machine and pulled out a can of soda. He hadn't even noticed she was down the hall getting ready to enter her final class.

Thank God.

Slipping into the class before Darryl did see her outside, she went straight to her work table. Abriella sat down in her designated chair, pushed the waiting slides and microscope aside, and leaned over to her partner.

"Where's your phone?" she asked the girl.

Carrie nodded down at her bag. "There."

"Can I use it?"

"Can you make it fast?"

"Of course," Abriella said. "I lost mine in a friend's car. I just want to let them know it's there."

"No problem."

Abriella waited as her lab partner found her phone and handed it over. The professor walked in just as Abriella sent off the first text. Their teacher was an asshole about electronics during the class, so she had to be careful.

Tommy, her text read, *my phone and book is in your car.*

A minute later, Tommas' text came through.

Who is this?

Abriella's brow furrowed. She was using a different number, sure, but no one else had been in Tommas' car other than her. Who else would be messaging him to tell him their stuff was in his damn car?

It's Abriella. I think I dropped my phone and book in your car.

The phone buzzed again. *What book and phone?*

Abriella's brow furrowed. *Mine, Tommy. Just figure out a way to get it to me, okay?*

Okay.

That was it.

More confused than ever, Abriella handed the phone back to her partner. Tommas had never ended any kind of conversation with Abriella, even through text messages, without telling her that he loved her.

She remembered that he had to go pick up his mother.

Maybe that was it.

Maybe his mother had him distracted.

Abriella pushed her worry aside.

Tommas would handle it.

"Abriella Trentini," came an unknown voice from behind her.

Abriella turned fast on her heel only to come face to face with two unknown men dressed in plain black suits. She'd just left her second period class a little early, as she had a meeting with her professor from her first class before her next one was to start.

Cocking a brow, Abriella said, "I can't say we're on the same level, as I don't have a damned clue who either of you are."

The shorter of the two men smiled.

It didn't look friendly.

Something terrible welled in Abriella's gut. She held tighter to her messenger bag, wondering where in the hell Darryl was. Something stunk about these two men. Something that smelled like cop.

A person couldn't wash that shit out.

"Detectives Delog and Crown," said the taller man. "My partner thought meeting you at school would be a good time, seeing as how you somehow manage to get away from your enforcer here quite often."

Abriella's heart jumped into her throat. "I beg your pardon?"

"Two days ago. Tommas Rossi. Ring any bells?" Crown asked.

She couldn't fucking breathe.

How did these idiots know that?

"I have no idea what—"

"Trentinis are always good for a lie when the need arises," Delog interrupted smoothly. "Fact is, we know you were with Tommas two days ago. You forgot some things in his car. We did a little checking after we heard about your meeting with him. Seems you've been messing with Tommas for a while. He's even got a little apartment set up for you, huh? The people in that building recognized your picture right away. The neighbor knows you as Ella."

Abriella refused to let these two fools see the panic they were causing her. "Again, I don't know what you're talking about."

"Sure, sure," Crown said, shrugging. "We want to chat. Are you up for a little talk before your next class?"

"Absolutely not."

"You know, we could always give your brother a call and drag you both down to the station. I am sure Joel Trentini would love to find out his sister has been fucking his number one enemy. Wouldn't he?"

"What in the hell are you trying to prove?" Abriella asked, spitting out the question. "I have nothing for you."

"We want to talk," the other detective said.

"About what?"

"Tommas, for starters."

Abriella swallowed back her anxiety. She had to get away from these men and as fast as was humanly fucking possible. If Darryl found her with detectives, she might as well put the gun to her own head and save Joel the trouble. Worse, if her brother didn't kill her for talking to police, he might find out about her relationship with Tommas.

Tommas.

Oh, God.

She needed to talk to him.

Now.

"I have nothing to say to the cops," Abriella said firmly.

She turned on her heel to leave. A hand grabbed her arm and spun her around.

"Just you wait one goddamn min—"

"Let me go."

Abriella's words had come out deadly sharp and quiet. The detective released her almost instantly with wider eyes.

"Keep your hands off my body," Abriella said. "And stay the hell away from me."

"We will be chatting again, Abriella," Delog said.

"Actually, we won't. Ever."

With that, Abriella left the detectives behind her. She couldn't get down the hallway quick enough. Just around the corner where she knew the detectives couldn't see her, she stopped to take a breath.

Her heart wouldn't slow.

She was sick all over.

Darryl walked out of the men's bathroom two doors down. The idiot wiped his hands on his dark wash jeans as he noticed Abriella.

"Aren't you supposed to be in class?"

"Um …"

"Um," Darryl mocked. "Not an answer. What are you doing?"

"I want to go home," Abriella said quickly. "I don't feel well."

"You haven't even been here more than a couple of hours."

"So?"

Darryl scowled. "Whatever, let's go."

"Abriella?"

"Sorry, Dad," Abriella called as she streaked past the kitchen. "I'll be right in to make some dinner for you."

"Hey, wait a second."

"I just want to grab something from Mom's room. Okay?"

Peter made a sad sound. "Okay, Ella."

Abriella ignored her rush of guilt at lying to her father. When she arrived home, Joel was there with a dozen of his men. She couldn't run the risk of calling Tommas from one of their wing's phones, so she used the excuse that she wanted to go check on Peter.

Joel didn't question her.

Once Abriella was in a safe spot in her father's wing, she hid in a spare room, closed the door, and grabbed the phone off the bedside table. Dialing Tommas' cell, the call rang and rang until his answering machine picked up.

Frustrated, Abriella hung up and then dialed again.

Breathless, Tommas picked up the second time. "Yeah, hello?"

"Tommy, it's me. We've got a problem."

Tommas groaned. Abriella swore she heard something hit a wall with a dull thud. "Ella, baby … I don't want to hear those words right now. I need to have no problems for a while. None, okay?"

"Sorry, but this is important."

"What happened?"

"Where are you?" she asked instead.

"Our place. I thought it might help or something. I don't know."

"Help with what?"

"My crazy ass, that's what. It's not important. Talk to me."

"The cops came to my school today. Detectives, I guess. I think they said their names were Crawn or Crain … something."

"Crown?" Tommas asked, a dangerous edge to his tone.

Abriella flinched. "Yeah. Why?"

"Was the other one Delog?"

"Yes."

Now, Abriella felt worse than ever.

"Tell me everything," Tommas demanded.

Abriella quickly recapped the events for her lover, keeping an eye on the door all the while. She was sure her father would keep quiet if he caught her, but she didn't want to put her father in that position, either.

"Remember when I texted you about my phone and book?" Abriella asked at the end.

Tommas made a disgruntled noise. "No."

"Tommy, come on. I messaged you not thirty minutes after you dropped me off. I left my phone and—"

"Your book in the car. Yeah, I noticed them after I dropped my mother off at her meeting. They were shoved under the seat a little. I planned on getting them to you sometime this week if I could manage it. But I didn't get any messages from you, Ella."

"Yes, you did. I used a friend's phone. You messaged me back a couple of times. The point is that the detectives knew about the phone and book in your car. They knew it was there and that I'd forgotten it. How do they know that?"

Silence answered Abriella back a second before something crashed on Tommas' end of the call. She jumped at the sound, but kept her squeak of surprise muffled by her hand.

"Tommy?"

"That fucking bitch," Tommas growled.

"What?"

"Just … just wait a second."

Abriella did as he said. She couldn't hear his soft breathing, but she did hear the click of keys. A minute later, Tommas was back on the line.

"I think the person you were messaging with was my mother," Tommas muttered. "I found the messages. They were deleted from the main unknown contact, but not the log. I stopped to grab a pack of smokes from the store for her after I picked her up."

"Oh."

"I left my bag in the car. Nate stepped out for a smoke while I went into the store. I think it was her, Ella."

"The detectives …"

"I'll handle it, baby."

What did this all mean?

Abriella wished she could calm down enough and think.

"I'm sorry, Tommy."

"God, for what?"

Abriella didn't know.

"Be careful, okay," she said.

"Always. And stay away from those fucking pigs."

"I will."

No matter what.

CHAPTER FIFTEEN

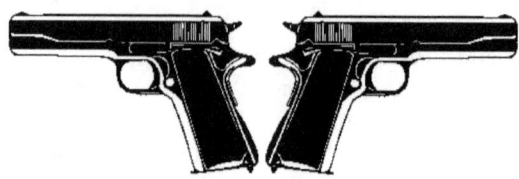

"You good?" Damian asked.

Tommas nodded, but his lie was as clear as day. "Yeah."

"I can do it, Tommy."

"You've done enough. This is my mess."

Damian slapped a hand down on the hood of the car and pushed away. "If you say so. After everything that woman put me through, it's not like this would keep me up at night. It wouldn't be a problem, that's all I'm saying."

"I know, but I need to do it."

"All right, man. Call me later, let me know it's done."

Tommas agreed to Damian's request, and then watched his cousin stroll down the quiet Melrose street. It was late enough that most of the houses on the block were shrouded in darkness. The people within were likely sleeping, their bodies prepping for another day of life.

Strangely, Tommas didn't feel sad about the fact that he was going to end one of those people's lives tonight. He was angry over the information he'd learned, disbelieving in a way that his mother would do such a thing, but he mostly, he was resigned.

Another duty.

The Outfit always won.

Turning the Jaguar off, Tommas slipped out of his car and tightened his coat. The cold wind nipped at his exposed skin, promising another cold morning was yet to come. He'd be glad when the summer months rolled around and stayed for a while.

Tommas checked the street, taking note of every vehicle parked in driveways and on the side of the road. Having grown up on the street, he could name which vehicle belonged to whom. It let him know that no one had followed him and no one was watching his mother's house.

The cop detail that had been situated across the street after Tommas had killed his father was long gone. Tommas had made sure that little to no business and visitors from the Outfit side of things came to his mother's place. He wanted the attention gone as quickly as possible.

Thankfully, it went without much trouble.

Crossing the street, Tommas tugged on a pair of black leather driving gloves. He pulled out a pair of house keys from his pocket, knowing his mother hadn't changed the locks in years. The alcoholism shared by his parents had made them forget the most basic things in life. Alcoholism turned them into desperate creatures who would do anything if they thought it would save their own asses.

Tommas was ashamed that his blood had come from them. He was embarrassed that he shared their last name. Above all else, Tommas wanted something to be proud of again.

Anything.

Correcting his mother's wrongs would be a step forward. One step. What he couldn't understand, was why his mother had turned rat. It didn't make sense. Serena had always been a vocal woman against others who turned to the officials for protection, or for a way out of the Outfit. Nothing Tommas came up with explained away his mother's actions.

Sliding the key into the lock of his childhood home, Tommas unlocked the deadbolt, and pushed the front door open. The quietness of the house came as no surprise, and neither did the darkness of the place. If it weren't for Tommas paying the light, phone, and heating bills every month, his mother would live in the squalor of her own alcohol and vomit.

What had the police used to get his mother to turn rat?

What did they have on her?

The woman did nothing but drink!

Refusing to let the anger overtake his emotions, Tommas pushed those questions aside, wiped his shoes off on the rug, and went in search of his mother. The familiar stale smell of the home was diluted slightly, but only because Tommas had hired a twice-weekly maid to go in and clean the place. The girl reported back to Tommas that Serena rarely, if ever, noticed she was there doing her job.

Nonetheless, the faint smell of old alcohol and cigarette smoke still lingered in every hall Tommas walked down and in each room he checked. So did his memories.

Bruised with abuse.

Blackened with neglect.

Healed, but still sore, with scars.

He could see still see his red-headed, quiet sisters playing under the stairwell with their matching dolls and their dirty dresses. They had barely made a sound growing up for fear that being too loud would earn them something painful. He could still remember walking down the stairs for his high school graduation and giving his cousin and sister a ride to the auditorium because his parents were passed out on the couch.

Empty cupboards.

Filthy floors.

Forgotten children.

That was the home that addiction raised.

Tommas ignored the nagging ache in his chest as he continued his search for his mother. The living room was empty, devoid of life but for the flicker of a rerun television series playing on the flat screen. Upstairs, the master bedroom was just as quiet and dead.

Finally, Tommas found his mother in the upstairs bathroom at the very end of the hall. Serena rested, naked and seemingly asleep, in a bathtub full of cold, murky water. A nearly emptied bottle of cheap vodka rested on the ledge beside a pack of cigarettes, a lighter, and a woman's shaver.

Leaning in the doorway, Tommas focused on the shaver instead of his mother's naked form. It wasn't the first time he'd seen her without clothes on, given her moral standards were low as shit when she was drunk, but it still bothered him all the same. The pink shaver looked like someone had attempted to pry it open. Speckles of a rusty brown littered the item, while deeper red droplets had splattered on the edge of the tub and the floor.

Serena's hand, draped over the edge and hanging out of the tub, explained the blood. Tiny cuts marred the tips of her fingers.

For a second, Tommas almost wished his mother had succeeded in getting the blade out and finishing the job. It might have made this godforsaken night a little easier on him if she had been able to get it done.

"Ma," Tommas said loudly.

The volume of his voice echoed off the dingy tiled walls. There was no way on earth his mother hadn't heard it.

Serena's glassy gaze flew wide as her arms flailed, and she shrieked. The pale tone of her skin and bluish tint around her lips said that she had been in the cold water for quite a while. Instantly, Serena's teeth began to chatter when she found her son leaning in the doorway.

"Tommas," Serena mumbled drowsily. "What are you doing here?"

"I come here more often than you're aware, Ma."

"Funny, I never see you."

"Maybe if you popped your head out of the bottle every once in a while—"

"Hey, watch your fucking tone," Serena barked, more awake than before.

Tommas recognized the fire in his mother's eyes, but he wouldn't back down. He wasn't a child, now. She didn't frighten him. His little sisters no longer needed his protection.

"When did you get in the tub, Ma?" Tommas asked.

Serena blinked around at her surroundings. "Before the four o'clock news."

"It's three in the morning. What else did you take other than the vodka?"

"None of your business, Tommas. Get the hell out and let me get dressed."

"No," Tommas said quietly. "There was a bottle of pain meds in the living room. The cap was off. Is that what you took?"

Serena scowled. "So what if it was?"

"Just getting my ducks in a row, Ma."

"I don't understand what you mean."

"You don't need to yet." Tommas nodded at the bloody razor. "That's what, failed attempt number seven since I was fourteen or so?"

Serena's stare dropped to the razor. "Tommas—"

"Lucky for you that Dad was around to save you. Seems like lately, I've been picking up where he left off in that regard. What was the problem tonight? Did your hands shake too much? Did the meds make you too weak to get the blade out? What was it?"

"You wouldn't even care if I had slit my wrists and drowned in my own blood, Tommas. You've never cared! You don't understand what it's like for me, Tommas, and I tried for years to be better. But all you did was push me away and make it worse! I hate you."

Manipulation.

Tommas could recognize that shit anywhere. It was Serena's specialty. She was damned good at it.

"You know, that worked better when I was a child and your words had some ring of truth, Ma. Now that I'm older, I've heard your spiels one too many times. It's like water off my back. It doesn't even make me wet anymore."

Serena struggled to get out of the tub, spewing more vile words at the same time. "You fucking little asshole, I'll—"

"Sit down." Tommas pulled the gun out that he'd tucked into a holster at his back. He clicked the safety off and rested the gun against his side, watching his mother's eyes widen with shock and her brow furrow. "Shut up, and let this be easy. For fuck's sake, Ma, for once, let something between us be easy."

"You wouldn't …"

Tommas laughed sadly. "Wouldn't I?"

"I'm sorry," Serena rushed to say. "I didn't mean what I said. You surprised me and—"

"And the more you say, the less I care. Whatever you have to do, you'll do it, right? Anything to save your ass, you will make it happen. It won't matter who you hurt in the process as long as you get what you want from it, Ma. What did they promise you? What did they have on you?"

Serena stared up at Tommas, water filling her gaze and her hands shaking against the ledge of the tub. "What?"

"The detectives, Ma. The detectives. The fucking pigs. Who else?

189

What did they have on you? Did they offer to get you in with the FBI as an informant if you could feed them enough info on us all? What was it that was so bad you couldn't come to me? Instead, you played their little agent, going through my fucking cars, my house, and reporting back on whatever they needed or asked for. *Why*, Ma?"

Tommas' last two words were shouted so loudly that Serena flinched back into the water. The sight of her fear did nothing for him. Her trembling and her tears made him deader than ever and numb from the inside out.

He despised this woman.

He hated her very breath.

"The detectives went to Ella," Tommas continued quieter.

"I didn't, Tommy."

"Liar. They fucking put Ella in a corner, thinking it was going to make me jump through hoops for them. They knew about her, and that I've been fucking around with her for years. They had information that no one else would have known, like my second apartment and the note Ella left in my goddamn house. They asked her about the textbook left in my car. She called me the second she could. And that's when I knew, Ma. You always were nosy, but I figured you weren't paying enough attention to put it all together. Shame on me, right? You really fucking fooled me.

"Those bastards have been hounding me for years, but they messed up going after her," Tommas finished darkly.

Serena gaped. "I ..."

"I don't want your useless fucking excuses. I just want to know why, Ma. You almost ruined everything for me. Had I not figured it out, had they not mentioned the textbook and phone in my car, I wouldn't even have looked at you twice for this. *Tell me why*!"

"Because you took Laurent."

The statement had been hissed so quietly that Tommas strained to hear his mother's confession. Her glare burned with the fire and hatred of a woman who felt nothing for the son she carried and birthed. Her fists clenched on the side of the tub, and her face crumpled in her grief and anger.

"Because you took him from me, Tommas!" Serena cried. "So I took something from you!"

Tommas took the second he needed to let the shock of his mother's admission soak in. He hadn't realized how much his mother depended and loved his father until Laurent wasn't there anymore. He wasn't the least bit surprised that she knew it had been her own son who killed her husband. The whispers were out there in the Outfit—people simply had to listen hard enough to hear them.

"I hate you," Serena mumbled. "I hated you from the very second I knew I was pregnant for you. I hated your sisters, I hated this fucking house, and I hated that stupid man. And then when you were all gone, I was alone."

"You hate yourself far more," Tommas replied coldly. "We were just byproducts of your hate, Ma. Stop blaming us. We tried. You failed."

Serena laughed bitterly, splashing water up the wall. "What are you going to do now, Tommas? Are you going to kill me?"

"Yes."

"Hurry up then."

Tommas pushed off the wall and grabbed the razor from the tub. He popped the blade from the plastic cartridge and tossed it into the bathtub. It sunk under the water with a plop.

"We'll call it assisted suicide," Tommas murmured. "I'll let you cut your final marks, Ma. You can do it, or I can. One way or the other, I will not leave this house with your heart still beating."

Serena's gaze flew between her son and the tiny piece of sharp metal resting at the bottom of the tub. "I ... I ..."

"Pick it up. Hell, I'll go get you a few more pills if you want to take the edge off."

"Who are you?" Serena asked.

"The man you raised, Ma. Your worst fucking nightmare. You did this—don't be so surprised. This was a long time coming."

"But Laurent ... y-you shot him in the face. You did it yourself. Are you frightened of me, Tommas? Does the thought of killing me yourself hurt you that badly inside?"

"No," Tommas admitted. "I feel nothing for you. I don't even want to touch you, or breathe your air. You're nothing to me, Ma. With Laurent, all I felt was rage. It made me fucking hot inside, it made me sick to my stomach. I couldn't shove that gun into his face hard enough. I couldn't make him cry beg loud enough. I broke every one of his teeth with the barrel of my gun. I made him vomit because he was sobbing so hard."

Serena choked on her grief, but it flew right past Tommas.

"He begged for you, Ma," Tommas added. "If that helps—if you care at all. He begged for you. But do you know what you were doing? You were upstairs while he was bleeding and begging on the kitchen floor for his life and for yours. You were passed out upstairs in a puddle of your own piss, too drunk to care about anything but yourself. That, Ma, is our life. It has always been our life."

"I'm sorry," Serena whispered.

"Maybe you are. But I'm certainly not. I just don't care anymore. Pick up the blade, Ma. Finish the job that you've been working on for years."

Crying, Serena did as she was told. Tommas felt his back hit the door and his ass hit the floor as the first slice was made. Serena's hands shook.

Her blood spilled.

The water turned red.

Not once did Tommas try to stop her.

Tommas pulled the front door closed and locked the house. He walked, numb and cold, to his Jaguar. Once he was inside the car and the heat was turned on full blast, he finally began to blink awake from the daze that he'd been in.

Pulling out his phone, he called his cousin.

Damian picked up on the second ring.

"Well?" Damian asked without even a proper greeting.

"It's done," Tommas said.

"You're sure?"

"Positive."

Damian let out a quiet sigh. "Good."

The sound of a car starting echoed through the phone. Down at the end of the block, Tommas took note of a familiar blue Porsche pulling out of a driveway.

"You didn't have to stay," Tommas said.

"Maybe not, but I wanted to."

"In case I couldn't do it?"

Damian chuckled. "No, in case you wanted a familiar voice when it was over. You never mentioned a thing about Laurent to me, and I just wondered …"

"Don't," Tommas said. "There's nothing to wonder about, man."

"Seems we're good at this. Too good, maybe."

"What is that?"

"Killing," his cousin answered quietly.

"I've never taken a life that didn't deserve to go where I was sending them," Tommas said.

"I wish I could say the same."

Tommas sucked in a heavy breath of air. "Terrance?"

"And a few others."

"But mostly him."

"Mostly," Damian echoed. "It still makes me wake up at night. I'm still angry that I let myself get put in that position, Tommas. He was good to me, the boss, I mean. He treated us well growing up. I fucked that one up big time."

"But he wasn't really all good," Tommas replied quietly. "He overlooked abuse. He didn't help people like Theo and Dino, or us for that matter. Terrance Trentini was too busy trying to cover his own mistakes in his family that he was willing to pretend like the foulness around him wasn't happening as long as others turned their cheeks, too. He helped to perpetuate that generation of people and their misdeeds."

"I'd never looked at it like that."

"Stop feeling guilty, D. We're cleaning house. There is no middle ground here. There is no dead-man's zone. You can't be a little good and a little bad. You're one or the other."

"We're not exactly the good guys here, Tommy."

"But we're not *that* kind of bad, either."

"Truth." Damian hummed under his breath before asking, "What did she tell you at the end? Did she say anything to you at all?"

"To go to hell."

"Damn."

Tommas smiled. "I told her that I would meet her there."

Tommas barely got his shoes kicked off and his coat hung up before his cell phone rang. He shot a look at the decorative clock on the wall. Who in the hell would be calling him at four-thirty in the morning?

He'd left his mother's body in the tub, hoping the cold water would fuck up the time of death enough that no one would suspect someone else's involvement. Really, his only involvement was not stopping her. Nonetheless, he didn't expect a call about Serena's unfortunate death until mid-afternoon the next day when the maid was scheduled to clean the house.

Tommas would have to remember to put an extra bonus on the girl's final paycheck. Finding Serena's dead body in a tub full of bloody water wouldn't be an easy sight to forget, that was for sure.

Tommas dug the phone out of his jacket pocket and picked the call up on the sixth ring. "Rossi speaking."

"Evening, Tommas. It's time to chat."

Tommas straightened like someone had shoved a metal rod up his spine. The familiar voice on the other end of the phone call was not who he expected. In fact, it was the very last person he thought would ever make a phone call to him.

"Joel," Tommas greeted with forced civility. "I can't say this is a great time for you to be calling, but what do I owe the pleasure."

"Nothing, I simply thought it was time to end this nonsense."

Swallowing back the distrust that left a bad taste in his mouth, Tommas took Joel's words with a grain of salt and nothing more. He wouldn't give any faith to the man. Joel had a terrible habit of biting the hands that fed him.

The moment someone turned their back to Joel Trentini, the man stabbed them.

"End it, huh?" Tommas asked.

"Yes. A truce. How does that sound to you?"

Like you're working on something.

"Why, Joel? What's changed?"

"The attention on the Outfit is heavier, for one thing," his former friend answered.

"And for another?"

"My mother was killed in all this, Tommas. The families are two words away from going at one another again. Is that what you want? Another street war? Your cousin's wife is pregnant. My sister is due for her baby soon. Should those women be left without husbands to care for their children simply because we can't work something out?"

Each word that Joel spoke felt falser than the one before. None of it rang true to Tommas. Joel cared nothing for the people around him. He would slit the throat of anyone who stepped in his way of getting what they wanted.

Yes, the man was definitely planning something.

Tommas just didn't know what.

"Tell me about this truce," Tommas said.

"Well …"

"I don't have time to waste, Joel. You either want a serious discussion about whatever it is you're considering, or you're prepared for the next wave of hell that I throw at you. I can do this forever. Or at least until you're dead."

Joel chuckled. "This is why we were such good friends all those years ago. I like the way you think, Tommas. You never failed to disappoint me."

"Is that so?"

"Very," Joel replied. "The truce, like I said, would benefit us both."

"Unless it ends with me taking the boss's seat, I don't want to talk about it."

"It does, actually."

Tommas stilled while a drop of tension crawled down his spine. Again, the whole conversation felt entirely wrong to him in some way. Why, after all that Joel had done, would he give Tommas the seat?

"Now you're just trying to lull me into some sense of comfort, Joel," Tommas said. "Let me call your bullshit out before you go any further. No one but Joel Trentini means a damn thing to Joel Trentini. If you're going to use other people as a reason for why you care enough to stop the war, then you might as well just go right on ahead and use your own name and not someone else's. For another thing, you want it too much, Joel. The Outfit, the families, the control, and the power—it's yours, right? That's what you've always said."

"It's not that simple."

"Don't treat me like I'm an idiot, Joel. You're trying to trick me into a situation where only one of us comes out alive. I know your games. I have always played them better. This one is no different."

"I'm proposing a truce that benefits us both," Joel repeated calmly.

"I don't believe that."

"That's because you trust no one."

"I wonder why," Tommas murmured more to himself than to Joel. "Tell me your offer. I'm listening, but my attention span is only as long as you can keep me interested, Joel."

"Two organizations," Joel said quietly. "Split the families, and the territories, or let them choose. Two bosses. Peace on the streets. Simple."

Tommas took the information in. Joel's voice held every ounce of serenity and solemnity that it could.

"You're serious," Tommas said.

"As a heart attack. You're right, I care little for everyone else. If I thought it would benefit me somehow, I could easily kill them all or force them to kill one another to get me where I want to go. The bigger problem, Tommas, is that doing so will leave me with nothing. In the end, once the dust clears and the blood is washed away, I will be left with little but a struggling organization that can no longer stand on its own two legs."

"What good is a boss with no family to run?"

"Exactly," Joel agreed. "I've had a while to think all this over. I would rather have a piece of a large pie, than nothing at all. Are you amicable to sitting down and having a proper discussion about this offer?"

No.

Tommas still didn't trust Joel.

The situation still felt bad.

"The last sit-down we had didn't exactly end with either of us getting what he wanted," Tommas mused. "What makes you believe this one will?"

"We can arrive at the same time. Outside at a location of your choosing. Men, decided on beforehand, from both sides can check for weapons. Whoever you and I choose to bring to the meeting can be there. Have your cousin bring his wife if you want a female to ensure the peace."

"Right, because that would deter you, I'm sure. Don't even try it, Joel."

But, Tommas was listening. Joel had essentially offered Tommas a lot in a few sentences. He'd given him control over where, how, and when the meeting could happen. He'd allowed Tommas all the power.

"You're amicable to separating the Outfit?" Tommas asked.

"Yes," Joel replied.

It sounded like the truth. Tommas knew nothing with Joel was truthful.

The bigger problem Tommas faced was figuring out exactly what Joel was planning. It would be damn near impossible. He also had to consider Abriella. He promised his girl a forever—one of their own choosing and making. No matter what, he needed to give Abriella her forever with him.

Tommas only really had one option.

"I'll call you with the details within a couple of weeks," Tommas said.

"I look forward to it, Tommas."

CHAPTER SIXTEEN

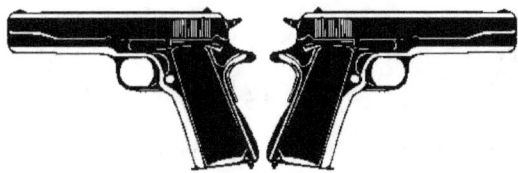

"**D**ad?" Abriella called down the long hallway.

Her father didn't answer. Concerned for Peter's emotional health, Abriella slipped into the wing that had always belonged to her parents and shut the connecting door. Peter had taken the murder of his wife harder than Abriella thought he would. Her father had rarely left the Trentini mansion since they buried Sara, and he had yet to return to his law practice.

She knew her father loved Sara. She simply hadn't realized how much.

Almost every day, Abriella made her way into the other wing of the mansion just to sit with her father so he didn't feel alone in the large space. When Joel wasn't around spreading his usual nastiness, Abriella went over to cook for her dad and to eat with him.

Peter, for the most part, was quiet. He didn't speak a lot. He didn't cry in front of Abriella, either. But his heartbreak, his grief, was palpable.

Even walking through the wing in search of her father, Abriella could practically feel the man's pain embedded into the walls.

Did he cry when he was alone?

Did he talk to her mother?

Did he want to follow Sara?

Shaking those thoughts away, Abriella trekked into the kitchen. She found her father sitting at the table with a full cup of coffee between his hands and his expression unreadable. Blank like a white piece of paper.

Emotionless.

Dead, even.

A cold shiver rolled across Abriella's shoulders.

"Hey, Dad," she said quietly.

Peter glanced up from his coffee, his hands tightening around the mug. "Morning, Ella."

She smiled, but it didn't quite ring true. "Do you want me to cook you something for breakfast? Eggs, bacon, toast? Whatever you want, Dad."

"I'm not very hungry right now."

Abriella crossed the room and pulled out a chair to sit beside her father at the long oak table. Reaching over, she grabbed her father's wrist and held tight. The side of her hand brushed the coffee mug, but it wasn't hot. In fact, it was cold.

"How long have you been awake?" Abriella asked.

Peter stared down at the black coffee. "I didn't go to sleep, I guess. I've been thinking about a lot of things. I must have lost track of time."

"Oh, Dad …"

Her father winced. "Don't do that, Ella. Don't worry about me."

"Kind of hard not to."

"I'm sorry. I shouldn't be causing you any stress. You probably have enough to deal with where your brother is concerned."

Abriella laughed bleakly. "Joel's craziness is nothing new. He's old news. It's you that I'm worried about, Dad. I know you're sad and that you miss Mom, but—"

"More than you know," Peter interrupted softly.

The heart in Abriella's chest, the one she was sure had frozen over long ago, cracked with a splinter of pain. The wetness in her father's eyes was enough to melt even the coldest of souls.

"How many more?" Peter asked.

"I don't understand what you mean."

"How many more people have to bury the ones they love for this chess game the Outfit plays?" Peter shook his head and rubbed at the spot over his heart like it was aching, and he wanted to soothe it somehow. "My youngest child is going to make me a grandfather soon, but I can't even see her because your brother hates her husband. My other daughter is being set on the sidelines until something good comes along, and she can be used to benefit her family's name. And my oldest, the boy who isn't really mine even though I tried to love him like he was, is the cause of it all, Ella."

"Dad—"

"We failed," Peter murmured. "Sara and I, we failed at taking care of the babies we brought into this world. We weren't always given a choice, we were forced into a marriage, into a life we didn't ask for, and we tried to make the best of it."

"You didn't fail, Dad."

"We did, Ella. We never fought to have our own lives and control, and by default, we lost. I'm sorry that we weren't better for you."

Abriella grabbed her father's wrist harder. "You're the best dad."

Her parents had certainly made mistakes throughout the years. They had overlooked things, let others have the control over their family and children, and they followed the herd like they had been told to do.

She didn't blame them for that.

They didn't know any different.

"I love you," Abriella said, wanting her father to know. "Alessa loves you, too. Please don't feel like we blame you for the way our lives have turned out. We don't, Dad, and we never have."

Peter smiled sadly. "You're a good girl, Ella."

Abriella snorted. "Not highly."

"You're good where it counts. I wish your brother would see it, too. You deserve the world and so much more, sweetheart. I want to see you happy, Abriella. All your mother ever wanted was to see her children happy, not confused and heartbroken like she had been for most of her life."

"I'm happy," Abriella said, lying in hopes that her father would feel better.

How could she possibly be happy with her life in shambles like it was? How could anyone be happy in the midst of a war that just kept on taking and killing? She was struggling to breathe day after day, and missing something vitally important for her happiness in her heart.

Peter stood and patted Abriella on the cheek with a gentle, loving touch as he passed her by to go to the sink. He dumped the contents of his cold coffee before turning on the electric kettle to boil more water.

"I think I will have some breakfast after all," Peter told her. "How about waffles instead of eggs and the usual?"

"Sure, Dad."

Abriella stood from the table and helped her father gather the things they needed to cook. As they worked side by side in silence, Abriella felt closer to her father than she had in years. They were both still heartbroken. They both missed people—one dead in the ground, and one just beyond reach.

Maybe it was a kindred thing as much as it was their shared blood.

For a moment, Abriella did feel some sense of happiness. But she needed more. She wanted more. She craved peace. She was hungry for the safety of those she cared about and for the friendships that had been forced away. She missed dinners filled with friends who cared, and the familiar connection of people who lived a lifestyle that no one on the outside could ever possibly understand.

Had the Outfit ever really felt like those things?

Abriella couldn't remember a time when it had without some sort of underlying issue causing problems, but it could be like that. She knew it could. Her friends, her family, and the lives they were starting was proof that it could be better. They wanted it to be better.

It could be *happy*.

"Dad," Abriella said, never taking her eyes off her work.

"Yes?"

"I'm not happy, but I want to be."

"I know, Ella."

"Tommy."

"Hey, Ella."

Tommas' voice was a soothing balm to Abriella's tired heart. After being cornered by the detectives at her college the day before, she had been on edge ever since. When she arrived back to her wing of the mansion, she found Joel gone. According to the cook, Joel said he had business to do and didn't offer any information about when he would be back.

Abriella took the chance to call Tommas with the mansion's home phone. She still hadn't gotten her burner phone back from Tommas after forgetting it and her text book in his car.

"It was my mother," Tommas said.

Abriella's brow furrowed at his random statement. "What?"

"My mother—she was the one who gave the info about our relationship to the officials."

"Are you sure?"

That didn't sound right to her. Serena Rossi was a vile woman, to be sure, but turning rat on her own son seemed low even for her. Not to mention, what good would it do for people to know that Tommas had been in a long-term relationship of sorts with Abriella?

Other than to piss off Joel, that was.

"Positive," Tommas finally replied. "I took care of it. Don't worry about that nonsense. Joel hasn't given you back your cell?"

Abriella scowled. "No."

"It's been a couple months since he took it."

"I know. But Joel left this morning to do business. Or that was the message he left behind about where he was going. No one is here but me and the cook. Dad is in the other wing."

"How's Peter doing?"

"Terribly."

Tommas hummed a sad sound. "I'm sorry, Ella. I tried to stop it once I knew your mother was—"

"I know you did, Tommy."

And that, more than anything, meant the world to Abriella. Just the fact that Tommas had his plans for Joel set in stone; the fact that he could have had the seat as the boss, and he attempted to call it off to keep her mother from possibly being hurt in the process meant everything.

He *tried*.

He hadn't meant to hurt Abriella.

Tommas proved he would have given up what was right at the tips of his fingers if it meant that Abriella wouldn't have lost her mother.

"I know you tried, Tommy," Abriella said again.

"Still kills me," Tommas murmured.

"Talk about something else, hmm?"

"I'm buying a new restaurant this week."

Abriella laughed. "Why?"

"I've been looking at a specific one for a while, but I've gone back and forth on whether the risk and cost of opening was worth the price. I thought you might like a seafood place or something."

"Maybe."

"But that's not the only reason I'm buying it," he admitted.

"Why are you being strange, Tommy?"

"I'm always strange, Ella. Nonetheless, I need a restaurant that is untouched and unknown by your brother. He called me early in the morning—too early, frankly. He wants a sit-down."

Abriella's head snapped up at those words. "You can't be serious."

"As a heart attack. I don't trust him, but he's given me control of all the planning for it and how it should go down. He's agreeable as long as I let him have his men check mine when we arrive. He suggested something ..."

"Tell me."

"The Outfit, Ella. He suggested we split the Outfit between us."

Abriella's heart stopped dead in her chest. "Split ... Like two bosses?"

"Exactly."

"But—"

"He made it sound good," Tommas cut in quickly. "As if that's what would be the best thing. Joel made it seem like he didn't want this feud to continue, because there might not be a damn thing left standing when it's done. And he's got a point. A good one, Abriella."

"Sure," she admitted, though it left a bad taste in her mouth.

"He's playing on it. He's toying with it, and he wants me to believe it."

"But you don't."

"Of course not."

Abriella's heart started beating again as relief washed through her bloodstream. Tommas was not a stupid man. Joel liked to play his manipulative games, but Tommas could see those manipulations coming long before it could hurt him in some way.

"What is my brother planning?" Abriella asked.

"I don't know," Tommas said. "What I do know, however, is that this might be a chance for me to finish it. Somehow, I don't know. I want to be careful with everything."

"Yeah, I get that."

"Especially with me and you."

Abriella stilled on the spot, and she clutched the cordless phone tighter. "What in the hell does that mean?"

"It means that I'm going to keep a distance for the next little while. Just until I get wind of what Joel might be planning. Call me if it's safe, or if you can. But I won't be showing up like I have been over these last couple of months. I don't want to risk it. As it is, the detectives have information about us. Unfounded right now, sure, but what if that gets out?"

Abriella shuddered. "It won't."

"It could," Tommas pressed. "I have to stay away for a while."

Her heart cracked all over again.

"But ... I don't get to see you as it is. Not enough."

"I'm sorry, baby. In a few years, once this is all said and done, maybe you'll wake up one day and wish that you didn't have to see my face as much as you do. When that happens, I will remind you of this. Sound good?"

"No," Abriella said sadly.

"It won't be for long."

"You don't know that."

"I do," Tommas said, so confident, smooth, and sure. "Because your brother started the ball rolling on something. Joel, like he always has, plans and plans until he's ready for action. He's clearly ready. Keep an eye and an ear out for me, okay?"

"You know I will."

"Loyal like nobody else," Tommas said, chuckling. "I love you, Ella."

Abriella smiled. "I love you, too, Tommy."

"No crazy stunts, right?"

"I promise. Hey, about your mother?"

"What about her?"

The coldness in his tone shocked Abriella, but she brushed it aside.

"You're positive it was her that talked to the detectives?" she asked.

"Yeah, baby. No doubt. She's been doing it since my dad died. In her mind, it was payback for what I had done to her."

That was just ... sickening.

"And how did you handle her?"

Tommas rattled off a television station. "Watch the news. I have to go. Nate is waiting to take me to the lawyer's office to sign some paperwork. He's fucking impatient."

Abriella didn't want to hang up, but this was their reality. It sucked sometimes, but mostly, it was wonderful.

She was tired of hiding.

"Okay. Be careful, Tommas."

Tommas laughed darkly. "I don't know how to be anything else, Ella."

After hanging up the phone, Abriella grabbed the remote for the television and turned the flat screen on. She perched on the edge of the couch as she flicked through the satellite channels to find the one that Tommas had mentioned. The moment she found it, she knew something was wrong.

Abriella watched, fascinated and horrified, as a stretcher was rolled out of a familiar house. The news report flashed back and forth between the reporter on the case, the surrounding images, and the anchors back at the station.

There was only one person who could be the one being wheeled out of that house, dead in the body bag. It was surreal. The more the reporter talked, the sicker Abriella felt. He'd handled it. That's what Tommas said.

Abriella knew how much her lover despised his mother. He'd told her stories of his past, the abuse and the addiction; he explained the neglect and the pain.

Could he have done this?

Did Tommas kill his mother?

The middle-aged female reporter flashed back on the screen. "Serena Rossi, now deceased, was the longtime wife of Outfit member, Laurent Rossi. Laurent's death months ago has been under an active investigation when the man suffered a gunshot wound pointblank to the face. His wife was sleeping upstairs, although the investigators cleared her of any suspicion in her husband's murder.

"We're just being told now that cause of death is likely suicide, although the investigators refuse to give more information on exactly how Serena Rossi took her own life," the reporter continued. "We do know that the body was found in the upstairs bathroom and that the house was locked and empty as it usually is when the maid comes to clean. It is possible that this death is in no way related to Laurent's, or the current issues the Outfit has been facing with the street war happening between influential families. We will keep you updated as this breaking news develops."

Abriella turned off the television. She didn't need to know more.

This was more than enough.

The rest of the day passed Abriella by in silence. Well, it felt that way. She heard nothing from Tommas. Her father had left the mansion after their breakfast together without a word. Even her brother had come home, went to his office without stopping to talk to her, and thankfully, left Abriella alone.

Unfortunately, Joel still managed to wrangle Abriella in for a meal at the table with him. Like it always had been, the dinner was awkward and thick with tension.

"Leave us for a minute," she heard her brother say.

Abriella looked up from her plate. She found it easier to focus on the food being served and eating than she did trying to strike up some kind of awful conversation with her brother. Talking with Joel never ended well.

With a nod, the cook placed the chicken dish on the table and scurried from the dining room.

"And you, Darryl," Joel added. "If you wouldn't mind."

The enforcer sitting at the middle of the table between the siblings had been coming around to the house a lot more often. Mostly, the guy left Abriella alone unless she was out of the house for school. Then, he was on her ass like he was her new best friend.

"I could use a smoke before supper, I guess," the enforcer said.

"Ten minutes at the most," Joel replied. "We should be done by then."

Done what?

Confused, Abriella watched the enforcer leave the room. Joel plucked up the napkin resting beside his plate, flicked it open, and tossed it over his lap. His casual nature and calm expression almost lulled Abriella into the idea that her brother might be in a good mood.

Almost.

She didn't trust Joel enough to relax around him.

"I wanted to give you a decent forewarning about what will be coming in the next couple of weeks," Joel stated.

Abriella arched a brow, choosing to wade into the conversation carefully. "Oh? What's happening?"

"A sit-down between Tommas Rossi and me. Actually, the majority of the Outfit will be invited, or the people who matter the most, anyway. Tommas and I, well, we've decided to come to a truce of sorts. Or that's how it seems."

Nothing about this little chat felt right to Abriella. She allowed her brother to continue.

"You see, Tommas asked for something at the last sit-down," Joel said.

Abriella swallowed back the nervousness tightening in her throat. "He asked for a marriage to be arranged between him and I, right?"

"He did. Guarantee was the word he used."

"So?"

Joel's gaze snapped up, cutting into Abriella with a fierce knowing. "So, it started the ball rolling for me. It made me wonder why a man like Tommas, so intent and focused on his desire to become the boss, would offer something as crazy as giving up the seat in exchange for a guarantee like a marriage. Not just any marriage, mind you, but one to my sister."

Abriella's hands balled into tight fists on her lap. "I don't understand what you're getting at, Joel."

"When did you catch the man's eye?"

"I haven't—"

"Before you think to lie, don't bother. I simply want you to tell me when you caught Tommas Rossi's attention, Abriella."

Abriella wet her lips, considering her words. "I don't know when."

"But he is interested."

"Why would you think that?"

"I told you why," Joel said, his jaw tightening. "The ball began to roll, and I followed it. There are rumors in the Outfit of Tommas' involvement with a woman that he keeps on the low. The night his vehicle was caught up in that unfortunate bomb, it is highly likely that a woman was with him. I had people ask around, but no one had a clear answer for me. And now …"

"What now, Joel?"

"Now, with his mother showing up dead this afternoon, it makes a person wonder. Especially considering her death was an apparent suicide, yet the officials are all over that like flies on shit. That's all."

"You're talking me in circles, Joel."

"It's not nice to be left out of the loop, is it, Ella?" her brother asked scathingly.

Abriella felt the familiar drip of dread fall down her spine. "What am I missing?"

"You had visitors while you were at school. Again, I guess. That's what they explained to Darryl when he stopped them from accosting you. He couldn't say for sure if they had gotten past him later in the day as the halls were full of people during your class switches."

Air caught painfully in her throat.

"The detectives, you mean?" she asked.

Joel nodded once. "Yes, them. They wouldn't say very much to Darryl, but when I went in to find out why my sister had suddenly become such an interest to police detectives, imagine my surprise to find out they believed you to be in a relationship with Tommas Rossi."

"I—"

"I had already started to go back through some things before this, you see," Joel interrupted, cocking a brow.

The sight alone made Abriella wince. It felt like violence and Joel's tone rang of rage.

"Like what?" she dared to ask.

"Phone records, for one. Being in control of the account for your cell phone allows me that privilege. You seemed to make a lot of calls to a number I don't recognize."

Abriella chewed on her inner cheek, refusing to give Joel a reaction. "So?"

"I called it early this morning. Guess who picked up?"

A sting radiated over Abriella's eyes, but she fought the tears for all she was worth.

"Tommas," she said.

"Yes. I offered a sit-down the moment he picked up. He didn't even realize that I had called his private cell phone, and not his home. That forewarning," Joel said sharply, making Abriella wince. "I think you should know it now."

Abriella struggled for words, and thoughts. This had been a very real possibility that Joel would get word of what the officials knew about her and Tommas. She almost expected it to come out, despite Tommas wanting them to keep a distance from one another and be careful.

Sometimes, you just couldn't be careful enough.

"What do you want, Joel?" Abriella asked.

"When this sit-down happens, I'm going to give Tommas exactly what he wants."

Abriella blinked, stunned. "The marriage?"

"Yes." Impassive and unreadable, Joel watched Abriella like she might bolt at any minute. "And you will happily go along with whatever is arranged. You will keep quiet, you will be agreeable, and you will somehow manage to keep that mouth of yours shut about what I know."

"But ... why?"

"Because this is how it needs to be," Joel said frankly.

Abriella was so confused that it wasn't even funny. "How what needs to be, Joel?"

"The Outfit, of course. And let me be very clear on something, Ella. If you can't manage to do those four very simple things for me, then I have no problem with finishing this feud out in an entirely different way. You see, if Tommas has been stupid enough to be messing around with you, then you have also been dumb enough to play around with him. He's not the only one who cares between the two of you. So, you'll do as I ask, and you'll do it well, or I will finish it."

Nothing about what her brother just said made sense. Tommas was right, Abriella realized. Joel was planning something. The bigger problem was that no one knew what exactly his plans were. That made things all the more dangerous.

"Why?" Abriella asked again.

"I already told you."

This is how it needs to be ...

Tommas wouldn't give up the boss's seat. Abriella knew it. Joel had to know it, too. Her brother wouldn't give up what he wanted, either. For Abriella, that could only mean one thing.

Joel was going to make his final move.

But what was it?

"Oh, and Ella?"

Abriella slammed back into reality with a bang. Her brother smiled coldly at her from the other end of the table.

"Yes?" she asked.

"To make sure you follow my rules, since you're so damned good at breaking them, and to guarantee this conversation of ours doesn't get out before the sit-down happens, you won't be leaving the house."

Abriella stiffened in the chair. "At all?"

"No actually, you won't be leaving the upstairs wing. You have all you need up there, after all. The cook can bring you food. As we speak, Darryl is removing all the phones, computers, and whatever else might let you contact someone. Think of it as a timeout. A moment to get your priorities straight and think about what you really want, Ella."

He was locking her in.

Like a fucking *animal*.

"I'll give you another thing to consider as well that goes along with the first offer," Joel added, still smiling in that sickening way of his. "Something else for you to think about while you walk the halls for a week or two."

"Don't bother," Abriella spat.

The heat in her tone couldn't be hidden. She didn't care anymore. She wanted her brother to know how much she despised him and what he was doing. He was going to put her into a proverbial corner and force her hand into somehow hurting Tommas. Joel was making goddamn sure his plans, whatever they were, wouldn't be spoiled.

What more could he fucking do?

"Oh, you might like this one," Joel replied. "Freedom, Ella. I'll give it to you."

Abriella's brow crumpled. "Freedom."

"I'll give you tickets to wherever you want to go, I'll sign over every red cent of your inheritance for you to use whatever way you wish, and you can leave. Go out of Chicago, start somewhere new, or whatever you want to do."

"In exchange for what?"

Joel shrugged. "In exchange for giving me what I want."

Abriella knew exactly what her brother wanted. It was the same thing he had always wanted.

To be the boss.

"Think about it," Joel said quietly.

"What if I won't go along with your ... whatever this is?"

"It's like this, Ella, either one person can go, or a bunch of them can. I want to make this as easy as possible, but that doesn't mean it's going to be painless. It isn't my fault that you've gotten yourself tangled up with a man that you had no business being with. If your feelings got involved, it was by your choice, not mine."

Her chest ached from her heart beating so fast.

This wasn't fair.

"Those aren't options at all, Joel," Abriella hissed. "You're going to trick Tommas with me. You're an asshole."

"I think the options are perfectly fine. Simple, even. You only have to make a choice. Lose one person, hurt for a while, but have the freedom to eventually move on. Or, try to save that one person in some way, and this nonsense will continue until everyone is dead in the ground."

Abriella clenched her teeth. "Why are you doing this?"

"Because as someone once told me, this life isn't about getting what you want, Ella. You can't have what you want just because you said so."

More confused than ever, Abriella met her brother's cold gaze from across the table. She knew he must be angry, but he hid it far too well.

This wasn't the Joel she thought she knew. The Joel she knew was a vile man in his own right. This man was even worse. This was someone else entirely.

"The last time you caught me with a man, you barely held back from beating me black and blue," Abriella said, sneering. "What's changed?"

Joel glanced down at his plate. "You made me feel like a fool. There's no question that I would like to show you exactly how whores like you should be treated, but I can't. There's something I need from you, Ella. All you have to do is give me what I have asked for, and the rest will go away. This is mine—the Outfit, the families. They're mine."

Her heart for his.

The truth burned as she swallowed it down.

"Think about it all," Joel said quietly. "You have time. Starting now."

Abriella didn't get the chance to ask her brother another thing.

Darryl came out of nowhere from behind her, grabbed her by the arm, and pulled her up from the chair. The last thing she saw in the dining room before she was dragged from it cursing and kicking was a two-fingered wave from Joel.

She smacked Darryl hard in the side of the face. The man's eyes flashed with anger and his grip turned painful.

"Let me go!"

"Stop it, or you'll get a taste of your own medicine, you little bitch," the enforcer snarled.

Abriella chose to stop fighting. Not because she was weak or had given up, but because she needed a plan. Joel was right.

She needed time to think.

More than anything, Abriella felt like she was out of options that she could control.

CHAPTER SEVENTEEN

"Ten minutes," Damian said, looking down at his watch.

Tommas still checked the time on the dashboard even knowing that his cousin was right. "It's been a rough year, man."

Damian's gaze drifted from Tommas in the driver's seat, to the windy, quiet Chicago street outside of the car. "It has been, you're right."

"I'll be happy to put an end to it all."

"Have you seen or talked to Abriella at all?" Damian asked.

"No," Tommas answered, offering little else.

The nagging anxiety in his chest refused to relent whenever he thought about his girl, however. It bothered him more than he could explain that Abriella hadn't contacted him since the last time they spoke.

Sure, he'd told her that they needed to keep a safe distance for obvious reasons, but the thing about Abriella was that she didn't follow the rules very well.

Still, no calls.

Concerned about his lover, but knowing there wasn't much he could do but wait, Tommas decided to let it all work out on its own. He didn't have a choice either way.

"Tommy?"

"What?"

Damian sighed, shooting his cousin a look from the side. "You know it doesn't have to go down like this, right? You don't have to do it this way, man."

"Conceding isn't always losing," Tommas murmured. "Sometimes, smart men have to play a game in such a way that conceding is the only possible option in the end. It's what Joel wants, anyway. For me to concede to this arrangement. He's looking for that, and he must have a reason for it. It's a safer way to win right now, D. Nothing more."

"And what about in a few months?"

"What about it?"

"When Joel decides he's tired of having the city split into two organizations, or when he tries another bomb episode on you again. What if he wins then, huh?"

Tommas smiled, and waved his cousin's concerns off. "You should learn to trust me more."

"I'm trying really hard, but you make it difficult when you go on to do something like this with Joel Trentini, Tommas."

Damian had not been happy at all to hear about the offer Joel laid on the table for Tommas to consider a week and a half ago. In fact, Damian might as well have called Tommas a fool for even agreeing to a sit-down with Joel to discuss separating the Outfit into two new organizations with separate bosses on both sides.

"Trust," Tommas repeated. "It will take you everywhere with me."

"Easy for you to say, Tommy."

"I'm not an idiot. I know what I'm doing."

"That's the whole problem. I have no idea what you're doing."

"You don't need to," Tommas replied quietly.

Damian rubbed at his forehead, obviously tired and over the conversation. "What have you been doing these last couple of weeks, anyway?"

Planning.

Considering.

Deciding.

"Making the right choice," Tommas settled on saying. "Even if that choice isn't what everyone else might choose or want to see happen. Sometimes the right decision is often the hardest and most difficult."

And bloody, he added silently.

"I hope, for everyone's sake, that you're right in doing this with Joel," Damian said.

"But you don't think I am."

"No, I think you're giving up, and you're so much fucking better than that, Tommas."

With that statement, Damian got out of the Jaguar and slammed the passenger door hard enough to rock the car. Tommas watched his cousin stroll down the street in the direction of where the sit-down would take place in just a few short minutes.

Tommas didn't blame Damian.

No one really knew much about what would happen today other than what Tommas offered to tell. It wasn't a lot. He'd invited Capos to sit in and watch. He'd asked for the Capos to bring whoever they felt comfortable with having along for the ride, as this day would be a valuable lesson to everyone involved.

Tommas decided to have it go down this way, because he wanted a point to be made. He wanted the Outfit people to see how things should be handled in *la famiglia* when wars happened.

Scores had to be settled. Sometimes it was bloody, but not every time.

"How was the last couple of weeks?" Joel asked.

Tommas spread his arms wide, allowing Joel's man to pat him down and check all through his coat, his pants pockets, and wherever else the man felt necessary. "Quiet, actually."

"Nice, isn't it?"

"Yes," Tommas agreed. "It's been too long since the streets were peaceful."

"It has been a while," Joel said, smiling falsely.

The man checking him moved down to a crouch so he could check Tommas' legs. His hands slid a little too high for Tommas' liking.

"Do you want a handful of my cock?" Tommas asked the guy.

The enforcer cleared his throat. "No."

"Then let me help you out." Tommas brushed his pant legs with his hands, clearly showing he had no weapon at his groin. Then, he grabbed his dick through his slacks and said, "Just this in here, sorry."

Joel chuckled. "Always good for a show, old friend."

Tommas looked to Damian. "And?"

"He's clean," Damian said. "Checked him myself. Checked all the guys he brought. They're good as well. The street is clean of people. No one will be outside waiting. It's … good, boss."

Joel's nostrils flared at Damian's casual offer of the boss title to Tommas. It didn't escape Tommas' notice how Joel quickly tampered down his reaction to hide it.

"And her?" Tommas asked, tilting his head toward Abriella.

Tommas had done all he could to ignore his lover since he'd walked down the street to see her and Joel getting out of a black town car together. It didn't surprise him that Joel had brought Abriella along.

Even when Joel was attempting something worthy of peace, he still liked to play mind games. How Abriella factored into those games, Tommas wasn't sure.

Abriella, on the other hand, had kept her head down and she stayed quiet. She wouldn't even meet Tommas' stare when he blatantly asked about her. His fingers itched and ached to reach out and grab Abriella to bring her close.

Why was she looking at the fucking ground?

She wasn't smiling—that was never good.

Tommas forced his hands to stay at his sides, and dragged his attention from his lover so that his worries weren't so goddamn obvious.

"She's good," Damian said, shrugging. "Nothing on her, Tommy."

"Good," Tommas said. "Everyone is inside?"

"The Capos and a few of their middle men, yes."

Joel passed a glance at the restaurant that was in desperate need of an overhaul on the outside. Chips of paint fell on the pavement, one window could use a replacement, and the old door spoke of years past.

"Who does this place belong to?" Joel asked.

"Me," Tommas answered. "I bought it this week. Someone I know has a taste for seafood. I wanted to be able to enjoy it with them when it was up and running again. For now, it'll serve its purpose of getting us through this meeting without drawing attention from the police or anyone else. Your men checked it out earlier, didn't they?"

Joel nodded. "Sure."

"And?"

"And you already know," Joel said. "There was nothing to find."

"I'm being amicable, Joel. This is what you wanted."

"Then let's do it, old friend."

Tommas really wished Joel would lay off the 'old friend' nonsense. It was tiring. It was untrue and ridiculous. A certain understanding between men did not make for a friendship, and they certainly didn't have much to be friendly about now.

"Yes, let's do that," Tommas said, waving toward the quiet restaurant.

Damian grabbed the door and pulled it open, allowing others to walk in ahead of him. During the entire conversation and check outside, Tommas had felt the eyes of more than a dozen people inside the restaurant watching him and Joel.

No doubt, he probably knew exactly what they were thinking.

How was this going to end?

Are the rumors true?

Is it over?

Tommas hoped he could answer all three of those questions before the meeting was out.

Joel stepped in ahead of Tommas, and Abriella followed quietly behind her brother. Moving behind Joel, Tommas joined in.

"Wait a sec," came an older voice from behind them.

Finally, Abriella lifted her head. A familiar fire colored up her blue eyes, instantly making Tommas feel at home, even if they were anywhere but safe, quiet, and together. His girl was there, but she was doing what she had to do—whatever it was.

"Dad?" Abriella asked, seeing her father standing outside of the restaurant.

"I thought you weren't coming inside with us?" Joel asked, moving his sister aside so he could talk to his step-father.

Peter Trentini gave Tommas a passing glance as he said, "I haven't changed my mind, Joel. I have no reason to go inside with you today. I drove here, showed my face, and that's more than enough. I buried my wife for this, and that was too much."

"Well, what are you doing?" Joel barked.

The older man waved a handbag, decked out with the faces of Abriella's favorite Sugar Skulls. It was just a clutch, nothing big.

"Abriella forgot this in the car. I just happened to notice it."

Peter passed the bag into Abriella's hand. Tommas took note of the way her brow crumpled in question, but she stayed quiet when Joel glared down at her. Tommas beat back the urge to slap Joel just at the sight alone.

"Thank you," Abriella said softly.

"Never go anywhere without your purse," Peter said, chuckling. "That's what your mother always said."

"We're wasting time," Joel muttered.

Joel and Abriella disappeared inside the restaurant without a goodbye to their father. Tommas offered Peter a nod that was subtly returned.

A thank you of sorts.

"It's too bad the restaurant isn't open for business," Joel noted. "It would have been nice to have a meal."

"I'll save a spot for you on opening night," Tommas said.

Joel smiled. "I'll see to it that you make sure of it."

Sure he would.

Settled into one of the many tables and chairs in the middle of the room, Tommas watched his rival from across the way. Abriella, poised as ever, sat pretty and quiet beside her brother. The men around them, the major players in the Outfit, watched the scene unfold with rapt attention and closed mouths.

Thankfully.

The less issues this meeting was met with, the better.

Tommas took note of the people sitting at various tables with their people. Theo DeLuca had brought along a couple of guys Tommas recognized from the DeLuca crew. Damian had asked for two of his men to tag along and help with checking Joel's men and to watch the outside of the restaurant. Adriano Conti, typically calm and reserved, sat in the far corner with three men at his table and looking like the restaurant was the last place he wanted to be.

Adding the couple of men Tommas brought, and the guys who tagged along with Joel, the restaurant was full.

"I'd like to get this over as quickly as possible," Joel started to say, glancing up at Tommas.

"As would I."

"Good. Semantics, right? That's what this whole thing is. We'll get the main point of it all out there for everyone to know what's going to happen. We'll decide which Capo and territory belongs to you or I. Simple, Tommas."

It could be.

Tommas didn't believe it would be.

"Separate the organization into two entities," Tommas said, drumming his fingers on the table. "That's what you wanted."

"Yes."

"What about the Commission? They've only got enough room at the table for one boss from Chicago."

Joel shrugged. "Our business hasn't been tied to New York for years ever since the little disagreement we had with the Marcellos. Terrance kept his seat at the table simply for show and to be up-to-date with the happenings of the other families. It's an unneeded process, in my opinion."

Tommas disagreed entirely. The Commission was hugely important for building allies in other families, having a line of communication across the continent with other organizations, and some of their work was still tied up with places like Canada and Las Vegas.

What was Joel trying to prove?

"Someone needs to be at the Commission," Tommas pointed out. "It's not unneeded, as you said. It's vital for all of the families to have that direct line to one another, Joel."

"Then go to it," Joel replied flippantly.

Go to it ...

Tommas' gaze cut to Abriella, who was also watching her brother curiously. He wondered what, if anything, she might know about her brother's plans.

"I'll go," Tommas said.

"Good. The crews. Let's break it up here and now."

"DeLuca and Rossi crews are unquestionably mine," Tommas said.

Abriella's brow furrowed like she wanted to say something, but her lips pressed into a thin line like she was forcing herself to be quiet. She glanced between the two men at the table, waiting on her brother's reply.

"Of course," Joel finally said. "I wouldn't assume differently."

In the corner of the restaurant, Adriano Conti cleared his throat.

"What about my crew, don't I get a say in who I prefer to work under?"

Tommas chuckled at the sight of Joel's narrowed gaze.

"We're family now, Adriano," Joel said. "It would do you good to remember that."

Adriano scoffed quietly. "When you begin treating me and my wife like family, then I'll give you respect back, Joel. My crew goes to Tommas, but it won't go to you."

"Well," Tommas drawled quietly, bringing Joel's attention back to him. "What do we do about that?"

"Take him," Joel spat. "He's fucking young and useless, anyway."

"He's a fantastic Capo."

"If you think so."

"I know he is," Tommas said calmly, refusing to feed into the rage brimming in Joel's eyes. "How he's managed to keep out of this entire war for the most part showcases exactly how good of a Capo that Adriano can be. Any man would give their left arm for a man who desires nothing more than peace on his streets and money in his boss's hand."

"I guess I don't see it the same way, old friend."

Joel was hitting his breaking point already. That was the thing about Joel Trentini. He could only pretend for so long, and then his anger diffused like a damn bomb.

"That leaves you with what?" Tommas asked. "Only your crew, huh?"

"Keep in mind that my territory dominates on shipping the products that the other territories sell, Tommas."

"And we'll pay accordingly for the privilege until we can figure something else out."

"That works for me," Joel said.

"What else is there?" Tommas asked.

Joel lifted a hand and gestured toward Abriella. "You asked for something at our last meeting. I've given it some consideration, and thought you might want to chat about it."

For a moment, Tommas' throat thickened at the possibility of what Joel might be talking about. It didn't help that his lover met his gaze from across the table with a deadness in her stare—something he'd never seen from her before. It was like for that brief second, she'd dropped from time because she didn't want to be there at all.

"A marriage?" Tommas asked.

Abriella wet her bottom lip and looked down at her lap. The muscles in her arms jumped like she was squeezing the purse in her lap for all she was worth.

"Yes," Joel confirmed. "If anything, it would guarantee a peace of sorts between us. Family and all that nonsense."

Nonsense was exactly what it was. Joel cared nothing for family or what the word meant. Family was only useful to him if he was capable of using it to hurt someone else or for his personal gain.

Tommas wanted Abriella more than anything.

God knew he would have her.

He would.

But first … first he needed to hurt her again. Hopefully, she would see this for what it had been, and she would understand. She would hopefully accept one last person's blood spilling to the ground for the sake of everyone else.

"I don't accept," Tommas said quietly.

Joel's head snapped up, confusion lighting up his features. "What?"

Abriella, wide-eyed and silent, watched Tommas with an understanding dawning as she glanced back and forth between her lap and her lover's face.

"Just as I said," Tommas replied with a confident smile. "I don't accept the offer of marriage. I don't feel it's necessary. There's nothing I want from Abriella that frankly, I haven't already gotten."

Abriella sucked in a hard breath. "Tommas, don't …"

Two words.

That was all it took for Tommas to confirm everything he'd been wondering for the last week and a half since he'd last talked to his lover. Her voice was raspy, and tired, like she hadn't been sleeping or talking all that much. There wasn't enough makeup in the world to hide the worry on her face, or the sadness in her frown.

"But I must say," Tommas drawled, standing from the table slowly, "… that I enjoyed every damn minute of what I was given from your sister."

Joel stood, too, his fists clenching hard at his sides. "You're admitting it then?"

"I have no reason to hide it."

"Her reputation, her safety?" Joel asked scathingly. "Did you consider that maybe my offer was a way to save her from shame?"

"Your offer is a way to lull me into a false sense of security, just like everything else has been, Joel. I'm not an idiot, but we'll do this the way you want. I'll let you think that this show of separating the Outfit is real. I'll walk out of here stupid in love, happy in my heart, and blind to whatever is it that you have planned next because you've handed her over to me. The one thing I want more than anything is Abriella away from you and happy with me. You think you're so much better at this game, but you're not. I am not an idiot. When something feels too good to be true, it usually is."

"You're wrong," Joel spat. "I would have done this, but you've proven to me that you're not ready for this war to be over."

"I am," Tommas said. "I am more than ready."

Abriella blinked up at Tommas from where she was still sitting. Her eyes had always spoken far louder than her mouth did, although she was never without something to say.

Crazy, her gaze screamed.

He was being crazy.

Didn't she already know?

Abriella had made him this way.

"Aren't you at all curious why no one around us seems shocked to find out that I was fucking your sister?" Tommas asked, smirking. "It's because most of them knew in one way or another, Joel. Don't you realize that both of your sisters played you for years?"

Abriella stood fast from the table, her anger burning into Tommas from feet away. "That's enough. Stop it."

"Why should I? Joel has done nothing for you, Ella, and even less for me. Joel thinks he knows everything there is to know about me, but actually, he knows very little." Tommas' gaze drifted to Abriella as he said, "He doesn't know that everything I do is for the only thing that I want. And for those who do know me, they will know exactly what that is, and they know that if not today, I will get what I want tomorrow."

Abriella was the only thing he had ever wanted, after all. She came with a whole list of amazing things, and a few terrible ones added on, too. He loved her all the same. A future with her also carried the weight of expectations, now, he knew. Things that Tommas hadn't given much thought to before—being a boss, for one.

She knew ...

Abriella had to know it was *always* for her.

Joel's hand smacked the table hard. "We're done, Tommas."

"We've been done for a long time, Joel. There's no real offer here. Whatever you were trying to do with me, whatever you had planned, is over."

"There was an offer," Abriella whispered.

Joel grabbed Abriella's arm and yanked hard. It took all that Tommas had inside his soul not to beat the man to death with his fists.

"Shut up," Joel hissed to his sister.

Abriella jerked from her brother's grasp with a glare. "There was an offer, and my choice just got easier."

"We're leaving right now."

"Then let's go," Abriella replied.

The moment Joel turned from the table, Tommas knew something was wrong. Abriella didn't move to follow her brother. Instead, she flipped open the clutch purse her father had handed over before the meeting. It drew Tommas' gaze down to her steady, delicate fingers wrapping around the butt of a small handgun.

Where had that come from?

Her father?

Why?

"Ella," Tommas said. "Ella, don't do that."

His voice was a breath.

Stunned, barely there, and not even heard.

Abriella pulled the gun out, lifted it, cocked back the hammer, and pulled the trigger. Tommas wasn't even sure if she aimed before she fired.

But the girl hit her mark.

The bullet entered the back of Joel's head just above the hair on his neckline. A soft, fleshy part of the head where the bullet could penetrate easier, and instantly hit the spinal cord. The small caliber handgun wasn't big enough to cause a major shock on impact, but Joel still let out a gasp a second before he fell forward.

Blood pooled.

Silence echoed.

Abriella lowered the weapon, and her hand began to tremble at the same time she let out a loud, broken, agonizing sob. The sound alone was enough to slice Tommas' heart open for her. She shouldn't have had to make that choice. She shouldn't have needed to hold that weapon or to pull the trigger.

Everyone seemed to move at once, charging for the woman with the gun and to the man on the floor. People from the outside flooded into the building at the sound of a gunshot going off. The roar of the new people entering the restaurant and trying to figure out what had happened was damn near deafening.

Tommas was already jumping over the table toward his lover. In the process, he knocked whoever was in his way to the ground. He didn't even care. Joel's fools would want to protect their boss, but it was probably too late.

He simply needed to protect Abriella.

"Ella!"

Abriella spun out of a man's grasp and pointed the gun again. Tommas slid an arm around her waist, pulled her back into him, and slipped the gun from her hand at the same time. He aimed it straight at the face of the fool who had come directly at Abriella. Almost everyone in the restaurant stilled the moment Tommas had control of the only weapon around.

His lover shook in his arms, like a little leaf ready to blow away in the wind.

"It's okay," Tommas whispered in her ear.

Not once did he drop his weapon from the face of the enforcer that had checked him earlier. Darryl was the guy's name. He looked after Abriella for Joel, too. No doubt, the man was close to Joel and loyal to him like nobody else.

Abriella sobbed again. "I'm sorry. I didn't know what he was gonna do, Tommy. I didn't know, but—"

"*Shhh*, baby. I got you, Ella. I'm always going to have you."

She quieted, but her trembling continued.

"This is done," Tommas said loud enough for every person standing frozen around him, unsure of what to do. "The fighting, this war, it is done. No more. Stop hurting people for your own agenda, and stop letting others use you for the same reason. Be better—we are better than this. No more blood, not in Chicago. I won't allow another drop to spill for this war."

"Aye," came a quiet call from the corner.

Adriano Conti.

"Aye."

Damian.

"Aye," echoed Theo DeLuca from the floor.

Tommas looked down at Theo. The man had been helping another man flip Joel over.

"He dead?" Tommas asked.

"Yeah," Theo confirmed.

Abriella made a pained, muffled sound that caught in her throat. Tommas held her tighter, feeling her body weaken under her own weight. She needed to get out of here. That gunshot had been terribly loud for such a small weapon. He wanted this meeting to stay under the radar of the cops and agents, but now it probably wouldn't. The restaurant was in a decent part of the city where the sound of gunshots wasn't common. The cops would be on their way soon.

"This is done." Tommas still hadn't lowered his weapon from Darryl.

"Done," the enforcer said quietly, but strained.

"Play the right cards," Tommas told the man, "and you'll get another day, man."

Darryl dropped his hands, empty with nothing to fight back, to his sides.

He was a stupid man to do it.

Tommas would have him killed before the night was out. Darryl had been too close to Joel, and Tommas knew some of the stuff that had been said to Abriella by the enforcer.

"D?" Tommas called.

"Right here, boss," Damian said, stepping around the men he'd brought along to the sit-down.

No one seemed to know what to do.

"We need to fix this and fast."

"I'll take her."

"No," Abriella said, looking back at Tommas with wide eyes. "I don't want to—"

Tommas, uncaring of those watching, pressed a kiss to her trembling lips to quiet her. "Go with Ghost. Please."

"But, *Tommy*."

Her tears welled, and his heart broke.

"I'm sorry," he said right before Damian grabbed Abriella's arm and pulled her away.

His lover was dragged from the restaurant to the stunned silence of everyone else.

When the door swung shut, Tommas said, "Is there any objections to my seat?"

No one said a thing.

He still had that goddamn gun, after all.

Outside, Tommas heard the screech of tires and the faint scream of sirens.

Shit.

Shit. Shit. *Shit*.

These men couldn't be here. Most of them were good, honorable men for the Outfit.

"Fucking *go*," Tommas barked. "Get out of here!"

He didn't have to say it again. His mind raced to catch up with what was happening as men started to scramble from the restaurant. Some went straight out the front, but most went out the back. Tommas' shoe slipped on a small puddle of blood, but he caught himself quickly as he turned to leave as well.

The sound of the door opening stopped him.

Behind him, Tommas found Peter Trentini waiting. The man held his hand out.

"Give it to me," Peter said.

Tommas held tighter to the gun, his one failsafe in that moment.

"Give me the gun, Tommas. She did the right thing, didn't she? My girl did the right thing."

"Yeah," Tommas said, confused and sad at the sight of the man's pain.

"I love my girls. Both of them. I'd do anything for them."

The confession came easily for Tommas. "I love her, too."

Peter laughed bleakly. "I know. Joel thought I was a fool, that I didn't know how to do anything. He treated me like it, too. This last week and a half, Ella didn't come around. She's been coming over to my wing ever since her mother was killed just to keep me company, make sure I was fed, and give me someone to talk to. I knew something was wrong when she stopped coming."

Tommas sucked in a deep breath; the air burned in his lungs.

"I logged onto the cameras for the house using the program the tech guys put in, and watched it all. I heard what Joel said to Ella about things."

"What things?"

"You, how he was going to use her to trick you into something, but he didn't really say what, and that he needed to make sure you didn't find out about it. He locked her in the wing upstairs, and took away all of her things. All week I've been watching her cry in the hallways. She just wants to be happy, Tommas."

God.

Tommas ached inside. "I know she does."

"Please make her happy."

"I will."

"And tell her I'm sorry."

Tommas didn't get the chance to respond. Peter had slowly moved closer to Tommas as the men talked until he was just a foot away, and snatched the gun from his hand. Turning fast on his heel, Peter ran for the front door. The blare of the sirens roared directly outside the restaurant and red and blue flashed in the windows. Peter pushed the door open and stepped outside, still holding the gun tightly in his palm.

What was he going to do?

"Put the gun down!"

The shout shocked Tommas. It came from a loud speaker somewhere outside.

Peter lifted the weapon and wrapped his finger around the trigger.

Tommas choked.

"Tell her I'm sorry, but Joel wouldn't have ever seen her coming," Peter said. "He expected you, Tommas, or someone else, but not her."

The gun would have Abriella's father's fingerprints on it, Tommas realized. Gunpowder residue, fresh from the weapon as it had just been shot, would be on his hands. A murder-suicide would be the headline. A vengeful father who blamed his son, maybe.

Peter had planned it all.

Sometimes, allies showed up in the most unlikely of places.

Knowing all of that didn't make it easier when Peter pulled the trigger, and the guns from the police answered him back.

CHAPTER EIGHTEEN

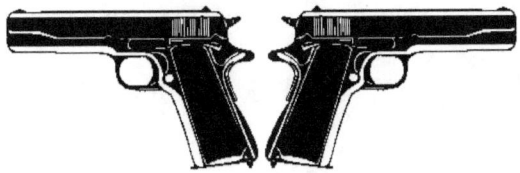

"**A**briella, are you okay?"

Blinking out of her daze, Abriella turned in the passenger seat to stare at Damian Rossi. The tight, grim set of the man's mouth spoke of his concern. He'd been mostly quiet ever since he shoved her into the car except to tell her that he was taking her home.

Where was home?

God knew the Trentini mansion certainly hadn't felt like home for a long, long time.

"Are you okay?" Damian asked again.

"Do you care?"

Damian's brow furrowed. "Why wouldn't I care?"

"I shot a man—it's over now. Why should you care how I feel about what I did?"

"Because that man was your brother."

Abriella glanced back out the window, a strange mix of sadness and confusion swirling around her heart and suffocating the very life out of each beat. She'd been so confused when her father brought her that small clutch outside the restaurant. She hadn't brought a clutch along, and she hadn't noticed her father with one in the car on the drive to the sit-down.

When she felt something hard in the purse during the dinner, and opened it up to find a small gun inside, Abriella knew right then what she needed to do.

Joel had forced her into confinement for a week and a half. He'd refused her access to her father, to a computer, or even a phone. The only thing she was left with for her time was herself, her thoughts, and her choices.

By the time the sit-down arrived, she still hadn't been able to choose.

Peter gave her another option.

"I didn't have a choice," Abriella whispered.

"To kill Joel?"

"Yeah."

"Someone else would have done it, I'm sure. No one is going to blame you for any wrong doing, as far as that goes. This has been a long time coming."

Damian was right.

Abriella knew it.

She wished that helped the odd guilt swimming in her veins, but it really didn't.

"He's still your brother," Damian said, softer than she had ever heard him speak. "You're allowed to grieve for him. Or rather, what you could have had with him, Ella."

Abriella hadn't thought of it that way. Maybe that was her problem; maybe that was the issue keeping her throat thick, her heart hurting, and her mind in a hazy bubble.

"It'll take a while, but that feeling you're experiencing will go away," Damian told her quietly.

"Will it?"

"Eventually."

Abriella stared down at her clenched fists resting in her lap. "Joel wanted me to make a choice this week. One was to be free, and the other was to free everyone else. Either way, he was going to take something from me, Damian."

"Tommas?"

"Yes."

"You made the right choice," Damian said.

"But it wasn't one of Joel's choices. That was a choice that was given to me last minute and it was out of my brother's control. And it hurts ... in here," Abriella said, pointing at her heart. "Because out of Joel's options, I didn't know which one to choose. I couldn't make the choice."

"Ella, maybe you couldn't choose because they weren't really options for you. It was never a matter of what you would do, but how you wouldn't do it. Do you understand what I'm saying?"

"No."

Damian frowned. "Maybe when you wake up tomorrow with Tommas by your side, and the freedom that was offered in your hand, it'll make more sense."

God.

Abriella hoped so.

"Damn, Tommas, it took you long enough," Damian growled the second he answered his ringing cell phone.

Abriella had just kicked off her heels and dropped the clutch she was still holding on the floor. She spun fast on her heel at the sound of her lover's name, wanting to know where he was, what had happened, or … anything.

She just needed *anything*.

"Where is he?" Abriella demanded.

Damian held a finger high, silently asking for her to be quiet. "Yeah, man, I'll call the lawyer and get him down there for you."

Oh, God.

A lawyer?

She had heard the police sirens before Damian dragged her away and drove off, but she had stupidly hoped that was just her mind making up things. Apparently not. This was a problem Tommas, and the Outfit, didn't need.

Even worse, what about her?

She held the gun, she shot it, and Tommas had taken it from her.

"He's … dead?" Damian asked, shooting Abriella a wary look.

"What?"

Damian turned his back to her. "So, they're just holding you for nothing because Peter—"

Something made Damian stop talking.

Then, Damian said, "What do you want me to … Yeah, okay. I'll get the lawyer down there, and I'll come, too."

Once the phone call ended, Damian spun back around to face Abriella. A solemn, dark sadness colored the man's features. Abriella's stomach instantly felt heavier and sicker than it had the entire day. Damian's face was a mask of apology—like his next words would cut her deep, and he didn't want to do it.

"Ella, I have to tell you something," Damian said slowly.

The numbness from earlier settled back into her nervous system again. Her body and mind wanted to protect itself, and Abriella didn't blame her reaction a bit. Nothing about this day had been easy. It only seemed to get worse at every turn.

Why should this be any different?

"Where is Tommas?" Abriella asked.

"The police are holding him, but they don't have much of a reason to. The scene was pretty clear when they went in, and I guess Peter wiped the gun down enough to erase what was left other than his fingerprints. They're holding Tommas because they want to get as much information from him on what was going on in the restaurant before the shooting, and why Joel is dead."

Abriella didn't understand. "My dad? He wasn't in the restaurant."

"He was after," Damian replied gently.

Her heart clenched painfully.

"So, he's at the police station, too?"

"No."

"But—"

"He took the gun from Tommas after the place cleared out," Damian interrupted, stepping closer to Abriella with his hands outstretched like she might run. "The cops were outside, just a couple of cars at first. He pulled the gun on them."

"No," Abriella mumbled, moving backwards.

"I'm sorry, Ella."

"No. My dad wasn't in the restaurant, Damian. He wasn't! He was outside waiting in the car."

"Your dad gave you the purse outside the restaurant. I watched him do it. The purse had the gun in it. He planned this, Ella. He knew how this was going to end. I'm sorry."

"You're wrong," Abriella said, her voice breaking on the final word. "He wouldn't do that to me and Alessa."

They had already lost their mother.

Peter wouldn't leave them, too.

"He did," Damian said. "I'm sorry."

No.

Abriella's heart might as well have fell from her chest and shattered across the foyer of the Trentini mansion. Her pain came rushing out of her lungs in a sob that echoed as she tripped backwards, and caught herself on an end table.

Why her father?

She loved him.

"But …. b-but …"

Abriella couldn't make the words form. Her throat constricted over and over, catching her grief and sobs as the tears stung her eyes. This was not how it was supposed to be. She didn't make the choice given to her so that something else—someone she loved—could be taken away.

It wasn't supposed to be a give and take.

"This isn't right," Abriella mumbled, staring at Damian through watery eyes.

"I … I'm so sorry," Damian said lamely. "I have to go and get Tommas his lawyer. I'll have Lily come over, maybe she can get Eve and your sister, too."

"Just go," Abriella forced herself to say.

Her pain was enough.

It was too much.

She was breaking apart at the seams, and she didn't want anyone else to see it. For the last week and a half, her days and nights had been spent in a perpetual head game that she played alone. She tried, failing miserably, to figure out what her brother was planning, and how it all might end.

Abriella had made the right choice.

She chose to let Tommas win.

She still lost.

The sound of the front door closing vaguely registered to Abriella's overloaded senses. It was only then that she realized Damian had left.

Her fingers tightened and loosened around the edge of the decorative table she held onto. Her legs acted as if they were going to give out on her at any second. When her stomach threatened to revolt from the churning sensation tying her up in knots, she barely managed to keep the bile down.

Abriella's heart and soul screamed out for people that weren't there. People who comforted her, who had loved her, and would always protect her.

Her mother.

Her father.

Tommas.

She could have him now, couldn't she?

Freedom wasn't free.

This life came with a cost.

Abriella had paid far too much for hers.

Anger and agony rushed Abriella's gut in a wave of hot lava. She swept the pictures and knickknacks from the table in one fell swoop, screaming her rage and sadness to an empty house.

It would *always* be empty now.

The sounds of shattering glass as the picture frames broke on the floor soothed her inner war for a moment, but it wasn't enough. She grabbed the first thing she could, a painting on the wall of her great-grandfather, and ripped it down to throw it on the floor.

This house had been raised and kept in a swamp of lies. Manipulation, control, and shifting power had been a game they all played. It had started a long time ago, when her mother made an honest mistake, and then paid dearly for it.

It was over.

But it still made Abriella so goddamn mad.

And *agonized.*

God, the pain.

She wanted to feel better, so she grabbed the next thing on the wall and tore it down, too. She tossed pictures from the hallway onto the floor, destroying memories that weren't entirely true, and pictures of men whose greed had ruined so many lives.

This was their fault.

They made her choose, not just Joel.

Shouting and crying her anger for no one to hear, Abriella tore through the wing of the mansion that had been her gilded cage for far too long. She let every broken picture frame, every ruined piece of history, hit the ground like the trash it was.

She could start over, after all.

She could be better tomorrow.

She could be free with Tommas.

It was worth it.

The price was worth it.

Right?

Quiet murmurings from outside of the living room woke Abriella. Sitting up on the couch, an Afghan blanket fell around her waist. She hadn't covered up before passing out. She'd broke the lock on the liquor cabinet after she trashed a few more family heirlooms and pictures, drank a bit of bourbon, and promptly drifted off to sleep quickly after.

But she hadn't covered up.

"Thank you for coming over," Abriella heard a familiar voice say out in the hallway.

Tommas.

"Of course," said someone else.

Lily.

"We'll be back tomorrow afternoon," said another.

Evelina.

"And we'll bring Alessa," Lily added quickly.

"Adriano demanded she stay home, just in case something went crazy," Tommas explained. "I don't blame him. I'm sure she'll want to come over tomorrow with you, but maybe let Abriella have some time to herself. She needs to … I don't know."

"Absorb things," Evelina said quietly. "I know the feeling."

"Me, too," Lily agreed. "But she's the toughest one of us all, Tommas. Give her some credit."

Tommas laughed. "I have always given Abriella her dues, believe me. You'll both make it home all right?"

"I called Theo to come get me," Evelina said.

"Damian said I could drive my car home," Lily said. "He's … out, I guess. He didn't tell me where he was."

"Thank you for coming, really. I'll make sure Abriella gives you both a call. For now, just stay quiet, let this mess blow over, and then I'm sure she would love to have her friends close."

"Absolutely."

"Sure," Evelina agreed.

Abriella listened as the footsteps faded down the hallway. She was surprised that her friends had come over, and had stayed with her, yet she hadn't noticed a thing and slept through it all.

Pushing off the couch, Abriella padded out of the living room and down the hall. She made her way to the front of the house just in time to see Tommas shut the front door. With a sigh, her lover pressed his palm on the door, and leaned forward like a weight had just fallen on his shoulders.

Still … he seemed calmer than he ever had before.

Like it was over.

The war, the fighting, the blood … *over.*

Just like that.

Tommas dug in his pocket, pulled out a cell phone, and hit a number. Putting the phone to his ear, he didn't turn around as he waited the call out.

"Hey, Ghost," Tommas said. "Where are you at?"

Abriella knew she should probably turn around and leave him to his private conversation, but she didn't want to. Being closer was better, especially after the day they had.

"Good," Tommas replied to whatever Damian had said. "I need you to finish him out tonight—Darryl, I mean. He was working something with Joel, I know he was. I don't know what, but it doesn't matter. Loyalty is what it is, right?"

Swallowing the lump forming in her throat, Abriella leaned against the wall and wished the sudden coldness in her bones would leave. It didn't.

"Check around his place a bit and maybe see if there's anything that'll explain what Joel was up to," Tommas continued, oblivious to Abriella's presence. "Give me a call if anything comes up. The official side of things is going to be hot and heavy on us for a while, especially with me being here at Abriella's place. I don't care, but we might as well expect it. I have to stay quiet for a bit, maybe a week. Keep an eye on shit for me … Yeah, and besides, she needs me more."

"All right, later, man," he finished.

Tommas ended the call, shoved the phone back into his pocket, and spun on his heel. Abriella waved two fingers the moment his gaze landed on her quiet form.

"Hey," she whispered.

Tommas smiled an honest, brilliant sight. It quickly faded. "You trashed this place."

"How do you know I did it?"

"Because it screams of you, baby. You've been angry for so long, Abriella. Bottling it up, keeping tabs, and marking the score of everyone's wrongs around you. Eventually that has to come out, sweet girl. It's never pretty when it does. Inside your heart and deep in your soul, you've been like black ice waiting to kill somebody when they slipped on you."

She flinched at his choice of words.

"It just … hurt," Abriella said lamely.

Tommas nodded. "Your dad?"

"And Joel a little. My whole family mostly. Everything, Tommy."

"I love you, Ella."

Abriella glanced down at the floor. "I wanted to choose you."

"What?"

The pain and confusion of the last week and a half locked up in a wing of the Trentini mansion came spilling out of Abriella in a rush of words. She explained what her brother had told her, the options he gave, and what had followed. She told Tommas how she cried, how she felt like she had failed, and the final choice that came at the last moment.

"I wanted to choose you," Abriella repeated, "but Joel didn't give me a choice that would leave me you, Tommy. And then when my dad did, and I realized what he wanted me to do, it was so fucking easy, like breathing. Just pull the trigger and it'll be done. I got you, and everyone else gets peace. For a split second, it was easy."

"But it's not easy," Tommas said gently.

Abriella shook her head. "No."

"I'm sorry, baby."

"My dad …?"

Tommas dipped his head down. "Desperate men are dangerous men, Ella."

Was that how Tommas had been for all these years?

Desperate. Craving. Without.

A pain settled deep in Abriella's chest. She pressed her hand over her heart, willing it to go away, and needing it to stop.

"God," she mumbled, "I don't want to feel like this."

Tommas glanced up as he took a few steps forward, closer to her. "Like what?"

"Aching in my heart. When I was angry and breaking things, it went away. When I was screaming and crying, I was distracted."

"And when you drank a quarter of a bottle of bourbon?"

"I was numb."

Jesus.

A quarter of a bottle?

Why wasn't she still drunk?

"What time is it?" Abriella asked.

Tommas frowned. "Five in the morning."

Time just slipped through her fingers.

"When will the police be coming here?"

"Soon," Tommas answered. "For your father's death and your brother's. For you, however, they'll need nothing. No one knows you were there. No one will say a thing. It looked pretty clear about what had happened. Your father shot Joel, his fingerprints were all over the gun, his hands were full of gunpowder residue because he fired the weapon at police, and he got himself killed in a shootout. No one is looking at you."

But they should.

She was guilty.

"Ella?" Tommas asked.

She stared up at him, realizing he'd come to stand right in front of her. His hand came up to graze her cheek with the softest touch.

It was still enough to light a fire on her skin.

In her soul, she was calmed for a moment. In her heart, she was at home. Only Tommas had ever done that for her.

"I still hurt," Abriella told him.

Tommas nodded. "It'll get better in a while."

"I don't want to feel like this right now with you."

"Then you don't have to."

Abriella didn't get to ask why or what he meant. Without warning, Abriella found herself wrapped in Tommas' warm, strong embrace. A blink of time later, and his mouth was crushing down on hers with a wicked intent.

She wondered if this was the right time.

Shouldn't she let herself wallow for what she had done?

Shouldn't they ...

Abriella decided she didn't care when Tommas' tongue swept the seam of her lips, demanding more. When he wanted something from her, she always gave it to him. Allowing Tommas entrance to the heat of her mouth, he wasted no time claiming it with nips of his teeth to her bottom lip before his tongue tangled with hers. His hand slipped into her hair and grabbed tight at the nape of her neck, holding her in place.

With every bite of his teeth, she felt better. With every sweep of his lips, she was hotter. With every strike of his tongue, her pain was forgotten.

"Oh, my God," Abriella breathed when Tommas began a trek down her neck.

His lips kissed a burning path over her skin.

Promising.

Sweet.

Need.

She *needed* this man.

Abriella's head fell back, and her body sang the harder Tommas' hands held her. He knew what she needed without asking, and he was giving it to her.

"More," Abriella demanded, tugging on Tommas' hair to make him look at her.

His heated gaze met hers, and in that one second, Abriella was lost and found at the same time. Tommas was capable of making her forget, taking her to the greatest heights, and grounding her with just a look.

Nothing more.

"I love you," Abriella whispered.

"I've always known you loved me, Ella."

"I've not told you nearly enough."

"You have the rest of your life to make up for it, sweet girl."

She did.

Abriella had a feeling it would take a while for that fact to really sink in.

Suddenly, Tommas was pulling at her dress until it was flying up over her head and somewhere on the floor. The cool temperature of the house wrapped her skin in a soft touch, pebbling her flesh until Tommas' hands soothed it away.

Abriella ignored the mess still on the floor from her earlier tantrum as Tommas dropped to his knees, pulling her underwear down with him. Her breath caught in her chest when his fingers grazed the soft lips of her sex with a ghost of a touch.

"You're so hot under my fingers," Tommas murmured, his voice a husky drawl.

A shiver worked its way down Abriella's spine. "Am I?"

"Mmm, yes. Hot, smooth, and wet, baby."

Abriella widened her legs enough for his hand to slip in between easily. Two of his fingers swept her folds from her entrance to her clit, firmer than his first touch. It was enough that his digits pressed a little into her sex, promising what was yet to come.

"Very wet," Tommas noted, letting his now slippery fingers circle her clit teasingly.

She rocked into his hand, needing his touch. The more he worked her, the hotter she would get until she couldn't take it anymore. Tommas' fingers pinched her clit without warning, making Abriella moan loudly.

The sting of his pinch made her want to come.

"And needy," Tommas said, chuckling.

"You did this to me, you know."

"I like you like this, Ella. Wanting my dirty words, needing my cock pounding into your tight little pussy, and never knowing when you've had enough. I love you like this, baby. Love you when you're on your back, your knees, or any way in between. Love it when you let me fuck you until your throat is raw from screaming, and you're pussy is sore and soaked with us. It's always been the hottest, the most fucking perfect thing I have ever seen."

"Ever?" she asked.

"Ever," he confirmed, dragging his digits through her folds again.

Slowly, Tommas eased his fingers into her clenching pussy, keeping his gaze up on her all the while. Abriella practically fell onto his hand, rolling her hips into his touch to get more. She needed him deeper, filling, stretching, and fucking her until this awful day was over and she didn't have to go back.

"What do you want, hmm?" Tommas asked, leaning forward to kiss her bare thigh.

"I want you to make me scream until my throat is raw, fuck me all night, and put me to bed when I can't hold my own weight up anymore."

Tommas smirked a sexy sight. "That's quite a list."

"It's a reasonable one. I don't ask for more."

"True."

Abriella trembled as his fingers worked her pussy hard with deep, quick thrusts. Tommas would press into her wet, tight walls every so often, like he was reminding her that he knew the exact spot to make her come in seconds if he wanted to. She could hear the sound of her wet pussy sucking in his fingers, and she could smell the tartly sweet aroma of her own arousal wafting upwards.

Staring down at her lover, watching him so enraptured with her pleasure he was creating, Abriella realized something. She didn't have to hide him anymore. They didn't have to play pretend on safe weekends, run between apartments for an hour of time together, or act like they weren't totally and completely in love with one another.

It released every bit of worry and pain in her heart.

All of it was gone.

"Come on, Ella," Tommas urged, his teeth scraping her thigh as he spoke. "Your pussy is so tight, baby, fucking me damn good. I want your come on my fingers before I drag you down to this floor and fuck you just the way you like."

"Like your dirty little slut."

Her words came out as a breathless, shaking whisper.

His fingers worked her harder, scissoring on the withdrawal and curling on the thrust. He was going to make her come fast and rough, like his touch.

Tommas' grin deepened into something wicked. "But I love you that way, Ella. Nobody else gets to see you like that, or have you begging for their cock to fuck you until you see stars while their fingers are knuckle deep in your ass. Nobody but me gets to leave bite marks on your body. Just me, sweet girl. You've only ever been mine."

He was so right, it was scary.

It was wonderful, too.

"There, Tommy," Abriella mumbled. "I'm right there …"

Tommas' fingers dug into her inner thigh. "This is mine, Ella, so fucking give it to me or I'll take it from you."

She came with a loud whine, her body uncoiling with release as pleasure licked up her spine, stabbed in her womb, and sparks flew behind her lids. She nearly sobbed her way through the orgasm, it felt that fucking good. She had needed it so bad that once it was raging through her bloodstream, she couldn't feel anything else.

She barely even felt Tommas' fingers leave her sex.

The sound of shuffling fabric resounded in the background of her dazed thoughts, while her vision was hazy from unshed tears.

Then, Abriella was being pulled away from the wall and pushed on the floor without a word. Broken items and clothes were pushed aside as Tommas rolled Abriella to her back. His nakedness covered her form heavily, taking away her breath again.

His hands held her face while his mouth descended on hers. His second kiss wasn't like the first—it was softer, sweeter, and he took his time loving her mouth with his own. The coolness of the floor soothed the war heating up her body.

The darkened blue of Tommas' gaze pinned her on the floor as he pushed up and hovered over her.

"Thank you for choosing me," Tommas murmured.

Abriella blinked, letting the tears gathering in the corners of her eyes fall from her lids. "All I had to do was find a way."

"I know, baby."

"I still don't want to feel right now," she admitted.

"You don't have to."

"Make it stay away, Tommy."

His fingers traced her lips. "Only for a short while."

"It's enough."

He hooked her legs around his waist, and positioned the head of his cock at her slit. Abriella tilted her hips up, feeling the tip of his member fill her entrance with just enough of him to make her crave more. Her body reacted to anything he gave, whenever he gave it to her. With a press of her heels to his back, his hips flexed forward and his cock buried deep into her soaked, tender sex.

Tommas' hands grabbed her inner thighs and pushed her legs wide until her muscles burned. She shook under the weight and pain, still wanting more.

"Ask me for it," Tommas whispered.

Abriella arched off the floor, a delicious coil tightening in her stomach. "Fuck me good."

"And hard."

"So deep, Tommy. I want to feel it in my fucking bones. *Please.*"

Abriella didn't get a warning before her lover started a pace that drove her body into the floor with every thrust. Tommas' hand found her throat, and grabbed tight enough to make her eyes fly open to find him watching her from up above. She loved his hands on her neck, holding her still and keeping her stare on only him while he fucked her.

Tommas didn't show her mercy when he took her like this. It was brutal between them with her fingernails cutting into his wrist, her teeth biting into her lip, and his hands holding her down while he fucked her like she was a damned animal for his taking.

A mate.

The one perfect, forever person in the world meant just for her.

Nobody had to understand them.

She only wanted him.

Swallowing her emotions, and taking in the sensations of being filled, stretched, and fucked to yet another completion, Abriella gasped for air. She took in the smell of her lover, the feeling of the cold floor bruising her back, and the orgasm building.

Tommas' muscles jumped under her touch, and his eyes blazed with lust and love.

"Don't you want this again?" Ella asked, taunting him. "Don't you want to make me come again?"

He laughed darkly.

"It's all mine anyway, girl."

"Then make me give it to you, Tommy."

Abriella felt him pull from her body a second before she was flipped over to her knees. There was glass shards on the floor and a mess all around them. Her palms slipped and scraped. Pain walked with bliss. Like Tommas always had done with her, he didn't treat her like a china doll. Tommas' hands pressed to her shoulders and forced her upper body on the floor while her ass was high. She couldn't move.

She loved it.

All she needed was his cock driving into her again and she would fly. Before he started pounding into her again, she felt the tips of his fingers, the ones he'd used to fuck her with, press into the tight hole of her ass. Abriella sucked in a sharp whine as his fingers sunk into her ass, pushing past the tight ring of muscles and making her burn all over.

Then, he started fucking her. Filling her pussy and her ass at the same time. Stretching her open and using her for what he wanted, for what his body needed. Abriella knew by the end of it, she would have what she needed, too.

"Your ass is fucking beautiful, Ella, but it needs to be a little redder."

Abriella's moan melted into a shuddering cry when his palm slapped down across her ass hard. It was followed by another harder, faster swat. Her skin burned with a sweet sting.

It was pain.

It was dirty.

It was fucking bliss.

"Take it from me, Tommy," Abriella begged.

His fist curled into her hair, pulling hard. His cock pounded into her harder, making her knees scrape against the floor. There were security cameras on them. They were in full view of the mansion's large front bay windows.

She didn't give a single fuck.

How could she?

Tommas' whispers of *come on my cock, girl* and *make me fucking come, Ella* as he fucked her like that's all she was good for and it's all she needed were the only things she could hear and think about. It was the only thing she cared about.

Pleasure raged. It stabbed through her body until she couldn't breathe, her throat was raw from crying out and calling his name. Her orgasm went on and on, like it wasn't going to fucking end.

Then, he was pulling on her hair harder.

"Ask me for it," Tommas demanded.

Abriella sucked in a breath. *"Please."*

"Ask me."

"Give it to me, please."

She knew it was coming. His loss of control. The shake in his hand tangled in her hair and the groan in his throat.

"Make me fucking come," Tommas growled out.

"Please give it to me, Tommy."

A few more strokes was all he needed. She could tell by the tension in his muscles and the way he grunted his words. His groan was thick, drawn out, and rumbling straight from his chest.

"Jesus, Ella ... *baby* ... Christ."

Then he was pulling out, and his come painted her back in warm, thick streams.

Her pain was gone instantly. Her thoughts were lost.

All she felt was him on her body.

He'd used her dirty, on a floor of broken memories.

And that was exactly what she needed.

"Get dressed," Tommas said.

Abriella glanced up from the mug of coffee she was hugging to her chest. In a too-large sweater and leggings, she was huddled in the corner of the couch, watching reruns and ignoring phone calls.

She'd done her thing, talked to police, kept a low profile, and everything else that was asked of her. She planned two funerals, made face to bury her father and brother a week after they had died, and didn't say a bad word about either.

Abriella just wanted to hide away for a little bit longer.

Tommas was at her side every step of the way.

"What?" Abriella asked.

Tommas lifted his wrist and checked his watch. "It's seven. You need to get dressed."

It was only then that Abriella noticed her lover was dressed in a suit that hugged his fit frame perfectly and made him look all the more sexy. He looked fit for the position he had taken over in the Outfit as the boss of the operation. Tommas had always looked the part, but the years of learned confidence and his current happiness radiated off him and made it all the more apparent.

How was this man hers?

It was something entirely different to wake up to this man day after day. It didn't feel new, if that made sense. It simply seemed like Tommas had filled the hole in Abriella's life that she always knew was missing.

Surreal, yes, but lovely.

"For what?" Abriella asked.

"It's Sunday."

"So?"

"Church," Tommas clarified.

Abriella opened her mouth to argue, but his raised hand stopped her before she could get a word in edgewise.

"Before you start," Tommas said, "you should consider something."

"Like what?"

"Like the fact I have to do certain things because of who I am now, Ella. I have to go to church, talk to my men, see their families, and go to dinner when I am invited. I have let you hide away for two weeks and do whatever it was that you needed to feel better, and get back to yourself. You're my girl, and I really need you to start realizing that and show everyone else that you know who and what you are to me."

Abriella's brow furrowed. "But … it's just church."

"It's more than church. It's us being together outside of a home. It's not hiding because of a few older generation of people are whispering about what's been going on between us for years. It's a sign of solidarity and happiness, Ella."

"You make it sound like we're married or something."

Tommas quieted instantly.

Oh.

Shit.

The boss needs a wife.

She should have known that was what Tommas was dancing around. It was a long standing tradition in Italian based mafia families that the men who ran the organization be married. It was believed that a woman settled a man in a way that a single man couldn't be. It looked good for the public, and *la famiglia* as well.

Wildness was frowned upon in a boss. Standards was praised in one.

Tommas had earned his spot, he was both feared and respected, but he still had things to make it final. Things like marrying an appropriate wife.

Abriella cleared her throat, and stood from the couch. "We're not married, Tommy. Taking me out and showing me off as your significant other is only going to make people talk. And not necessarily in a good way after all that's happened."

"Actually, I look at it like this is a way for me to show off the woman I intend to be my wife."

Maybe it was the fact that Abriella had always felt like her relationship with Tommas would be a stain on both their names, and that was why she hadn't ever thought so far ahead. She had never assumed that the role of being his wife would be hers even though she had wanted it for years.

"There's never been anyone but you, Ella," Tommas said as if he could read her mind.

"I don't want people to talk about you or me."

"Let them. It's not their choice."

Abriella laughed. "Oh?"

"No. I'm the damned boss, Ella. It's all about me now."

Her smile bloomed instantly. "And me, apparently."

Tommas shrugged. "You don't really need me to say that, do you? You already know—"

"Everything you do is for me. I do know, Tommy."

"Then get dressed. Pastels, I think. It's church, but you don't have to look like you're at a fucking funeral again. I love you in light colors. It reminds me of spring, beauty, and young life."

"Does it?"

Tommas smiled. "It reminds me of you."

Her heart swelled.

Yeah, this man was totally hers.

Abriella glanced at the clock. "We might be a little late."

"Good. I love making an entrance."

CHAPTER NINETEEN

The sermon dedicated to forgiveness of past transgressions, and moving on to a beautiful tomorrow felt incredibly fitting for a portion of the people gathered in the pews. At Tommas' side, Abriella sat quiet with her eyes drawn down to the sympathy card in her hand. Another three rested on her lap.

He smiled as she flipped the card open and read the scrawled words inside.

We're so sorry for your loss.
Love,
Theo & Eve

It was a simple card, but Tommas knew it was significant to his lover. Someone had thought about her, several people, actually. The other cards came from Alessa and Adriano, and Lily and Damian. His girl had been so distant for the last couple of weeks.

Tommas grabbed her hand in his and pulled it into his side where he could hold a piece of her close. His affection and love for Abriella wasn't a secret, but it was Tommas' choice of how much of his adoration that others would get to see.

In a way, he wanted to shout his possession and jealousy to the world and make sure every man knew that Abriella was his and stayed away. But on the other hand, he knew that he didn't really have to do any of that at all.

She was already his.

People knew it.

Let them assume what they wanted.

Tommas didn't care.

"I love you, *bella mia*," Tommas murmured in Abriella's ear.

Her smile was a sweet, honest sight.

"I know you do."

"Don't forget it."

"I won't, but you might. You're thirty, Tommy. Your age might start catching up to you."

Faking a half-growl, Tommas lifted Abriella's hand and brought it to his mouth in what looked like a kiss. Gently, he nipped her skin with his teeth, warning her silently.

"Nasty," she said.

"Very," he replied. "No jokes about my age."

"It's all in how you feel, right?"

Tommas didn't know how to answer that question. In his mind, he felt decades and decades older than what he really was. He'd seen enough, done enough, and felt enough to be two-hundred instead of almost thirty-one. But in his heart, he was young enough to believe that there was always hope for something better, and that the darkness of a person's past didn't have to color the light in their future.

"I think," Tommas murmured, drawing Abriella closer to him in the pew, "… that how you see yourself is what's more important, Ella."

"So … you're saying that you feel old."

"Stop it."

"Do you?"

"No. How could I when you remind me what it's like to be twenty-two with your whole life ahead of you, just waiting for you make a choice?"

Abriella's hand tightened in his. "That's an interesting way of looking at things."

"I try."

Subtly, Abriella glanced around at the people in the pews surrounding theirs. A good portion of the Outfit families had come to attend the Sunday Mass. Some, like Abriella and Tommas, talked quietly amongst themselves, while others focused in on the priest still delivering his words of hope and compassion.

"Everyone seems happy," Abriella noted.

"They are."

And he wanted to keep them that way.

Tommas took the chance to gage the people around them like Abriella had done. While the couple had shown up twenty minutes late to Mass, a seat in the very front pew had been saved for them without question. Down from Tommas' left, he found Damian and Lily sitting quietly together. As usual, Damian had a hand resting on his wife's rounded stomach, keeping a proverbial eye on his unborn son, while his other was on his wife. Lily was only a couple of months away from her due date.

A new generation for their families would soon be born.

Just behind Damian was Theo and Evelina. The couple didn't look entirely interested in being at church, but they did seem happy to be together.

A tap on Tommas' shoulder had him looking behind to find Adriano.

"Hey, boss," Adriano said quietly.

Beside the man sat his very pregnant, tired wife. Alessa was a week over her due date, as far as Tommas understood. That couldn't be fun for the young woman.

"Yes?" Tommas asked.

"Plans still the same after church?"

Tommas nodded. "Of course."

"Just checking."

Adriano rested back in the pew without another word. Tommas turned back to stare at the priest, knowing that likely no one had given the quick conversation with his Capo a second thought.

Tommas smiled.

His Capo.

It had only been a couple of weeks since Tommas took the seat as the boss of the Outfit, but occasionally, it still sneaked up on him and surprised him all the same. At the same time, taking responsibility for *la famiglia* meant something far more to Tommas.

He was responsible for these people.

He needed to protect them.

Hopefully, after today, he could do that for at least one aspect of problems their families had been facing. The police and FBI attention had been a little much. Tommas still had two particular detectives that just wouldn't back the hell off. If he considered all of the issues the two detectives had caused for him and Abriella over the last little while, he figured they deserved everything they were going to get.

"At least we don't have to worry about someone's car blowing up when the service is over," Abriella said.

Tommas didn't respond. He figured she meant it hypothetically, but recent past events made it all a little too raw for him.

"Lily invited you to dinner later, right?" Tommas asked.

Abriella shrugged. "Yeah, but—"

"Go, enjoy yourself. You've been hiding away for two weeks. It's time to get back to normal, Ella."

"Nothing is really normal, Tommy. It can't be."

"You can have a new normal," he said softly.

"As long as it includes you."

Tommas smirked. "It sure as hell isn't going to include anyone else."

"No swearing in church, Tommas. My God."

Pressing his lips together tightly to keep from laughing, Tommas simply shook his head. "Whatever you say, my little rebel queen."

Abriella scowled. "Don't say that, either."

"But you are."

"Keep it up."

Tommas chuckled. "You're so sexy when you're angry."

Abriella smiled. "And I bet you're sexy when you sleep alone."

Oh. Damn.

Well, then …

"You win," Tommas said, letting his lover have the battle.

Abriella put her head on his shoulder. "I always do."

"Where are you planning on living after this?" Adriano asked.

Damian laughed in the driver's seat as he passed a lighter back to Theo. "Same place he's been living for the last two weeks."

"Thanks," Theo said, snatching the lighter.

"Don't stub the cigarette in the back. I'd like to return this damn thing without anyone noticing I took it for a spin."

"You still owe me a new car," Theo muttered around the cigarette in his mouth.

Tommas eyed Theo beside him. "I'm surprised Eve doesn't tell you those things are bad for you."

"She does. I pretend like I don't hear her."

"But you do," Tommas pressed.

Theo smirked. "Sure, but it helps with the stress."

"You had massive heart surgery a couple of months ago," Damian pointed out. "Cigarettes was not on the list of what you should be doing, Theo."

"Hey, when I pay you to babysit my ass, then I'll give a shit about your opinions," Theo said.

"Enough bickering, Jesus," Tommas mumbled, rubbing at his forehead. "D, you could have stolen a bigger car. This is ridiculous. I feel like I'm in a fucking sardine can."

"Truth," Adriano agreed. "Who drives these little hatchbacks, anyway?"

"Green people," Theo said. "Whatever that means."

"Would you shut up?" Damian growled. "It was the easiest to take because the people are gone for a week. You didn't want to be in a noticeable, recognizable car. This piece of shit does the job, Tommas."

Laughing, Tommas conceded to his cousin's points. That didn't mean he liked having his knees driving into his chest because the back seat was so small.

"Oh, here we go …" Damian said, trailing off with a nod down the street.

Parked where they were in a driveway down the block, their car with dark tinted windows wouldn't be noticeable. It probably looked like any person's car.

Tommas found who Damian had mentioned quickly enough. Down the street, a familiar unmarked, black cop car pulled into the driveway of Tommas' home.

"So, you're going to be living at the mansion?" Adriano asked.

"Why not? It belongs to Abriella," Tommas said.

"Yeah, but you have a house."

Tommas chuckled. "Not for long."

"You checked it all out, right?" Damian asked.

"Yep," Tommas confirmed. "Seems Darryl had a job to do leading up to the day of the sit-down with Joel. That little search you did in his apartment the night you killed him gave me everything I needed to know, D."

"Good."

Tommas had taken a special care to stay the hell away from his house ever since Damian took Darryl out. Apparently, Joel's enforcer had left Tommas a nice little gift in his foyer that would leave a nasty mess once the front door was open.

"I'd been staying at the apartment," Tommas said, sighing heavily. "I had Nate watching my car and the apartment instead of the house. I didn't think Joel would be brave enough to try something on my house like that right out in the open. Maybe I did know, but I was too busy being stupid."

"Hey," Theo said, catching Tommas' gaze. "You finished it out, Tommas. Everybody's fucking safe, they're happy. There's nothing wrong with that."

Maybe not.

Tommas had still come terribly close to losing his life.

"Nonetheless," Tommas murmured, shrugging, "I'll make an anonymous phone call to the police tomorrow, telling them to check Darryl's apartment. There's a dead body that still hasn't been found, after all. Plus, all that evidence leading straight to—"

"Be quiet ... look," Damian said.

Tommas watched the detectives stroll across the driveway and climb the front steps of Tommas' home. Delog and Crown had no idea what was waiting for them. Tommas suspected blame would be on him for a short while, at least until the evidence in Darryl's apartment was found along with the man's dead body. Direct information and instructions had been sent in emails between Darryl and Joel for the enforcer to set the bomb in Tommas' townhome the day of the sit-down.

"Are you going to miss the house at all, boss?" Adriano asked.

Tommas leaned back in the seat, considering the young Capo's words. "No."

"Why not?"

"It was never really home."

Damian caught Tommas' gaze in the mirror, a knowing glint burning behind the man's eyes. No, the house had never felt like home, but Tommas did have one that was. His apartment across town where he had spent years hiding his relationship with Abriella had become his safe haven, the protector of his secret love and truths.

No matter what, Tommas would keep the apartment. He could live in the Trentini mansion with Abriella for their entire lives, until the day he was dead and gone, but that apartment would still be there for the weekends his girl wanted to get away, or for the dinner dates that ended early and home just … wasn't close enough.

"Darryl left the door unlocked, right?" Tommas asked when the detective knocked again.

"Yep," Damian said.

"I told the fools to just come on in if I didn't answer. I said I might be down in basement or something."

Theo laughed. "Do you think they told anyone that they were going to meet up with you?"

"Nope," Tommas replied, sure of that fact. "I made it clear I wanted to talk, but I wasn't going to do it on the record or in an official capacity right away. They're desperate, and they've done desperate things already, so they bit at the chance to get me to turn rat."

"Good riddance," Damian said in the front seat.

Yes, good fucking riddance, indeed.

Tommas might have let the detectives live had they not caused him as many issues as they had. He might have turned his cheek to their badgering and trailing him, but he couldn't. Because if he was watched, then his Outfit was also being watched.

He had a duty as these men's boss.

Protecting his Outfit was the most important thing.

"Here we go," Tommas said as one of the detectives pushed open the front door of the home.

The men in the small hatchback car, watching the scene unfold a few houses down, felt the blast rock their tiny vehicle to and fro with pressure. The ball of flames that rushed out of the front of the house was spectacular in nature, and any chance of survival was unlikely.

"That's that," Damian noted.

"Easy cleanup," Theo said.

"You should probably get out of town for a week or two," Adriano added.

Tommas watched, silent and uncaring, as his house quickly began to burn and the flames ate away at a part of his past. "I think I'm good right where I am. D?"

"Yes, boss?" Damian asked.

Pulling the velvet box from the inside of his suit jacket, Tommas popped open the top and looked over the ring resting inside. The princess cut diamond was nestled in a crown of smaller diamonds and set on top of a white gold band would fit Abriella's hand perfectly. He'd known it when he walked past a storefront window two years ago, and the glittering piece caught his eye. The three carat diamond was big and appropriate enough to be worn on the hand of a boss's wife, but small enough that his girl would still like the style.

Tommas didn't wonder if Abriella would say yes.

He knew she would.

After all their wasted years hiding and sneaking around, Tommas refused to wait one more goddamn minute for what had always been his.

"Take me to dinner," Tommas said, still looking at the ring. "It's time for a surprise."

Two months later ...

Nervousness slipped through Tommas' veins, making him restless and agitated at the same time. The quiet cry of a newborn drew his attention to Damian as the man strolled down the aisle with his baby boy swaddled in white. Lily followed at her husband's side, talking sweetly to the fussy infant.

"He's not happy at all," Damian grumbled.

"He's only been outside of his mother for a few days," Tommas said. "Give the kid some credit. He's still trying to figure this life thing out."

Lily smiled brilliantly. "See, that's what I told him."

Damian glanced down at his son with tender eyes and a small smile. "I worry, that's all. I want him to be happy all the time."

"He's a baby. All he knows how to do is cry, eat, and shit, man."

"He knows more than that."

Tommas sighed. "Okay, Damian. Give him to your wife now. We have important business here."

Lily took the baby from her husband's outstretched arms. "Ten minutes, Tommas. You look good. Smile a little more."

Tommas did as his soon-to-be wife's bridesmaid demanded. Once Lily was gone back down the aisle to hide behind the closed oak doors where Abriella was waiting in her wedding gown and with her party, his nervousness returned.

Fidgeting on the spot, Tommas took note of the priest coming out.

"What is wrong with you?" Damian asked.

Tommas shrugged. "Big day."

"Where's Adriano?"

"Feeding Corrine because Alessa was helping Abriella," Tommas explained.

Adriano and Alessa's baby girl finally made her way into the world eleven days past her due date. It had been a two day labor that Tommas and Abriella waited out in the family waiting room in the Labor and Delivery ward. The baby girl was healthy, happy, and big. She took after her mother in appearance, but she had her father's happy, sweet-natured attitude. Tommas adored his little niece.

Well, and his new nephew, too. Damian's son wasn't actually his nephew, but a cousin, but Tommas didn't see the boy that way.

"Are you ready, Tommas?" the priest asked, coming to stand behind him.

Tommas nodded.

More than ready.

"I've been ready for years," Tommas confessed.

"Never would have guessed it," the priest joked. "And, Damian, your baby boy is having his baptism today, yes?"

"He is," Damian said.

"A wedding and a baptism." The priest smiled widely. "Seems fitting for a Sunday morning."

Soon after, Theo joined Damian and Tommas on the altar. Adriano made his way not long before the ceremony was to begin. Thankfully, the priest had allowed them to change up a few things, despite the church being so strict on the tradition of marriage.

Mostly, Tommas was just happy to have his best men surrounding him on the most important day of his life. Damian, his underboss, best friend, and cousin. Theo, his new front boss and friend. And Adriano, a damn good Capo, a new father, and a part of Tommas' family.

It was a whole new generation of men for the Outfit.

Better men.

Honorable men.

When their backs were turned to the priest, and they waited for the doors at the back to open, Damian whispered, "Are you ready for the Wednesday meeting in New York with the Commission?"

Tommas didn't answer his cousin as the back doors of the church opened, revealing a line of women in pastel pinks, waiting to walk down the aisle. At the very back, he could see Abriella, her sheer veil, and the off-white color of her lace wedding dress.

When something as beautiful as Abriella walked in, she was the most important thing in the room. Nothing else mattered to Tommas.

He pushed aside his restlessness, his worries, and the nervousness that had been eating at him all day. He forgot about his upcoming meeting with the Commission, the one that would essentially decide if the Chicago Outfit still had a seat at the table with the rest of the crime syndicates.

None of that mattered.

Alessa walked down first with Corrine in hand, followed by Evelina, and then Lily holding her son, Joseph. Other than the babies, no children had been included in the wedding party.

Well ... not in the way that anyone knew.

Tommas realized he was smiling like a damned fool when Abriella stepped up to the doors. The lace dress she wore hugged her curves and fell with a regal grace to sweep the floor. The veil covering her face also trailed down her back to the floor, and had a train that was at least a few feet long behind her.

So beautiful.

His heart ached, but it was goddamn *good*.

"Go," the priest said from behind him.

Tommas laughed, remembering his job in that moment. He took the altar steps two at a time, ignoring the chuckles echoing throughout the church from the parishioners and the wedding guests. He practically jogged down the aisle to meet his soon-to-be wife at the end.

Abriella didn't have to walk alone.

Tommas promised her that.

There was no one to give her away, but she'd already handed herself over to him a long, *long* time ago.

At the end of the aisle, Abriella's smile bloomed when Tommas came to a stop in front of his lover. He held his hand out, palm up. Hers slid into his without question as the red camber of her lips deepened.

She'd woken him up with a similar smile that morning, kissing down his chest to the hardness of his cock hiding beneath their soft sheets that smelled like them. She'd whispered promises against his skin, wishes in his ear, and rode him into oblivion with morning sunlight streaking across their bed.

Nothing could be better than that.

Right?

Wrong.

The best thing was hearing his lover tell him that two little pink lines had shown up on a pregnancy test that morning. No one else knew. They would keep it to themselves for a little while.

Best wedding gift ever.

"Tommas?" Abriella asked.

He still hadn't moved, or turned to start them back down the aisle. Tommas was far too caught up in taking the beauty of Abriella in, and the life they were finally beginning to have together.

"Yeah?" he asked.

"I'm ready," she whispered.

Tommas glanced up at the large cross hanging above the opened doors.

God knew ...

God knew Tommas had been ready for this day forever.

Without a word, Tommas interweaved their fingers, moved to Abriella's side, and faced the waiting church. No, his girl didn't have to walk alone.

He had her.

He would always have her.

Dante Marcello stepped forward, breaking from the line of the three men who were standing side by side. "Tommas, we weren't sure if the Outfit would be joining the meeting this year."

"Neither were we," Tommas said, a hint of a joke in his tone.

Dante passed a quiet Damian a look behind Tommas. "I'm happy to see the fighting come to an end, and of course, see who came out on top."

"So to speak," said one of the two men from behind Dante.

Tommas recognized the man instantly.

"Lucian," Tommas greeted.

"Rossi," Lucian said with forced politeness.

Dante didn't act like his brother had said a thing. The other Marcello brother, the youngest, stayed quiet beside Lucian. Giovanni did give a nod to Theo who was standing with Damian. From what Tommas understood, the two men had an old friendship.

"Lucian," Tommas started, "I hear that apologies are in order."

Lucian cleared his throat, seemingly surprised. "They have been in order for years, yet we've not received a single one."

"Let me correct that quickly. I apologize for the unfortunate events that took the lives of your crew by men in the Outfit. It's unacceptable and it never should have happened. I know it's been quite a while, but if there's anything that would help smooth this resentment away—"

"Actually, there is," Lucian interrupted.

"Try me."

"There's a trust fund set up for the two men's children. I made it myself. Those kids are without fathers now because someone's hotheaded men couldn't work with my men. Those children didn't ask for that, and I felt a need to help them in whatever way I could."

"I'll gladly contribute," Tommas said.

Lucian nodded. "Apology accepted."

A sense of relief flooded Tommas. It was a small thing, to be sure, but the bitterness between the Marcello family and the Chicago Outfit had been standing between their mutual businesses for years. It was just one thing that Tommas wanted to correct in his new position as boss.

"Clarify who you've brought and why," Dante said.

"Damian is my underboss, and Theo is the front boss as of last month. It was a bit of a … situation, we'll say … to get him to agree to the spot."

"I liked being a Capo," Theo muttered.

Dante chuckled. "You'll make a good front boss, Theo. Duty and responsibility look well on you."

"Thank you for seeing me before the meeting," Tommas said.

"You'll have no problems inside with the Commission," Dante assured. "We're missing a family this year, but it won't be an issue when they rejoin."

"Oh, which one?"

"The Guzzis."

Canada.

Tommas' thoughts instantly went to his surviving sister who lived in Toronto.

"Is there something happening up there?" Tommas asked.

"We don't really know," Giovanni said. "It was just explained that they had no need to be included this year, and the families should proceed as they normally would with the meeting."

It still bothered Tommas, but he chose to ignore it until he could make a few calls.

Reaching out, Dante snagged Tommas' arm and lifted his wrist. The man eyed the new white gold band on Tommas' ring finger.

"Thank you for assuring he was married when he came, Damian," Dante said.

Damian laughed. "I had little to do with that."

Tommas took his arm back, and fixed his suit jacket. "It's quite new, actually."

"Just three days old, hmm?" Dante asked.

"You've been keeping track, I see," Tommas replied.

"Good bosses always do." Dante shrugged like it didn't make a difference, but the air of the boss of bosses still radiated off the man. He demanded respect, and he already had Tommas' in the bucketful. "And where is your wife, Tommas?"

"Enjoying the presidential suite across the city, and waiting for me to return to finish out our honeymoon."

Dante smirked. "It's never good to keep a woman waiting. Let's get this started and over with, yes?"

"Absolutely," Tommas agreed.

"These are horse pills," Abriella complained. "Fucking impossible, Tommy."

Amused by her pout, but knowing better than to tell her he was, Tommas slipped the large, pink prenatal vitamin from Abriella's hand. He looked it over. "It's not that big."

"Then you take it."

"Ella, I'm not the one who is pregnant."

"But if you were, would you swallow that thing?" she asked.

Tommas eyed the pill again. "No."

"See!"

Laughing under his breath, Tommas made quick work of chopping the pill using the butter knife from their breakfast tray. He split the pink pill into four pieces.

"There, baby, manageable," he said, handing the pieces over.

Scowling playfully at having been bested, Abriella tossed the pills back with her remaining orange juice. Swathed in Egyptian cotton sheets, the peek of her skin and curves was enough to make Tommas harder than steel and dry in the mouth.

God, he loved this woman.

After Tommas had moved the tray from the bed, stripped down to nothing but his skin, and joined his wife in bed again, he was content. Her legs tangled with his, keeping him pinned in place and close to her smooth, sweet-smelling skin.

"Well?" Abriella asked.

"Well what?"

"How did it go yesterday? You haven't said a thing about it."

Tommas kissed the tip of her nose, earning himself a pretty smile. "It went okay. Better than I expected."

"I told you it would."

For as long as Tommas could remember, Abriella had been his confidant where the Outfit and mafia business was concerned. She let him talk, never judged his choices, and was one of the better people to go to for advice if he needed it.

"Thank you for coming with me," Tommas said. "You could have stayed in Chicago, but I wanted you here, so thank you."

Abriella snuggled in until she was tucked into his chest. One of his hands rested on the small of her back, keeping her close, while his other laid over the toned contour of her stomach.

"You couldn't leave me behind if you tried."

No, he probably couldn't.

"You're my everything, Ella. You can't leave something like that behind."

Abriella stilled in his arms, her blue eyes twinkling with an honest love. "Everything?"

"Everything worth bleeding for."

"I guess it's a damned good thing you're what makes me breathe, huh?"

Tommas didn't tell her, but she kept him breathing, too.

That's how love worked.

EPILOGUE

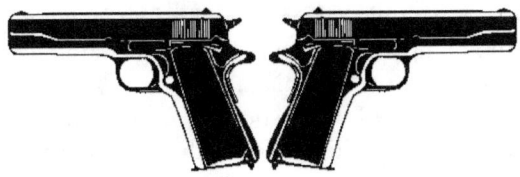

"I love you, Tommy."

Tommas' lips curved into a smile against Abriella's skin. "Do you?"

"So very much."

"I love you, too."

Abriella had spent so much time keeping those three simple words from Tommas that she made goddamn sure it was the first thing he heard from her mouth every morning, and one of the last things he heard from her at night.

She hummed contentedly at the sensations coursing through her body. Tommas' dark chuckles filled the quiet bedroom with a heady, sexy melody. His wandering fingers and teasing kisses on her stomach seemed determined to wake her up. Abriella refused to open her eyes. Feeling was far better, anyway.

"Ella," Tommas whispered against her hip.

"Hmm?"

"Wake up."

"I am."

"Let me rephrase …"

Abriella laughed when the very tips of Tommas' fingers ticked up her side. "Please do."

"Open your eyes, Ella, and watch me while I fuck you good morning properly."

"We're not having sex. We're sleep—"

Abriella's words cut off the second she felt a familiar vibration against her thigh. It wasn't a second later that the vibrator slipped between her thighs, the hum of the toy muffled under the blanket, and then slid between the fleshy lips of her pussy. Abriella's gasp echoed in the room the moment the toy filled her sex. Tommas' exploration of her body had made her wet and hot, and it allowed the toy easy entrance as the vibrations turned up a notch or two.

"Jesus," Abriella mumbled into her palm.

She felt Tommas' mouth press on the hood of her clit, adding an extra layer of intensity to the vibrator working her pussy. His tongue flicked hard against her clit over and over, leaving her begging for breath and right on the precipice of an orgasm.

It wasn't often that Tommas surprised her with something like a toy in bed. He preferred his body against hers, his hands working her to a peak, and his mouth lapping up anything that was left behind.

Abriella wasn't about to complain.

Her muscles clenched in response to Tommas' gravely hum of contentment against her sensitive clit. With every twist of the toy in his hands, her body was ready to give up the fight and freefall into bliss. He knew exactly how to play her body, and how to make it so much better if he wanted.

"*There* ... Oh, my God, Tommy, there."

Tommas sucked the hard nub of her clit between his teeth as he tilted the toy on the next thrust. The stimulation of Abriella's G-spot mixed in with the shock of pain from her clit was enough to send the orgasm racing through her bloodstream.

She froze for a brief second, stunned and shocked at how fast and how intense she came. She twisted off the bed with a shout stuck in the back of her throat as Tommas' fingers bit into her thighs, forcing them open as she shook through the orgasm.

"*Cazzo perfetto*," Tommas praised lowly.

His husky tone beat through the haze of Abriella's senses. She vaguely felt the toy slide from between her legs and her body be turned under demanding hands. Still trembling and feeling a bead of sweat gather on her spine, Tommas' warm fingers danced over her backside. It was only a flicker of his touch, a passing moment of his affection for her with his hands, but she had still felt it.

Then he was pushing in.

Abriella's muscles tightened all over again at the sensation of her sensitive tissues between stretched and opened for her husband's cock.

"Tommy, wait ..."

Tommas hesitated, but barely. He was already half-way in and a blink away from pushing his cock in to the hilt. "What?"

Abriella giggled at how whiney he sounded behind her. Like she'd just interrupted the one thing he wanted more than anything. "Just ... wait a sec."

"*Abriella*," Tommas said through what sounded like his teeth.

She glanced over her shoulder, finding his jaw tight and his eyes blazing. Sliding her hand between their bodies, she glided the tips of her fingers over the base of her husband's cock. Bare and wet from her pussy, his dick twitched under her touch.

"No condom," Abriella told him.

Abriella hadn't been on birth control for a while. She'd been terribly careful about using condoms for fear of getting pregnant. Apparently,

Tommas was done with that nonsense.

Tommas sighed, the action jostling his cock a little further into her soaked core. "Ella, come on."

"I don't—"

"Before you even start, I do, babe."

Abriella's refusal caught in her throat and melted into a moan as Tommas pushed the rest of the way in and hit all the best spots inside her sex. "God, Tommy. It's not even been a *year.*"

"I know. Shut up and let me fuck you."

"But—"

"Ella, I'm warning you, sweet girl. I will turn you over, shove my cock in your mouth, and fuck you quiet that way instead of like this. We both know you want this far more right now. But if you're a good girl and let me pound into your pussy like I need to right now, I'll still let you suck me clean once I've filled you full."

Abriella shivered, her pussy flexing and hugging him tighter as he began to withdrawal his cock slowly. Tommas' responded with a groan.

"Diapers," she mumbled.

"What?"

"Diapers. Bottles. Twelve, two, and four AM feedings. Car seats. Teething. Fevers. Late night runs to the store. Colic. Crying. No sleep. Midnight drives to make them sleep."

Tommas pulled Abriella back into his length, making her ass slap to his skin. "So?"

"Labor," she whispered. "Hours and hours of labor, Tommy. You remember that, right? You remember being scared, exhausted, and not wanting to do it again—*twice.* Because I sure do."

His fingers dug into her sides. "Stop it."

"Well, that's what you want."

"It is. With you, of course it is. We make beautiful babies, Ella."

Abriella bit her lip and buried her face into the bed in an attempt to muffle the volume of her moan. It didn't help much. She didn't get the chance to make another noise before Tommas' hand was covering her mouth and his wet fingers, slick with her arousal, pushed in between her lips to find her tongue.

She sucked his digits clean as he fucked her hard from behind. Abriella whined, happy and blissed, when Tommas fisted her hair and pulled her head to the side. The roughness in his actions only made her wetter—it got her off even more. She backed into every thrust, feeling him hit her deeper with each one. The rougher he fucked her, the better it was.

There was no love-making in their bed.

Not the usual kind.

Softness wasn't good for her when she needed to feel him still between her thighs long after he left their home for the day. Sweetness did nothing for her when she liked his dirty talk, and his names, and his dark promises ringing through her mind for hours.

This was perfect.

This was them.

"There's my girl," Tommas growled into her ear. "Fucking me so good, Ella. You're tight as hell, baby. Love this pussy."

His words were punctuated by a hard slap to her ass. The heat of the sting traveled from her backside straight to her wet pussy. Abriella responded to his tap by biting down on his fingers. He liked to take it as much as he gave it. It only added to their tempo and the sound of their bodies meeting again and again.

And then his whispers came dark and dirty in her ear.

Just how she liked.

Little slut.

Fuck that cock, Ella.

Take it, baby. Fucking take it.

Tommas' hand slipped away from her mouth to grab Abriella under her throat. She never worried about him hurting her, or that his hand might squeeze too tightly for once. He wouldn't ever do something to ruin the trust that she gave to him every time he used her in bed. Because for as much as Tommas did use her for however he saw fit, he also needed what she gave. The compliance. His dirty girl. His friend and lover.

She was still his slut in their bed. That had never changed. Nearly ten years did nothing to affect their sex life inside of a bedroom ... or even outside of it. Abriella would still drop to her knees for this man in a back alley and suck his cock when he told her to. She would still let him finger-fuck her under a table full of guests. She would always pull him into the closest room and let him bend her over whatever was he could, even if there was a room full of people next door.

Abriella would always be whatever Tommas wanted in the bedroom, because he let her be whatever she needed.

And outside?

Outside, she was still his equal.

Using one hand to keep her steady on the bed, Abriella reached back with her other to find Tommas' fingers weaved into her hair. She grabbed onto his wrist and held tight, letting her nails score into his skin as their pace became frantic and brutal.

"Make me come," Abriella whispered.

"So fucking hard," Tommas breathed.

Her second orgasm came on much like the first had. Suspended in time, airless, weightless, and there in a blink of time.

"Oh, *God.*"

"Yes," Tommas ground out. "Make me fucking come, Ella. Come on, sweet girl."

He fucked her through the tremors until her body protested in the best way, and she couldn't breathe. Her pussy milked him into his own release, and Abriella felt the ropey stream of his come fill her deep.

She gasped for air and came up with nothing.

Not a drop.

Breathless.

This man made her breathless.

They were damn dirty, bloodstained by his own hands, and by hers.

Perfection was a myth.

Beauty was in the flaws.

A stream of light woke Abriella. Strong, warm arms tightened around her frame as she blinked at the early morning sunlight coming in from the crack in the curtain.

"Tommas?"

"Mmhmm?"

"What time is it?"

"Six-thirty."

Abriella groaned. "What time did you wake me up earlier?"

"Like four?"

"Asshole."

Tommas laughed against her shoulder blade before pressing a soft kiss to her skin. "You needed it, I think."

"You did, too."

"Clearly."

Abriella turned under his urging hands to face her husband. A gentle smile played at the edges of his mouth. "Did you even go back to bed?"

"No."

"Why not?"

"Better to spend my time watching you than waste it sleeping," Tommas said, his tone a deep timber that woke Abriella up even more.

It was Monday. That always meant a ton of running around, Tommas being gone from the house until late in the evening as the boss of the Outfit, and every other little thing that somehow managed to always pop up last minute. Their life was hectic and busy. Abriella had breakfast to cook, school drop-off to make, soccer practice for their ten-year-old son, Tommaso, and then supper. In between, she had an almost one-year-old to chase after, a house to manage, and people to entertain because they never stopped showing up.

Last minute.

It might as well have been the story of their lives.

"You're too smooth for your own good, Tommy," Abriella told him.

Tommas flashed a sinful smirk. "I'm aware. Do you think we have time for a second round before—"

A quiet knock on the bedroom door interrupted Tommas' question. Abriella giggled at the sight of her husband's crestfallen frown. He might as well have had 'cock-blocked' stamped on his forehead.

That was life with kids.

God knew Tommas loved his kids. He was a fantastic father. Hands-on, loving, caring, and attentive. His attention was sometimes spread thin between *la famiglia* and his own family, but he never made Abriella and the kids feel like they were anything less than the most important thing in his life.

Abriella suspected that Tommas' good-naturedness, his big heart, and his love for his family stemmed from the fact that his family had been so poisonous to him growing up. His father had been a drunk, as had his mother. Abuse and neglect had run rampant through his life. He'd been left to care for his younger twin sisters, and he never had much of a childhood.

He was making damn sure that his kids had a beautiful one. Abriella was more than grateful.

"Mom, Dad?" came a quiet, muffled voice outside the door. "Are you awake?"

"Yes," Tommas grumbled.

Abriella smacked her husband with the back of her hand. "Just a second, Tommaso."

She quickly pulled on her husband's dress shirt that had been slung over the bedpost and tugged on her panties. Tommas was left with his boxers and unbuttoned pants as Abriella pulled the door open to find her ten-year-old son rubbing at his eyes with one hand and holding his baby sister in the other.

"Sara woke up?" Abriella asked, reaching for the baby girl. "I didn't hear her crying."

"I didn't hear her, either," Tommas said.

Tommaso handed Sara off. "She wasn't. She was chewing on her bear. I got her out."

Abriella tousled her boy's hair and leaned down to kiss his cheek. "Thank you, sweet boy."

"*Ah*, Ma," Tommaso mumbled, waving her off. "Don't."

At ten, it seemed like Abriella's son was already starting to push her away in small actions. The boy probably didn't even realize it, but it broke Abriella's heart. Tommaso had always been something akin to a momma's boy. He had spent every waking moment of the first three years of his life under Abriella's feet.

Then he turned four.

Tommas began taking his son out with him in the daytime. Abriella never said a word about it, but she watched her son go from a momma's boy to his father's understudy faster than she wanted to admit. Tommaso walked like his father, he liked his hair a little longer like his father did, and he even shared the same striking gray-blue eyes.

Twins.

"Go use the bathroom and get ready for breakfast," Abriella told her son.

Tommaso went off without needing to be told again. With her son gone, Abriella turned her attention to her almost one-year-old daughter. Sara Ella Rossi was a beautiful, spoiled creature. Her mother was partly to blame, but her father had caused just as much by feeding to the child's every whim. She was a princess through and through.

After Tommaso was born, Abriella had put off having another child. Tommas begged her every day from the time their son turned one, until Abriella finally gave in nine years later for a second baby. Maybe people had thought that they waited too long between their children, and that the siblings wouldn't be close, but Tommaso was the perfect big brother. Sara adored her TomTom.

"You're up early," Abriella said, grinning at her daughter's wide smile.

"Mamama," the baby babbled.

"Pretty Sara." Abriella fixed the baby's wayward curls. "And no chewing on your bear, baby girl."

"Dada's girl," Tommas said, coming up from behind Abriella.

Sara squealed loud enough to crack the windows. The baby flung her arms out the moment her father was in view. Tommas took his daughter into his arms but not before he placed a fast, searing kiss to Abriella's lips.

"Ready for another day?" he asked his wife.

Sara placed slobbery kiss after kiss to her father's scruffy cheek.

Abriella laughed.

Their life was messy.

Crazy.

Sometimes dangerous.

But it never lacked in fun.

Smiling, Abriella said, "So ready."

"Sit, sit," Tommas shouted.

The laughing, loud voices quieted as people started to fill into the large dining area. Abriella's husband had a strange way about him when it came to the people and families of the Outfit. Typically, Tommas was quiet and more observant of those around him. He didn't often join in discussions, but rather, stood off in the corner of the room and watched them happen.

For a boss, he was an unlikely one at first glance

But he was a damn good one when you took another look.

When he did speak, he commanded. He demanded attention. He forced respect. People liked him, and when his presence was fully invested into a party, dinner, or conversation, he was admired.

"Go, Cory," Evelina said as she patted her ten-year-old nephew on the back, urging him toward the table. "Go find your mother."

Cory Rossi gave his aunt a brilliant smile. "Get me an extra piece of cake."

"For my favorite nephew? Of course."

Abriella laughed as Evelina saddled up beside her against the wall. Little Sara stood at her mother's feet, hanging on to the ends of Abriella's dress for dear life like her mother might leave her sights.

"God, does Lily know how badly you spoil that kid?" Abriella asked.

Evelina shrugged. "Yep."

"What about Joseph?"

"Even worse. Theo gets the claim to fame for that one, however."

Abriella shook her head. Both of her nephews from Lily and Damian's side of the family were good boys—great, even. They were a hell of a lot like their father, quiet and unassuming, but they were also very much like their mother, too, with their outgoing personalities when the time was warranted and their sweet natures.

"And what about you?" Abriella asked.

Evelina cocked a brow. "Huh?"

"You, Eve. Aren't you and Theo going to ... you know what I mean?"

"Not really."

"You've been married for a decade. No kids."

Evelina's smile didn't falter. "We have what matters, Ella. Each other. Good family. Health. Happiness. We spoil the hell out of everyone else's kids and then send them back home to you when they're hopped up on chocolate and ready to crash."

"Thanks."

"Seriously, though, this is what makes us happy," Evelina said quietly. "We're not like everyone else. We're not looking for the white picket fence, the two-point-five kids, and the dog. This is our kind of happily ever after, and it's perfect for us."

Abriella was pleased that her old friend had found her happiness in a man like Theo DeLuca. Passing the people a glance as they began to take their seats, Abriella found Theo chatting with Tommas at the head of the table. As Tommas' front boss, Theo was never too far away. He'd gone from a Capo to one of the highest people in the Outfit without ever breaking a stride. Tommas simply said he trusted the man—Abriella had faith in her husband that he would pick the right men to stand with him and protect him.

"Alessa is ready to pop," Evelina said, rubbing her hands together.

Abriella found her sister in the crowd. Alessa wrangled her two daughters into seats at the table while holding onto her eight-month swell at the same time.

"Another niece for you to spoil, huh?"

Evelina nodded. "You know it."

"Hard to believe that Adriano had three girls. Are they done?"

"According to my brother, they absolutely are."

"He's a good dad," Abriella said. "Those girls have him wrapped around their pinkies, and he loves it."

"He is, and he does. Are you still going to the opera show with us all tomorrow?"

"Wouldn't miss it. Go grab a plate before the kids eat us out of house and home," Abriella told her friend.

"Going," Evelina said with a laugh.

Abriella watched her friend go, and took note of Evelina's brother coming to his wife's rescue. Adriano Conti helped Alessa sit their youngest five-year-old daughter into a chair beside her eleven-year-old sister. Then, the man shot his wife a tired grin and stood to speak with the man who had come up behind him: Damian Rossi.

The two men's conversation was had quietly, and by the looks of it, no one around them took note of it happening. Guessing by the serious expressions the two men wore, the conversation was not a light one, and it probably had something to do with Adriano's position as a Capo, and Damian's higher one as the Outfit's underboss.

Abriella had to say, she liked this better.

Business was not everyone else's *business*. It should be had quietly, and without the concern of others' sticking their noses where it didn't belong.

Less issues were had between the families when everyone worked together to keep things peaceful and respectful, especially Outfit business.

It certainly helped that everyone now seemed to have someone else in another family. At one time, these people were all separated by their bloodlines and their misplaced loyalties, leaving no family deathless. Reckless actions pushed them even further apart. The Chicago War left no one scarless. Each soul burned by the bloodshed came out of the fire a little breathless, but far smarter and more loyal than before.

Honor kept them honest.

Family was everything.

It was hard to kill your blood, after all. Lily, a once DeLuca, married a Rossi. Theo DeLuca married a Conti. Adriano Conti married a Trentini. And Abriella married a Rossi. Their families were so interwoven with their children and friendships that fighting would only mean killing themselves in the end.

"Not that I'm complaining," Tommas whispered into Abriella's ear.

She hadn't even heard her husband come up beside her until he was speaking. A shiver raced down her spine as his lips ghosted over her ear.

"What's that?"

"Not that I'm complaining, Ella, because you look damn good standing in a room full of people. Beautiful people draw attention, and we both know how much you shine, baby. But you're supposed to be saying grace for me. We're starving. You're keeping us waiting."

Abriella smiled, and turned her head just enough to press a quick kiss to Tommas' mouth. She could feel at least twenty pairs of eyes watching their private, close exchange. She didn't mind showing the closeness she shared with her husband off for others to see. It was a good reminder that as much as some had tried to shame her and Tommas, and for every *whore* that was whispered behind her back by the older generation of Outfit people, Tommas and Abriella still survived.

They were still them.

"A queen always makes people wait, doesn't she?"

"Not when the king is hungry, Ella."

"Spoiled man."

Tommas grinned. "You made me this way."

She had.

"Oh, you've got to be kidding me," Damian grumbled.

"Sorry, man," Tommas said, dangling his wiggling daughter on his hip. "Babysitter flaked. Abriella couldn't find anyone else at the last minute."

Damian cringed as something toppled and crashed in the other room. "Dammit."

Abriella cocked a brow in Lily's direction. "That was one of your kids."

"Probably," Lily said, entirely unashamed. "Tommaso is too proper to cause trouble."

"He just follows the rules," Tommas argued.

Damian shrugged. "Better he does."

"It's a little strange for a boy of his age, though, isn't it?" Lily asked. "I mean, he never does anything wrong."

"Clearly you've never seen him on the soccer field," Abriella replied. "Because he's brutal out there."

"That's my boy." Tommas chuckled as he dodged a wet slap from his daughter. "No, Sara, that's gross. You had your whole hand in your mouth and it doesn't belong inside mine, too."

"Back to the issue at hand," Damian said. "Theo and Eve will be here in twenty minutes. I have the goddamn—"

"Damian, language," Lily snapped.

Damian winced. "Sorry. I've got the tickets for the show. They're non-refundable. You promised a babysitter. Get one, Tommas."

"Watch it."

"Sorry, boss."

Tommas scowled, and passed Sara to Abriella. "Give me a few minutes."

"Twenty. I'll give you twenty because that's when Theo and Eve will get here and want to leave. If you're not ready to go, without the kids, you're staying behind to watch them. Abriella can come with us."

"Sounds like a plan to me," Abriella chimed in.

Lily giggled.

Tommas didn't look at all pleased with the turn of events. He stalked off, shouting into the living room for the kids to quiet down and pick up the mess as he passed by.

Shaking her head, Abriella put her hands on her hips and asked, "Anyone want coffee while we wait for Tommas to work his magic?"

"Can't," Lily said.

Damian passed his wife a look. "One won't hurt you."

"Caffeine is bad, Damian."

"Bad for what?" Abriella asked.

Lily bit the inside of her cheek, grinning. "Well ..."

Abriella didn't even need her friend to finish. Lily was pregnant with her third child. "Again?"

"Yeah, again."

Damian barely moved out of the way when Abriella rushed Lily into a bear hug.

"Congrats!"

"Two boys," Lily said, laughing. "It's time for a girl for me. God, she better be a girl."

"Decaf, then?"

Damian chuckled. "Yeah, she'll tolerate that garbage."

"Great," Abriella said, still hugging her friend. "You can make them, Damian."

No one refused Tommas Rossi's wife in her home.

Not even Ghost.

Fifteen minutes later, the doorbell to the Trentini mansion rang loudly throughout the wing. Curious, she tossed her husband a questioning look. Tommas gave her no answer in response, simply tipped what was left of his coffee down the drain and pushed away from the sink.

"Are we ready to go?" he asked.

"Theo and Eve aren't here yet," Damian said.

"Theo just messaged me. He's waiting at the end of the driveway. We're already running late."

"There's no babysitter," Abriella said.

Tommas smirked. "I'd be willing to bet that he just arrived."

Confused as hell, Abriella followed her guests and husband to the front of the house. Joseph, Cory, and Tommaso had set up the entertainment system in the living room and were thoroughly engrossed in some war game. Sara had been put down for bed earlier. Mostly, the house was quiet.

On the front entrance steps, Adriano Conti waited until the door was opened. The Capo's gaze widened at the sight of Abriella, Tommas, Lily, and Damian dressed up to the nines and walking out of the house.

"Hey," Adriano said as the four walked down the steps.

"You're babysitting," Tommas called without turning back.

"What?"

"Babysitting. I didn't stutter, Adriano."

"But—"

"You owe Damian a favor, from what I remember," Tommas interrupted. "Isn't that right? Something about him catching you dry fucking Alessa against a wall during his wedding reception all those years ago. You owe him. I'm cashing in on it. I don't think my cousin minds."

Abriella caught the sight of Adriano's furrowed brow as an understanding dawned in the man's eyes. "You're fucking kidding me! That was over a decade ago!"

"Pay up, man," Damian said, laughing. "I can't help that you forgot about it."

"I didn't forget," Adriano grumbled. "I just thought that it would be for something different."

Abriella let Tommas kiss her on the cheek when he opened the passenger door to their Mercedes. She slid into the passenger seat, ready for a break from life and the chance to have some fun. Sometimes, fun was never a part of the equation.

"Four kids inside," Tommas informed. "Sara is sleeping, she's out for the night. Give us a call if there's blood or broken bones."

Adriano scowled. "I'm never answering your call again, boss."

"Yes, you will," Tommas said simply.

He wasn't wrong.

Abriella jerked the moment her husband's hand came in contact with her bare thigh under her dress. She barely refrained from smacking him away when his fingertips trailed a little higher. Four people sat in ruby-colored leather chairs in front of them, only feet away. They were thoroughly engrossed in the opera playing out below their balcony, but it was too close for comfort.

"Tommy, stop," Abriella warned.

Her husband chuckled, squeezed her thigh tightly, but didn't remove his hand. In fact, he moved it higher until he was stroking her pussy over the silk panties she wore. Again and again, harder and harder until her legs were shaking and her fingers were digging into his arm to keep from grabbing the back of the chair in front of her.

Then, his fingers were slipping under her panties to find her wet sex. Abriella bit her lip while Tommas played with her pussy. His light touches and teasing strokes made her want to whine for more.

Why did he do this to her?

Make her so goddamn crazy?

A single finger slid into her clenching pussy, testing her body and playing with her constraint. Tommas didn't relent in his little game until Abriella was swallowing hard, her eyes were rolling, and she'd shoved her knuckles between her teeth to hide her sigh as she shook through an orgasm that felt as bad as it did good.

Their best friends chatted quietly ahead of them, discussing the show and what they had seen so far. It had been decent enough, if not a little tiring after a while.

Removing his hand from between her legs, Tommas winked as he cleaned his finger with his mouth. If she'd had told him to stop, he would have. But she didn't want him to. Abriella couldn't believe her husband, but then again, she didn't know him to be any different.

He loved using her like this.

She needed him to do it.

"Wonderful," Tommas said.

Abriella sighed. "Thank you."

"Always, Ella. I like this."

"Hmm, what?"

"This," he repeated. "Being here with them. It makes us feel closer. I think so, anyway."

Abriella understood what he meant. Tommas was close to his underboss and his front boss. Damian and Theo held the highest seats in the Outfit next to Tommas. Their daily business and control over the family walked hand in hand.

However, unlike the others who had come before them, the people who had simply faked friendships for the sake of the show, they actually had real trust and devotion to one another in ways people couldn't possibly understand.

No one but them had to see it.

Tommas reached over and stroked Abriella's cheek gently. "You're bored. I could see it in your eyes. That's why I woke you up with a little game, hmm."

It wasn't even a question.

"A little."

"And missing the kids?"

Abriella smiled softly. "Yeah."

"It's almost over. Do you want to go get a drink at the bar? By the time we're done, this will be over, too."

"As long as it's something strong. My ears are ringing from listening to this nonsense for the last two hours."

"Not rum," he said.

Abriella rolled her eyes. "Fun sucker."

"So be it."

Tommas leaned forward in his seat to tap Damian on the shoulder. Damian turned his head slightly as Tommas murmured something Abriella couldn't hear. Then, Tommas was standing from his chair and helping Abriella from hers.

Once they were outside the private balcony and walking down a quiet, red carpeted hallway, Abriella asked, "What did you tell him?"

"That we would meet them tomorrow for dinner at their house."

"But you said we would see them after the show."

"I lied," Tommas said with a wicked smile.

Abriella stared at her husband, confused. "What?"

"Remember what I told you that I wanted yesterday morning?"

It only took Abriella a couple of seconds to recall the conversation during their early morning sexcapade.

"Another baby."

"We're still working on that, babe. Here and now seems like a damn good time."

Tommas' hand found Abriella's lower back, and the closest door was pushed open. He shoved her inside what looked to be a storage closet of some sort. Abriella heard the jingle of keys in the dark before a light flicked on.

Silently, her husband locked the door.

"Where did you get those?" she asked, breathless and laughing.

Tommas didn't answer her. He started pulling her dress up, making her spin to face a row of shelves.

"Tommas!"

"Hush."

Abriella turned to face her husband again, glaring playfully. "Where did you get those keys?"

"Paid off a guy downstairs when you were checking in your coat."

Huh.

"Sneaky," she murmured.

"I had plans."

"I can see that."

"Well, you surely will." Tommas flashed his teeth in a sinful smile as he popped open the button on his slacks, pointed at the floor, and said, "Get down on your knees, open wide, make me good and hard, and then I'll bend you over and get a start on those plans."

Abriella didn't even hesitate to drop down like he'd told her to. She winked up at him from below. They were a little bit dirty—wicked in the best ways. She loved them best like this, because when he took the time to drag her into some dark room, promising something sinful was waiting behind a closed door, it made her feel forever young.

"I love you, Tommy."

First thing in the morning.

The last thing at night.

Tommas' hand found the underside of her jaw. "I love you, too. Now, open your pretty fucking mouth and show me how much."

Gladly.

ACKNOWLEDGMENTS

The Chicago War series was a project that began with just Tommas and Abriella's story in Breathless & Bloodstained. And then it grew to become four couples divided by misplaced loyalties, family, and bad blood. The people who encouraged me to tell this series as it should be told, as it deserved to be told, should get all the credit for this series becoming what it was, truly. Without them telling me to write it, I would have written Tommas and Abriella, and nothing else. I don't think the series, or the final book, would have had the impact it did without the previous stories.

To my family who went without me for sometimes days while I penned these novels out over the last six months, thank you. I am the luckiest woman in the world to have people in my corner who give me the chance to be this insane, creative person that I am.

To Jay Aheer … I know you thought I was crazy for the ideas I had banging around in my head for this series and the covers. I know you were worried, and unsure, and wondering what I must have taken to come up with something like the War covers. You're unexplainably awesome. Your talent is immeasurable. I am so incredibly proud to have your artwork representing my books, characters, and words. Thank you for indulging my idea, and going for it. All my love and respect.

To Eli, you're invaluable. Really, you are. Your advice and time has been imperative to this series. You've pushed me through the blocks that popped up, so thank you.

Tracy, from the bottom of my heart, thank you for being my best friend in this publishing world, and for being one of my biggest fans. Thank you for taking the time to proof, pre-read, and help me. All my love.

Sheila and Dominique, thank you for your work editing, proofing, and pre-reading with this series. You both helped to make it so much better.

And to the fans … my God. My readers, the ones who loved all these War men, for every message, every teaser you made, and the time you took from your life to give to me while you read this series, thank you. My readers are my greatest success. And it would not be half the fun without you.

--Kris

ABOUT THE AUTHOR

Bethany-Kris is a Canadian author, lover of much, and mother to three very young sons, one cat, and two dogs. A small town in Eastern Canada where she was born and raised is where she has always called home. With her boys under her feet, a snuggling cat, barking dogs, and a spouse calling over his shoulder, she is nearly always writing something ... when she can find the time.

Find Bethany-Kris at:
Her website www.bethanykris.com,
or on Facebook at www.facebook.com/bethanykriswrites,
on her blog at www.bethanykris.blogspot.ca,
or on Twitter - @BethanyKris.

Sign up to Bethany-Kris's New Release Newsletter here:
http://eepurl.com/bf9lzD

OTHER BOOKS IN THIS SERIES

OTHER BOOKS BY THIS AUTHOR

The Russian Guns Series

The Arrangement, Book One
The Life, Book Two
The Score, Book Three
Demyan & Ana, Book Four
Shattered, Book Five

Filthy Marcellos Series

Filthy Marcellos: Antony
Filthy Marcellos: Lucian
Filthy Marcellos: Giovanni
Filthy Marcellos: Dante
Filthy Marcellos: Legacy
Filthy Marcellos: The Complete Collection

www.ingramcontent.com/pod-product-compliance
Lightning Source LLC
Chambersburg PA
CBHW051336020726
47501CB00007B/2113